# Sunflowers

# By Sheramy Bundrick

## SUNFLOWERS

# Sunflowers

Sheramy Bundrick

AVON

*An Imprint of* HarperCollins*Publishers*

HarperCollins books may be purchased for educational, business, or sales promotional use. For information please write: Special Markets Department, HarperCollins Publishers, 10 East 53rd Street, New York, NY 10022.

FIRST AVON PAPERBACK EDITION PUBLISHED 2009.

*Designed by Diahann Sturge*

Library of Congress Cataloging-in-Publication Data
   Bundrick, Sheramy D.
     Sunflowers / Sheramy Bundrick. — 1st ed.
       p.   cm.
     ISBN 978-0-06-176527-8
     1. Gogh, Vincent van, 1853-1890—Fiction.  2. Painters—Fiction.  I. Title.
   PS3602.U49S86   2009
   813'.6—dc22                                           2009012865

09  10  11  12  13     OV/RRD     10  9  8  7  6  5  4  3  2  1

OCT 14 2009

*For my family*
*and*
*for Vincent*

It is truly the discovery of a new hemisphere in a person's life when he falls seriously in love.
—Vincent van Gogh

# CHAPTER ONE

# The Painter

Arles, July 1888

*I prefer painting people's eyes to cathedrals, for there is something in the eyes that is not in the cathedral... a human soul, be it that of a poor beggar or a streetwalker, is more interesting to me.*

—Vincent to his brother Theo,
Antwerp, December 1885

I'd heard about him but had never seen him, the foreigner with the funny name who wandered the countryside painting pictures. Hour after hour in the hot sun, people said, pipe in his mouth, muttering under his breath like a crazy man. Nighttime found him in the cafés clustered around the train station, and some of the girls had spotted him in the Rue du Bout d'Arles, although he'd never visited our house. He was poor, people said. He probably couldn't afford it.

The day I met the painter, the countryside called me as I would learn it always called to him. Fields and weathered farmhouses lined the road leading out of the city: a half hour's walk, and I could watch farmers pitch sheaves of wheat into *cabanon* lofts, breathe deeply of air that smelled of harvested grain instead of cheap cigarettes and cheap perfume. Pretend I lived in a cottage framed by cypresses, instead of Madame Virginie's *maison de tolérance*. That day, the life I led choked me like the heat.

While the other girls napped behind closed doors and shuttered windows, I slipped down the narrow street that followed the old medieval walls, then between the towers of the old medieval gate, the Porte de la Cavalerie. Here on the fringes of Arles lay the Place Lamartine, its public garden ringed by shops and hotels, the road I sought just beyond. A few wagons rattled past, carrying remnants of the morning's market, and a few stragglers sipped drinks in front of the Café du Prado, fanning themselves with hats. I had sidestepped one of the wagons and was crossing the garden when a loud voice stopped me.

"What is *she* doing here?"

The pair of ladies in their high-collared dresses looked like blackbirds and squawked like hens. "Luc, come to Maman," the second one called to her little boy from the park bench. "Where are the *gendarmes*? Shouldn't they protect decent people from such trash?"

A braver girl would have laughed and kept on her way, but I stood stupidly in the middle of the path, glancing from the good ladies to the police station on the other side of Place Lamartine. *Filles de maison* were supposed to stay in the *quartier reservé*, the corner of town where the law put the brothels—I'd be marched back to Madame Virginie's quick as anything if the *gendarmes* found me. Why hadn't I pinned up my hair or put on a hat, done something to disguise myself, like any *fille* with some sense?

A policeman!

He had emerged from the *gendarmerie* and was strolling in our direction. The ladies waved their parasols to get his attention, but I bolted before he could see me, ducking through a hedge to another part of the garden. I knew every tree there, every acacia, every pine, and I wove through the grasses to the furthermost edge by the canal, where I sank under a bush and listened for footsteps. No one came. I heard nothing but the bells of Saint-Trophime chiming four and laundresses finishing their work nearby.

"I'm nervous about . . . you know," a young voice floated over the splashes. "What do I *do,* exactly?"

An older voice replied, "Lie there and think about the babies you'll have. It's not so bad when you get used to it."

"My man grunts like a pig, I've never gotten used to that!" a third woman jumped in, to giggles and more playful splashing.

The soldier I'd entertained the night before, back from North Africa with desert madness in his eyes, had grunted too, like a wild boar rooting for mushrooms. He growled in my ear about what it felt like to shoot a man, and when he was done, he sneered, "What's with you, girl? Didn't you like it?" I forced myself to nod yes so he wouldn't hit me, and even after he left, I couldn't cry. I crouched in the tin washtub to scrub his sweat away, then tiptoed back to my room and a restless night in the chair by my window.

The tears fell freely now in the garden's quiet. *What's with you, girl?* The soldier's words rang in my head; so did the words of the ladies on the bench. *Decent people. Decent people.* Only when I'd cried all I could cry and was wiping my eyes with the hem of my dress did I listen to the chatter of cicadas instead.

*Stay awhile,* they murmured in their buzzing drone, *stay awhile.* The grass was soft and fragrant, the shadow of the cedar bush cool and comforting. It'd be hours before Madame Virginie expected me at supper and Raoul lit the lantern to signal we were open for business. *Sleep,* said the cicadas. *Sleep.*

It took five chimes of Saint-Trophime's bells to wake me, and I opened my eyes to find I was no longer alone. A man sat under a nearby beech tree with pencil and paper in his hands, face hidden under a yellow straw hat like the farmers wore.

He was drawing me.

His head jerked up when I jumped to my feet, then he stood too, dropping his things to the ground. "Don't come any closer," I warned, "or I'll—!"

"Please, let me explain. I won't hurt you. My name is—"

"I know who you are. You're that foreigner, that painter, and you've got no right . . . What kind of girl do you think I am?"

"The kind of girl who sleeps in a public garden," he said, and he was trying not to laugh. I snorted and took a step toward the path.

"Wait, I'm sorry," he added. "What's your name?" He tilted his head and studied me. "I'd guess you belong on *la rue des bonnes petites femmes* across the way, the street of the good little women, as I call it."

He didn't seem crazy to me, but still, I crossed my arms and refused to tell him my name. "That's a silly hat," I said instead.

He pulled off the yellow straw hat to reveal a ruffled shock of red hair that matched the red of his unkempt beard. Our southern sun had certainly had its way with him, kissing his hair and beard with gold, splashing his nose with freckles. His face had character—a bit serious, with the lines etched on his forehead and mouth drooping at the corners, but not unpleasant. His clothes, though. Blue workman's jacket spattered with paint, shabby white trousers that needed mending in the knees, mud-caked shoes . . .

He smiled again, and his melancholy look vanished. "Now will you tell me who you are?"

"My name is Rachel," I gave in, "and yes, I live on the street of the good little women, as you call it."

"I'm Vincent," he said with a bob of the head, "and I am sorry I startled you. I was working nearby, then I saw you and wanted to draw you."

"What for?"

He shrugged. "You were here, you weren't moving, and I can always use the practice."

I held out my hand. "May I see it? I think you owe me that."

"It's not very good, it's just a *krabbeltje*"—he searched for the word in French—"a scribble." I didn't budge, didn't lower my hand. He blushed pink under his freckles, then picked up his sketchbook with a nervous "Careful, it'll smudge."

The painter had drawn quickly with his black pencil, but the tangle of lines was me, mussed skirts, mussed hair, face restless in sleep under the cedar branches. I peeked over at him; he was rubbing his shoe into the grass with an expression I couldn't understand. "It looks like me," I said politely. "It's a good drawing."

His eyebrows shot up. "You think so?"

I flipped through the other pages, some with writing, most with pictures: a man working in the fields, a woman with a baby, a bunch of flowers, a bottle of wine. At the look on his face, I stopped and handed him the sketchbook. "I'm sorry, it's rude of me to—"

"It's nothing." He tilted his head and studied me once more. "Perhaps one day I can paint you."

"Paint me? What for?"

He laughed. "Because I'd like to, that's what for. It's hard finding models here."

"We'll see," I said and backed toward the garden path. "It's getting late, Monsieur, I should probably—"

The painter bent to gather the rest of his things and looked at me eagerly. "Are you going to your *maison* now? I could walk you, if you like."

"It's not far, and I walk alone all the time. But thank you."

He cleared his throat, the sketchbook now clutched to his chest. "Then can you tell me which *maison* it is? Since you knew who I was, you may have heard I am an occasional patron of *la rue des bonnes petites femmes,* although I have not yet visited your particular establishment. I hope you will permit me to call on you."

How funny and old-fashioned he sounded, as if we'd be having afternoon tea. "I'd be pleased to welcome you, Monsieur," I said after the briefest pause. "No. 1, Rue du Bout d'Arles, Madame Virginie's. Last on the right if you're coming from the Rue des Ricolets."

The painter clapped the yellow hat on his head with an awkward bow and a big smile. "I look forward to it, Mademoiselle. *Bonne journée.*"

I nodded in return and walked through the grass toward the Porte de la Cavalerie. Before I ducked back through the hedges to the garden path, I glanced over my shoulder. He was still watching me.

"The greatest city of Roman Gaul," Papa used to say about Arles, "when Paris was only a city of mud." The schoolteacher in our village, respectful of history, he wanted to take me to Arles to see the ancient ruins. Maman refused. "Filthy railroad town," she sniffed, "no place for a little girl." "There must be little girls in Arles, my dear," Papa said with a chuckle, but Maman sniffed again, and that was that.

When I finally did step off the train at the Arles station years later, Papa was not beside me. I'd lost him a few months before, Maman before that when I was eleven, and I'd come to the city to begin again, best as I could. An unexpected snowfall had blanketed the buildings in sugary white, and like any *touriste,* I gaped at the Roman amphitheater and medieval bell towers, wishing Papa had been there to see them with me. I gaped at the tourists themselves as they promenaded down the Boulevard des Lices in greatcoats and furs; I gazed in shop windows around the Place du Forum at things I couldn't afford and wondered how long it would take to find a new life.

But as the days and weeks slipped by and the fistful of francs in my valise melted with the snow, I learned Maman and Papa had both been right about Arles. The city had two faces: the one travelers and rich people saw, and the one everyone else saw, with dingy cafés and tatty backstreets in sore need of sweeping. A girl with no family and no money wouldn't get very far —no farther, as it happened, than the *quartier reservé.*

That was six months ago.

"Rachel, are you listening to me?"

Friday night at Madame Virginie's *maison,* and I stood with one of the other girls at the bar, shelving glasses and dusting bottles as the first customers trooped in. Once the most popular *fille* in the Rue du Bout d'Arles, Françoise had a faded prettiness about her that kept her regulars loyal, and a fierce efficiency that kept the rest of the girls in line. She gave me a little frown. "I knew you weren't listening. Did you read the editorial this morning in *Le Forum Républicain?*"

I shook my head. "What'd it say?"

"The usual thing. Griping how the cafés near the train station are full of whores at night, whining that the *gendarmes* don't do their job. The town's infected with a moral plague that must be stamped out!" She made a face and laughed, but I gave the glass in my hand an irritable wipe. Nearly a week, and I still heard the woman in the garden. *What is she doing here?*

"That business about the *gendarmes* has nothing to do with us," Françoise added. "We're legal. Madame paid good money for her license, and as long as we follow the rules—"

I set down the glass with a sigh. "I don't want to do this anymore. I've had enough."

"You still fretting about that soldier? Raoul's got orders not to let him back in, you won't be seeing him again."

"It's not about him. It's about all of them."

Françoise put her hands on her hips and gave me the same lecture I'd heard my first night at the *maison,* when I'd balked at the sight of my first customer. Did I want to be a seamstress and lose my sight squinting at stitches? Be a laundress with chapped hands and crooked back? We made a lot more money, she sternly reminded me, and the work was easier than washing clothes in the Roubine du Roi. I should count myself lucky to have a roof over my head and plenty to eat. Didn't I know other girls starved in the streets?

"Yes, Françoise," I said, "but—"

"But what?" Her voice calmed. "You've had bad luck lately, that's all. You need more regulars, nice *mecs* who'll take up your time. But you won't find them with a sulky face like that."

"I'm not being sulky, I'm—"

The entrance of a new customer distracted her. "*Tiens,* here comes someone now. Oh, it's that foreigner. You can do better than that."

I'd forgotten the painter's shy wish to visit me and my hasty agreement—I'd even forgotten his name. He'd swapped his dusty clothes for a rumpled black suit, and he carried a black felt hat that looked like it'd seen better days. His unruly hair was slicked back, his beard newly trimmed, and with his hat he held a makeshift bouquet of wildflowers, wilting from the heat. He didn't look like a man eager to forget a week's work between a friendly girl's legs. He looked like a man come courting.

Françoise didn't notice my smile as the painter gazed around the room and another *fille* sidled up to greet him. "There goes Jacqui," she sighed. "She's been here longer than you, she knows damn well Madame Virginie makes the introductions. Poison, that one. I told Madame not to hire her, but she was so bent on getting a blonde in the house when old Louis up the street's got two."

Jacqui's singsong *"Boooonsoir, Monsieur"* echoed through the room as she preened for the painter. A tall, blue-eyed northerner instead of a short *Provençale* with black hair, black eyes, and olive complexion, Jacqui never failed to give herself airs, bragging about living in Paris and working at a *maison de luxe* near the Opéra. Françoise and I couldn't hear the conversation, but we watched as Jacqui looped her arm through his, and Madame Virginie appeared to settle the arrangement. The painter politely shook his head, not-so-politely pulled his arm free, and said something that brought an ugly scowl to Jacqui's pretty face. He held a hand to his shoulder as if to say "A girl about so high," then waved both his hands, wildflower petals drifting to the floor, to say the girl had long hair and an hourglass figure. Madame Virginie looked puzzled until the painter produced his sketchbook and pointed at a page.

"It's you he wants?" Françoise asked when Madame beckoned and Jacqui flounced away. "You know him?"

I took my time untying my apron and smoothing my new

yellow dress. "I met him last week in the Place Lamartine garden."

"Aren't you sly, keeping that to yourself!" She cast a wary look in the painter's direction. "Make sure he gives you the money first, and don't do it if he starts acting strange."

"He won't act strange. He's nice. He drew a picture of me."

I left Françoise standing openmouthed among the wine bottles and ventured to the painter. "This gentleman seeks your company," Madame Virginie said with the lofty tone she saved for new customers. "Enjoy your evening, Monsieur." She bustled to the door to greet a trio of Zouaves, and I escorted the painter to an empty corner table.

"*Qu'est-ce que je vous sers?*" I asked. "Wine? Absinthe?"

"Red wine, please." His voice was deeper than I remembered. "Not too expensive."

I couldn't resist a sway to my walk as I fetched two glasses and a carafe of house wine from the bar, couldn't resist setting down the tray and leaning over to fix my shoe before making my way back. Had he been watching me the whole time? No, he hadn't. When I returned and poured our wine, he shoved his sketchbook in his pocket. He'd been drawing the Zouaves instead.

He thrust the wildflower bouquet at me before I could sit down. "Thank you," I said, laying the flowers on the table and pulling my chair close to his. "So you found me."

"Your directions were excellent." We sat with our drinks for a moment, then his brow furrowed. "Rouge makes you look different."

"It makes me look pretty, I hope."

"You're prettier without it." I must have looked as taken aback as I felt, because he flushed and said, "But you smell good, and yellow's my favorite color."

"And I see you left that straw hat at home. It's a good thing, otherwise Raoul might have taken you for some vagabond and not let you in."

The painter looked taken aback himself, then smiled when he realized I was teasing. He settled more comfortably in his chair, eyes roaming over the *salon* as he pulled a pipe and matches from his pocket. The three Zouaves had chosen one of the center tables and were busy with girls and drinks; Jacqui sat on the lap of one of them, his tasseled *chechia* perched coquettishly on her head. "Feels like a village school with the whitewashed walls and plain furniture," the painter said after the first puff on his pipe. "No velvet drapes, no gilt mirrors?"

I laughed. "You won't find velvet drapes in this street, Monsieur."

"It's much cleaner than that *maison* around the corner in the Rue des Ricolets."

"Oh, Leon Batailler's place." Leon's house was the cheapest and dirtiest in the *quartier,* and I couldn't keep the snobbery from my voice. "Is that where you usually go?"

The painter flushed again and didn't reply. "And less gloomy than the *maisons* of Paris."

"Paris!" I gasped. "I've always dreamed of going to Paris. The cafés, the dance halls, all the grand buildings . . . it must be the most magical place! And you've been there? Are there really stores like in *Au Bonheur des Dames,* filled with everything you could possibly want?"

"You read Zola?"

"I can read," I bristled. "I'm not some—"

"No, I meant—" He stopped himself and puffed on his pipe. "I lived in Paris for two years before I came here, and it's not what you think. Too much noise, too many temptations. That's what *Au Bonheur des Dames* is actually about, isn't it, how easy it is to be seduced by such fripperies."

"What kind of temptations—women? Is that why you came south, a doomed *affaire*?"

He scowled at me. "Do you always ask so many questions?"

"Why, I just want to get to know you better, Monsieur. That's all."

His mouth twitched at my smile. "Please don't call me Monsieur. Vincent will do."

"That's a nice name. What's the rest of it?"

"Van Gogh."

It was hard to say. "Van Gogue?"

"No—Gogh. Gogh. It's Dutch."

"Gogh. I've never met anybody from Holland before."

His mouth twitched again. "I don't suppose you have. . . . Rachel, is it?" I nodded. He said it like a Parisian would, choking on the *r* instead of letting it glide across his tongue.

Our glasses were nearly empty, and Madame Virginie watched us from the bar. She didn't like the girls to linger too long with customers on a busy night, especially not if the customer bought the cheapest wine and only one drink at that. When I stood and gestured toward the stairs, the painter tossed some centimes on the table for the wine and rose from his chair. I remembered to pick up the wildflowers before reaching for his hand; he squeezed my fingers and gave me a look that calmed the fluttering inside. Jacqui snorted as we passed her table, whispering something in her Zouave's ear to make him laugh heartily.

Upstairs, while I lit the lamp and found a vase for the flowers, the painter ambled around and peered at things. The blue and yellow flowery wallpaper Madame had gotten at a bargain, the worn blue rug with a cigarette-singed hole, the rose-colored shawl folded neatly over the footboard of my bed. "You're very tidy," he said as he studied the bottles and brushes on the washstand.

"You must not be, or you wouldn't notice. Please, Monsieur . . ." I took his hat and waved him to a chair.

"Vincent," he corrected and took a seat, watching intently as I pulled the pins from my hair to let its darkness ripple down my back. A spark ignited in his eyes when I strolled toward him, then straddled his thighs and unbuttoned my dress so my breasts strained against my corset.

"What's your pleasure this evening?" I purred.

"Whatever you're willing to give me." His hands stole round my waist to caress my back. My goodness, he had lovely eyes. Blue-green, like I imagined the sea must look . . .

"That'll be two francs."

He winced at the price—Leon Batailler's girls charged half that—but pressed the coins into my palm. Then he cupped my face in his hands and tried to kiss me, but I turned my head. "Even the Paris girls will kiss a man for two francs," he complained.

"This isn't Paris," I snapped and started doing my buttons back up.

"You have me in rather an awkward position," he said with a sigh. "I suppose that will have to do." He traced my lower lip with his fingertip and added, "It's unfortunate. Kissing is rather indispensable, otherwise serious disorders might result."

Françoise would have scolded him for that, maybe even chucked him out, but the cheap wine had gone to my head. "Three francs, then, for a nice man like yourself."

"You drive a hard bargain," he chuckled and dug in his pocket. He started to complain again when I slid from his lap to go to my bureau, but I silenced him with a wagging finger, tucking one franc into a box for Madame Virginie, the other two into a box for me.

Six months at the *maison,* and I still felt bashful taking off my clothes for a new man. You didn't know what would happen once he got a good look at you, whether he'd be sweet or turn into a pawing beast. Usually they sat and smiled as I slid my stockings down my legs and discarded my dress, and sometimes they couldn't wait for my corset to be unhooked before reaching for me and finishing the task themselves. But Vincent didn't grin, and he didn't grope. He regarded me seriously, eyes brushing every curve, and when I finished, he stood to walk around me. "Coffee-tinted skin, would use some yellow ocher," he muttered and glanced at my hair. "Carmine red and Prussian blue."

"Excuse me?"

"A black like that would take carmine red mixed with Prussian blue. And your eyes"—he peered into them—"I'd use orange with Prussian blue. Dark, but warm."

He was looking at me like he would a painting. "Oh," I managed to say and grabbed my chemise to hold it against my chest.

"Forgive me if I embarrass you, but I have to look at you. I'll draw you right now if you permit me."

His smile was so kind. I let the chemise drop to the floor. "You want to draw me? Why, I thought you wanted to kiss me."

Because I didn't let customers kiss me—except the first one, when I hadn't known any better; *mon Dieu*, he'd tasted of garlic—I hadn't been kissed very much. I let Vincent lead the way as I surrendered my mouth to his, wrapping my arms around his neck, his beard scratching my skin. He didn't taste like garlic, he tasted like tobacco and *vin rouge*. "Who taught you to kiss like that?" I asked, a little breathless, a little surprised to ache for him as I did.

"An Italian *signora* in Paris who thought me in dire need of an education."

I giggled and tugged him toward the bed.

The first time was over before we barely started—"I'm sorry, it's been almost a month," he said shamefacedly—and I broke Madame Virginie's rules by suggesting he stay and get his money's worth. He accepted, and soon I forgot all about the three francs as we passed a pleasurable half hour in the dim light of the kerosene lamp. I laughed at the pasty white of the skin beneath his clothes, he smiled at my gasps when he touched me in ways other *mecs* didn't, and all the time I worried we'd disturb Minette and her customer next door.

"I don't usually enjoy myself this much," I admitted as he retrieved his black suit, more rumpled now from being tossed to the floor.

"I've enjoyed myself too." His smile was almost proud. "The three francs were exceptionally well spent."

I mussed his hair before finding my own clothes. "Then you'll come back. Sunday nights are best, when it's not busy and I can spend more time with you."

We finished dressing, and I caught him watching me again. "Are you sure you won't let me draw you?" he asked as I unrolled my stockings over my knees and secured them with pink-ribboned garters. I told him no and threw his hat at him.

Whispers from customers who recognized him followed us to the door downstairs, and Jacqui's haughty stare felt heavy on our backs. Vincent didn't seem to notice—I giddily didn't care. He kissed me before leaving, and I leaned against the doorjamb to watch him go, something I never did, something none of the girls ever did. At the end of the street, he turned to tip his hat with a grin visible under the gaslamp.

Françoise appeared beside me with raised eyebrows. "*Oh là,* must have been a hell of a time. Who'd have guessed?"

# CHAPTER TWO

# Vincent

*My God, if I had only known this country at the age of 25!*
—Vincent to artist Émile Bernard,
Arles, late June 1888

A dull Tuesday evening over a fortnight later found me pacing the *salon*. From a table where two of the girls played cards with Raoul, to the bar to stare in a mirror, to the doorway to look up and down the Rue du Bout d'Arles. Lanterns flickered to attract customers, but business was slow everywhere, and bored girls bantered across the cobblestones. A boy passed with a pair of scruffy sailors in tow—Leon Batailler's son, sent round the cafés to drum up *mecs* when the police weren't looking. A tipsy *Bonsoir* from one of the sailors drove me back inside, but not before I stole a last glance toward Place Lamartine. No one else was coming.

Françoise called me from where she sat with Joseph Roulin, the postman from the railway station and one of her regulars.

She slid a mug of beer at me as I dropped into a chair. "You're making me jumpy," she said. "What's gotten into you? Not still thinking about leaving, are you?"

"Leaving, Mademoiselle Rachel? Madame Virginie's wouldn't be the same without you," Monsieur Roulin said gallantly.

"No, I—"

"Or were you thinking about that customer of yours?" Françoise teased. "She's got a new fellow, Joseph, he's come to see her twice already. He brings her flowers. And she kisses him."

"Kisses him?" Monsieur Roulin whistled. "Who is he, a handsome lieutenant from the Zouave regiment? A dashing butcher's boy?"

"That painter," Françoise replied, and I wanted to kick her under the table.

Monsieur Roulin's bushy eyebrows knotted together. "Vincent?"

"You know him?" I asked.

"*Bien sûr,* I know him. He lives over the Café de la Gare, where I've been known to, ahem, spend some time." Everybody knew about Monsieur Roulin's love of gossip, billiards, and beer. "Good man."

"They say he's an odd one," Françoise said. "Talks to himself and such."

Roulin shrugged. "No odder than anyone else. He talks to himself while he paints, but other than that . . . Don't be fooled by how he looks. He's a smart one. From a fine family, too."

That got Françoise's attention. "Rich?"

"Rich uncles, I think he said. He gets his money from his brother, though, has none of his own. He has a hard time selling his paintings."

She raised an eyebrow. "So he's a loafer who lives off his brother."

"Theo's an art dealer in Paris," I said. "He sends Vincent money, and Vincent sends him paintings. One day Vincent will be able to sell his pictures, and he'll pay Theo back. That's what he told me."

"Sharing secrets already, is he?" Françoise asked, and I felt myself blush.

"Vincent's no loafer," Roulin said. "He works hard. Up early, outside all day—"

"Spending his brother's money in cafés and brothels?"

"Every man's got a right to relax," Roulin reproached her.

"Why would some *mec* from a well-off family come all the way here to live poor over the Café de la Gare? Just to paint? He think he's too good for a real job?" Françoise looked to me for the answer, but I had to shrug.

Roulin dropped his voice. "He's got a history. He told me part of it, but I'm not sure I should repeat it." At our curious faces, though, he gave in. Two years in Paris had left Vincent nearly mad, Roulin said, drinking and whoring too much, arguing with his brother, his painting suffering as a result. The city was eating him alive, and he fled south, hoping the Provençal sun would help him see things in a different light. "I'll tell you something else," Roulin said, and Françoise and I leaned in closer. "Before he became a painter, he was a preacher."

"He was not!" Françoise exclaimed. "You're pulling our legs now."

"Ask him. A Protestant preacher. His pa was a preacher too."

I tried to imagine Vincent with a Bible in hand, pounding a pulpit and shouting about sin. "That must have been a long time ago."

"I tell you, he's got a history," Roulin said and took a deep swallow of beer. "He's lived more places than I could remember right now. He told me about it when he painted me."

"He painted you?"

Roulin stroked his beard with pride. "Twice. In my uniform."

"You and that uniform." Françoise tweaked his gold-braided blue sleeve. "You'd wear it to screw if I didn't make you take it off."

Roulin ignored her. "Posing for him was hard. I had to sit still a long time, and he fussed when I moved. 'Damn it, Roulin,' he'd say with that accent of his."

"That doesn't sound pleasant," I mumbled into my mug. "I'm glad I told him no."

Roulin looked at Françoise, Françoise looked at me, and I played with the folds of my skirt to avoid her stare. "How long since he came to see you, Rachel?" she asked.

"Ten days," I said absently.

She pursed her lips. "You've been counting. Haven't I told you—"

"Leave her alone, Françoise," Roulin chuckled. "A girl her age is going to have a little *toquade*, a little crush now and again. She doesn't have your experience."

"Or good sense. I know better than to mess with a red-headed loafer."

"Maybe I need to tell Vincent how much he's missed," Roulin joked with a wink. "Next time I see him at the café."

"Don't you dare!" I said in horror, and they both burst into laughter. "He's just a customer. Anyway, don't you two have somewhere you'd like to be?"

Roulin pulled a watch from his pocket. "She's right, I need to get a move on or I'll hear it from my wife. She gets ticked real easy these days with the baby keeping her awake." He puffed up so much at my surprised smile, it's a wonder his jacket buttons didn't pop off. "Augustine gave birth to our third child last week, a little girl. We called her Marcelle."

"That's wonderful. Congratulations!" I said, and Françoise pursed her lips again.

"Vincent wants to paint Marcelle when she gets older," Roulin said. "He's quite keen on painting a baby. Come on, *ma chouchoute,*" he told Françoise. "*Bonne soirée,* Mademoiselle Rachel."

After they went upstairs, I sat alone in the *salon* and thought about Vincent's last visit. We'd talked little before going to my room, Vincent explaining he was tired from his long walk to Montmajour that day to draw. As we dressed after another agreeable half hour, he said again he'd like to paint me. I'd be keeping my clothes on, he said, and he told me he'd pay a few francs. But I refused. "Why not?" he asked. "I would like to paint an Arlésienne." I couldn't explain. It just didn't seem right: only rich people had their pictures painted, and I couldn't see why he'd find me interesting. "Nonsense" was his reply, and he told me then about Theo in Paris, and his wish to paint ordinary people, like Dutch artists of the past but in a modern way that Parisian collectors might appreciate. "Portraiture is *the* thing of the future," he announced, "and we must win over the public!" He looked so earnest delivering this lecture in only his long-drawers, waving the trousers in his hand like a battle flag, that I struggled not to laugh. He said nothing more when I insisted I would not pose, and when he left, he didn't kiss me at the door, and he did not look back. Had I made a mistake, I wondered now. Had Vincent found someone else to paint, another girl more willing than I?

I'd given up thinking he'd return to Madame Virginie's

when he did, the following Sunday. Sunday was the slowest night of the week in the *quartier reservé,* when most husbands stayed home with their wives and most of the Zouave soldiers stayed in the barracks to recover from the Saturday. Vincent must have remembered what I said about Sundays our first night, because he'd chosen that evening to appear again in his rumpled suit and felt hat, catching my eye where I tidied up behind the bar. I brought some wine, and we settled ourselves at a corner table. "Welcome back, it's been a while," I said, then hoped I didn't sound sullen, hoped too that Monsieur Roulin hadn't told him to come.

"I had to wait for Theo's latest letter." He looked embarrassed, then reached into his pocket. "I passed an orchard this afternoon when I was out walking, and I brought you a fig."

"Thank you." We smiled at each other over our drinks, and I glanced at his hand on the table, spotted with red and blue paint. "Were you painting today?"

"I just finished a girl's portrait. It took longer than it should have, nearly a week."

"One of Leon Batailler's *filles?*"

I sounded worse than sullen, I sounded prickly. I turned as red as the dried paint on Vincent's fingers, but he seemed amused. "A girl of about twelve or thirteen, chaperoned by her mother. I saw her in the Place Lamartine garden, and I wanted to paint her because she reminded me of a character in a book I read. She was flattered and said yes at once." He gave me a look under cocked eyebrows that made me flush deeper, then went on to describe the picture, the colors of the girl's dress, the colors of the background. Malachite green, royal blue, Prussian blue . . . all of it a language as foreign to me as his native Dutch. "Everything is so colorful here," he said. "Not like Paris, not like Holland, where everything is so gray."

"Is it true you were a preacher in Holland?"

Again the cocked eyebrow, and his tone turned serious. "You've been talking to the good Monsieur Roulin. What else did he tell you?"

"Oh, nothing much," I said, "only that you've moved around a lot and haven't always been a painter."

"It's true, I haven't always been a painter. I was an art dealer for several years in Holland, London, and Paris—"

"Like your brother?"

He pressed his lips together so tightly that they disappeared into his beard. "He's better at it than I was. I became a school-teacher for a while after that, then a preacher—in Belgium, not Holland—before the church sacked me. *Then* I became an artist." On his fingers, he ticked off the names of places he'd lived—Brussels, Etten, The Hague, Drenthe, Nuenen, Antwerp, Paris—Paris alone being someplace I knew anything about. He pressed his lips together again when he said "Etten" and "Nuenen," muttering that he'd lived with his parents there; "The Hague" he practically whispered while staring at the tabletop.

"Why aren't you married?" I asked lightly. "Couldn't you find some nice girl to settle down with, all those places you went?"

A shadow crossed his face. "What makes you so certain I've never been married?"

"I don't know, I just thought—I'm sorry, I didn't mean to offend—"

"As it happens, you are correct. I've never been married." He gulped his wine before pulling pipe and tobacco pouch from his pocket, and we sat awkwardly for some moments.

"Monsieur Roulin told me you painted his portrait," I said at last.

Vincent's face brightened. "An interesting subject, like

something out of Daumier. Just the sort of thing I've wanted to do here." He played with the pipe in his hands and gazed at his half-empty glass. "I would be honored, Rachel, if you came one day to see my work. I would be pleased to show you Monsieur Roulin's portraits and other paintings besides. Tell you about them. That is, if it interests you."

"It would interest me very much, but—" Men came to visit me, we had our time together, then they went home or wherever they came from. To go off with a man outside the *maison* would be more foolish than having him paint my picture. I tried to be gentle. "To go places with customers just isn't done."

"I see." His tone had turned frosty.

"I'd say no to anyone who asked, Vincent. I have to."

"They don't own you."

"I can't lose my post. I have nowhere else to go."

His hand crept to cover mine. "How long have you been here?" he asked, his voice thawing.

"Since January."

"Are you from Arles? Where's your family?" he asked then, and every part of me tensed. I'd asked him all manner of questions, but he hadn't asked me anything like that until now. I told him I came from a village not far away, without saying the name, and I told him how my sister and her husband still lived there, how Maman died of consumption, Papa of the cholera. I told him with as few words as I could, hiding most of it and fighting to keep from saying, *I'm alone. They left me and I'm all alone.*

"I'm sorry," Vincent said. "My own father died over three years ago. You were close to your papa?" When I nodded, he patted my hand and said again, "I'm sorry."

If I spoke any more about it, I would cry, and I couldn't let him see me cry. He'd take me in his arms and let me weep on his shoulder, and that'd be a terrible mistake. I pulled my hand away. "What will you be painting next?" I asked and forced a smile.

He tilted his head and smiled back. "I'd paint you if you'd let me, but since you won't, I'm thinking of painting flowers—sunflowers. There's a good patch of them near the public bathing-house, and I think they'd make a fine color effect."

"Sunflowers," I breathed. "*Li viro-souleù.*" Just saying the word cheered me. Fields of sunflowers had circled my village and my family's house, so stately as they followed the sun with patient devotion, so beautiful I wanted to pick them all and keep them forever. "They wilt quickly without the sun to guide their way," Maman explained when I brought home an armful, only to find them shriveled and bent the next morning.

Vincent was giving me an odd look. "'*Viro-souleù*'?"

"*Viro-souleù,*" I corrected his pronunciation. "The Provençal word for sunflowers."

"I can't speak a word of Provençal," he said with a sigh, "and it's gotten me into trouble, because sometimes people can't understand my French. I never end up with the right postage at the post office."

I could imagine the pretend blank stares making him speak slowly for amusement's sake, the smirks behind his back after he left. "Most people understand you, especially the younger ones, they're just giving you a hard time. A lot of folks around here don't care for foreigners, and that includes anybody who speaks French like a Parisian."

"Perhaps if I learned to speak Provençal, folks would like me better, no?"

I ignored his teasing attempt to imitate my accent and pretended to consider this. "I suppose I could teach you. But you'll need to visit more often if you're to make any progress."

"So speaks the village schoolteacher. Yes, ma'am." He took my hand again and played with my fingers. "Might I suggest we commence my tutelage upstairs?"

"Let's go, then," I said, trying not to sound too eager. *"Anen aro, Vincèns."* And that began a most entertaining lesson.

# Chapter Three

## *Le café de nuit*

*There are colors which cause each other to shine brilliantly, which form a couple, which complete each other like a man and woman.*

—Vincent to his sister Willemien,
Arles, June 1888

July passed pleasantly into August, August into September, as Vincent came to see me whenever he could afford it. I always knew when Theo had sent a new letter with new francs, for Vincent appeared unannounced, fingers streaked with new paints, the familiar gleam in his eyes. Those nights he bought extra drinks, which pleased Madame Virginie, and those nights I usually found an extra franc hidden someplace after he left—a franc he always denied giving me and refused to take back.

If it wasn't busy, we talked over our wine, and he told me about his paintings. Everything about him changed when he spoke of his work—he came alive, prattling with a rat-a-tat rhythm and waving his hands until he almost spilled his drink. He tried to tempt me into posing or at least visiting his studio, and tempted I nearly was, many times. "You should see it," he'd say as he described a portrait of an old cowherder or painting of oleanders in a jug. When I asked whether he'd painted the sunflowers, the sly answer was always the same. "Perhaps."

He fascinated me with his accent and his stories and all the things he knew. I'd never met anybody who'd read as many books, who'd been as many places, who knew as many languages—not even Papa. When I spoke, he listened intently, and he treated me with respect, as if I'd been a decent lady, not a *fille de maison*. I taught him some Provençal, Vincent repeating the phrases over and over until he got them just right. He tried teaching me some Dutch, but I had such a hard time wrapping my mouth around the words that we wound up laughing instead. When he took my hand and played with my fingers, that meant he wanted to go upstairs, and I'd be lying if I said I didn't enjoy his company there too.

"I've got an idea for a new study," he said one September evening. "I'm going to paint the Café de la Gare."

I wrinkled my nose. "That tacky place?"

"It'll be a very modern subject. I want to paint it in the middle of night, when no one is around but the derelicts and vagabonds."

The Café de la Gare, owned by Joseph and Marie Ginoux, was one of the cafés around the train station that stayed open all hours, a *café de nuit*. During the day it was nice enough, all sorts of folks gathering there for a drink or a meal, but under the gaslights in the wee hours, you'd find those who had no place to stay, or anybody who'd rather spend their francs on absinthe than on a bed. The habitués of the night café wiled away the hours drinking, smoking, shooting billiards, or staring into nothingness. I ought to know—once I'd been one of them.

"It'll take two or three nights to get it right, I think," Vincent continued. "I'll sleep during the day and paint after dark." He wound a lock of my hair around his thumb. "You could keep me company part of the time, if you want." I didn't answer, and he said, "All this time, and you will not see me outside this place. At least think about it."

I did think about it, and the last night Vincent was painting at the café, curiosity got the better of me. The Café de la Gare wasn't far, a brisk few minutes' walk through Place Lamartine, but at that hour it was far enough. Pimps and pickpockets lurked in the mist rising from the river, along with drunken sailors and desperate whores, occasionally a *gendarme* whistling and swinging his nightstick. Even the public garden changed from a sunny, innocent spot to the sort of place where you heard moans and giggles in the bushes. As I passed by, a prostitute with missing teeth and a black eye called, "Half a franc, kitten, the *mecs* can't do you like I can," and I walked faster.

The café doors stood open on such a warm evening, and the eyes of the men slumped over the tables stalked me like hungry animals. One of them tried to get my attention, but I stuck my nose in the air and pretended not to see. Only the man with palette and paintbrushes interested me, the one frowning at his canvas, pipe hanging from his mouth.

"Rachel! You came!" Vincent exclaimed when he saw me. "Let me buy you a coffee." He motioned for Monsieur Ginoux, his delight making me bashful. I waited for him to ask why I'd changed my mind, but he didn't. When I asked if I could see his picture, he declared, "Of course, of course" and sprang up so I could sit in front of it.

I had imagined his paintings to be sweet and calm and

gentle, like he was with me. Not sinister and brooding like this. Bright colors shouted from the canvas—red walls, green ceiling, yellow floor—yet the mood in his café scene was anything but bright. The clock in the background read ten minutes after midnight, and most customers had gone home. Empty chairs and mostly empty glasses said they'd been there, but only dregs of absinthe and the dregs of society remained. Faceless figures hunched over tables; a pimp chatted up a whore. The billiard table sat ready, but no one was playing. Monsieur Ginoux stood there instead, staring out from the painting, and the gaslamps overhead watched too like unblinking eyes. The gay pink bouquet on the sideboard struck the only note of innocence, the only note of hope.

"What are you playing at, Vincent?" Monsieur Ginoux had brought the coffee and was scowling over my shoulder. "You've made my place look like a—"

Vincent waved his hand good-naturedly. "I told you, you shouldn't have made such a ruckus over being late with the rent. Don't worry, it won't sell, nobody will see it."

Monsieur Ginoux muttered something under his breath in Provençal and went to the billiard table, where he grabbed the cue to stab at billiard balls. *Clack!* Vincent ignored him, and so did I—I couldn't take my eyes from the painting. I saw myself in that room, as clearly as if Vincent had put me with the rest of the night crawlers: a frightened young woman whose money had run out, who couldn't afford the simplest inn and was tired of fending off sour-breathed men offering centimes to lift her skirt. Who regretted she'd ever boarded the train to Arles and missed her papa so much it hurt. "I can help you," Françoise had said when she'd found me there at the café. How could I have said no?

Vincent was watching my face, waiting for me to speak.

"You got the mood of the place," I said, trying to be nice.

"It's not supposed to be a happy picture," he said, and he actually sounded pleased. "I wanted to show that this *café de nuit* was a place where one could ruin oneself, go mad, or commit a crime. It's so different here late at night, filled with the terrible passions of humanity."

"The ceiling's not green," I said skeptically. "The walls aren't as red as that either." He'd made the walls in the painting crimson as blood, instead of a faded brick color that hid the dirt and smoke stains. "No wonder Monsieur Ginoux—"

"Red and green are what we call complementary colors," Vincent interrupted, sounding like my papa teaching at school. "When juxtaposed, they vibrate and clash against each other, but ultimately they belong together and form a strange kind of harmony."

I squinted at one of the figures sitting at a table, wearing a big yellow hat with a bit of red hair sticking out. "Is that man supposed to be you?"

Vincent smiled. "Do you want it to be me?"

"Maybe," I replied with a wink.

Now his smile reached the crinkles around his eyes. "Let me sit for a second," he said, then dabbed his brush in a smear of brown paint to sign "Vincent" and "*le café de nuit*" at the bottom of the picture, below the man in the yellow hat.

"Why 'Vincent'? Why not your whole name?"

"Because no one can pronounce it." He wiped his brushes and palette clean with a stained rag, shut everything in a wooden box, and yawned as he collapsed his easel. "Sorry, I'm not used to staying up this late. I was about to go to bed, but why don't I walk you to the *maison* first? I'd invite you upstairs, but I'm afraid I wouldn't be good company."

"You must be so tired. It's silly for you to do that when you live right here."

"There are rough characters about, and I don't want you walking alone. Just let me put my things away."

I agreed and waited for him by the door, still ignoring Monsieur Ginoux and the absinthe-sodden drunkards.

We didn't speak as we walked across the square, through the garden and past the pond, where moonlight tickled the water. The toothless prostitute was sitting under a streetlamp now, and she called, "Found yourself a redhead, eh, kitten? You know what they say about redheads." Vincent reached for my hand at her cackle. Such a liberty, to hold my hand—yes, I took his hand to lead him upstairs in the *maison,* but this made my heart race in a different way, made me wish we had further to go than the Rue du Bout d'Arles.

"*Bonne nuit,* Rachel," Vincent said when we arrived at Madame Virginie's doorstep.

"I want to pose for you," I blurted.

He stared at me, eyes wide. "Truly?"

I nodded. "But you won't make me look . . . you know . . ."

"Ugly?" He chuckled and took my chin in his fingers. I thought he might kiss me, but instead he turned my head to examine my profile. "The night café is one of the ugliest pictures I've done. It's unfortunate you saw that one first. You—you I cannot make ugly. I only hope I can paint you as I feel you."

"Feel me?" My heart began to race again.

His reply was quiet. "You are extraordinary. Like something by Delacroix."

"Is that good?"

"Delacroix was among the best." He turned my head the other way, to look at the other side of my face, then let go of my chin. "Meet me at the Café de la Gare in two days, around nine in the morning. Then I shall take you to my studio."

"I'll be there," I promised. "*Bonne nuit*, Vincent." He gave me one of his awkward bows and, with a last stifled yawn, disappeared into the mist.

Someone must have seen us. At luncheon the next day Minette asked about my rendezvous, and everyone else stopped talking to listen. I tried to make it sound as if my meeting Vincent at the café had been an accident, and I tried to describe his painting, although I said nothing about agreeing to pose for him. "Sounds like he's a lousy painter," Jacqui sneered. "No wonder nobody wants his pictures."

I shook my head. "No, he made it ugly on purpose. He wanted to show—"

"Ugly on *purpose*? What kind of fool would do that?"

I frowned at my plate and gave up. I could feel the other girls swapping glances around me, and I could read their thoughts: *Of all the men who come to Madame Virginie's, why did Rachel choose him?*

Françoise pulled me aside after we cleared the table. "You must stop spending so much time with him. It's dangerous."

"Dangerous?" I scoffed. "Don't be silly. He wouldn't hurt a flea."

"You know what I mean. You're playing with fire."

"You're the one who told me to find some regulars."

Her nostrils flared. "To have regulars is fine. To have someone special who brings you presents and treats you good, is fine. But once you start running around outside the *maison*, you invite all kinds of trouble. Do you see me going anywhere with Joseph? Or anybody else?"

"Monsieur Roulin is married and has three children. Vincent—"

"He could take advantage of you, get you to see him for free." Before I could fire back, she ranted on, "If you fall for him, you won't want to screw anybody else, and Madame Virginie will sack you. That painter doesn't have a franc to his name, he can't take care of you. You could lose your post, lose him, to end up where? On the street?"

"He told me about his painting, and he walked me here. That's all."

"I'm not blind, Rachel. And I'm not stupid."

A flush colored my cheeks. "Why should you care?"

"I don't want you getting hurt." The sudden tremble in her voice made me stare. "Years ago, I met this *mec*. Oh, what a sweet talker he was. I sneaked out, saw him for free, he strung me along for months. Then I got pregnant. When I told him I loved him and wanted to get married, he was gone, poof! The other girls warned me, but did I listen?"

I laid my hand on her arm. "What happened to the baby?"

"What do you think happened?" she said harshly and shook off my touch.

It wasn't hard to guess. Madame Virginie had told me months before about the old woman who lived out the road to Tarascon, who had herbs *filles de maison* might want. "It won't be like that," I whispered. "I'm not in love with him."

Tears swam in Françoise's eyes, thick-skinned, barb-tongued Françoise who always seemed untouched by anyone. "Be careful, Rachel. I only want to save you."

# Chapter Four

# The Yellow House

*I want to make it really an artists' house——not precious,*
*on the contrary nothing precious, but everything from the*
*chairs to the pictures having character.*
   —Vincent to Theo, Arles, September 1888

*B*e *careful. Be careful.*
     Françoise's words kept me awake that night and haunted
me the next day. I couldn't concentrate on anything, not the
mending I needed to do or the book I wanted to read, and
when I gave up and went to the market, I wandered aim-
lessly among the stalls, looking over my shoulder for a yellow
straw hat. When the *maison* opened for the evening, Françoise
watched every move I made, and when I broke not one glass
but two, cleaning up the bar at closing time, she hissed, "Get
your head out of the clouds!"
     I did not meet Vincent at the Café de la Gare. After break-

fast that day, I went upstairs and sat on my bed, listening to the clock in the hall chime nine and trying not to think about him sitting alone at an empty table. Part of me hoped he would visit the *maison* that night to learn where I was; another part of me hoped he would stay away. And he did. For over a week there was no sign of him. Joseph Roulin came to see Françoise during that time, and when I passed by their table with a tray of drinks for a customer, he said gruffly, "Vincent waited for you at the café. For two hours."

I nearly dropped the tray. "I don't want to talk about it," I said, ignoring the accusation in his eyes and the curiosity in Françoise's face.

One sunny afternoon, the kind of day that held the last gasps of summer, my restless thoughts and footsteps led me to the place in the Place Lamartine garden where Vincent and I met. The oleanders were in full bloom, their pink and white petals seductive, but I knew better than to touch them, for inhaling their perfume too deeply could make you faint. Instead I picked a dandelion and blew away the seeds like a schoolgirl, uncertain for what I was wishing.

I stopped walking as I rounded the last corner and let the empty stem drop from my fingers. Vincent was there, standing in front of his easel and painting, a young boy with a basket beside him. I ducked behind a tree before they could see me.

"But the sky's not green, Monsieur Vincent, why'd you make the sky green?"

I bit back a laugh at the childish voice and listened as Vincent explained his picture. His voice was patient, even affectionate, as if he didn't mind being bothered and knew the boy well. Finally he said, "Isn't your Maman waiting for those eggs?"

A sigh loud enough for me to hear. "I want to stay. Maman makes me do chores."

"I think you should run along, or we'll both be in trouble with your Maman. Tell her I said hello, won't you?"

"I will, Monsieur Vincent, *salut!*" With that the boy scampered off.

I stood a little longer behind the tree, watching Vincent touch his brushes to the canvas, or take off his hat to run his hand through his hair. I could have slipped away, but my shoes seemed stuck to the grass. "Are you going to stay back there all day?" he asked without turning around.

"I'm sorry to eavesdrop," I said sheepishly and walked toward him. "I didn't think the boy should see me. Who is he?"

"Camille Roulin, Joseph's middle child. A kind family, the Roulins, all of them." He tossed his hat to the ground and gave me the same look Camille's father had. "You didn't turn up. I waited for you."

I avoided his eyes to stare at the dandelions by my feet. "I know. I'm sorry."

"Where were you? Why didn't you send word?"

"I—I changed my mind. I can't pose for you, Vincent. Please don't ask me again."

He did not speak for what seemed an eternity. I was afraid to look at him, but when I finally did, his expression had softened. "What happened to you," he asked, "that you still cannot trust me?"

I did not answer and instead walked closer to the easel to see his painting. It couldn't have been more different than the picture of the night café. All kinds of yellows and greens lit up the plants of the garden—the weeping beech, cedar bush, pink-flowered oleanders—while patches of sunlight warmed the grass. Over the trees peered Saint-Trophime's stone tower, the only reminder of the surrounding city, and only I was missing, sleeping under the cedar in my pink dress and waiting for Vincent to find me.

"You've painted the place where we met," I said. "Why?"

A blush turned his face as pink as the oleanders. "Yes . . . well . . . it's a lovely spot. A garden like this makes me think of Boccaccio or even Petrarch. Petrarch lived near here in Avignon . . ." He babbled on about poetry and troubadours, but I heard, *"He's been thinking about me,"* and I felt more guilty than ever.

"Rachel, is something the matter?" He'd stopped talking about the garden. "Are you feeling unwell? Let's get you out of the sun." He gave a quick wipe to his paintbrushes with a rag, then led me to the beech tree before I could object. He spread his jacket on the ground so I wouldn't muss my dress and handed me a glass bottle before sitting opposite. "Water from the pump behind the café. Drink slowly." The water was warm but tasted fresh.

"Why are you so nice to me?" The question burst from my lips, and Vincent stared with raised eyebrows. "I've never had a man be as kind to me as you, except Papa. You used to be a preacher, and yet . . . ?" I fluttered my hand toward the painting, unsure how to explain.

He threw back his head and laughed. "You wonder why I treat a fallen woman like a human being, when good society shuns her."

My cheeks burned. "I don't see why that's funny."

"It's not funny, I'm sorry." His voice shifted, serious yet kind. "I don't give a damn about good society, Rachel, and it's not my place to judge you. Oh, it's easy for the high-and-mighty to say it's immorality, or laziness, or lust that drives women to prostitution, but I've never thought that way. No matter how good or noble a woman may be by nature, if she has no means and is not protected by her family, she is in great danger of being drowned in the pool of prostitution. Such women should be pitied and protected, not condemned."

"I don't need you to pity me. I don't need anybody to—"

He held up his hand. "I don't mean that in a bad way. I mean, I won't—I can't—condemn you or anyone else for the circumstances in which you've found yourselves. Besides, you're not like other *filles* I've known. You've picked up the rough language and all the rest, but it's not who you are, not really."

"Who am I?" I asked and clasped the glass bottle tightly.

"One of the few people who treats *me* like a human being instead of some odd foreigner." He changed position to sit beside me, so close that his arm touched my shoulder and I could smell the paint on his clothes. "One of the few people here I like spending time with. That I'd like to spend more time with."

"I like spending time with you too," I said, and meant it. "I truly am sorry, Vincent, about what I did. I'm sorry if I—"

"It's nothing," he interrupted. "I've been busy anyway, too busy to be working on a portrait. I'm moving into my new house, and it's taking up my time and money."

"Your new . . . ?"

"The yellow house here in Place Lamartine, on the corner next to the grocery shop." He pointed to the other side of the square. "I've been renting it since May, using one room as a studio, but there wasn't any furniture and it needed repairs I couldn't afford. My uncle Cent died recently and left Theo an inheritance, so Theo sent me three hundred francs. I've bought some furniture, begun fixing it up, and I'm hoping to move in a few days." He sighed happily. "It's one thing to roam from place to place as a free-spirited lad of twenty, but a man of thirty-five should have his own house."

"Is that how old you are?"

"You thought I was older, didn't you?" He was right: the lines on his face and the creases around his eyes had fooled me. "You're just *une petite* yourself."

"I'm not that young. I'm twenty-one."

He reached for my hand with another sigh. "I remember twenty-one. I was a different man then. You have years ahead, but one day you'll wake up and wonder where they went. Don't let the things you want escape you."

I resisted the urge to pull my hand away. "Your new house—is it a big house?"

"Not very, but there's good light, that's the important thing. Not a bad price, either, fifteen francs a month." He paused and looked shy. "I was wondering, would you mind helping me settle in? The house could use a woman's touch. I could show you all my paintings, too."

Françoise's voice muttered in my ear: "First he says he's short of money, then he invites you to his house. That's how it starts." *All I'd be doing is cleaning and tidying things up,* I told the voice. *I'd be back for the evening business.*

"I think you owe me that," Vincent added with a teasing glance, and I had to smile. I told him I'd love to help, and he exclaimed, "Splendid! Are you feeling better? Shall I walk you back?"

Now I did pull my hand free, as politely as I could, and I stood to brush grass from my skirt. "I'm fine, thank you, stay and finish your picture."

"Until next time, then." He climbed to his feet and gave me a swift kiss, his nose bumping mine.

"*À bientôt,*" I stammered and made a hasty retreat.

"Rachel?" he called after me. "You didn't say whether you like my painting."

I turned at the hedges to call back my answer. "I love it."

★ ★ ★

A yellow envelope appeared at the *maison* a few days later, my name written in a loopy scrawl. Inside was a sketch of Vincent's house and the single word "Today?" with its bold and insistent question mark. I would not fail him again—this time I would keep my promise. I tucked the note into the bosom of my dress and fetched an apron, a basket, and clean cloths for dusting.

"Where are you going?" asked Jacqui, lounging in the *salon* with a fashion gazette, the only girl about.

"The market," I lied over my shoulder as I walked out the door.

I must have passed the house a thousand times since coming to Arles, when I walked up the Avenue de Montmajour to the bathing-house, or when the girls and I dressed respectably to enjoy an afternoon coffee at the Café de l'Alcazar across the street. Madame Virginie had registered me as one of her *filles* at the *gendarmerie,* also across the street; I'd had to fill out a long form, answer questions about my family, and let the police doctor examine me in a back room. I remembered looking toward the little dilapidated house on the corner that day, thinking someone should live there and take care of it. It had seemed lost among the other buildings of the Place Lamartine, as lost as I'd felt. But today, with fresh paint the color of fresh butter, the house shone, and the shutters were bright green now, too. It wasn't lost anymore.

Vincent threw open the door with a cheery greeting and didn't stop talking as I walked inside. A slender corridor stretched ahead, two doors on the right leading to the studio and the kitchen, a flight of stairs rising to the second floor. He chattered about what would go here, what would go there, flinging his arms left and right. "A house of my own! I got some beds for the upstairs and a mirror . . . I still need a dress-

ing table for the guest bedroom, though . . . and I need to hang
up my pictures and Japanese prints. . . . I'll eat here and I'll save
so much money . . . just think of the work I'll be able to do
with all this space! . . . *Et voilà,* the studio . . ." He opened the
first door and waved me inside. "I took down the shutters so
there'd be plenty of light, and I'm having gaslamps installed so
I can work late."

"Don't you worry about everybody watching you?" I asked,
glancing at the large windows facing onto the busy street.

Vincent shrugged. "I have nothing to hide."

I wouldn't want anyone to see such a mess. Half-squeezed
paint tubes and black stubs of charcoal littered the red-tiled
floor. Stained cloths were piled on the worktable, together with
wilted flowers, empty ink bottles, bouquets of pencils and reed
pens. A stack of drawings and prints lay on a chair, others were
tacked to the walls, a piercing smell of turpentine perfuming
the chaos. My fingers itched to clean, and I had to stop myself
from finding a broom.

But the *paintings.* I clapped my hands at Monsieur Roulin in
his uniform, face wise and serious with his bountiful beard, cap
emblazoned with the proud word "*Postes.*" In another picture
stood an old man in a straw hat, careworn eyes in a careworn
face, and I knew this had to have been Patience Escalier, the
former Camargue cowherd Vincent spoke about with such respect. A sunset scene with coal barges by the Rhône, beyond it
the public garden, the night café, and Vincent himself, dressed
up in a brown suit and gazing from a canvas with tranquil eyes.
So many more, more than I could absorb all at once, and I felt
almost dizzy.

I looked at the painting on the easel and smiled. "That's
one of the cafés downtown in the Place du Forum." The café's
terrace glowed yellow from a single gas lantern, and under the

awning a white-aproned waiter bustled among the tables. A finer establishment than the cafés of the Place Lamartine, the sort of place where *filles de maison* dared not go.

Vincent had been standing silent in the doorway, but he came to join me. "I've wanted to try a starry sky for some time," he said. "In the dark I may take a blue for a green, a blue-lilac for a pink-lilac, but I can fix it in the studio if need be. Soon I'll try a night painting by the river."

"They look so happy."

"Who?"

"The people in the painting. You can tell they're happy from the way they're sitting. Not like in the night café. It's two different worlds." I nodded toward the painting of the Café de la Gare.

"You're very perceptive," Vincent said.

"It's not hard to see things if you only look."

He tilted his head to study me, and I sensed he was seeing something—in me—that he hadn't noticed before. He took my hand and drew me across the room. "Come, I want to show you something."

There it was. The painting I'd been waiting weeks to see, propped against a windowsill, framed in the afternoon light. The sunflowers.

Blazing sunflowers that should have looked forlorn and sad, plucked from the earth where they'd grown, trapped inside an earthenware jug. But they didn't. They writhed with life, the yellow so passionate, so untamed—oh, I wanted to touch that painting. I wanted to run my fingers over the canvas and savor its texture, every peak and valley of paint, every swirl and dash. Caress every line, every curve where his hand had been, trace the blue letters of his name.

I thought I knew this man who talked with me and made

love with me, but I didn't. I knew his body and something of his mind, nothing of his soul. Here was his soul, here, and here; in every painting in this room he'd left pieces of his spirit. *Soun bèu esperit*, his beautiful spirit, as we say in Provençal. This was no ordinary vase of flowers. The sunflowers were his voice, and for the first time since the day we met, I started to truly listen. "I've never seen anything like it," I murmured. "It's more beautiful than I could have imagined. All of it, more than I could have dreamed."

His hand was gentle on my shoulder, his voice soft in my ear. "You don't know what it means to me, for you to say that."

I threw my arms around him and buried my face in his chest, wanting suddenly to touch him as I longed to touch the painting. He was surprised but returned my embrace, and his lips brushed my hair, his fingers my spine. I closed my eyes to relish the rising and falling of his breath, and we stood in silence until embarrassment overcame me and I pulled away. "Shall we get to work?" I asked, my voice pitched too high, and I bent to gather paint tubes so he couldn't see my face.

Bit by bit, Vincent's ramshackle house began to look like a home. While he brought the rest of his things from the Café de la Gare and arranged them upstairs, I tried to work my artistry in the kitchen: blue enamel coffeepot and saltcellar on the table, mismatched dishes in the cupboard, tobacco box on the mantel. Vincent had a new stove—"on credit," he said with a roll of his eyes—and the sink had a pump for running cold water, more than I had expected to find. I set two chairs by the fireplace, where he could read and smoke his pipe in the evenings; I nipped to the garden for zinnias to tuck in a jug on the windowsill, and attacked the floor tiles with a soapy brush, pleased to see them gleam red instead of a dull, dusty gray.

There was nothing to eat in the cupboards, so I stepped out to buy vegetables and herbs for a *soupe au pistou* and some fresh bread. It was the strangest feeling going to the grocery shop next door with a basket on my arm and an apron around my waist, hair done up like I was somebody's wife instead of a *fille* from the Rue du Bout d'Arles. "*Bonjour,* Madame," I said to the grocer, who was sweeping her threshold when I approached. She smiled in a friendly way and helped me with my purchases, but she must have wondered who I was and what brought me to Vincent's.

I lit the fire in the stove and started supper when I returned, humming to myself as I chopped vegetables and pounded herbs. Like any Provençal girl, I started learning from Maman before I was tall enough to reach the stewpot, and like any Provençal woman, Maman had a way with herbs and spices, which she passed on to me. In no time the pungent aromas of basil and garlic challenged the smell of turpentine, and in no time, Vincent was lured downstairs. "You're cooking for me?" he asked.

I smiled as I gave the soup a leisurely stir. "You should have a good supper on your first night. How do you like your new kitchen?"

"*Mon Dieu,* you've worked a miracle." He frowned at the glistening red tiles. "But you didn't have to clean the floor, *ma petite,* I could have done that."

"I wanted everything to be perfect," I replied, then turned back to the stewpot to hide my blush. *Ma petite.* He'd called me his little one. He'd never done that before.

He lured me away from the stove to see his bedroom. It was too small to put much in it, so he'd filled it with color: blue walls, red blanket on the wooden bed, cheerful paintings and prints. In the corner stood a plain table instead of a washstand, and above it hung a mirror for shaving. He'd tacked pegs behind the bed for his clothes, including his yellow straw hat, and squeezed a chest of drawers next to the fireplace. He'd brought up two rush-seated chairs even though they made for a tight fit, and he'd put two pillows on the bed, like he didn't expect to sleep alone.

I walked to the wide-open shutters to lean on the sill. Some of the men strolling through the Place Lamartine garden were probably on their way to visit their mistresses or have a beer at a café, while their wives hurried home, baskets overflowing with food for supper. Friends called to one another, children laughed during their games, and in the distance whistled the afternoon train arriving from Marseille. So many stories beyond this window. Every morning Vincent could watch the dawn awaken the city, and every night, he'd see the stars from where he lay.

"You should have seen how it looked before," he said. "A rat wouldn't have slept here. Things cost more than I expected, but I wanted good, solid country beds, something durable that will last." He nodded toward a closed door. "The other bedroom is through there, but I'll work on that another day."

As he kept puttering around his bedroom, I finished supper. Bread sliced, table set, soup hot. Wiping my hands on my apron, I called up from the hallway, "*À table!*"

The stairs creaked under Vincent's feet as he descended. "Smells good," he said, catching me round the waist before plunking himself down at the table. "You should see what happens when I try to cook."

"Does it taste like paint?" I teased as I brought over a pair of bowls, and he laughed the musical laugh of a completely contented man. He ate two helpings of my *soupe au pistou,* and I was so glad he liked it that I pretended not to notice his gleeful slurping and the dribbles in his beard. After we finished eating I made coffee in the pert blue coffeepot—he told me he'd painted a picture of his coffeepot, he'd been so proud to buy it—and we talked at the table until the sun had nearly lowered. He helped wash the dishes and put things away, then, cheeks rosy with embarrassment, he asked if I'd mend his painting trousers.

I had to smile at this grown man of thirty-five who desperately needed a woman looking after him. He lit a fire in the kitchen fireplace so I could have good light while I worked, then dropped the trousers into my lap together with a battered red lacquer teabox and a muttered "There should be a needle and thread inside."

I opened the box to find a collection of yarn balls, each wound with a pair, trio, or quartet of colors. "Are you taking up knitting?"

"No," he said, kneeling before me and taking a ball of yarn from my hand. "When I lived in Nuenen, I was fascinated by the weavers who worked there, because they took ordinary wool and turned it into wonderful paintings of cloth. I thought, what better way to experiment with color combinations than to use wool yarn?"

I picked up another. "You have red and green in this one, like in the night café picture."

"Precisely, and this one has mostly yellow and violet, the second complementary color pair. Blue and orange make the third, and you can find that . . ." His face shone like an eager schoolboy's as he dug for another ball of yarn, and I watched him instead of the wool in his hand. He caught my eye and said, "You think it's strange, don't you?"

"I think it's wonderful." I took the yarn from him to put back in the box, then touched his cheek, his whiskers bristly under my fingers. The firelight turned his hair to copper flame, his eyes to deep blue, almost black.

The logs in the fireplace rearranged themselves with a flurry of sparks, and we both jumped. This time he was the one to pull away, retreating to his chair and a book as I set to work on his trousers. He'd tried to mend the holes in the knees himself but had made a mess of it, so I ripped out his clumsy stitches and started afresh. I couldn't make the trousers look new—that *would* be a miracle—but at least they'd look better. When I'd almost finished I peeked at him: brow furrowed, he appeared lost in his reading. "Vincent?" I said quietly.

He didn't look up. "Yes?"

"You once asked me where I came from, and I wouldn't tell you. I'd like to now."

He looked up at that, then closed his book and leaned forward.

"I grew up in a village not far from here called Saint-Rémy," I began. "My papa was the schoolteacher, and my family lived in a house just outside town. Next door, on his family's farm, lived a boy named Philippe."

Things nobody else knew, not Françoise, not Madame Virginie, poured from my mouth as if I'd been confessing in church. Names I hadn't said aloud in months, moments I tried to forget. Through it all Vincent said little, only regarded me with serious eyes.

*"You said you loved me."*

*Philippe clears his throat. "If I marry you, Father will disown me, and I'll lose everything."*

*"All because of your mother!" I cry.*

*"Because you and I sinned," he corrects me. "Because we shouldn't have done what we did in the barn that night."*

*"You didn't think it sinful at the time. If she hadn't seen us—" I shudder to remember Philippe hastily pulling*

*up his trousers, the blood spots on my white nightdress, his*
*mother's face pale and shocked under the moon.*

*"Rachel, it's over. I'm sorry."*

*He turns to leave, but I grab his arm. "Philippe, I love*
*you. If you don't marry me, my sister will send me away. She*
*says I can't be around her family anymore, she says I'm—"*

*"I'm sorry," he says again, then he's gone.*

*I don't wait for Pauline to throw me out. Tante Lu-*
*dovine in Avignon, that's what she threatened, pious Tante*
*Ludovine, with her rustly black dresses and constant talk of*
*hellfire. I pack my valise and hurry to the railway station,*
*taking only what I think I'll need, the money Papa left*
*me when he died, and a few mementoes of happier days.*
*Someplace else, there must be someplace else. When the*
*train reaches Tarascon, I walk inside the station and read*
*the names on the chalkboard.*

*Arles. I'll go to Arles.*

"That's why you didn't like my painting of the night café,"
Vincent said pensively when I finished. "It reminded you of
what happened and how Mademoiselle Françoise found you."

I looked at my hands, folded in my lap and still clutching
his mended trousers. I'd stopped my story at the Café de la
Gare and hadn't told him what happened next. When Françoise brought me to the *maison,* Madame Virginie gripped my
chin in her plump fingers and said, "Sweet-looking, nice manners, good figure, good teeth. They'll like you, you'll make us
both good money." She complimented Françoise, "Excellent
choice," as if I'd been a dress, a bonnet, or cut of meat from
the butcher's.

"I'm so ashamed, even now," I said to Vincent. "How could
I have been such a fool?"

Vincent shook his head. "The young man was the fool. He behaved like the worst kind of cad, using a chaste girl of good family then abandoning her."

"But I seduced him, I tried to trap him into marrying me. I loved him, and I thought—"

"A man of honor would have gently but firmly refused until marriage, rather than take advantage of your innocence." Vincent came to kneel before me again and held out his left hand. A pink scar lingered there that I'd never noticed, among the calluses on his palm. "Love makes us do desperate things, Rachel. That day"—he nodded at the scar—"I thought holding my hand in a candle flame would prove me worthy of a lady's affections. I was wrong."

A chill crawled through me at the thought of Vincent hurting himself that way. I traced the mark with my fingers, as if I could mend it and make it disappear. "Who was she?"

He stared at the fire, and his answer was a whisper. "Her name was Kee." He looked back at me and smiled a little. "What happened wasn't your fault. You sought only to love and be loved. That's no sin. And someday . . ." He stopped himself as the clock in the hall chimed nine times. *Ting-ting, ting-ting.*

"I should be going," I said, handing Vincent his trousers and the teabox.

He stood when I did. "Don't go. Stay with me."

I thought of the two pillows, two chairs in the bedroom. "I could stay long enough to try out that new bed, I suppose"—I winked at him—"but then I really . . ."

"Stay the whole night."

"Madame Virginie would be so angry. It might be busy—"

"I can give you four francs, that should satisfy her. Please."

More than anything, I wanted to stay. "*D'accord,*" I finally agreed. "I will."

Being with him that night, joining my body to his, felt different from all those times at Madame Virginie's. No stomping of soldiers' boots in the corridor to distract us, no girlish giggles through the walls, just his breath and mine mingling in the dark. Only afterward, when he'd relit the candle and was digging in his bureau to lend me a nightshirt, did I think about what came next. I'd never slept next to a man before. The customers always went home, he always went home, and I slept alone with nobody to bother me. To sleep in Vincent's bed seemed such an intimate thing to do, and I felt more nervous than I ever had around him.

He pulled on his long drawers, climbed back into bed, and looked at me expectantly. "What is it?" he asked.

How silly I must have looked, standing there naked and holding his nightshirt. "Nothing," I said and tugged the nightshirt over my head. It was too long and had a few holes in it— perhaps I'd fix them one day—but at least it was clean. I plaited my hair with shaking fingers, then blew out the candle and climbed into bed. I chose to lay near the edge, facing away into the room's center, but he inched close to fold me in his arms and nestle against my back. The rhythm of his breathing told me he fell asleep almost at once, while I stared into the dark, my mind too unsettled for rest.

*Isn't this what you wanted?* asked the voice inside my head. *Someone to hold you, someone to make you feel safe?* I hadn't felt safe since Papa died, not until today. *Someone to listen, someone to understand?* Vincent understood. I'd told him the truth of my life, and he understood. *Close your eyes, Rachel. Close your eyes.*

In my dreams I saw his sunflowers again. I saw us at the table, by the fire, every second of that wonderful day. I woke in the night and touched his peaceful face, reassuring myself he was no dream before burrowing into the warm circle of his embrace.

# CHAPTER FIVE

## Secrets and Warnings

*I do not want to deceive or abandon any woman.*
　　　—Vincent to Theo, The Hague, May 1882

I was alone when sunlight kissed me awake the next morning. Sunlight and the clackety-clack of the Paris-Lyon-Méditerranée express train steaming across the nearby railway bridge. A sudden clatter from the studio below told me Vincent had risen early to work, but I lay under the blanket a while longer, listening to the hubbub in the Place Lamartine and gazing at the paintings and prints on the walls.

I knew things about him now that I hadn't known the day before, that he snored when he slept on his left side, that his feet were cold even under warm covers. That he . . . sang? Yes, that was his voice drifting up the stairs, not totally on key but filled with good intentions. I rose from the bed and leaned in the doorway to listen. It was a Dutch song, so I couldn't understand much, but he sounded happy.

While I'd been sleeping, he'd brought a porcelain pitcher of water and a basin so I could wash my face. I let my fingers play over the other things on the table—hairbrush, bar of soap, razor—and after I dressed, I used his comb to smooth my hair. Birds trilled in the plane trees outside the window, and between their song and Vincent's, I couldn't help but hum as I put away his nightshirt and made the bed.

His eyes lit up when I entered the studio. He was dressed in his painting clothes, and I was pleased to see that the mended trousers looked just fine. *"Bonjour, ma petite,"* he said with a smile that looked as shy as I felt.

*"Bonjour, mon cher,"* I said, stumbling over the "my dear." "What are you doing?"

"Preparing canvases." He waved his hand toward a roll of canvas and stack of wooden stretchers. "I was out of stretchers, so I had to take off some of the nearly dry paintings before I could tack new canvas. I'm sorry if my hammering woke you."

"It didn't. I needed to get up." I reached out to rub the canvas between my fingers. "Did you get this here?"

"Oh no, that's primed linen canvas from Paris. Theo sends it to me, my paints too. Here I can only get cheap paints and jute canvas I have to prime myself. Which will do if I have nothing else, but I don't prefer it."

I glanced around the studio at the paintings he'd shuffled. I didn't notice the smell of turpentine anymore—I was getting used to it. "And you did all these since February?"

He laughed. "Since July. I've sent Theo two shipments of paintings already, and I'll send him more once everything dries."

He'd painted about two dozen pictures in only two months? "You do work hard," I said in wonder, which made him laugh again.

"People around here think it's odd, don't they, a man painting all day instead of doing what they call real work?" Françoise had said exactly that, Jacqui and some of the other girls thought it, and I knew Vincent could read their opinions in my face. He shrugged as he carried the roll of canvas to his worktable and measured a length. "It was the same back in Holland. *Het schildermenneke,* the farmers called me in Nuenen, 'the little painter fellow.' That's one thing I liked about Paris"—his knife sliced cleanly through the white fabric—"I wasn't the only painter. The *quartier* where Theo and I lived was full of them. This summer I met a Belgian and an American painter over in Fontvieille, but they've both left now."

"It must be lonely," I said, "not having any artists to talk to."

He looked over at me and smiled. "Not so much anymore. I can talk to you."

Talk to me he did as he kept working, telling me things about each painting I approached, stories about the people he'd met and the places he'd gone. How the waiter at the café in the Place du Forum was rude but tolerated his being there, how the gypsies in the camp outside town were friendly and gave him homemade blackberry wine. "Today," he said as he tacked the last nails into the last canvas, "I thought I'd do another study of the cedar bush in the public garden."

"The place where we met? Again?" I teased. "Have you had any breakfast yet?"

He shrugged. "Coffee."

"You can't work on an empty stomach."

"I do it all the time."

"I'll make some breakfast," I said firmly, "and you're going to eat it."

"If you insist," he replied. "It's been a long time since a woman fussed at me about breakfast!"

*It's been a long time since I've had someone to make breakfast for,* I thought as I sliced potatoes to fry, revived the fire in the stove, and started a fresh pot of coffee. I'd made breakfast for Papa every day after Maman had died—sometimes he hadn't wanted it either, but at my complaints he'd given in, every time. "*À table!*" I called a short time later, only to hear a muffled "*Une minute,*" followed by a Dutch curse as something fell heavily to the studio floor. Two minutes passed. Five. "Breakfast, Vincent," I called again. "*Viens,* it's hot!"

He strolled in then, wiping his hands on his trousers before I pointed to the sink. "I could get used to this," he said. "Hot coffee, hot food . . . warm bed." He winked as he reached for the coffeepot, and I passed him a plate with potatoes and toasted bread.

"You'll work much better now," I told him, and he nodded, mouth too full to answer. He ate in a hurry, not talking anymore but gazing around the kitchen, into the ashes of the fireplace, out the window at the carriages rattling down the Avenue de Montmajour. After he finished, I stood to get him more potatoes, but he shook his head. I thought he was anxious to go painting, until he looked grave and started drawing on the table with his fork. "Rachel, there's something I'd like to talk to you about."

I sat back down, my heart stirring in my chest. "Yes?"

"That night when I asked you about your past, you asked me something too. You asked why I wasn't married. The truth is, I almost was." He saw me glance at his left hand, resting on the table where I couldn't see the scar. "Not her. Someone I met later in The Hague, a prostitute named Sien."

"A prostitute?" I said numbly. "From a brothel?"

"From the streets."

His story didn't spill from him the way mine had from me.

It came slowly, phrase after careful phrase, and he kept his eyes lowered to his plate. He met Sien one lonely night in a darkened alley, where she looked for men and money to add to the pittance she earned from doing laundry. She was pregnant, he said, discarded like an old rag by some man who'd promised her a better life, and she already had a little daughter. Vincent wanted to help her, so he paid her to model for his drawings, and soon he invited them to live with him and share his bread. He kept her a secret as long as he could, because he knew what his family would say: that she wasn't beautiful, wasn't refined, that she was using him. She could barely read and write; she smoked cigars, drank gin, and cursed like a sailor. A hard life had marked her figure and bearing, smallpox scars her face. She was many steps down the social ladder as far as his family was concerned, no worthy match for a van Gogh.

"Did you love her?" I dared to ask.

"Very much, and I wanted to marry her."

"Why didn't you?"

"*He* wouldn't have let me," Vincent replied, and I knew he meant his father. "Eventually I told Theo about Sien because I needed his help. He didn't approve any more than my parents would, but he helped me anyway because he's a good man and a good brother. Sien gave birth to a healthy baby boy, and although we couldn't marry, we lived as man and wife—as a family—for well over a year." He looked up, not at me but into the past, a wistful smile on his face.

Over a year. She'd taken care of him, he'd taken care of her. She cleaned his house and cooked his meals, and they lived together in a real home. She slept beside him in his bed the way I had, like me she fussed at him about breakfast. "What happened?"

He drew on the table with his fork again, and his voice

changed. "It didn't last. When I finally told my parents, my father thought I'd gone mad. Sien and I never had enough money, and she complained that I spent too much on my paintings and drawings. We started fighting more and more. Theo came to visit, and he helped me see that the situation was hopeless, that for the sake of my work and my health I needed to leave. I went to Drenthe to live on the heath, then to Nuenen to live with my parents. I saw Sien and the children once more, when I returned to The Hague to collect some things I left behind."

"You left her?" I gasped. "Just like that?"

"She didn't love me anymore, and if Theo had cut me off . . ." His eyes were liquid. "For months I wondered if I did right, and sometimes I still do. It broke my heart to leave the children. If they'd been mine, no force on earth could have taken me from them, but . . ."

Of course for a man of his age there had to have been other women—I wasn't so naïve to believe otherwise—but I hadn't expected this. He'd created a home with Sien then left her because Theo had said he should. *What would Theo say if he knew about me?* I wondered. Was I any better a match than Sien Hoornik?

Vincent reached across the table to take my hand in his. "Rachel, what happened between me and Sien was a long time ago. I made a lot of mistakes that I wouldn't make again, mistakes that shame me now, but I felt you had to know. Especially after yesterday. I hope this won't change things between us, although I'd understand if . . ." He let the thought fade away.

I could leave without looking back. I could forget him, the sunflowers, the feeling of his arms around me, pretend it never happened. Or I could believe, as I wanted to believe, that I was more to him than just another whore from the brothels, that I wouldn't end up like Françoise when her man had left her, or like Sien. I stood at a crossroads, two paths winding before me to a distant, misty horizon. In my mind, I knew I had a choice. But in my heart, I knew I didn't.

We said good-bye at the public garden, Vincent continuing toward the beech tree and cedar bush in his yellow straw hat, me in yesterday's dress heading to the Rue du Bout d'Arles. "Do you want to see me again?" he asked in a low voice before I walked away, and I assured him that nothing had changed. He looked relieved and kissed me on the forehead.

I figured I'd get a scolding back at the *maison,* but I didn't expect Françoise to be the one waiting for me. "Where have you been? Madame Virginie's furious, as well she should be. Staying out all night without a word to anyone."

Jacqui couldn't resist joining in. "She's been with that crazy painter." At my shocked expression, she added, "Yesterday wasn't market day, *idiote.* I followed you to the Place Lamartine. His house is just as ugly as he is."

"Rachel, what were you thinking?" Françoise cried. "Don't you remember what I—"

"He needed help moving," I broke in. "I cooked him supper and mended his clothes. To be nice." Françoise crossed her arms without comment, and I glared at Jacqui. "He's *not* crazy."

"Playing house, were you?" Jacqui jeered. "All night long? I can't imagine why anybody'd want to sleep with that. Unless he has a really big—paintbrush!"

"You'll never know," I snapped before turning back to Françoise. "He paid me four francs, and I'm giving half to Madame Virginie like I'm supposed to."

Jacqui jumped in again. "Four francs! That's a laugh, I earned *ten* francs last night. Oh, I bet he told you that you were the prettiest girl in Arles and that he was so lonely and sad." She tried to imitate Vincent's accent. "Rachel, you inspire me sooo much—"

My face grew hot. "It's not like that."

"—and you fell for it. Cooking him supper, for God's sake!"

"You're just mad because he didn't want you!" I exploded. "You think you're so special, but he wouldn't give you the time of day!"

Her mouth twisted with anger, and she drew close to loom over me. "*Petite salope,* why would I give a damn what that redheaded loon thinks?"

"Don't call him that!"

Our shouting summoned the other girls to the landing or down the stairs, and Françoise stepped between us. "Stop it! Madame Virginie is going to catch you both out, and Rachel, you're in enough trouble as it is."

"What do I care anyway," Jacqui said with a shrug and slinked away. "She'll catch fleas or the clap, then who'll want her?"

Françoise caught my arm before I could scurry upstairs. "You're wasting your time. One day he'll go back where he came from and forget all about you. He's no different from the rest of them."

"You're wrong. He's kind and gentle and caring." I tried not to think about Sien as I spoke. *That was different. She was different.*

"He's still a man."

Madame Virginie's voice thundered across the room, shouting my name, and she hurried toward us. "What do you have to say for yourself, missy? Where have you been?"

"With that painter," Jacqui said smugly from the bar. "All night."

I bit my lip so hard that I tasted blood, but I kept my temper and reached into my basket. "He paid me, Madame."

Madame Virginie stared at the coins in her hand. "You were gone the whole night, and all you have to show for it is two francs? It was busy here, you could have made a lot more than that. You work for me, young lady, not him!"

I shoved the other two francs at her. "Then take my share too, and leave me alone!"

No one spoke to Madame Virginie that way. Her face turned purple, and her eerily calm tone made me take a step back. "If I threw you out, where would you go? Your name is on the police register, and until you have enough money to get it taken off, it's a brothel or the streets for you. And you know what that means."

I did know. At Leon Batailler's the girls slept on hard cots in a damp attic, and they didn't get half their fees, either. Half a franc each time, more like, and they did things for men that Madame Virginie wouldn't let happen at her house. The other *maisons* weren't much better. To work the streets like those *filles soumises* drunk on absinthe and wearing too much rouge, whining to passing sailors for a few centimes . . . it'd be weeks, maybe months, before I wound up in hospital with the clap or the madhouse with syphilis. Or in the cemetery.

"Rachel's a good girl, Madame," Françoise said, sliding an arm around my shoulders. "She made a mistake, that's all. She won't do it again." She squeezed me to get me to talk, but I couldn't speak.

Madame Virginie looked from her to me, and her face went back to its normal color. "Then you best not dally with that foreigner any more, unless he pays a fair price. You have to earn your keep. Do you hear me?"

I wanted to walk out the door, go someplace, anyplace, maybe to the yellow house and beg Vincent to take me in. He couldn't support me, though, Françoise was right about that, and going to Pauline in Saint-Rémy or Tante Ludovine in Avignon was out of the question. No, I had to stay at Madame Virginie's until I saved enough money to get my name off the police register and make an honest living. What choice did I have?

"Do you hear me?" Madame repeated.

Françoise gave me another nudge, and I forced myself to look submissively at the floor and apologize. That evening, as I entertained yet another soldier, yet another farmer to "earn my keep," I closed my eyes and saw Vincent's face.

# CHAPTER SIX

## A Starry Night by the Rhône

*I often think that the night is more alive and richly colored than the day.*
—Vincent to Theo, Arles, September 1888

First it was little things. At luncheon, Madame Virginie called Minette to sit next to her, the place that used to be mine, while I was banished to the other end of the table. I stayed behind and helped the cook clean the kitchen while everyone else left for the market and monthly trip to the apothecary. Then it became clear: I was on Madame's list. "Where do you think you're going?" she'd demand if I went anywhere near the front door, so there was no chance of slipping out to see Vincent. "How many customers did you have last night?" she'd ask each morning, even though she made sure the other girls had more than I did. Jacqui tried her best to make things worse, taunting me under her breath, sneaking into my room to steal my hair ribbons or use my perfume without asking.

Oh, I would have liked to talk back to Madame, give a piece of my mind to Jacqui, but I didn't. Françoise understood. She quietly made sure I got new hair ribbons and gave me encouraging smiles whenever she passed me. "Madame'll get over it," she whispered. "Keep being a good girl."

One night, when Madame Virginie was safely in her parlor and everybody but me was upstairs with a customer, Raoul brought me a message at the bar. "*Monsieur le peintre* is outside and asks for you."

Vincent stood on the sidewalk under the lantern, wearing his work clothes—even his straw hat. He had a pipe in his mouth, artist's box in his hand, canvas and easel strapped to his back. "It's time to try a night picture by the river," he said. "Would you like to come with me?"

I glanced back inside. "I can't. Madame Virginie threatened to throw me out after I got back last time."

An angry spark leaped into Vincent's eyes. "What did she say?"

"That I couldn't go off with you anymore and lose a night's business."

"I can give you some money—"

"I don't want to take your money." I thought about the little box in my bureau. If I got caught, I could give her a few of my own francs. "Wait a minute," I told him and pulled Raoul aside. "If Madame Virginie asks, I'm with a customer. There's a franc in it for you." He agreed with a grin and a "*Oui, Mademoiselle.*"

"Let's go," I said to Vincent, "but let's hurry before someone sees me." We rounded the corner toward the city gate and the Place Lamartine, but instead of crossing the garden in the direction of the yellow house, he steered us toward the river. The burden on his back was making him hunch over, and I asked, "Would you like me to carry something?"

"No, thank you." He smiled at me as we passed under a streetlight. "I look like a porcupine, but I'm used to it."

The Place Lamartine ended at the edge of the Rhône in a high sloping wall, built some years before to protect the city from floods. Vincent unfolded his easel and secured a canvas so the breeze wouldn't blow it off. "You don't want to go to the riverbank?" I asked, peering down a stairway to the stony shore below. I could take off my shoes and stockings and dip my toes in the water.

"Too dark down there," he said. "Better vantage point from up here."

From where we stood at the bend of the river, you could see all the lights of Arles and the bridge linking the city to the suburb of Trinquetaille. A full moon flooded the southern sky with light and drowned out the stars, but you found them if you turned to the north, a carpet of them twinkling like diamonds. Most nights, pimps and whores wandered the embankment, or fishermen wanting a late-night catch, but not tonight. We were alone with the stars.

Vincent pulled a palette from the box he'd brought, then rummaged among his tubes of paint. "I'm sorry you got in trouble with your *patronne* because of me."

"It's not your fault," I sighed. "I'm the one who stayed out without permission."

"I wish"—he paused with a paint tube in each hand and a frown on his face—"I wish I could help you in some way."

"Don't you worry about me, I'll be fine." I tipped back my head and tried to count the stars in their silvery-gold brilliance. I didn't want to think about Madame Virginie or the *maison de tolérance,* I wanted to think of nothing but being right there, right then. The wind off the water made me shiver; in my haste to leave I'd forgotten my shawl. Vincent saw me tremble and came to drape his jacket over my shoulders. A gentle scent of paint and pipe smoke drifted around me. His scent.

After squeezing blues, greens, and yellows onto his palette and using a small knife to blend the colors, Vincent picked up his brushes and started to paint. It was dim, but the moon cast enough light so he could work. I sat on the wall and dangled my feet, peering again down to the riverbank. I could make out a coal barge, anchored and waiting to be unloaded the next morning, somebody probably sleeping on deck to keep away thieves. The river paid no attention as it made its dogged and determined way south.

"Have you ever seen the sea?" I asked Vincent.

He had a paintbrush in his mouth and spoke around the handle. "Many times in Holland. There's a fishing village called Scheveningen near where I lived in The Hague. I did some seascape studies there a few times, and we used to take the children to the beach."

We. He and Sien. Had he carried Sien's little girl on his shoulders across the sand, kissed Sien as they walked barefoot through the waves? I kicked my heel against the stone wall. "Have you been to the sea here?"

"Once, for several days at Saintes-Maries-de-la-Mer. Back in the spring."

"What's it like?"

"Beautiful. The Mediterranean changes color every second, from green to violet to blue, then the next moment it's taken on a tinge of pink or gray. Very fine effects. I've wanted to go back but"—he cleared his throat—"that takes money."

We fell silent then, Vincent busy with his painting, me chasing images of the little family at Scheveningen from my mind. I turned from the river to watch him as he worked. Sometimes he stopped to look up and around, tilting his head and muttering under his breath. Once or twice he laid down his things altogether and held up his hands in a kind of frame, screening off what he wanted to see before smiling and taking up his brush again. His hand was graceful as it swept from palette to canvas, here with small dashes of paint, there with long swooping strokes. Once he took a tube of yellow color and squirted little blobs right on the picture.

"There, you see, Rachel," he said, "it's not enough to put white dots on the canvas. Some stars are citron-yellow, others pink, while others have a blue forget-me-not glow. They aren't all the same." He sighed and gazed at the sky. "The stars make me dream, like when I look at a map and dream about the places I've never been to. Just as we take the train to Tarascon or Paris, we take death to reach the stars, and there we'll live forever. Ah, to feel the infinite high and clear above you, then life is almost enchanted after all."

It was easy to believe in dreams, there by the Rhône on such a night. The stars seemed to hold ancient secrets as they hovered and winked above our heads, secrets only they knew and that we could but guess. Was someone up there watching, looking after us, as I'd always been taught and almost always believed? Had that someone brought Vincent to me? My eyes returned to him—brush held aloft, contemplating the picture with furrowed brow—and I thanked the stars that exactly that had come to pass.

He happened to glance over at me in the same second. "What is it? You have the most extraordinary look on your face right now."

"I was thinking about how much I love you."

Astonishment flickered across his face. He stared at me for a moment, then turned back to his canvas and tapped his brush on the palette with a soft "Oh."

The water lapped. The wind blew. I waited, but Vincent said nothing, only painted. I pulled up my knees and hugged them without another word, tears pooling in my eyes. I couldn't look at him anymore and turned to the river instead.

"Come and see," he said gently after a while. That was all: *Come and see.* Wiping my eyes on the sleeve of his jacket, I slid off the wall to stand beside him, not touching him, not speaking, trying vainly to pretend I hadn't spoken in the first place.

The painting pulsed with energy and movement, the gaslights of Arles golden beacons under the midnight sky. Restless reflections shimmered and shone in the restless waters, stars blooming above like flowers, constellations unfurling across the horizon. Empty boats rocked against the shore, and on the riverbank he'd painted a pair of lovers strolling arm in arm where in real life no one stood. The woman had a blue dress like mine, and the man wore blue too. With a yellow straw hat.

Vincent turned to me, and on his face was, as he put it, the most extraordinary look. "How do you call the stars in Provençal?"

"*L'estelan,*" I murmured.

"*L'estelan,*" he repeated, then took my chin in his fingers and kissed me. It was the slightest brush of the lips—as soft as the breeze on my face—but the sweetest kiss, more loving in its tenderness than any words he could have spoken. Words were not necessary. His eyes told me, his kiss told me what I wanted to know. So did his painting.

# CHAPTER SEVEN

# The Studio of the South

*If I set up a studio and refuge right at the gates of the south,
it's not such a crazy scheme.*
　　　　　—Vincent to Theo, Arles, September 1888

Vincent showered me with little attentions after that night
by the river. Flowers he picked on his walks, novels with
tattered yellow covers—one visit he surprised me with a bird's
nest he found lying in an orchard. "I kept over a dozen nests in
my studio at Nuenen," he said shyly when he handed it to me.
"Birds are artists in their own right, no?" Jacqui, sitting at the
next table with a customer, erupted into giggles overhearing
him, but I ignored her and kissed him thank-you in front of
everybody. I didn't care what she thought, I didn't care what
anyone thought. The flowers watched over me from the vase
on my bureau, and the bird's nest earned a place of honor on
my windowsill.

　　The yellow house became my refuge, the nest where I flew

when I was free. Vincent and I shared suppers I cooked on my evenings off. We chatted by the fire, satisfied each other in the blue-walled bedroom. Some nights I imagined what it would be like to stay forever, not leaving in the morning for the Rue du Bout d'Arles, giving myself to no one but him. Some nights I dared to think what it would mean to bear his child, have a family together like he'd had with Sien. Then dawn would come, he'd rise from the bed to go to the studio, and my fancies would fade with the moonlight.

Some days I joined him on his painting trips. I sat with him in the Place Lamartine when he painted a picture of the house; I walked with him to the vineyards outside town when he wanted to paint the grape harvesters. With my hair up and face hidden under a parasol, no one took any notice of me, although Vincent was ogled by the curious everywhere we went. He talked to me as he worked, telling me the names of the colors he used and why he arranged the picture a certain way. "There, you see, Rachel"—he'd always begin—"if I painted all the trees that stand in front of my house, you couldn't see my house. Bless me, look at that sky! Pure cobalt. A fine effect."

Madame Virginie had become too distracted to notice how much time I spent with Vincent. One of the girls, Claudette— who'd been at the *maison* for two years and ought to have known better—got herself arrested for soliciting outside the *quartier reservé,* down by the Place du Forum. The police came to the brothel to investigate, and Madame feared she'd lose her license. Then word came that old Louis Farce, Madame Virginie's biggest rival, remodeled his place up the street with gilt mirrors and heavy red curtains, and was trying to steal our customers. Among all this, I was one of the good girls again, and as long as I brought money in, Madame couldn't care less what I did or with whom.

The question of taking Vincent's money troubled me as the weeks passed. One night at the *maison*, when I perched on his lap clad in my chemise and he reached into his pocket for three francs, I folded his fingers over the coins and shook my head. "I don't want you buying me like the others."

"I'm helping you," he said, "so that one day you can leave this place. I'd help you more if I could. Please, I want you to have it."

I thought about this. "Only when you visit me here, not when I visit your house. And two francs, not three. I'll kiss you for nothing."

"You drive a hard bargain," he teased and tucked a coin back in his pocket.

Oh, those were happy days as summer drew to a close and autumn made its unhurried way to Provence. Then the mistral arrived.

A fierce north wind that swept through the Rhône valley on its way to the sea, the mistral appeared any time of year but was ruthless during the autumn and winter months. The locals called it *le vent du fada*, "the idiot wind," because a mistral that howled through the streets and beat at the windows had the power to bring even the sanest soul close to lunacy. The wise stayed home and the weakest took to their beds, afflicted with headache brought by the wind's force. Even Vincent, who always thought painting more important than weather, accepted defeat when the mistral blew its hardest and worked indoors.

The banging of the window shutters startled me from a deep sleep one night near the end of October, and the shutters didn't stop banging for six days. The girls were bored silly with our business down to a trickle, and Madame Virginie stomped around the *maison* cursing the mistral instead of old Louis. I heard nothing from Vincent, so once the winds died, I crossed the Place Lamartine to find him.

A testy *"Oui, oui, j'arrive"* filtered from the hall before the door flew open. "Rachel!" The irritated frown on Vincent's face became a weak smile, but even that couldn't disguise his haggard appearance.

"Vincent, are you all right?" I asked in alarm. "Have you been ill?"

"I've had a queer turn, but I'm fine now. I've been working too hard, that's all, and with that devil of a wind wailing all night, I couldn't sleep."

I bustled past him into the kitchen, tossing my shawl over the banister on the way. "Have you been eating like you should?" Stained cups surrounded the empty coffeepot on the table, the stewpot stood abandoned on the stove. I lifted the lid to find a congealed mass of . . . something . . . that looked like it'd been there a while.

"I ran out of money," he said from the doorway. "Theo's latest letter didn't arrive until today. Anyway, I didn't feel like eating."

"Why didn't you send a note? I could have taken care of you."

"It's nothing. Sometimes this happens when I work too hard, then I have a long sleep and I feel better. I slept sixteen hours straight after the winds stopped, and I had some soup earlier at the Restaurant Vénissat."

"Vincent . . ."

"Rachel, please. You mustn't worry." The irritated frown briefly returned, then his face brightened. "Come upstairs, I want to show you what I've been doing. I've nearly finished decorating the second bedroom."

I followed him with a heavy sigh, then stopped with a gasp in the doorway of the second bedroom. It was smaller than his own, but he'd lavished it with attention, the bed sturdy walnut and expensive-looking, the chest of drawers with fine brass fittings. The sunflowers—*my* sunflowers—hung proudly over the bed, and a second sunflower picture too, with a blue background instead of yellow. "I didn't know you'd painted two," I said, walking up to them and longing again to touch.

"I have two more downstairs. They make a fine effect, no?"

On the opposite wall hung four paintings of the Place Lamartine garden—four! I'd only seen the first one. The second showed the place where he'd found me sleeping, the cedar bush under a bright blue sky, small figures dawdling along the path. The third, another corner of the garden where the path curved beside a tall fir tree and a pair of lovers held hands. A pair of lovers appeared in the fourth painting too, strolling among cypresses as a glowing moon watched them from a sunset pink sky. Their faces were featureless, but the man wore a yellow hat.

"I ran out of money because of the frames," Vincent said as I stared at the pictures. "But it was worth it."

I wasn't listening. "It's us," I whispered. "You painted us."

The room was for me, I knew it was. He was going to ask me to share his life in the yellow house. Share his life as Sien had shared his life, but this time it'd work, together we'd *make* it work. Maybe he'd already explained everything to Theo and his family. I could leave Madame Virginie's and be with him always. We'd take care of each other and be so happy. . . .

"Do you like the room?" Vincent asked.

I tried not to let my excitement show, but "yes" hovered on my lips. "I love it."

"Good. I think Gauguin will like it too."

My "yes" faded away. "Who?"

"Paul Gauguin—a painter, a great painter." Vincent walked to one of the paintings and straightened the frame. "Theo has arranged for him to live here. We've been negotiating for months, but he's agreed to come, and he'll arrive next week."

Negotiating for *months*? I turned so he couldn't see my tears and marched toward the stairs. "Rachel!" he called. "Where are you going?"

"Leave me alone!"

"No, wait! Tell me what's wrong!" He hurried downstairs behind me and reached for my arm as my fingers brushed the doorknob.

I jerked myself free and whirled to face him. "You're ashamed of me. You're ashamed of being with me."

"What are you talking about?"

"You haven't told your brother about me, have you? All those letters I see you writing, not one word about me, right? You say such lovely things, you act like you care for me—"

He tried again to reach for my hand, but I shrank against the door.

"Rachel, I *do* care for you, what is all this?"

"— and the room—I thought the room was for me."

His eyes were wide and puzzled. "For you?"

"The paintings! The sunflowers, our garden . . . I thought you'd ask me to live with you. What a fool I was. They were right, everybody was right!"

"What do you mean—who's right?"

I wiped my cheeks with my sleeve. "Everybody thinks you're using me."

"That's not true, I swear it's not true. Please, don't go."

My other hand was still on the doorknob.

"Don't go," he repeated. "I beg you. Come into the studio, and let's talk about this."

Only the pleading in his voice made me stay. I followed him into the studio and waited while he calmly circled the room and closed the windowpanes. It felt like all his pictures were staring at me. "No, I haven't told Theo about you," he began. "It's not the time, not yet. You have to understand, he's not likely to approve, and it's best if I—"

I didn't let him finish. "You're ashamed of me. Just like you were ashamed of Sien."

He yanked the last window shut with a *bang!* that made the others rattle. "Don't you talk to me about Sien! You know nothing about what I went through with her!"

"I know what you told me! You said you kept your relationship with her a secret. It's because you were ashamed of her!"

"I knew my family would make me leave her!"

"You didn't leave her because of your family, you left her because of your painting!"

It was like I had slapped him. His face blanched, and he picked up a rag from the worktable to mop his forehead. When he spoke, his voice was quiet and sad. "Yes, I was concerned Theo would cut me off, but everything had already fallen apart by then. My work was one thing among many."

My voice was quiet now too. "You left her, Vincent, and someday you'll leave me."

Realization dawned in his eyes. "Is that what you think? Is that what this is all about?"

"You won't tell me you love me, although I know you do." I flung my hand toward the starry night over the Rhône. "Look at the couples you paint—you won't even give them real faces. You're ashamed of me because I'm a whore." I collapsed into a chair and hid my face in my hands.

He rushed to kneel before me. "I'm the last man in the world to think such a thing. Surely you must know that by now."

"Then why won't—"

"My dear girl," he said wearily, "if you only knew." He

opened his palm so I could see his scar. "When I told Kee how much I loved her and wanted to marry her, do you know what she said? 'No, never, never,' and she left town to escape me. All my life that's how it's been. I've been rejected, laughed at, my heart's been broken more times than I care to remember. By the time I came here, I resigned myself to thinking I'd never— I didn't expect any of this."

"Didn't expect what? Me?"

He turned from me to glance at his paintings. "It's like . . . it's like the wheatfields. Right now in the plains of La Crau the farmers are tilling the soil and sowing the seeds. They'll take root, brave the winter, then the wheat will grow and ripen to the harvest. But it doesn't happen right away. The farmer has to be patient and have faith, let things happen in their own time." He gazed into my eyes and wrapped my hands in his. "Do you understand what I'm trying to tell you?"

He looked so lost. Like the youth he must have been in Holland, not the man he was in Arles. A wave of tenderness swept over me, and I pulled my hands free to run my fingers down his cheek. "You have nothing to fear, Vincent. You know that I would never—"

"I do know, but you must be patient with me, *chérie*. When the time is right . . ." He touched my cheek in return, then tugged me to my feet. "As for you thinking I'm leaving . . . I want to establish an artists' colony here, an *atelier du midi,* a studio of the south. I've dreamed of it since I left Paris, and now it will happen. First Gauguin will come, then others in the spring if we can lure them." He shook his head. "I'm not going anywhere."

"But why didn't you tell me?" I asked. "Why hide it?"

"I didn't know for certain Gauguin was coming until the other day." He handed me the rag from his worktable. "It'll be splendid to have another painter to discuss ideas with. I think you'll like him, he's quite sociable."

I dabbed at my eyes and blew my nose. "Have you known him a long time?"

"I met him briefly in Paris, but right now he's in Brittany with another friend of ours. I have a self-portrait he painted and sent to me. It says more about him than I ever could." Vincent fetched a canvas from the corner and propped it on the chair.

One look and I didn't trust the man in the picture. With his reddened complexion and shifty eyes, Gauguin looked like a drunken sailor, the type of *mec* who thought he was something with his upturned moustache and affected goatee. The type of man who thought a girl should fall all over him but would treat her like his hired plaything once he got her upstairs.

"I see despair in this portrait," Vincent said from behind my shoulder, "a man who is ill and tormented, a prisoner. Someone who needs peace and calm as much as I did when I first came south. Arles will do him good."

I saw someone who couldn't think of anyone except himself. I'd met Gauguin's kind before, more times than I cared to remember. "It won't be the same with him here," I said wistfully.

Vincent started drawing a picture on my back with his fingertips. "Nonsense. It won't change a thing."

"But you'll be so busy working with him, what if you forget about me?"

He brushed aside my hair to nuzzle my ear, and his hands grew bolder. "No chance of that, I assure you."

I leaned into him, my body forgetting its anger to tingle under his fingers. "Mmm . . . stop, someone might see us through the window."

"You think I give a damn?" He scooped me up in his arms

as I giggled and squirmed. "Quit wiggling, I'll drop you!" I stopped squirming and only laughed as he carried me upstairs.

Paul Gauguin arrived in Arles about a week later, although the gossip reached Madame Virginie's before he did. Joseph Roulin met him first, bright and early after he arrived on the 5:00 a.m. train. Vincent, in his absentmindedness, had forgotten to tell Gauguin where he lived, so Gauguin stopped at the Café de la Gare to ask the address. Figuring he might do this, Vincent had lent Gauguin's portrait to Monsieur Ginoux so he could keep watch. Monsieur Roulin was enjoying a last coffee before his shift when Gauguin entered the café looking tired and cross, only to be greeted by Monsieur Ginoux's "Ah! You're Vincent's friend!" Gauguin laughed when Monsieur Ginoux produced the painting from behind the bar, and Roulin introduced himself at once.

"He's a true sailor," Roulin told Françoise and me. "He's been all over the world . . . Brittany, Denmark, Martinique, and he was born in Peru. He used to be a rich man, but he gave it up to paint. Can you imagine that?" He shook his head. "That's the bourgeoisie for you."

My first meeting with Gauguin came a few nights after that. The door of the *maison* swung open with a jovial bang, and all eyes turned to the two painters. Vincent tried not to attract attention, going quietly to a corner table as he always did, but Gauguin clearly enjoyed the stares. His walk was a strut, a swagger, his survey of the room amused as he stroked his moustache. He looked me up and down when Vincent introduced me as "my friend, Rachel." Then Gauguin removed his hat with an exaggerated bow. "I've heard many tales of the beauty of the Arlésiennes, Mademoiselle," he said, speaking more to my breasts than to me. "Now I believe them."

"You are too kind, Monsieur," I replied with a tight smile. "Shall I bring you a drink?"

"Absinthe, if you please, Mademoiselle. Vincent, an absinthe for you as well?"

"A beer, please," Vincent said. "I had too much absinthe last night."

"I didn't know you drank absinthe," I said.

"You must not know him very well," Gauguin laughed. As I walked away, he said to Vincent with a low whistle, "Fine-looking girl, nice hips, nice ass. Tits to sink your teeth into." I didn't hear Vincent's reply.

To my relief, they were discussing their work when I returned. "What do you think of Vincent's paintings?" I asked Gauguin, my voice full of pride.

Gauguin shrugged as he mixed his absinthe. "He's coming along. The sunflowers he placed in my room is his best work yet." Vincent beamed like he'd received the most extravagant compliment, not the most halfhearted, and I didn't know what to say. Who did this Paul Gauguin think he was?

"He needs to learn about keeping things neat and minding the money, though," Gauguin added. "I've created a system so we can track our expenses and not run short before Theo's monthly allowance arrives. I was once a stockbroker"—he gave his moustache another stroke—"so I know about money and business in a way Vincent does not." I expected Vincent to defend himself, but instead he nodded in agreement.

"And what do you think of Arles, Monsieur Gauguin?" I asked.

"It's dirtier than I expected." He gave another shrug. "Southerners are a breed unto themselves. Can't understand a word of their provincial patois, and all the sun makes them lazy." He told a story about how he and Vincent had gone to buy jute canvas the day before, how slow the service at the shop had been, and how he'd had to repeat the order three times before anyone had understood. "Never have problems like that in Paris," he concluded.

Now I expected Vincent to defend Arles and its people, but he was gazing into his beer mug as if he hadn't even been listening. "You'll find us no different from anyone else once you get to know us, Monsieur," I said, struggling to remain polite. "Besides, Arles was the greatest city in Roman Gaul when Paris was just a city of mud. Everybody knows that."

"Why don't you join us for one of our painting trips, Rachel?" Vincent jumped in before Gauguin could respond. "We're going back to the Alyscamps tomorrow."

An ancient cemetery south of the city, the Alyscamps was abandoned but still housed old Roman coffins and medieval Christian chapels. "*Non, merci,* I'd rather not."

Vincent probably thought I was saying no because of Gauguin. "Why? You've come painting with me before."

"It's scary at the Alyscamps," I said reluctantly.

"Scary?" Vincent and Gauguin asked at once.

"Haven't you heard the stories? They call that bell tower on the church of Saint-Honorat *la lanterne des morts*—'the light of the dead'—and they say at night a ghostly flame leads the way to the underworld." Vincent and Gauguin exchanged looks that made my cheeks warm, but I kept on. "Ever since the railroad was built, they say the ancient dead whose graves were disturbed haunt the place."

Gauguin rolled his eyes. "I didn't come here tonight to talk about southern superstitions." He stood and my heart stopped. *Please don't ask me, please don't ask me.* "Can you recommend a good girl for me, Mademoiselle?"

"What kind of girl do you like, sweet or fiery?"

"Fiery," he replied with a look that said he was undressing me in his head. "A girl who needs taming. A girl as pretty as you."

I gave him a look that said to leave me alone. "Ask for Jacqui, she's fiery enough."

Noisily clacking his walking stick on the floor, Gauguin sauntered up to Madame Virginie while Vincent and I watched. Madame beckoned to Jacqui, who gave Gauguin her best sultry smile and let him slide his arm around her waist. As they turned to go upstairs, he groped her *derrière* before giving us a big grin of approval.

"He wanted to go with you," Vincent muttered with a glare to Gauguin's back. "He hasn't taken his eyes off you since we walked through the door."

I laughed. "I can handle *mecs* like him, don't you worry about me." Vincent snorted and frowned into his beer. "Why, you're jealous," I added in surprise.

"Not exactly, but . . . he's had a lot of women. Women like him."

I covered his hand with mine. "I think it's sweet you're jealous. It means you care."

His eyes softened. "Did you doubt it?"

"You must doubt me, if you think I'd choose him instead of you. Come with me, *mon cher,* and I'll show you that you have nothing to be jealous about."

Instead of taking me by the hand when we stood, Vincent put his arm around my waist as Gauguin had done with Jacqui—protectively, possessively, like he didn't want me to get away. I did my best to assure him there was no chance of that.

# CHAPTER EIGHT

# The Alyscamps

*I venture to hope that in six months, Gauguin and you and I will see that we have founded a little studio which will last.*

— Vincent to Theo, Arles, late October 1888

In the bright light of morning, I wondered if I should join Vincent and Gauguin. I didn't want them thinking of me as a superstitious provincial bumpkin, as surely they probably did, and I didn't like the thought of staying behind. So I sneaked into the kitchen to fill a basket with bread, sausages, and a bottle of wine, tucked a novel Vincent had given me into the basket too, and walked outside the city walls toward the Alyscamps.

The iron gate at the cemetery's entrance creaked unhappily when I pushed it open. Ahead stretched a long path framed by twin rows of firs and red-streaked poplars; with every breath of wind, autumn leaves flitted down to cloak the ground. The

Alyscamps felt like a world unto itself, but the chimneys of the PLM railway workshops stood beyond the treetops, the faint banging of metal against metal competing with the calls of birds, a plume of smoke curling into the sky. Far down the path stood the ruined church of Saint-Honorat with its stout walls and legendary bell tower. *La lanterne des morts.*

There was no sign of Vincent and Gauguin—or indeed, of anyone—and I rambled up the road looking left and right for the two painters. Stone Roman coffins stood among the trees, some gaping open, their lids broken or long since lost, others pushed onto their sides, others shut, harboring who knew what. "Don't be a goose, it's just a bunch of old coffins," Françoise had said when she'd brought me here back in the spring. "I had my first kiss over by that tree. There's nothing to be afraid of."

Maybe those coffins were all centuries old, maybe plenty of girls shared kisses with their beaux under the trees, but death still hung over the Alyscamps like a shadow. Back in the summer, *Le Forum Républicain* had reported the discovery of a body in the neighboring Canal de Craponne, that of an eighteen-year-old girl of good family who'd drowned herself, abandoned by her married lover and disgraced by pregnancy. When I read the story, I imagined the girl's desperation as she stood on the bank and stared into the murky depth, how she must have felt when the water closed over her head. Would I ever love anyone so much to believe I couldn't live without him? I asked myself then. Philippe had hurt me, but not enough to want to die. Did I love Vincent that much? I asked myself now, and the thought made me shiver.

I shivered, too, remembering what day it was. Tomorrow was the feast of all saints, and soon Provençals would set places for dead relatives at a special meal, *le repas des armettos*, the supper of the wandering souls. Maman had taught me to put chestnuts under my pillow to satisfy the spirits, something I still did every year. Soon families would take flowers or maybe baskets of food to cemeteries to share with the dead—and here I carried just such a basket, in the oldest cemetery of Arles.

The wind picked up, and a stray cloud masked the sun. Suddenly I couldn't hear the sounds of the railway workshops, or any more birds. Aside from the wind, it was silent. I gritted my teeth and quickened my pace down the path. "Vincent?" I stopped and looked about. "Vincent?"

A chill passed over me, the unmistakable sense that I was not alone, and I could swear footsteps rustled the leaves behind me. I started to run, to where I wasn't sure, tripping over the rocks in the path and nearly dropping my basket. The wind in the trees became seductive whispers rasping out my name, Rachel, Rachel.

I had to find him before the spirits found me.

"Vincent!" I called. "Where are you? Answer me!"

"*C'est toi*, Rachel?" Vincent appeared from behind the trees and scrambled down the high bank edging the canal. I stumbled toward him, and he held me tightly. "You're shaking, what's the matter?"

"I couldn't find you . . . I thought I heard something . . . I thought I lost you . . ."

"Shhh, your imagination ran away with you, that's all. I've not gone anywhere. Everything is fine." The birds chirped again, and the clouds drifted away to restore the sun.

"Where were you?" I asked when I'd composed myself.

"Painting on the bank. Gauguin's working there, too." Studying my face, he added, "You did have a fright, didn't you? *Pauvre petite.*"

I banished *la lanterne des morts* from my mind and tried to smile. "I'm being a goose. Imagining things, like you said."

"I thought you weren't coming. What have you brought?" He lifted the corner of the cloth covering my basket and peeked inside. "You're an angel," he murmured, then cupped his hands around his mouth and shouted for Gauguin.

"Don't tell him how silly I acted," I begged, and Vincent promised he wouldn't.

I spread the cloth on the ground and took everything out of the basket with Vincent's help. Gauguin joined us a few minutes later. "I don't know what a fine girl like her's doing with you, *mon ami,* but if it means we get fed . . ." He laughed and reached for the wine bottle.

"I don't know what she's doing with me either," Vincent said and smiled as I handed him a bit of garlic sausage and cheese, wrapped in a napkin.

I asked how the painting was going, and Gauguin was the first to answer. "I've been working on a view by the canal, which I'll finish in the studio tomorrow." Vincent chimed in that he'd almost finished his third canvas, which led Gauguin to mumble in my direction, "He paints too fast."

"I do not," Vincent said with a roll of his eyes.

"Yes, you do," Gauguin countered. "The way you build up the paint so thickly on the surface—it's sloppy. You need to work more slowly, from your imagination. Don't limit yourself to the things you can see."

With every sentence, Vincent's scowl deepened. "But it's the things I see that intrest me. Nature, the things that are real. Like Daumier, like Millet."

"Millet? A sentimentalist. Daumier? A hack. Give me Ingres! Degas!"

"What, those insipid ballerinas?" Vincent scoffed. "You can have them. Delacroix . . . now there's a man who knew about color. Ingres had no idea about color."

"*You* have no idea about color, slapping it on with no rhyme or reason." Gauguin made a face and imitated Vincent painting. "You must think about what you're doing."

Vincent's voice rose to the treetops. "I know exactly what I'm doing, damn it!"

"Boys! *Boys!*" I clapped my hands to get their attention. "Eat your food and behave yourselves." Vincent and Gauguin grinned awkwardly and stopped squabbling.

After luncheon, they climbed the canal bank to work, friendly camaraderie having won the day, while I plucked the novel I'd brought from my basket. A few idlers came to dawdle along the road, among them a fresh-faced Zouave and young girl, walking arm in arm. No prostitute, from the looks of her, a nice girl who must have fibbed to somebody to be out with a soldier without a chaperone. He probably hoped to steal a kiss in one of the old chapels, and I couldn't tell from her smile whether he'd succeed. I paid no heed to the time as the sun journeyed across the sky and I lost myself in the story I read. Until once again I had the sensation I wasn't alone. That I was being watched.

Vincent had come from the bank and was sitting on the ground, sketching me like the day we'd met. This time I smiled and didn't disrupt his work. "Hold the pose," he said. "Read your book and pretend I'm not here." I tried, but I was so aware of his presence that I couldn't resist glancing at him. He gave a teasing frown and motioned for me to put my head where it belonged.

He showed me the drawing when he finished. Gone was the blowzy *fille de maison* of his earlier sketch, the one with mussed hair and mussed skirts who frowned in her sleep. This demure young lady's hint of a smile said she had pleasant secrets locked inside her heart, secrets that had nothing to do with the book in her hands. Vincent knew what lay in my heart, just as I knew, without his saying it, what lay in his. Studying my portrait, seeing myself as he saw me, I hoped this Rachel—the happy, contented, so-much-in-love Rachel—was the Rachel I could always be.

# CHAPTER NINE

# Absinthe

*I have done a rough sketch of the brothel, and I quite in-tend to do a brothel picture.*
—Vincent to Theo, Arles, November 1888

Vincent and Gauguin's painterly partnership seemed to flourish over the next few weeks. They worked together nearly every day, rising with the sun and continuing into the night with the help of the gaslamps Vincent had installed in the studio. Some evenings found them at Madame Virginie's, although Vincent's visits weren't as frequent as before. He apologized and insisted it was nothing to do with me, that he was just busy. I insisted I believed him.

Even when he did visit, things were different. Before Gauguin came, Vincent and I had been in our own world, talking over the wine and sharing things lovers share. But with Gauguin seizing attention for himself, I felt like an afterthought. They talked of art and Paris and things I knew nothing about;

most of the time I sat and listened like a mute china doll. Vincent tried to draw me into the conversation, but I suspected Gauguin excluded me on purpose, thinking me too ignorant to keep up with them.

I visited the yellow house once a few weeks after Gauguin's arrival, and although he was out for the evening, his invisible presence was everywhere. He'd taken over half the studio with his paintings and things, and even the tidiness of the house spoke of him rather than Vincent. Vincent told me Gauguin did all the cooking and was surprisingly good at it. I hated to think of him using the same pots and pans I used, setting the table the way I always did, treating my kitchen as if it belonged to him.

Unfortunately Gauguin returned early from wherever he'd gone that evening and strolled into Vincent's bedroom without knocking, catching us at an embarrassing moment. I shrieked and grabbed for the blanket. "Sorry, Brigadier, thought you'd be finished," Gauguin drawled as he crossed the room toward his own, kerosene lamp in hand. As if nothing had been going on, as if he hadn't been the least bit sorry to see us like that.

When Gauguin's door shut, Vincent chuckled and tried to resume what he'd been doing, only to protest when I pushed him away. "Where are you going?"

"Back to Madame Virginie's." I didn't bother with my corset; I pulled on my chemise and dress as fast as I could. "You think I'm staying after that?"

"It was funny, he didn't mean to—"

"He knew exactly what he was doing," I hissed, not caring if Gauguin heard me through the thin wall. "Who opens a closed door without knocking? He wanted to ruin our evening."

Vincent sighed and leaned back against the pillows. "Well, it's ruined now, isn't it? You're acting like a child."

"I am not. I've never been so humiliated, and I'd rather sleep

in the street than stay here with him. Goodnight, Vincent." I
darted down the stairs, pausing at the front door to tug on my
shoes and see if Vincent would come after me. He didn't.

The weather matched my mood as it rained for days at a
time, and the waters of the Rhône churned against the stone
embankments. In the *quartier reservé* we were safe behind the
city walls, but the Place Lamartine lay vulnerable to the river's
wrath. Two years before, Françoise said, the embankments had
been breached, and the square had flooded beyond the Café
de la Gare. If the river invaded again . . . I hoped Vincent
and Gauguin were taking precautions, but knowing Vincent,
he was irritated that he couldn't paint outdoors and gave the
matter no thought beyond that.

The skies cleared and the waters receded as November
dragged on, and the Arlesians heaved a sigh of relief. Business
at the *maison* picked up, the unceasing rain having kept many
customers home, then Vincent and Gauguin made their own
way back to the Rue du Bout d'Arles. I was so happy to see
Vincent that I forgot all my annoyance and threw my arms
around his neck. "I'm sorry about before," he whispered in my
ear, and I kissed him with an "I'm sorry, too."

"Two absinthes, please, Mademoiselle," Gauguin interrupted. "And one for you."

I tried not to think about the last time I'd seen him, how
he'd caught me naked in Vincent's bed. "*Merci,* I'll have wine,"
I said, and I knew I'd turned as red as the *vin rouge.*

"What kind of *fille* doesn't drink absinthe?" Gauguin asked
with raised eyebrow and slightest emphasis on the *"fille."* "They
all do in Paris."

"I've never had it," I admitted. "Papa always said it was the
devil's drink."

Gauguin burst out laughing, and Vincent said, "One won't hurt you."

"No, thank you," I repeated. I saw how completely some of the other girls were controlled by *la fée verte*, the green fairy, and our customers too, how greedily they guzzled the absinthe and how glassy-eyed they got. It bothered me enough that Vincent was drinking it in Gauguin's company, but I figured he wouldn't listen if I tried to stop him.

When I returned with our drinks and the accoutrements for preparing the absinthe, Vincent and Gauguin were deep in discussion. "I painted you the other day," Vincent told me cheerily as he poured absinthe into his glass.

I was about to reply when Gauguin broke in, "It's a brothel picture."

"It's a *pochade*," Vincent said, "an oil sketch to work out the composition. Next I need you to pose for me so I can begin the actual painting. Maybe you can persuade other girls to pose too. It'll be the most ambitious figure scene I've tried since I left Holland."

I frowned. "You want to put me in a brothel picture?"

Vincent whipped a sketchbook and stub of pencil out of his pocket. He explained his idea as he drew: girls and customers talking in the *salon* in couples and trios, maybe some Zouaves playing cards, lots of color, lots of gaiety. The more he talked, the less I listened, and when he showed me the sketch, I refused to look. "I don't care. I'm not doing it."

"But if you don't pose for me, I won't be able to get anyone else."

"You should be flattered he wants his favorite *fille* in the picture, Mademoiselle," Gauguin said with a chuckle. "Don't you want to be made immortal?"

Vincent scowled at Gauguin and shoved the sketchbook in his pocket. "It wouldn't really be you, *ma petite,* you'd just be the model," he wheedled. "Once we're finished, I'll paint your portrait all by yourself, how about that?"

"I could paint her also, like when Madame Ginoux posed for us," Gauguin said eagerly.

"Would you want me dressed like a whore then too?" I asked.

Vincent said, "No," Gauguin said, "Yes," Vincent glared at Gauguin, and I glared at both of them. "Maybe I'll have an absinthe after all," I muttered. Gauguin leaped up to fetch a third absinthe glass from the bar, and to Vincent's concerned look I said, "You heard him, all the whores in Paris drink absinthe. If you want to paint me as a *putain,* I have to play the role."

"Rachel, you've misunderstood me, I didn't mean—"

Gauguin plopped an empty glass in front of me. "*Faites attention,* Mademoiselle. The ritual of preparing the absinthe is as important as the act of drinking it." He extended the absinthe bottle to Vincent. "Since our little Mademoiselle is a virgin, you should have the pleasure of deflowering her."

Vincent sighed as he took the bottle from Gauguin. He poured enough green liquid to fill the reservoir at the bottom of my glass and reached for a slotted spoon lying on the table. Balancing the spoon across the mouth of the glass, he placed two cubes of sugar on top, then poured water over the sugar.

"Too fast," Gauguin scolded, "just like your painting. Don't pour it, let it drip."

Vincent ignored him and kept pouring. As the sugary water hit the absinthe below, the color started to change. "Observe, Mademoiselle," Gauguin said. "The emerald green turns citron yellow, then cloudy white. You must have very cold water to achieve the right effect, three to five parts, depending on your preference. Ah, is there anything more lovely than that swirl of color?"

Vincent finished pouring the water as the sugar melted. He dipped the spoon into the glass for a quick stir before handing it to me, and I took a cautious drink. It was *dreadful*. Too bitter, too strong—it made me choke, and Vincent had to slap me on the back.

Gauguin laughed as I pushed the glass toward him. "No, no, I insist you try again. Maybe you need more water, since Vincent didn't do it right." He poured a splash of water in the glass and pushed it back to me.

"I prepared her drink just fine," Vincent snapped, then added, to me, "you'll taste the sugar more the further along you get."

It didn't taste as bad on the second sip—rather like the licorice candy Papa used to bring me when I was a little girl. Gauguin asked if it was better, and when I nodded, he smirked, "Seems I know best how to satisfy you, Mademoiselle." I ignored him and kept sipping.

Gauguin turned to Vincent. "Have you seen those big spigot carafes in Paris, where you can leave your glass and let the water drip as slow as you want?"

"Yes," Vincent said, focused now on preparing his own drink. "Agostina Segatori got one for Le Tambourin while I was there."

My ears perked up. Agostina Segatori? Was she the Italian *signora* he'd mentioned our first night together, the one who'd taught him how to kiss and who knew what else?

"La Segatori!" Gauguin hooted. "Before or after she threw you out on your ass?"

Vincent looked at him sharply. "She didn't throw me out, one of the waiters did. It wasn't my fault. I gave her some pictures to hang in the café, they weren't selling, and I wanted them back. She was being obstinate."

Back and forth they went, Gauguin proclaiming that's not what he heard, Vincent retorting he'd heard wrong. "Everybody knew you two were having an affair," Gauguin said. "I don't know why you think it's a big secret. I heard she let you paint her in the nude, you rascal."

"Damn gossiping Lautrec," Vincent mumbled.

"So it's true!" Gauguin bellowed. "Mademoiselle Rachel, you should see this woman. Used to be an artist's model, posed for Corot and Manet. The blackest eyes, and even at her age the juiciest pair of . . ." He whistled, then laughed at Vincent's expression. "She's what, twelve, thirteen years older than you, *mon ami*? *Oh là,* you were a lucky man to get a screw like that. Welcome to Paris!" He guffawed and slapped the table, while I frowned at Vincent over my absinthe. The color rising in his cheeks, Vincent was trying not to look at either of us. Gauguin elbowed me and added, "Don't let the dewy-eyed Dutchman fool you. He's been around."

"How the hell would you know?" Vincent demanded. "Only time I ever saw you up there was at my brother's gallery."

"People talk, Brigadier," Gauguin said smoothly. "People talk."

Vincent tossed back his absinthe and reached for the bottle. "Too much damn talking, that's why I left."

"Young lady, you're drinking awfully slowly," Gauguin observed with a glance to my glass. With a glance to Vincent, he said, "La Segatori can *really* knock 'em back, can't she?"

I drained my absinthe in a gulp, just as Vincent had, and

slammed the glass on the table. "If she can, I can! I'll have another, Monsieur Gauguin, if you please."

"Rachel, are you sure this is a good idea?" Vincent asked.

"Don't tell me what to do, Vincent. Now, shall I fix it
myself?" Under Gauguin's watchful eye I steadied the spoon
on the glass, the sugar on the spoon, and mixed my second
glass of absinthe. Not long after that, my third. After *that* . . .
after that I don't remember much.

*Oh, God. I want to die.*

Where was I? My own bed. Where were my clothes? I was
wearing my chemise and drawers, but everything else was piled
on the floor. What time was it? Morning, the sun streaming
through the window to reveal Vincent sleeping in my armchair. "What are you doing here?" I asked, and he woke with
a start.

"I stayed to make sure you were all right," he said and walked
to the bed to sit beside me. "How are you feeling?"

"How much did I drink?"

"Three glasses full. I tried to stop you, but you told me to
mind my own business. You sang too." He chuckled despite
himself. "You couldn't walk, so I carried you up here."

My legs wrapped around his waist, my arms around his neck,
giggling into his ear, saying his name over and over, *Vincent,
Vincent*: I remembered that. "But we didn't . . . ?"

He shook his head. "I put you to bed and slept in the chair
in case you needed me." He went to the washstand and brought
back a damp cloth. "You don't have to prove anything, Rachel,"
he said gently as he wiped my face. "Not to Gauguin, and certainly not to me."

"But—Paris! You had a very exciting life there with very

exciting women. You must be bored silly with Arles and a country bumpkin like me." I sniffled.

"That's the absinthe talking. Paris was killing me. Another month and I would have been completely mad."

I sniffled again. "Did you love her?"

"Who, Agostina? I felt a great deal of affection for her, but I didn't love her. That was about"—he coughed and blushed— "having fun. I was lonely, and she . . ." He coughed again. "I'm sorry you had to hear about her from Gauguin. Do you want to try sitting up?"

When I nodded, he slid his arm behind my shoulders to help me and plumped the pillow so I could sit back. The room rocked and swayed. "Oh, God," I murmured. "I feel dreadful." Vincent returned to the washstand for a glass of water, then tipped it to my lips, steadying my head so I could drink. He'd taken care of sick people before, I realized. Back when he was a preacher, perhaps? I pictured him looking after a sick child or old man with a soothing touch and kind smile. The vision made me love him even more. Then it made me cry.

"*Tiens,* what's this?" He set the glass on the floor and cradled my head against his shoulder. "Poor little one, no more absinthe for you."

"I don't want to be in a brothel picture," I sobbed. "I don't want you to paint me as a whore. Is that how you see me, as a painted whore?"

"Of course not, I thought you'd be a pretty model, that's all. I promise I didn't mean to hurt your feelings. I'll paint your portrait as I do see you, *d'accord*?"

"Without Monsieur Gauguin?"

"Without Gauguin. Just you and me." He kissed my forehead and held me until I stopped crying. "I know I've neglected you, *chérie,* and I want to make it up to you."

He told me then about a Nativity play at the Folies Arlésiennes the next Saturday, about how Augustine Roulin had
invited him to go with her family and said he should bring
someone. He seemed excited at the idea, but I looked at him
like he'd lost his mind. "Vincent, I can't go to a play with the
Roulins. Monsieur Roulin knows who I am." So did his eldest
son, for that matter. I'd been a gift to Armand Roulin for his
seventeenth birthday back in May.

"Joseph wouldn't say anything inappropriate. He knows
better than that."

"But other people might recognize me. I'd embarrass you."

Vincent smiled and brushed my hair out of my eyes. "That's
ridiculous. Would you be embarrassed to be seen with 'that
painter,' 'that foreigner'?" I smiled back and shook my head.
"Please come, it'll be all right, I promise. You shouldn't let fear
keep you from doing something you want to do." I thought about
it, then nodded. "Good. We'll have a wonderful evening."

A knock sounded at the door, which Françoise opened
before I could say anything. "Rachel, I wanted to make sure
you were— What are *you* doing here?"

"Taking care of Rachel," Vincent replied. "She's sick."

Françoise folded her arms and glared at him. "No wonder, as
much absinthe as you gave her." I told her it was my fault, not his,
and she said, "Well, he shouldn't be here. You know Madame
Virginie doesn't allow customers upstairs during the day."

Vincent helped me lie down and offered to go, but I clutched
his arm and pleaded, "No, please don't."

"Yes, please do," Françoise said and gave him a little push so
she could arrange my blanket the way she thought it should be
arranged. Vincent meekly retreated to fetch his hat and jacket,
then caught my eye with a smile before slipping out the door.

"I wanted him to stay," I complained.

Françoise snatched up my clothes from the floor. "He's nothing but trouble, that one. He'll give you a *gueule de bois* worse
than any absinthe, mark my words."

"I think I'm going to be sick." She grabbed the basin and
held back my hair as I threw up into it. *At least he didn't see that.*
*Oh God, I want to die.*

She *tsk-tsk*ed. "No more absinthe for you."

# CHAPTER TEN

## *Pastorale*

Once I recovered from my grim flirtation with the green
fairy, it seemed Saturday would never come. I coaxed
Françoise into helping me dress like a true Arlésienne in the
traditional local costume, although she grumbled when I told
her why. "I haven't worn these things in years," she said as
she pulled a blue dress from her armoire and a dusty box from
under her bed. She helped me pin my hair into a chignon on
top of my head, then wrap the chignon in a white lace *cravate*
trailing two ends. Finally, the white lace *fichu*, draped over my
shoulders like a shawl, tucked into my belt in front and pinned
into a triangle down my back. From habit my hand reached for
the powder box, but I stopped myself. No powder, no rouge.
Tonight Vincent would see me and only me.

He was already waiting downstairs. "How lovely you look!"

"*Merci*," I said and fiddled with the *fichu*. "I've never dressed like this before." I noticed his dapper black velvet jacket and the new hat in his hand. "Look at you, so handsome!"

He smiled at the floor. "You're the only person who's ever told me that."

Our walk to the theater took us through the heart of the city, where the stone skeleton of the ancient arena stood ghostly under the rising moon. This was the Arles visiting *touristes* saw, Arles of the Romans, the powerful city favored by Augustus Caesar himself. I remembered sitting in Papa's classroom, reciting the Latin names for the towns of Provence—*Arlate, Nemausus, Massilia*—hearing him tell us how proud we should be, descended as we were from such greatness.

"Have you been to a Nativity play before?" Vincent asked. "Madame Roulin says it's not what I'll be expecting."

"We had them in Saint-Rémy, although I'm sure this one will be much grander." How excited I used to feel, when I dressed up in my church clothes and walked proudly with Maman and Papa through town to see the play. "It's not just the Bible story—the *pastorales* have all kinds of characters on their way to see baby Jesus. There's singing, and music, and the plays can be very funny. Sometimes they make fun of politicians and things like that. Oh goodness, I hope you'll be able to understand, because it'll be in Provençal, not French." Vincent assured me that even if he couldn't understand all the words, he'd enjoy the music and my company just the same.

We reached the Place de la République, presided over by the town hall and church of Saint-Trophime. Around the obelisk-topped fountain in the center of the square, local *santonniers* had set up their stalls for the Christmas season. Most were closed for the night, but one enterprising merchant was keeping his open to lure customers from among those on their way to the *pastorale.* Vincent stopped to admire the rows of painted ceramic figurines. "What are these?"

"*Santons* for the Christmas *crèche,*" I replied, "the Nativity scenes in people's houses. You can have whoever you want in your *crèche,* a fisherman, cheese-seller, knife-grinder . . ."

"Did you have a *crèche* in your house when you were a little girl?"

"Oh, yes. I fought with my sister about who got to put in the *santons.*" The memory made me giggle. "Madame Virginie will put a *crèche* in the *maison* too."

"This is fine work," Vincent told the *santonnier.* "Do you have any artists?"

"I'm sorry, Monsieur, no artists. Perhaps an ink-seller? Three francs."

"This one for the lady, I think." Vincent held up a miller clutching a sack of grain before fishing in his pocket. "*Voilà,* three francs."

"You didn't have to buy me anything," I protested as we walked away.

Vincent pressed the *santon* into my hand and closed my fingers over it. "I wanted to. So you will remember tonight, and remember me."

Inside the crowded theater, around the corner on the Boulevard des Lices, I held Vincent's arm tightly so we wouldn't be separated. Most of the women were dressed like me, their gowns a rainbow of colors under the gaslights. Everyone chatted and laughed as joyous anticipation filled the air. At first I looked nervously around, afraid one of my customers would appear, until Vincent patted my arm and whispered, "Anyone who might recognize you isn't going to admit it here. Relax and enjoy yourself."

Joseph Roulin's voice echoed through the hall, calling Vincent's name, and he pushed his way through the throng to meet us. It was odd seeing him in something besides his blue postman's uniform. Tonight he wore a black suit faded from many washings, his long beard trimmed and tidy. "*Bonsoir,* Roulin," Vincent said, and the two men shook hands. "May I present Mademoiselle Rachel Courteau."

Monsieur Roulin, bless him, gave no sign of having met me before, although his eyes twinkled. "*Enchanté,* Mademoiselle. And may I present my family—where'd they go? Ah, here they come. My wife, Augustine, our elder son, Armand, our younger son, Camille, and our baby girl, Marcelle."

Madame Roulin came up to her husband's chest, plump, matronly, the perfect Provençal *maman* with her baby in her arms. Lagging behind and gazing around in wonder, young Camille was nearly swallowed by an overcoat that probably once belonged to his brother. "*Bonsoir,* Monsieur Vincent," he said and waved. Armand brought up the rear, trying to pretend he wasn't with his parents while he scoped the crowd for pretty girls. Being the oldest meant his cheery yellow jacket was brand new, and his black hat was perched on his head at a jaunty angle. He'd grown a wispy moustache since I'd seen him last.

"We're so glad you could join us, Mademoiselle," Madame Roulin said with a pleasant country accent. Armand noticed me then and blushed crimson.

"Thank you, Madame. It was kind of you to invite me."

The baby reached for Vincent. "May I, Madame?" he asked, and at her nod, he took Marcelle in his arms. Straightaway she tried to pull his beard. "It's not as long as your papa's, little one," he said and chucked her under the chin. She giggled and hid her face in his shoulder.

As we entered the theater and found our seats, Madame Roulin asked, "Have you known Vincent long?"

She likely thought me something respectable, a seamstress or shopgirl. "Since July."

"We met him a little before that. He and my husband have become close friends."

I smiled at her. "I saw a portrait of Monsieur Roulin that Vincent painted. He said you've been posing for him too."

"Vincent has wanted to paint pictures of all of us since Marcelle was born. He painted Armand and Camille, and he insisted on painting the baby too." She glanced at Vincent, still dandling Marcelle on his knee. "He's very good with her, very comfortable with children. Now he needs a family of his own to paint." She looked at me pointedly with her gentle green eyes, and I blushed as red as Armand.

The gaslights lowered, and cheers and clapping rippled across the theater. Vincent passed Marcelle to her mother, then reached for my hand as the curtains parted. His eyes sparkled with excitement. I hadn't seen him look so happy in weeks.

The *pastorale* was like the ones I'd known back home, although much more elaborate. Children laughed at the clownish characters and gasped at a dramatic battle between Saint Michael and a dragon, while the adults roared at the satirical speeches of the "politicians" who appeared for no good reason, except to deliver satirical speeches. Much of the humor probably went over Vincent's head, but he was captivated nonetheless, only occasionally leaning over for a quick translation. I glanced at Camille Roulin during one of the musical interludes, and his eyes were as big as saucers. So were mine, for that matter, and so were Vincent's, especially at the end, when the character of the reformed sorceress sang a dazzling solo at baby Jesus' crib.

Vincent was the first among us to burst into enthusiastic applause. The entire audience leaped to its feet as the actors took their bows, a chorus of male and female voices calling out their appreciation in Provençal: *Osco! Osco!* After a round of *Bonne nuit*s and *Joyeux Nöel*s, handshakes and cheek kisses, the Roulins went home to get the younger children to bed. I saw Madame Roulin's knowing smile when Vincent took my arm, her glance from me to him and back again, and not for the first time that evening, I wished I was anything but a *fille de maison*.

When Vincent and I crossed the Place de la République on our way back through town, he stopped this time in front of Saint-Trophime, gazing up at the sculptures of the Last Judgment above the doorway, illuminated by streetlamps. He tilted his head and pondered them until I began to feel uncomfortable and gave his arm a tug. The Christ with his hands poised to welcome the blessed and condemn the damned had become a stranger to me, the apostles and saints terrifying judges waiting to decide my fate. But Vincent wouldn't move away, and he surprised me by suggesting we go inside. "Into the church?" I asked. "You and me?"

"Why not? I'd like to see the *crèche,* and I've never been inside."

"I haven't either, but that doesn't mean I want to go now."

He looked at me curiously, then stared at the sculptures again. "Would you mind if I go in for a minute?" I shook my head, and he bounded up the steps.

I sat down and put my chin in my hands with a sigh: what had come over him? To pass the time, I reached into my reticule and took out my *santon,* examining its cunning costume and details more closely. A miller with a sack of grain. I smiled as I remembered what Vincent had said about the wheatfields and the harvest, that day in the studio before Gauguin came. What was he trying to say in choosing this particular *santon*?

I expected him to emerge with a scowl, grumbling about clergymen and self-righteous hypocrites, but he looked calm, his eyes shining. He didn't comment about what he'd seen or done inside the church; he simply reached for my hands and helped me to my feet. Instead of heading toward the *maison* when we left the Place de la République, he turned us the other way. "Where are we going?" I asked, tugging at his arm again.

He grinned. "It's a surprise."

He was taking me to the café in the Place du Forum, the one in his painting. I knew it before we got there, and my excitement grew as we reached the square. I'd never been anyplace like this before, not here in Arles, not in Saint-Rémy, where there were only two cafés to speak of and neither of them fancy. Straight to the yellow awning Vincent led us, gallantly pulling out a chair at an empty table for me, seating himself opposite. The night was mild for December weather, and nearly all the chairs and tables were occupied.

I arranged my skirts and sat up straight like a lady would, not slouching, folding my hands neatly on the table. Couples around us were enjoying their own evening out, talking together and laughing. Love, not money, bound these men and women together. You could see it in their eyes, their faces, every line of their bodies. "It's like we've walked into your painting," I mused to Vincent. "It's a whole other world."

The waiter approached and greeted us respectfully before Vincent placed the order, "*Une bouteille de vin rouge, s'il vous plaît.*" After he left, Vincent whispered, "That's the same waiter from my painting, but I don't think he recognizes me."

"No one would recognize either of us tonight," I whispered back.

Vincent was still studying the waiter as he attended to the couple sitting next to us. Before I could ask Vincent what he was looking at, he held his finger to his lips and reached for the sketchbook and pencil he always carried. A half smile on his face, he drew for a few minutes, pencil scratching across the paper in quick strokes. When the waiter moved away, unaware that anyone had been watching him, Vincent handed me the sketchbook. There he was: neat buttoned waistcoat, crisp white apron, the drawing moving with the same controlled energy as the man. I laughed. "Do you always do that?"

Vincent pulled his pipe from his pocket and winked. "Only when they aren't looking."

We lingered on the café terrace for about an hour, maybe longer, after the waiter brought our wine. Pipe smoke curled lazily around our heads as we talked of everything and nothing, touching hands, smiling at each other under the yellow awning. I liked seeing Vincent's smile instead of the frown that had often appeared lately. I liked the way the wine played over my tongue, rich and fruity, better stuff than what I usually drank at Madame Virginie's. I liked having Vincent all to myself again.

The sky was clear enough to see the stars as we strolled from the Place du Forum toward the *maison.* Once again we passed *les arènes,* and I stared at the ancient amphitheater with the same awe I always felt. "Have you been inside the arena?" I asked. "There's a beautiful view from the top. You can see all the way to the Alpilles."

Vincent shrugged. "I went to a couple of bullfights back in April. One on Easter Sunday."

"I was there on Easter too! What did you think?"

He grimaced. "I didn't expect them to kill the bulls, they didn't at the other games I went to. But the crowd was something to see, everyone dressed in such bright colors under the sun. All the pretty Arlésiennes in their *fichus* and caps." He squeezed my arm. "What did *you* think? I can't imagine a woman enjoying it, although many women were there."

"Oh, I didn't like the bull being killed either. I left after the first fight." I'd cheered with the rest when the matador had appeared in his gay beaded costume and entered the taunting dance with the ebony-black bull. It seemed a game—the red cape, the glinting sword—until the sword plunged between the bull's shoulder blades, and blood flowed across his back onto the sand. Dazed, he staggered in a circle and fell to his knees, then the matador finished him with a blow to the heart. The crowd erupted into wild shouts, even the women jumping up and down with glee. I wanted to leave, but Françoise grabbed my arm. "Don't go yet," she said. "Look."

A picador drew near the fallen carcass, and sliced off one of the bull's ears with a long-bladed knife before wiping it clean and handing it to the matador. I clapped my hand to my mouth; I thought I'd be sick. "Look," Françoise insisted. A beautiful girl appeared in the arena, her pink dress cheerful, her smile unwavering. The matador put the bull's ear in a little box and, with a graceful bow, presented the box to the girl. "The matador always gives the ear to his lady love," Françoise explained. "Isn't it romantic?" I thought she must be as crazy as the rest of the clapping Arlesians, and I pushed my way through the crowd down the steps to the street. I'd still been able to hear the shouts as I'd walked away.

Vincent began to hum one of the songs from the *pastorale* as we turned into the Rue des Ricolets, then the Rue du Bout d'Arles. Suddenly he seized me in his arms to dance me to the door of the *maison,* whirling me around and around as I squealed with laughter. "Stop, stop! You're a terrible dancer!"

He did stop and laughed too. "I've never danced in my life."

"One day I'll teach you," I said and kissed him. His answering kiss was the sort of kiss we'd shared that very first night, the sort of kiss that said he'd like to come inside with me. I wanted him to come inside with me.

He lifted my chin with his fingers. "Rachel, I —" He cleared his throat and looked away. "I—I have to get up early, so I'm afraid I must say goodnight. Gauguin and I are traveling to Montpellier to see the museum."

It was the first time that night either of us had said Gauguin's name. I covered a frown with my best coquettish smile, the sort of smile that said it'd be well worth his time and he'd be a fool to say no. "Not even for a half hour, are you sure?"

"Another night, I promise. *Bonne nuit,* Rachel. I had a wonderful time."

"So did I, thank you for inviting me. *Bonne nuit.*"

He bowed, then set off down the street, still whistling the tune from the *pastorale.*

# CHAPTER ELEVEN

# Rain

*I think myself that Gauguin was a little out of sorts with
the good town of Arles, the little yellow house where we
live, and especially with me.*
    —Vincent to Theo, Arles, December 1888

Another night" became another, and another. "I tried to
tell you," Françoise said when I refused to come downstairs one evening and lay in bed with a headache. "He's just
like the rest of them." I turned away from her to face the wall.
Vincent had been about to tell me he loved me, I was certain
of it. But why had he stopped himself, and why was he staying
away now?

"Where's your painter?" Jacqui asked the next night, happy
to humiliate me. "He forget about you? Ohhh, I wish his friend
would come back—*nom de Dieu,* that one just about wore me
out! I walked funny after he left." She giggled. "You know

they got tossed out of a café on the Rue de la Cavalerie for fighting."

"You're making that up," I said crossly.

"A girl from old Louis' place was there and she told me. Your painter threw a glass of absinthe at the other one to start it. It took Joseph Roulin and the café owner to break them up, although I imagine what's his name—Paul?—could make short work of that skinny *mec* of yours if he wanted to. He sure made short work of me." She giggled again. I dismissed the story as one of her attempts to rile me, until one of the other girls mentioned it too, then I could only wonder. And wait.

A dismal night over a week after the *pastorale,* Raoul came to where I sat at the bar. "*Monsieur le peintre* is here, Mademoiselle, but I'm not sure I should let him in."

Vincent stood in the pouring rain under the door lantern, soaking wet with only a tattered umbrella to cover him. He looked like a rat who'd fallen in the Rhône and crawled out again. I waved Raoul away and pulled him inside. "Vincent, what on earth are you doing out on a night like this? You'll catch your death."

He mumbled something I couldn't understand as I stuffed his umbrella in the stand by the door and guided him to a table near the fire. Madame Virginie had gone to bed early, so she wasn't there to complain about this bedraggled person messing up her clean floor. "Look how wet you are," I scolded before fetching a towel and a small glass of brandy. "Don't gulp it, sip it. It'll drive the chill from your bones." I rubbed his wet hair with the towel until it stood on end. "Going out in the rain without a hat. My goodness. Even the soldiers are staying in the barracks instead of chasing women."

"I want an absinthe," he said. I refused, and his jaw tightened. "I said, bring me an absinthe."

"And I said no. That's the last thing you need."

He scowled, as if he'd argue with me, then his eyes flitted around the room. "Let's go upstairs. People are watching."

Aside from Claudette cozying up to a *mec* in the corner, the *salon* was empty. "There's nobody here—other men have more sense than you. Let's stay and get you dry."

"I'm dry enough. I want to go upstairs."

I sighed and took the empty glass from his hand. Some nights the door of my room was barely closed before his hands and mouth were everywhere and we freed ourselves from our clothes in a frenzy. Other nights were more calm, more tender, letting spark build slowly to flame. But that night, as I lit the lamp and pulled back the bedcovers, Vincent circled the room and ran his hands through his hair as if I hadn't been there at all. "It's cold in here," he muttered.

"I told you we should stay by the fire. Do you want to go back downstairs?" He shook his head. "Well, then why don't I warm you up?" I led him near the bed, slipped his suspenders off his shoulders, and started unbuttoning his shirt. My lips followed my fingers down his chest.

At first he seemed eager—head thrown back, heart pulsing beneath my touch—but then he backed away from me to gaze out the window at the dark rain. "I can't," he whispered as he buttoned his shirt back up.

"Vincent, what's wrong?" I asked, scared now. "You're acting so strange . . . oh, God, you found somebody else. Some other girl." The room lurched, and I leaned against the washstand to steady myself.

"There's nobody else, I swear. I mean . . . I *can't*." He turned from the window to look intently at me, face crimson.

Then I understood.

I couldn't help but feel relieved that's all it was, although

I didn't let it show. Men took these things so seriously; it wouldn't do to hurt his feelings. "I'm sorry," he mumbled. "I didn't think it'd ever happen with you."

I crossed the room to clasp his hands in mine. "It happens to every man once in a while, dearest, there's no need to apologize. Is something bothering you that you'd like to talk about? Maybe that would help."

"Theo sold two of Gauguin's Brittany pictures for six hundred francs. A third if Gauguin will retouch it, five hundred more francs. I haven't sold a damn thing." He sighed to the floor, and I squeezed his fingers. "Gauguin's also been invited to exhibit with Les Vingt in Brussels. That's an important opportunity for him to show with other painters working in the new styles." In a lower voice he added, "I hoped Theo would negotiate an invitation for me."

"I'm sure he tried . . ."

Vincent snorted without reply.

"I'm sorry, I know you must be disappointed."

"The only exhibition opportunity I've been offered is to hang some things in the Paris offices of an art journal called *La Revue Indépendante*."

"Well, that's something," I said brightly. "Will you do it?"

He glowered. "It's a black hole run by scoundrels. They want me to give them one of my paintings for the 'privilege'—as if I'd do that. Theo's pissed at me, but what's the point? I want to have a proper exhibition next year with all the new work, in a proper gallery space. Even a café would do. Someplace where regular people will see my paintings, not just—"

"It'll be a wonderful exhibition," I soothed. I'd never seen him like this, and I had no notion how to make him feel better. What did I know of art dealers and exhibitions, except what he told me?

"That's not all," he said with another sigh. "Now that he's earned more money, Gauguin's thinking of leaving."

"Why would he do that? He just got here."

Slowly Vincent began to tell me everything, how things between him and Gauguin had changed. How intensely Gauguin disliked Arles and the Arlesians, how tired he was of the yellow house. Gauguin thought Vincent talked too much, he didn't like the way Vincent painted, he thought Vincent too messy, on and on, day after day, a litany of complaints. The weather hadn't helped; they'd been cramped together in the studio with no place else to go. Even the trip to Montpellier to see the museum—which Vincent had hoped would improve matters—had led to arguments, the old squabbles over this artist or that artist. "You can't imagine what it's been like," Vincent kept saying, but I could. I'd seen enough, I'd heard enough to picture it all, and the thought of the yellow house as a battleground sickened me. "I know I'm not easy to live with," Vincent said, "but I've tried. I have."

I remembered Jacqui's story. "Is it true you fought with him in a café?"

"Oh God, you heard about that?" he moaned. "I was so drunk, I didn't mean any harm. I get so fed up with his—"

"Then why not let him go?" I asked. "He can return to Paris or wherever he pleases, and you and I can—"

Vincent shook his head. "He'll tell everyone how much he hated being here. He'll tell everyone it's all my fault, and what a failure I am. I'll be humiliated."

I cupped his face in my hands and forced him to look at me. "You're *not* a failure. Your paintings are beautiful, and someday everyone will love them as much as I do." He snorted again and pulled his eyes away. "Can't you invite someone else to come, one of your other painter friends?"

"Don't you see—if Gauguin leaves, no one else will want to come. He'll scare them away, and that'll end my plan to create a studio of the south. Only if he stays can it succeed."

I swallowed what I really wanted to say to that. "Then why don't you talk to him? Discuss it calmly, without getting upset? Or Theo could talk to him for you. Maybe you can—"

"Gauguin won't listen to me, and I doubt he'd listen to Theo either."

"Vincent, I'm trying to help you," I sighed. "I'm trying to understand."

"You can't understand!" His voice was sharp, hateful. "How could you possibly understand?"

I dropped my hands and turned my face. "I don't mean to be cross with you," he said then, the sharpness gone. "My nerves are stretched so thin, I don't know what I'm saying." He bent his head to kiss my hurt away, and for a moment it seemed we'd end up in bed after all, until he pulled back and blurted, "Gauguin thinks I'm mad."

"Mad? What makes you say that?"

"We painted portraits of each other. The way he painted me, the face, the expression—I look like an imbecile, or a madman. Gauguin wouldn't be the first to think so. My own father wanted me locked up after the thing with Sien." Vincent walked to the mirror above my washstand and stared at his reflection. "Maybe it's true. Eight years I've been doing this, and what do I have to show for it except rooms full of paintings that nobody wants? Surely that's mad, isn't it?"

I joined him at the mirror and touched his shoulder. "You must be patient, *mon cher*. I know it's hard, but—"

"I've been patient!" He stepped away to pace the room, gesturing wildly as he spoke. "I've worked and waited . . . I gave up *everything* to do this. I could have become a successful art dealer like Theo and had a normal life, but I gave it up and now look at me! Thirty-five and supported by my younger brother. I'm a failure, and I'm a burden to Theo." He added under his breath, "It's like goddamn Paris all over again," and felt his empty pockets with a frown.

I gave him a cigarette and matches from the supply I kept for customers. He inhaled deeply and blew out a cloud of smoke with a *whoosh* that was mostly a sigh. His hand was shaking. "Theo believes in you and wants to help you," I said. "What does he say about selling your paintings?"

Another long drag on the cigarette. Another *whoosh*. "What you say: be patient. Collectors are only now investing in the Impressionists, and public opinion is even slower to embrace new artists. Theo says the tide will turn."

"There, you see? I'd listen to him instead of Gauguin. What does Gauguin know?"

He stubbed out the cigarette with impatient fingers. "I don't know how much longer I can do this, Rachel. Sometimes I know exactly what I want and feel I can do it forever, other times I think it will be the death of me. But I can't stop. I can do without everything else—money, people, even God—but I can't do without my painting. Even if someday it kills me."

I reached for him, and he held me like a drowning man clinging to a flimsy raft in a typhoon, his face damp against my neck. "Forget about Gauguin, forget about everything," I whispered and pressed myself close. If only Gauguin *would* leave. The frightened man in my arms was not the man I'd met in the Place Lamartine garden, who'd laughed and smiled and been so hopeful in his yellow house. Gauguin was ruining everything.

"Stay with me tonight," I said. "You need your rest—I'll look after you."

His voice rumbled in my ear. "I've been enough bother."

"You're no bother, dearest. I want you to stay."

He smiled for the first time when I brought him a fleecy wool blanket, and he chuckled when I joked that he should borrow one of my nightdresses. But when I got ready for bed and prepared to blow out the lamp, he shook his head and said, "Leave it burning." I turned it as low as it would go, then climbed in beside him, tucking the covers into a cocoon around us. He curled up against me and pillowed his head on my breast like a child. "Everything will be fine, my love," I told him and kissed the top of his head. "You'll see."

He closed his eyes with a little sigh and went to sleep, but I lay awake, stroking his hair with light fingers as my thoughts wandered to unfamiliar places. What had he been like as a boy? Had his mother held him like this in the dark of the night, when storms had raged and the world had frightened him? I imagined him reading books while the other children played, or lounging alone in the grass, searching for pictures in the clouds. I wished I had known him then, or sometime before thirty-five years had marked his face with the lines barely visible in the lamplight.

Outside the rain continued to fall. When the oil in the lamp was almost gone, I leaned over and extinguished the flame.

# Chapter Twelve

## 23 December 1888

*Our arguments are terribly electric, sometimes we come
out of them with our heads as exhausted as a used electric
battery.*

—Vincent to Theo,
Arles, late December 1888

*Everything fine now. He's not leaving.*

I frowned at Vincent's hastily scrawled note—two lines,
that was all—and threw it in the fireplace. Every day I'd waited
for some word that Gauguin had hopped the train to Paris,
never to be seen in Arles again. Every night I'd waited for Vincent to come back to me, but he hadn't. What was Gauguin
trying to do, staying when he hated Arles so much? Did he
envy Vincent's talent even though he was the one selling paintings, did he find some perverse satisfaction in preying on Vincent's fears? Why couldn't Vincent see him for what he was?

I heard nothing more for over a week. "Here comes your

painter!" Jacqui called from the doorway one night, and I dashed to the threshold in time to see Vincent and Gauguin disappear inside old Louis' place up the street. Jacqui burst into laughter; I burst into tears and ran upstairs. Louis' girls prowled his *salon* clad in see-through peignoirs, Louis' girls did anything you paid them to do, no matter how disgusting. Maybe he was only there to drink, I told myself as I held the *santon* he'd given me to my chest, maybe he was only sketching for his brothel picture. A girl braver than I would have marched next door to find out, but I cried myself to sleep and nightmares of Vincent making love to someone else.

Sunday, December 23. For three days it'd been raining again, and with the coming holiday, business that night was slow. That morning Madame Virginie had set up the Christmas *crèche* in her parlor, and all the girls but me had gathered around it to light candles and sing songs. The cook had been baking all day to prepare for our Christmas Eve feast, and smells of ginger and vanilla filled the *maison*. Françoise tried to cheer me up by giving me an early Christmas gift—another *santon* from the man in the Place de la République, this one a laundress—and she tried to make me laugh by saying, "We make more money than she does."

The frigid north wind blew open the door with a *bang,* and from habit I turned to look. Vincent and Gauguin. I stared at them from the bar, not moving a muscle until Gauguin waved me over and placed an order for drinks. He greeted me as if nothing was amiss, but Vincent frowned with his head bent and didn't speak.

"Mademoiselle Rachel," Gauguin said when I returned with the tray and took a seat between them, "I have news that will break your heart. I'm leaving. I'm going back to Paris."

I glanced at Vincent, who was preparing his absinthe and acting as if he'd been by himself. "Oh, that's too bad. Why?"

Gauguin slowly dripped water into his own absinthe glass. "Maybe I'll return to Brittany, perhaps Martinique or even Tahiti. Vincent's brother sold some pictures for me, so I might be able to afford it. Eleven hundred francs. It's about damn time." He stirred his drink and announced, "I think we need a toast. First, to me and my future endeavors."

I raised my glass of wine but didn't say a word. Vincent ignored the toast altogether.

"Second, to Theo van Gogh and his future bride, Johanna Bonger, whose engagement we learned about this morning."

"Oh!" I gasped and turned to Vincent. "Theo's engaged!"

"Yes," Vincent muttered, his first word of the evening.

"Aren't you happy for your brother? Do you not like the girl?"

"I've never met her," Vincent said, still mumbling. "She's the sister of a friend of ours. She's Dutch."

Gauguin jumped in. "A nice, educated girl with spirit, according to Theo. The perfect wife for a young art dealer on his way up."

"That's wonderful news," I said to Vincent with an encouraging smile. "You should be glad for them." I tried to take his hand, but he shook me off without reply.

"I'll tell you what his problem is," Gauguin snapped. "He thinks once Theo marries and has a wife to support, then children, there won't be any money left for him. And it scares the hell out of him because his work's not selling."

Vincent glared at him. "Fuck off, Gauguin."

"It's the truth, isn't it? Theo's been supporting me too while I'm here, but now he's sold some work for me, I don't need his money. But you—you haven't sold anything."

"I said, fuck off. You haven't a goddamn idea what you're talking about." The eyes of the two men locked, and a tense electricity crackled between them.

I almost suggested to Vincent right then that we go upstairs. In my room we could talk everything over, he could calm down, I could help him see that his brother's marriage was nothing to envy, nothing to fear. But I didn't. Instead I turned to Gauguin and tried to sound cheerful as I said, "Tell us about your plans for Paris."

"A little of this, a lot of that," he said airily. "I've missed the Paris girls. Nothing like them anyplace else, except maybe in the tropics."

"Don't you have a wife waiting for you in Denmark?" Vincent sneered.

Gauguin ignored him and slipped his hand under the table to stroke my thigh. "You know, Mademoiselle Rachel, my gingerheaded friend has been most selfish, keeping you to himself. Seems he's forgotten the lessons of Christian charity from his preacher days. How about a little . . . going-away present?"

Vincent looked like he was about to explode. "Oh, you," I said with pretend playfulness and swatted Gauguin away. "Jacqui can keep you plenty entertained, you don't need me."

"I mean it." The hand migrated back to my leg and inched up the hem of my skirt. "That little preview I got at the house whetted my appetite. Or how about one last collaboration, Vincent, my friend? We could take turns and make her very happy—"

"Get your fucking hands off her!" Vincent shouted, leaping from his chair as I leaped from mine. He pulled me to his side, and we were both shaking: me with revulsion, him with rage. Everyone in the room was staring, and Raoul moved in from the doorway.

Gauguin raised his hands in sarcastic surrender. "Apologies, *mon ami,* I had no idea the lady was spoken for." He looked at us curiously, first Vincent, then me, then Vincent again. "Wait—

are you in love with her? Is the clergyman's son actually in love with a *fille de maison*?" He howled with laughter and slapped his knee. "Here I thought you just liked screwing her! Mijnheer van Gogh, whatever would your mother say? Your brother picks a virgin, you pick a whore!" Vincent's fingers dug into my hip, and I tightened my grip on his shoulder.

Gauguin reached into his pocket and slammed coins on the table. "Here's two francs to make up for my inexcusable rudeness in propositioning your girl. Take her upstairs and do whatever you want with her. As hot as she is under that skirt, I'm sure she'll let you." He leered at me as tears of shame filled my eyes.

"I don't need your fucking money," Vincent snarled, snatching up the two francs and hurling them at Gauguin. They clattered on the wooden floor.

"Why not? She feel sorry for you and give it for free?"

Jacqui appeared and draped her arm around Gauguin's shoulder. "You should have asked me, Paul. I'd show you boys a fine time you'd never forget."

"I bet," Gauguin said, smacking her bottom before pulling her onto his lap and making her giggle. "What color garters are you wearing tonight, lovely?"

She twitched her dress at him. "Why don't you take a peek and find out?"

"Let's go upstairs, Vincent," I said under my breath and urged him toward the staircase.

"Did you hear that, *mon ami*?" Gauguin asked as Jacqui giggled harder. "Your little lady is ready and waiting! You sure you don't want my money? Or can't you—ahem—keep up your end of the bargain?"

"Why can't you leave him alone?" I cried. "You're jealous because his paintings are better than yours—you're nothing but a parasite!"

"Jealous, eh? Parasite, eh?" Gauguin pushed Jacqui away to stand and take a step toward me. "Someone needs to teach you some manners, my girl."

Vincent stepped between us, and his voice was ice. "If you touch her, I swear to God I will kill you, you bastard."

I waited for Gauguin to charge at him, waited for a fight, but Gauguin backed away. "Stay here with your two-bit whore then, Brigadier, I'm getting my things and finding a hotel. I'm going to Paris tomorrow, I don't want to be in this blasted hellhole one more day. You and your goddamn brother can both fuck off!"

With that he strode toward the door, but before he could reach it, Vincent flung an empty glass across the *salon* at Gauguin's back. He barely missed, and the glass shattered against the wall. Then Gauguin did charge at Vincent, gripping him by the shoulders and shaking him until his teeth rattled. "Let him go!" I shrieked and tried to throw myself between them, but Gauguin shoved me aside. I fell to the ground with a cry, smacking my shoulder on the hard floor.

Bellowing like an enraged bull, Vincent seized the absinthe bottle and made to hit Gauguin over the head as Jacqui screamed curses and I screamed for him to stop. Joseph Roulin came running from upstairs and jumped in with Raoul to break them up, Raoul taking hold of Gauguin and Roulin wresting the bottle from Vincent's hand. Madame Virginie ran in from her parlor and screeched like a vengeful spirit, "Get them out of here! Out! Out!"

"Let me go, damn it!" Gauguin yelled, but Raoul was far stronger, and Gauguin wasn't going anywhere except outside. He settled for shouting at Vincent as Raoul hustled him out the door. "Fucking failure! Madman! The world will know!"

"Please let me go, Roulin," Vincent said. I'm sure we all

thought he'd chase after Gauguin, but instead he knelt beside me and asked if I was hurt.

I shook my head, although I knew I'd have an ugly bruise. "Don't listen to him," I pleaded and put my arms around his neck. "He's not worth it."

"Get him out of here," Madame Virginie ordered Roulin, still glaring at Vincent. She glared at me too, as if all this had been my fault.

"Come on, Vincent, my friend," Roulin said in his booming voice. "Best we get you home." Vincent meekly followed him, turning at the door to look at me one last time.

I started to go with them, but Françoise took my arm. She'd come downstairs with Roulin at all the shouting. "There's nothing else you can do, Rachel. Let's get you cleaned up." She scowled at the still-staring customers. "What are you all looking at?"

"Something else is going to happen. What if Gauguin goes after him? What if—"

"Raoul's taking Gauguin to a hotel, and Joseph's with Vincent. They'll sleep it off, and if we're lucky that Gauguin really will leave tomorrow. On the first damn train."

I followed Françoise up the stairs, as meekly as Vincent had followed Roulin. I let her help me into my nightdress and wipe my face, fuss over the yellowing spot on my shoulder. She tucked me in, put a glass of water by my bed, told me that everything would be all right. I nodded and dutifully pulled the blanket around my chin, but I kept seeing Vincent's eyes when he'd looked back from the doorway. Haunted. Sad. Like an animal caught in a trap.

"Don't worry," Françoise said and blew out the lamp. "Everything will sort itself out in the morning."

★ ★ ★

I couldn't have been sleeping very long when a persistent knock startled me awake. Wincing at my sore shoulder, I reached for my shawl and hurried to the door. It was Françoise again, her face white, asking that I come downstairs right away. "Vincent is here," she said. "He wants to see you. He—"

Before she could finish, I was padding on bare feet down the hall, past the clock on the landing, down the stairs. 11:30, the clock said, only 11:30. A few customers remained in the *salon,* waiting their turn with the girls, but no one was talking, no one was saying a word. Vincent stood silent and alone in the center of the room, and when I reached the bottom of the stairs, he slowly walked toward me.

Never, not even that night of the rain, had he looked like this. A ghost of his own self, paler than ever under a black beret. Since when did he wear a beret? Was it Gauguin's? Only when he came closer did I notice the paint-stained rag wrapped around his head—closer still, and I realized the thick red trickling down his neck and shoulder was not red paint.

*This can't be real. It's a dream. I must wake up.*

He was near enough for me to smell the blood now, a sticky, sweet smell that dizzied me.

*What should I do?*

I should have taken him in my arms, I should have called for help, but I couldn't speak, I couldn't move. His eyes held me rooted to the spot. His hand reached out to take mine, raise it and open it so that my palm faced upward. All of it so slow, so gentle, as if we had been alone together in my room or the yellow house and this had been just another caress, just another night.

He lifted his other hand, where he clutched something in his fist, wrapped in newspaper. He pressed it into my palm and closed my fingers over it, something moist and cold, never once taking his gaze from my face. *"Tu te souviendras de moi,"* he said, his voice hollow.

You will remember me.

He released my hand and backed away a few steps, watching, waiting. I stared at my fingers, smeared with blood, the packet in my hand smeared with blood, and nausea washed over me. Part of me wanted to fling whatever he'd given me far away, but another part of me . . .

*Don't look. Don't look.*

I opened my hand and unfolded the paper. The rest was darkness.

# CHAPTER THIRTEEN

# Nightmares

*I'm standing in the avenue of poplars at the Alyscamps.*

*The mistral is blowing, and the red leaves falling from the trees are bathing me in a crimson shower. Red leaves everywhere—covering the ground, spilling from ancient coffins. The wind whistles in my ears, and in the bell tower of Saint-Honorat a fiery light shines through the shadows. La lanterne des morts—beckoning to all who see it, leading the way to the underworld.*

*Vincent is there.*

*He's walking up the road toward the chapel, pipe in his mouth, canvas slung over his back. I call his name, but he can't hear me over the wind's ceaseless howling. Over and over I cry out, but he keeps walking . . . slowly, steadily . . . every footstep taking him farther from me.*

*He's almost reached the light.*

*I start to run after him, faster and faster, still calling his name.*

*Never stopping.*

★ ★ ★

I wasn't in the Alyscamps. A cold morning sun poured through the window of my own room, and I lay in my own bed. Someone slept in my chair, keeping watch over me. It was only a dream. He was there. He'd been there all along.

Françoise stirred when I said Vincent's name. "Rachel, thank God!" She hurried to me and felt my forehead. "Your fever's broken. *Merci à Dieu!* Are you thirsty, do you want some water?"

"Where's Vincent?" I asked. My tongue was tangled wool, my head a mess of cobwebs. "I had a terrible dream, Françoise, the strangest dream . . ."

She brushed the hair from my eyes. "It was no dream, little one."

*What does she mean?*

Monsieur Roulin led Vincent away after the fight, but he returned. Françoise came to my room to find me. We went down the stairs. His haunted eyes, then . . .

*My hand. The blood. The red, red blood . . .*

Dizziness flooded me as I gripped her arm and tried to sit up. "Gauguin did it! The police must arrest him before he leaves town!"

Françoise urged me back onto the pillow, but I'd have none of that. Didn't she hear what I said? The police, I kept telling her, you have to get the police. Gauguin cut him. Gauguin hurt him. My fault, all my fault, if I'd only gone with him . . .

"Lie down, dear," she begged, "please lie down and listen." She took my hand, and her voice was patient and gentle—more patient and gentle than I'd ever heard her sound. I listened to her words but could not understand them. They made no sense. Gauguin didn't do it, she said. He was in a hotel the whole time, he couldn't have. The police made sure of that during their investigation. No, it was not Gauguin.

Vincent had done it to himself.

I sat up again, the dizziness flooded me again. "That's a lie! A filthy lie! Where is he?"

"In the hospital—Rachel, please, you must calm down—"

"Take me to him! Take me now!"

She held my shoulders to keep me from climbing out of bed. He needs me, I shouted, he needs me, and I struggled against nausea and fatigue while I struggled against her. "Rachel, stop," Françoise ordered. "I'll call for Raoul if you don't stop. What good will it do if you make yourself more sick than you already are?"

I couldn't fight anymore. I let Françoise ease me onto the pillow, and when she brought a glass of water, I let her hold the glass to my lips. "There's a good girl," she murmured. "You must not worry. The doctors are looking after Vincent at the Hôtel-Dieu. He's safe there."

"Is he going to die?" I whispered.

She set the glass aside and avoided my eyes. "He's very ill. He lost a lot of blood."

"When can I see him?"

"Not yet, Dr. Dupin said you must rest quiet." She smoothed the blanket, still not looking at me. "Anyway, it's Christmas Day, they won't let you in."

"Christmas Day?" I exclaimed. "Why did I sleep so long?"

"Dr. Dupin gave you some medicine."

*There's something else. Something she is not telling me. Something I do not remember. Something I do not want to remember.*

"I fainted . . ."

Françoise brushed the hair from my forehead again, fingers warm against my damp skin. "Yes, dear, you fainted. You had a miscarriage."

Flashes of memory, flashes of pain rushed back to me, pain

in the night. I'd awakened from the faint with blood stain-
ing my nightdress, dripping down my legs. Someone ran for
the doctor, Raoul carried me upstairs as I cried out in terror—
Vincent's blood, fresh on my fingers, mingling with my own. I
couldn't stop screaming as I felt the life inside me slip away, as I
learned for the first time the life was there. Our baby, our baby,
I screamed, and I thrashed on the bed as Françoise and Madame
Virginie held me down, and Dr. Dupin gave me an injection.
Everything was red, the whole room was red.

I remembered everything.

I began to shake, expecting to see the sheets and blanket
covered in blood, my hands covered in blood. "No . . . no . . .
Vincent!" I cried as the room spun about me, as if he'd magi-
cally appear to keep me safe and chase the red away.

Françoise rocked me like a child and tried to soothe me,
whispering, "It wasn't meant to be" softly in my ear. Wasn't
meant to be, wasn't meant to be—words I tried to hear, tried to
understand, but in my mind I saw only pictures of what could
have been. A baby . . . a family . . . a home. Now the baby was
gone, and maybe Vincent would go too, maybe he'd die there
in the hospital, and I wouldn't get to say good-bye.

*Please don't die. Please don't leave me.*

It was another day and another night before I felt well enough
to sit up, or eat anything but the smallest spoonful of broth.
Françoise stayed with me every moment, even though I barely
spoke and kept my face turned to the wall. She held me when
I cried, wiped my forehead with cool cloths when I felt fe-
verish. I wandered in and out of sleep, dreams haunting me
when I closed my eyes, questions plaguing me when I woke.
How could I have been so blind? How could I have missed
the signs, how could I not have known? The blood that still

flowed frightened me: had I lost not only this child but any chance of another as well? And Vincent . . . I knew nothing of his condition, only that he was alive. Only that kept me from going mad.

When I felt strong enough, I asked Françoise to tell me everything that happened that night, everything that happened to Vincent after I fainted. "Oh, Rachel, no," she said, "it'll only upset you."

"I have to know. Tell me."

Vincent had stared when I'd collapsed at his feet, then knelt beside me and stroked my hair. "He had no idea who or where he was," Françoise said. She rushed to help me, while Joseph Roulin hustled Vincent back home and Minette ran for Dr. Dupin. Roulin returned and said the house was filled with blood-stained rags and towels, and Vincent had gone unconscious. Could the doctor come? The *gendarmes* appeared then, alerted by whom Françoise didn't know, and they hurried away with Roulin to take Vincent to the hospital. The next morning the police questioned Gauguin, convinced he had some role in it, but he'd been sleeping in the hotel all night, ever since Raoul took him there. Vincent had done the unthinkable—he'd injured himself. Had he not come to Madame Virginie's, had he not been discovered, he would have died for certain.

There was something else I had to ask. "Did the doctor . . . did Dr. Dupin say . . . how long? How long I . . ."

Françoise sighed and handed me a cup of tea. "Drink this. *Millepertuis* and verbena chases away the devil, my *grand-mère* always said so." I held the cup and waited for her to answer. "Nine weeks," she finally said, "maybe ten."

It must have been that day before Gauguin came, I thought, when we argued and we made up and Vincent whisked me to his bedroom to make love for hours. That day I didn't wash myself with vinegar afterward, that day we took no precautions.

Vincent would have wanted the baby, I knew it. I could imagine the smile on his face when I told him the news, the light in his eyes. He would have been so happy. All those other things—the feelings of failure, Theo's engagement, the strains of sharing the yellow house with Gauguin—those things wouldn't have hurt him, and even now we would be planning our life together. He wouldn't be lying in the hospital, I wouldn't be lying here. "I could have saved him," I whispered. "If only I'd known."

"What?" Françoise asked. "No, you stop that, right now. This is not your fault. Plenty of women don't realize— What happened is not your fault."

Old Dr. Dupin came to examine me again. "You will continue bleeding for some days, perhaps a week or even two. You must forgo intercourse until it ceases, and you must eat more so you'll regain your strength." He patted me on the arm and said gently, "You can have other babies, Mademoiselle Rachel, if you want them. You are young and strong."

"She has nightmares, Doctor," Françoise said. "Frightful dreams that make her cry."

Dr. Dupin frowned and peered into my eyes. "Shock," he said. "And it's no wonder. The cure for that is rest."

Françoise pulled the doctor aside so I couldn't hear what she asked him next. He shook his head, and I couldn't hear his reply. But I knew they spoke of Vincent, and I pressed my hand to my empty womb, slow tears streaming down my cheeks.

The two of them were still whispering together as Françoise escorted Dr. Dupin into the hall. When she came back, she tried to sound cheerful. "Oh, don't cry, he said you'll be just fine. Are you hungry, do you want some hot broth?"

"How is Vincent?"

She poured me a fresh glass of water. "Still at the hospital. His brother came to see him, though. Someone sent a telegram, Joseph, I guess."

"Theo's here?"

"He was. He's already gone back to Paris. Gauguin left too."

Why would Theo leave so quickly? Vincent was all alone. "Can I go see Vincent soon?"

"Dr. Dupin says you must rest a few more days. When you're better, we'll go see him together. Now let's get you to the chair, so I can change your sheets."

"Françoise?" I said quietly. "The baby was his. I know it was."

Her eyes filled with tears. "So do I."

## CHAPTER FOURTEEN

# The Hôtel-Dieu

*The prospect of losing my brother . . . made me realize what a terrible emptiness I would feel if he were no longer there.*

—Theo to fiancée Johanna Bonger,
Paris, 28 December 1888

December 29, the feast day of Saint-Trophime. At last I felt strong enough to go out, and I leaned on Françoise's arm as we walked toward the hospital. Before we left, she warned me that we might not be able to see Vincent, an announcement that nearly sent me into hysterics. Joseph Roulin had brought her news from the Hôtel-Dieu—Madame Roulin had visited Vincent a few days earlier and he'd seemed better, but afterward he'd gone into another fit. The doctor looking after him had forbidden any more visitors. I heard all this, and yet I insisted we try.

The faithful had attended Mass at the first sign of the sun, to ask for Saint-Trophime's continued protection of Arles and their families. Services now over, parents and their little ones, dressed in their churchgoing best, leisurely strolled the streets and gardens. Seeing them reminded me what I'd lost, and it brought a chill to my heart that mirrored the chill in the winter air. A wee boy dressed in yellow scampered past, his papa in pursuit; the boy's laughing blue eyes, smiling up at us, cut me to the quick.

As we passed the church of Saint-Trophime, the sight of the sculptures carried me to the last happy night Vincent and I had known together, and a strange pulling sensation compelled me to stop. Perhaps if the saint listened to the prayers of other Arlesians today, he'd listen to mine too.

Françoise looked skeptically at the church door when I said I wanted to go inside, the same way I had the night of the *pastorale*. "Do you need me to come with you?" she asked.

"No," I replied, "I'll go alone." I covered my hair with my shawl and ducked in a side door, avoiding the main portal under Christ in judgment. A seashell carving welcomed pilgrims on the road to Santiago de Compostela, as it had since medieval times. I was the only pilgrim here now.

Awe overtook me as I crept inside and my eyes adjusted to the dimness. I'd never seen a building like this—so much larger, so much older than my family's church in Saint-Rémy. The long vault overhead soared to fifty or even sixty feet, and huge pillars lined the aisles. A spicy smell of incense clinging to the stones revived memories of Masses when I knelt next to Maman and Papa, blending my voice with theirs as we recited the responses and sang the psalms. Small windows high in the thick walls and stained-glass windows behind the altar admitted enough light for me to see the church was empty. Only the myriad of glowing candles in iron stands betrayed that anyone had been here.

The Christmas *crèche* stood nearby, its tall wooden figures smiling and joyful. Soon the Three Kings would be added for Epiphany, and the *crèche* would be complete. Until then, *santons* dressed like Camargue shepherds watched shyly while Mary and Joseph gazed in adoration at their newborn child. After Maman died, I would look at Mary's serene face in every *crèche* I passed and envy baby Jesus for having a mother. Today, I envied Mary.

Another morning I might have slipped into a back pew, prayed, and hurried out before anyone saw me. That morning, I forced myself to walk boldly down the aisle between those huge pillars, summoning all my courage to ask for what I wanted. I stood before the altar and stared at a large painting of one of God's miracles, a painting darkened by centuries of candle smoke that had witnessed centuries of prayers. But my own prayers for my own miracle would not come. Even tears would not come. Anger swept over me in their place, a suspicion that we were all pawns in some divine chess game. I wanted to knock over the statues, tear the tapestries from the walls, and scream, *"Where were you? How could you let this happen?"*

What self-respecting saint would listen to a fallen woman whose illegitimate child had died and whose lover had gone mad? A whore who wanted him to be healed so she could feel his arms around her, who felt no remorse for loving him and desiring him with every fabric of her being? What had I ever done to merit Christ, the Virgin, Saint-Trophime, or anyone listening to me? I could say nothing. All I could do was stand there, clutching my shawl around me and trembling with emotion.

A priest with a kindly face and black cassock appeared beside me. I hadn't heard his footsteps. "Mademoiselle? Is there something you need?"

So many things I needed, so many things I wanted. But I

could not ask for them. I did not dare. I shook my head, then
hastened out of the dark church, back into the sunlight.

The hospital stood a few minutes' walk beyond the church. The
stone portal with "Hôtel-Dieu" above the doorway looked as
forbidding as the entrance to Saint-Trophime, and I balked in
front of it. "What's gotten into you?" Françoise asked. "You've
been wanting to see him for days, now's your chance."

I didn't know what frightened me more: seeing him, or not
seeing him. "What if . . . what if he . . ." She shushed me and
pulled me through the gateway.

Françoise gave a name to the porter on duty—"Dr. Félix
Rey, please"—and he told us where to go. As we crossed the
courtyard garden toward the men's ward, Françoise said Joseph
Roulin thought highly of the doctor, thought him a nice man
who knew all the latest treatments and medicines. If anyone
could help Vincent, he could. She told me this to make me
feel better, but when we reached his office, guided now by a
nun serving as a nurse, I was scared again. Françoise knocked
instead. "*Entrez*," came an efficient-sounding voice, and Françoise had to practically push me through the door.

I couldn't believe this was the doctor. He couldn't have been
much older than I. "I'm sorry, do we have an appointment?" he
asked. When Françoise told him my name and said we wanted
to see Vincent, I thought I saw recognition in his eyes. "Please
come in and have a seat," he said and waved us toward over-
stuffed chairs. "Would you like some tea?"

"Yes, please." I spoke for the first time, and he looked at
me curiously before handing us teacups and taking his place
behind the desk.

"Vincent is extremely unwell," he began.

"Will he live?" I asked at once.

"I'm trying my best to ensure that, Mademoiselle, but it has not been easy. The situation was critical when he arrived last week." He described Vincent's condition in a dispassionate voice—delusional with hallucinations, extreme mental shock, severe loss of blood—and added, "We couldn't do anything with the ear except dress the wound to prevent infection. It was too late to reattach the portion of the lobe he cut off, even though the *gendarme* had the foresight to bring it here."

My stomach twisted, and Françoise patted my hand. "Is he better now?" she asked.

"His brother came from Paris to see him, and that seemed to help. After Monsieur van Gogh left, the hallucinations mostly stopped, and Vincent began to eat again. Madame Roulin came to visit, and Vincent carried on a lucid conversation with her. But something triggered a relapse afterward. He started hallucinating again, became violent, and we confined him to an isolation room for his own safety. Once we did that, he wouldn't speak, he wouldn't eat, he did nothing but sit and stare at the wall or floor."

Vincent, my Vincent, caged like a dangerous beast. It couldn't be.

Dr. Rey looked at my face and cleared his throat. "A few hours ago, however, he tried to talk, and he ate some soup. He's resting now and hasn't had any hallucinations in over twenty-four hours. This represents a marked improvement." I asked if I could see him, and the doctor told me what Monsieur Roulin had told Françoise, that no visitors were allowed except the Protestant preacher, Reverend Salles. Then his voice softened. "Seeing you might overexcite him, Mademoiselle. He doesn't remember what he did, but he knows he frightened you, and it upsets him. We must avoid unnecessary adverse stimulation."

My hand flew to my heart. "You know who I am—he's mentioned me?"

"He kept calling your name when he was first brought here."

"Let her see him," Françoise begged. "You don't know what a state she's been in, fretting about him. And who's to say it won't help, seeing she's all right? Maybe he's been fretting about her!"

I gave Françoise a grateful look as Dr. Rey gazed from her to me and back again. He tapped his pen on the desk and sighed. "Let me see how he's doing. I shall return presently."

His clock ticked away the time as we waited. I tried to drink my tea, but it'd gone cold and bitter. Françoise amused herself by browsing the bookshelves. "What the hell is anti—anti-sepsis?" She pulled a volume from the shelf to flip through it. "*Tiens*, the doctor's got dirty books. Look at this picture."

"Françoise, stop!" I whispered fiercely. "If he catches you, he might not—"

She got the book put away and herself back in the chair just as Dr. Rey opened the door. "I will permit you to see him for a few minutes, Mademoiselle," he said to me. "I gave him a mild sedative earlier, so he's resting quiet. If he becomes agitated, you must leave immediately."

Françoise and I followed the doctor down the corridor to a vast room with two long rows of beds, each bed hung with thin white curtains. Most were occupied by patients: some sleeping, some sitting up and reading or else talking softly with visitors. Other patients played cards in a huddle around a potbellied stove, keeping their voices low so as not to disturb their breth-ren. Black-garbed nuns with white aprons flitted about like shadows, bringing drinks of water, bowls of broth, or smiles of comfort to the men in their care.

"This is the main ward," Dr. Rey said. "When Vincent seemed better this morning, I decided to move him from the isolation room. Being alone was only upsetting him more. I'll wait here so that you can have some privacy. His bed is at the end of this row."

Françoise said she'd stay with the doctor, so I walked alone down the length of the ward, trying not to let my shoes clatter against the floor tiles. Some of the windows had their shutters open to freshen the air, but still it smelled of sickness and sweat, of death. When I reached Vincent's bed, I brushed through the closed curtains and sat on the chair beside him. He was dozing, his face troubled in sleep. Dr. Rey had wrapped a thick bandage around his head, and his white face was haggard against the white sheets and pillows. The sight of him so frail made tears spring to my eyes, but I blinked them back. He could not see me cry.

He must have heard me or sensed my presence, for his eyes opened and tried to focus. Then he tried to sit up. "No, don't," I said quickly. "Save your strength and lie still."

He sank back onto the pillow with a sigh and smile. "I've waited and waited for you. I was so afraid you wouldn't come."

"Of course I came." I took his hand in one of mine and caressed his cheek with the other. His clammy skin frightened me. "I can only stay a few minutes. The doctor doesn't want you exhausting yourself."

His next words were the softest whisper. "I'm sorry. Please forgive me."

"There's nothing to forgive." His hand was so cold. "It's over. *C'est fini.*"

"You're pale. You've been ill."

I couldn't tell him about the baby. I would never tell him. "I'm fine now. Everything is going to be all right. You'll get well, and you'll paint beautiful things again. I'll stay with you in your yellow house whenever you need me. . . . Everything will be all right."

He closed his eyes and smiled to himself, seeing pictures in his head I could only imagine. He spoke so quietly that I had to lean forward to hear him. "I love you, Rachel."

His simple words conjured tears I could not stop. I knelt beside the bed and buried my face in the blankets, his limp hand touching my hair. The prayers that had eluded me inside the church rushed through me with a mistral's force, and with all the strength I possessed, I spoke to the God who might or might not listen. *Please hear me, please let him live. He cannot die. He must not die.*

Alarm filled Vincent's eyes, and a single tear coursed down his cheek. "Don't cry," he murmured. "Please don't cry."

I wiped his tears, then mine, with the edge of my shawl. "Don't you worry about me," I said and tried to smile. I pulled the chair close and sat down again, clasping his hand to my heart. "You must fight, Vincent. Promise me you'll fight." His answering nod was weak, but it was there. Dr. Rey appeared then and signaled it was time to leave. "I have to go. The doctor is here."

I stood, and he clung to my hand with sudden vigor. "Don't leave me."

"Dearest, I must, but I'll come back." I pressed my lips to his forehead. "I love you." Releasing his hand, I passed through the white curtains, pulling them together behind me.

# CHAPTER FIFTEEN

## Recovery

*When I left him, he was very sad, and I was sorry I could
do nothing to make his situation more bearable.*
      —Reverend Mr. Salles to Theo,
            Arles, 31 December 1888

I tried to keep my promise to Vincent, that I would return
to the Hôtel-Dieu. But when Françoise and I arrived the
following afternoon, the gate porter denied us entry with an
apologetic "No visitors on Sunday." Then Monday, although
he readily let us pass, the nun posted at the entrance to the
men's ward sent us away. The same nun had helped us before
and had taken us to Dr. Rey's office, but that afternoon found
her stern and rude. Françoise refused to give up and insisted we
wanted to see the doctor. Dr. Rey was busy in surgery and was
not available, we were told. No, we could not speak to someone else. No, the Sister could not take us to see Monsieur van
Gogh. No, she would not deliver a note.

I wanted to cry as we walked across the courtyard and into the street. "We have to try again tomorrow—we have to. I promised him I'd come. I don't understand."

"Uptight virgin nuns," Françoise was muttering, when Joseph Roulin walked toward us with long-legged strides. He greeted us and asked if we'd been to the hospital, and Françoise told him what had happened.

"They won't let me see him either," Roulin said. "Dr. Rey has been reporting to me, though, and so has Reverend Salles. I've been keeping Vincent's brother in Paris and his sister in Holland informed of his condition best as I can."

"Dr. Rey did let Rachel see him Saturday," Françoise said and nudged me.

"*Vraiment*? Was he still in the isolation room?"

"No, Dr. Rey had moved him to the main ward," I replied. "He was weak, and he'd been given a sedative. I wasn't allowed to stay long, but I spoke to him for a few minutes."

Roulin nodded approvingly. "That must have boosted his spirits! Listen, a group of us are meeting today at the Café de la Gare—my wife, myself, Joseph and Marie Ginoux—to talk about what we can do to help Vincent. Why don't you come?"

It was one thing to go to the *pastorale* with the Roulins when Vincent was with me, but another completely to meet them at the café. "I'm not sure that's a good—"

"Do come. My wife will be glad to see you. We're meeting at five." Françoise nudged me again, and I agreed. "The editors of *Le Forum Républicain* ought to be thankful I'm not paying them a visit today, but we've got bigger things to worry about," Roulin added with a scowl.

Françoise shot Roulin a warning look. "What's this about *Le Forum Républicain*?" I asked. "Françoise?"

"Nothing," she mumbled. "Let's get you home, it's cold. *Salut*, Joseph."

I held my tongue until we reached the *maison*, where, against Françoise's protests, I dove into a pile of old newspapers in Madame Virginie's parlor. "Rachel, I told you, it's nothing. Forget what Joseph said, it's just a——"

There it was. In the Sunday *Forum Républicain*, glaring at me in black and white the way it'd glared at everybody else in town. I sank into a chair by the fireplace, the words swimming before my eyes.

### LE FORUM RÉPUBLICAIN
Dimanche, 30 Décembre 1888

#### Chronique locale

Last Sunday at 11:30 pm, one Vincent Vangogh, painter of Dutch origin, presented himself at the *maison de tolérance* no. 1, asked for one Rachel and gave her his ear, saying "Guard this object very carefully." Then he disappeared.

"Those bastards," Françoise said with a scowl that mirrored Roulin's. "I tried to keep it from you. I didn't want you to see."

I forced myself to keep reading. The article said the police went to Vincent's house, and he was in the hospital—that was all, but it was enough. I should have guessed that night couldn't be kept a secret; I should have guessed the writers of *Le Forum Républicain* would enjoy printing such a gruesome tale. More evidence of how Arles was infected with a moral plague, one more reason for the good citizens to shake their heads in dismay. I could imagine the chatter over the breakfast table, the gasps of horror and disbelief. Or, God forbid, the laughter, the firm conviction that the crazy foreigner and the filthy whore had gotten exactly what they deserved.

"Vincent must not see this," I said. "He must not know. *Mon Dieu*, how will everyone treat him now?"

Françoise snatched the newspaper from my hand. "They didn't even get it right. That's not what he said."

"You think they care about getting it right? Oh, *that's* why the Sister at the hospital wouldn't let us in. She knows the whole story, everybody does!"

"You can't let this rattle you, or you'll make yourself sick again. You're going to meet Joseph and the others later, and you're going to help Vincent. Forget this nonsense." Françoise gave the pages a stern shake before tossing them into the fire.

"I can't go to the café. Who I am is right there for everybody to see! Madame Roulin . . ." She'd been so kind to me at the *pastorale,* where she'd treated me like any decent young lady. I couldn't bear to think of her snubbing me, as she surely would. As she had every right to do.

"Who cares what she thinks? Besides, if Joseph thought you shouldn't be around his wife"—Françoise's frown deepened at the word—"he wouldn't have invited you. You have to go. For Vincent."

I watched *Le Forum Républicain* curl in the fire and collapse into ashes. If only every copy could disappear so easily. "For Vincent. You're right."

"Now, I have some news that should cheer you up," Françoise said and perched herself on the settee. "I got Dr. Dupin to tell Madame Virginie you can't entertain anybody for at least a month, until your body heals and you've gotten over the shock." She looked positively smug, and I knew what she must have done. That old man! "And since you won't be earning any money, I want to share some of my wages with you."

"Françoise, thank you, but I can't do that. I can't take your money."

"Yes, you can. Out there folks don't understand, but in here, we girls have to help each other." She winked at me. "I went to a lot of trouble for you, you best take it. You'll need it."

The clock struck five as I walked through the door of the Café de la Gare, and Joseph Roulin waved from a corner table. Monsieur and Madame Ginoux were already there, along with Madame Roulin, and my stomach fluttered as I approached them. Would Madame Roulin look at me differently, the way ladies always looked at me? Get up and leave? But she surprised me, rising to kiss me on both cheeks, insisting I sit next to her. Maybe she didn't know who I was after all. Maybe Roulin— and Vincent, when she'd visited him—had hidden it from her. Maybe she didn't read the newspaper.

"My husband said Dr. Rey let you see Vincent," she said. "He was glad to see you?" Her smile was as friendly as the night of the *pastorale,* her eyes as gentle.

Before I could answer, Monsieur Roulin called, "Reverend Salles! Over here!" and an old man in a black suit hurried from the door. I wanted to crawl under the table—Roulin hadn't said anything about the preacher coming! He apologized for his lateness as he took a seat and greeted everyone. To me he said *bonjour* politely, studying my face until I squirmed in my chair. "What news, Reverend?" Roulin asked as Madame Ginoux brought coffee.

"It's truly miraculous," Reverend Salles said, still huffing and puffing. "When I last saw Vincent, he was lethargic, barely able to speak, but today he was perfectly calm and coherent. He was sitting up in bed and reading when I arrived." Madame Roulin patted my hand, and I smiled into my coffee. *Merci, mon Dieu.*

"Splendid!" Roulin exclaimed. "So he'll come home soon?"

The Reverend frowned. "I don't know. They've put him back in the isolation room."

Gasps of alarm came from around the table, and Roulin demanded, "Why the hell would they do that? Apologies, Reverend, ladies." Reverend Salles sounded worried as he explained that he'd spoken to two different doctors—not Dr. Rey, unfortunately—and neither had given him a satisfactory answer. Despite Vincent's improvement, the hospital administrators felt he should be transferred to an asylum, perhaps in Aix or Marseille. A report had already been sent to the mayor requesting the transfer. The mayor would lead an inquiry, the results would go to the prefect, and depending on what the prefect said, Vincent could be moved within a week.

"That's outrageous!" Roulin thundered, and everyone started talking at once. Everyone but me. An asylum. An asylum lay just beyond Saint-Rémy, out the road to Les Baux, in the shadow of the mountains. A *maison de santé,* the notices called it, as if it had simply been a place for a long rest, but everybody knew the high walls hid the insane, the *aliénés,* and any number of frightening secrets. Some villagers swore ghosts roamed the fields around the asylum at night, and a favorite dare of local boys was to try and find out. Papa always said that was ignorant nonsense, but he steered clear as much as anyone and warned me to do the same. And the doctors wanted to send Vincent to a place like that? No matter what he'd done to himself, he wasn't mad. I knew it.

"Maybe we'd be better off," Monsieur Ginoux muttered

under his breath. At the surprised look from his wife, he cleared his throat and said more distinctly, "Maybe he'd be better off. In Aix or Marseille."

"How can you say that?" Madame Ginoux asked. "When he's been a good friend to us?"

Monsieur Ginoux looked uncomfortable. "In Aix he'd be in a hospital where he could be well taken care of. He'd recover faster."

"Nothing could do Vincent more good than to get back to his paintings and his friends," Roulin declared, and everyone but Monsieur Ginoux nodded in agreement. I was as puzzled as Madame Ginoux—I'd heard what he'd said too. But why? Because Vincent and Gauguin had painted portraits of his wife? Was he still angry because Vincent had painted an ugly picture of his café?

"What does Vincent's brother say?" I asked timidly.

Reverend Salles looked at me, and his voice was kind. "If the ruling is made that Vincent must go to the asylum, there isn't much Monsieur van Gogh can do, unless he takes Vincent back to Paris. He is most anxious and hopes for Vincent's recovery as much as we do." He sighed. "Vincent asked me to write his brother about coming for another visit, but given Monsieur van Gogh's busy work schedule, I do not think it will happen."

His brother nearly dead in the hospital, and Theo came to Arles for only one day. Now Vincent was in danger of being sent to an asylum, and Theo wouldn't return to help? He had more power than the rest of us; he was family. Was he so frightened that he felt it best to stay away? Did he believe there was no hope?

"Does Vincent know what they're planning?" Madame Roulin asked.

"I think he's guessed. Even though he was calm, he was also very cross about his situation, and said several times he wanted to go home. I am concerned he may work himself into another *crise,* he is so indignant."

Roulin pounded the table with his fist. "I'll go to the hospital tomorrow and demand he be let out of that isolation room, because for damn sure it's not fair, those damn bourgeois doctors! Apologies, Reverend, ladies."

"I'll join you," the Reverend said. "Perhaps Dr. Rey can help us persuade the other doctors. He seems a sensible man, and he knows Vincent's condition best."

Madame Roulin shook her head. "Just when you say Vincent is getting better!"

"We must not lose heart, no matter how bleak things seem," Reverend Salles said. "All things work for the good, and we must have faith that God will look after our friend."

Roulin's reply was quiet but determined. "If God won't, we will."

# Chapter Sixteen

## Return to the Yellow House

*I am happy to inform you that my predictions have been realized, and that the overexcitement has been only temporary.*

—Dr. Félix Rey to Theo, Arles, 2 January 1889

The new year dawned. Vincent was still in the Arles hospital, still not fully recovered, but together, Monsieur Roulin, Reverend Salles, and Dr. Rey stopped his transfer to an asylum. He was even moved from the isolation room back to the main ward. Visitors were not permitted except for Reverend Salles—Dr. Rey could not change his superiors' minds about that—but Roulin faithfully got reports of Vincent's condition and faithfully sent news along to me. Each short message, telling me that Vincent had walked for an hour in the hospital courtyard that day, or that his appetite had returned, convinced me my prayers had been answered.

Two weeks after Vincent's collapse, Françoise appeared at

my door with another message. "Rachel, Joseph's outside and says he has a delivery for you."

The sly twinkle in her eyes had me grabbing my shawl and running downstairs in a flash. I hoped for a letter from Vincent, a real letter in his own hand telling me he was all right, but it was something much better. Outside on the sidewalk, Vincent himself stood beside Roulin, wrapped in his green overcoat, a fur hat pulled low to conceal his bandage.

I wanted to throw my arms around his neck, cover his face with kisses, clutch him to me and never let go. But the fear of hurting him held me back, and I could only gasp, "What are you doing here?"

"I'm going home for a while." His voice was stronger than that day in the hospital. He sounded like himself again. "Then I must return to the Hôtel-Dieu."

"I had a long talk with Dr. Rey and one of the other doctors yesterday," Roulin said, "and I told them my friend Vincent MUST be allowed to see his paintings." He delivered this pronouncement with a stern nod, beard wagging emphatically.

"I thought you might like to join us," Vincent said. He tilted his head and added with a smile, "I won't break. I'm no ceramic *santon,* although I could probably use a papier-mâché ear."

Roulin discreetly turned his back, and I flung myself into Vincent's waiting arms. How thin he was. I could feel it even through the wool overcoat, and when I looked up into his face I saw that his cheeks were sunken. Porridge and broth, that's probably all they gave him in the Hôtel-Dieu; he needed a good home-cooked meal, somebody besides nuns and doctors caring for him.

"How long can you stay?" I asked.

Roulin replied, "I told Dr. Rey we wouldn't be but an hour

or two, so we should move along. Vincent, you must say something if you start to feel tired."

Vincent waved his hand impatiently. "I'm fine. I just want to
see my paintings."

I took his arm so he could lean on me while we walked. At
first he did a little, and at first his footsteps were slow, but when
we reached the Place Lamartine, any weakness vanished. His
pace quickened, and I felt my spirits rising together with his as
we crossed the garden and neared the yellow house. Under the
gray skies it appeared yellower than usual, as if putting on its
best face to welcome him home.

Vincent shifted from foot to foot as Roulin fumbled in his
pockets for the key. "Patience, my friend," Roulin chuckled.
"The charwoman put everything back in order. She worked
hard to get the house ready for you."

"I'll make sure she's paid extra for cleaning up the mess I
made," Vincent said. I tried not to think about what that mess
had been.

When Roulin pushed open the door, Vincent broke from
my grasp and bolted through the hallway into the studio. "He's
been worrying over his pictures ever since he started feeling better," Roulin told me in a low voice as we gave him
a moment alone. "When it comes to his painting, *il est doux
comme un agneau.*" Sweet as a lamb.

"You haven't told him about that article, have you, Monsieur Roulin?" I asked.

Roulin looked offended. "I'm no fool, Mademoiselle Rachel."

Vincent was pulling canvases from stacks in the corner and
setting them around the walls: touching each one, crooning
under his breath to them like a father gone too long from his
children. "Right where I left them, safe and sound," he told us

with shining eyes. "I wish I could start something today. I can't wait to feel a brush in my hand again."

I was astonished how the paintings had multiplied since my last visit. Sowers under setting suns, the portrait of Madame Ginoux, another vineyard painting . . . so many of them. Not all were his, though. One stack in the corner he didn't touch, and I could tell from the look of them they were Gauguin's. He must have forgotten them in his haste to leave.

Vincent started dragging his worktable to the empty space where Gauguin's easel had been. "Careful," Roulin said and went to help. "Look, Mademoiselle Rachel, Vincent painted my whole family."

"Kept me busy on the rainy days," Vincent said and scooped paint tubes from the floor.

Vincent hadn't painted one picture of each member of the Roulin family: he'd painted multiple pictures of all of them. Joseph Roulin again in his postman's uniform, Madame Roulin plump and serene by a window, three pictures of Camille, and in two paintings beyond, Armand, once looking shyly away, once looking confident in his best hat and yellow jacket. The unfinished painting on Vincent's easel—the one he must have worked on before his illness—showed Madame Roulin in a green dress against a flowery background, rocking an unseen cradle by a cord.

"Still need to finish the hands," Vincent muttered as he passed the easel, "and the top layer on the skirt. Oh, I wish I could work today."

He'd painted chubby Marcelle most of all, twice in the arms of her *maman*, three times by herself. If our baby had lived, I thought as I stared at one of the pictures, he would have painted us. The doting mother against that yellow background would have been me, the child our son or daughter, wiggling and reaching for Papa while Papa tried to paint. "Hold the pose, little one," Vincent would have said with a fond laugh. When he finished the portrait, he would have hung it in a special place, maybe in the kitchen, where I could have seen it while I nursed the baby by the fire. Instead Marcelle stared from the canvas with accusing eyes, and the proud, motherly face belonged to somebody else.

Monsieur Roulin thought me fascinated. "Didn't he do a splendid job with my little girl? You've seen how he adores Marcelle."

"I had to work fast for that study," Vincent said, "because at first she didn't like posing. A child has the infinite in its eyes, *n'est-ce pas?*"

I couldn't bear any more. I disappeared into the kitchen to light the stove and make coffee, glad to escape the painted gazes of *la famille Roulin*. I heard Vincent and Roulin talking more about the pictures, Vincent delivering a spirited lecture about modern portraiture that boomed through the house and lasted until they followed me.

"*Et voilà, ma pipe!*" Vincent said happily as he retrieved pipe and tobacco pouch from the mantelpiece. He clenched the pipe in his teeth to fill the bowl with tobacco, lit a match from the stove, and closed his eyes to savor the first puff. "God, I've missed this. Dr. Rey won't let me smoke in the hospital."

"When can you come home for good?" I asked as I poured the coffee.

"In a few days, if I'm up to it. Then I'm to go to the hospital to have the dressing changed on my ear every two days until the wound is completely healed." Vincent frowned to himself and stared at the table, then abruptly announced, "I want to see my room."

"Would you like me to come with you?" I asked, and he

nodded. Roulin stayed behind to drink his coffee and smoke his own pipe.

Vincent's bedroom looked as pure and untouched as on the day he'd moved into the yellow house. The charwoman had cleaned the bedding, scrubbed the floor, and laid all his things in a row on his dressing table. Including his razor. That's what he must have used, I realized as I caught sight of it, and I shuddered.

"I remember nothing after the fight with Gauguin," Vincent said as he walked around the room, brushing his fingers against his things. "All I know is what the doctor told me I did, and I have no idea why." His voice fell to almost a whisper. "You must have been so frightened when . . . it was wrong of me to scare you like that."

"I was frightened for you more than anything else," I said and touched his shoulder. "You have no reason to be sorry."

He opened the window shutters for light and air, and we both smiled at the sounds of chattering laughter and clattering carriages floating up from the Place Lamartine. He started to talk softly about what he'd do when he came home, how the weather would soon be fine again, how he'd paint in the orchards outside town, when suddenly a panicked look crossed his face. He ran to the other bedroom and flung open the door. "He didn't take them," he breathed.

I hurried to stand beside him. "Who didn't take what?"

"Gauguin didn't take the sunflowers." Vincent opened the shutters and examined each piece of furniture, each painting as if taking an inventory. The charwoman had cleaned here too. No trace of Paul Gauguin remained.

"Why did you think he would?"

"He wanted them," Vincent said simply and latched the shutters tight to keep out the mistral. Then he turned to me.

"What was wrong in the studio, while we were talking about the baby's portrait?"

So he'd noticed after all. "Nothing's wrong."

"The look on your face, the way you rushed to the kitchen— I know there's something, *ma petite*. Please tell me."

"There's nothing," I insisted. He studied my face until I cast my eyes to the floor. "What were you doing at old Louis' place?" I asked.

"What? When?"

"Before you got sick. I saw you go inside."

He thought for a minute, then smiled. "Oh, that. Gauguin was trying to get Louis to pose for us. I tagged along for a drink."

"Only a drink?"

His answering look was steady. "Only a drink."

I smiled back at him. "We should go before Monsieur Roulin wonders what we're doing up here." That made him laugh out loud, and it was so good to hear the sound that I forgot all about old Louis, all about Marcelle Roulin.

"Rachel," Vincent said shyly as we crossed the landing, "I meant what I said in the hospital."

I stopped and peered up at him from under my eyelashes. "And what was that?"

"I love you," he murmured, flushing pink.

"How do you say it in Dutch?"

*"Ik hou van je."*

*"T'ame, moun amour,"* I told him in Provençal. He seized me round the waist and kissed me, a searching kiss that revived every night we spent together. He tasted of tobacco, of coffee—he tasted like home, and for the first time in far too long, I felt no sadness, no fear.

We were backing toward the bedroom door when a gruff cough from the hallway below startled us apart. "We need to get to the hospital, Vincent," Roulin called. I tucked my hair back into my chignon, Vincent straightened his clothes, and we sheepishly walked downstairs.

Vincent took a last turn around the studio and grabbed his sketchbook and pencils to keep him occupied in the hospital. He sighed as he locked the door of the yellow house and gave the key back to Roulin for safekeeping. "I'll write Theo and tell him all's well with the house," he said. "I can't thank you enough for all you've done." Roulin proclaimed it was his pleasure, and we began our walk to the Rue du Bout d'Arles. "By the way," Vincent asked, "have you written my mother and sister Willemien? I'll write them myself soon, but I don't want them to know what happened. You haven't told them, have you?"

"No, I've only written your brother." Roulin was lying to protect Vincent's feelings. A few days earlier he'd said he was passing news to Mademoiselle van Gogh.

"Good, I wouldn't want them to worry. It's bad enough Theo came for nothing."

"He hardly came for nothing," I broke in. "Vincent, you could have died!"

"But I didn't die," he said calmly, and added to himself, "I need to write Gauguin too."

"What for?" I demanded.

"To ask him to be discreet in talking about what happened, and to let him know I still consider him a friend."

"Humph—I don't know why!"

Vincent's voice was weary. "Rachel, please." I kept quiet but seethed inside at the thought of Gauguin. I wanted to snatch up his paintings and hurl them into the Rhône to rot. Had he once thought about Vincent after he fled to Paris? Bothered to find out whether Vincent lived or died?

I gave Vincent a last embrace when we reached the *maison,* whispering, "Come home soon." He nodded, too overcome with emotion to speak. Françoise came to join me in the doorway, and together we watched as Vincent and Roulin continued down the street toward the hospital.

A familiar envelope, my name written in a familiar scrawl, appeared at Madame Virginie's a few days later. No words accompanied the sketch of the house inside. No words were needed.

The door opened before I raised my hand to knock. "I watched for you through the window," Vincent said and kissed me on each cheek.

"When did you get back?" I asked as I followed him into the studio. The scent of turpentine, slight and faded earlier that week, was strong once more.

"Yesterday afternoon. It was wonderful to sleep in my own bed, even better to get back to work. I'm beginning with a still life to accustom myself to painting again." He gestured toward a carefully arranged collection of objects on the table: empty wine bottle, onions on a plate, a book, letter, candle, stick of sealing wax, and his pipe and tobacco pouch. "I'll stop soon for a break. Have a seat."

It was hard to believe that as sick as he'd been, as near to death as he'd been, he could stand there painting as if nothing had happened. Aside from being thinner and having the bandage around his head, he seemed no different than before. He seemed to be the Vincent I'd known back in the summer, before Gauguin had come. "And you're feeling fine?" I asked. "Not too tired, not too weak?"

He shrugged. "Perfectly fine. It was an artist's fit, nothing more."

"Artist's fit? What does that—"

"A temporary overexcitement, Dr. Rey says."

I watched him for a moment. His hand moved the same way it always had; his expression as he studied the canvas was the same as always too. "What does he say you need to do now?"

"Rest, take walks outdoors, eat well, don't work too hard. No drinking except a glass of wine with supper. And"—he turned to me with a pained look on his face—"no women."

"Oh. For how long?"

He stabbed at the canvas with his brush. "Until he says I can, I don't know, a few weeks? Too long, as far as I'm concerned."

"I suppose he's right," I said. "It's too soon."

"Easy for him to say. He doesn't have you waiting for him."

"It's more important for you to get well. We have all the time in the world." I walked closer to the easel and peered at the painting. "What do all these things mean?"

He ignored my question, setting down his brushes and palette to take my face in his hands. "*Mon Dieu,* I want to kiss you so much right now."

"Kissing is rather indispensable," I murmured with a giggle, "otherwise serious disorders might result."

A knock at the front door interrupted us a few minutes later, and I pulled away to answer it as Vincent groaned in annoyance. I stifled another giggle at finding staid Dr. Rey, who removed his hat and said politely, "*Bonjour,* Mademoiselle. Is Vincent here?"

"He's working in the studio, this way. May I take your hat and coat?"

"Yes, thank you." He coughed. "Pardon me, Mademoiselle, but you have paint on your cheek." I wiped away Vincent's fingerprints and wondered if the doctor had seen us misbehaving through the window. At least the paint was only on my face.

Dr. Rey's eyes widened when we entered the studio and he saw all the paintings. "*Bonjour, Docteur,*" Vincent said. "Welcome to my home."

"*Bonjour,* Vincent, I've come to ensure you are satisfactorily settled. I am pleased to see you working"—the doctor's brow furrowed as he considered the objects on the table—"but mind you don't work too hard."

"I'm taking things slowly, I promise. Would you like to see my paintings?"

Vincent toured the doctor around the studio, his voice growing more animated with every canvas he pulled out to show. The doctor seemed out of place with his fine suit, and I noticed he was careful not to brush against anything and spoil it with paint. From his bland expression I couldn't tell whether he liked Vincent's work, until his face lit up at one of the pictures. "That's one of my favorites," I said when he bent to take a closer look at the starry night over the Rhône.

Dr. Rey smiled at me for the first time. "You have exquisite taste, Mademoiselle. I can almost hear the water lapping."

"I was there when he painted it."

"Look at this one," Vincent broke in, producing the canvas with the night café.

"I'm sorry to say it, but I'm not sure I like that one," Dr. Rey said.

Vincent beamed with satisfaction before launching into an explanation of complementary colors. The doctor listened attentively, nodding his head and asking questions, and my already good opinion of him soared even higher. "I've often thought I should try my hand at painting," he mused, his eyes returning to the starry night.

Vincent shook his head. "A man of your means should turn collector, not painter, although even to do that, you have to train your eye." He chose a print from a pile on a chair and handed it to Dr. Rey.

"A surgeon! That's a fine picture."

"Rembrandt's *Anatomy Lesson of Dr. Tulp*. The original is in The Hague, where I used to live. I'll have my brother send a new print for you as a gift." Dr. Rey thanked him, and Vincent added, "I'd be honored if you'd allow me to paint your portrait, also as a gift."

The doctor paused so briefly that Vincent in his eagerness might not have noticed, but I did. "I wouldn't want you to work too hard."

"I could use the practice after my illness. Why don't you come back later in the week and sit for me?"

"I could come Sunday after church," the doctor said, still sounding doubtful. He gave a little bow in my direction. "Mademoiselle, I hope you will be joining us. Although I admit I'll be nervous, having my picture painted."

Vincent waved his hand. "It'll be fine. You spend your days cutting up people and peering inside them, now I shall peer inside you."

"I look forward to it. And now I must return to the hospital. *Au revoir,* Mademoiselle."

I smiled and handed Dr. Rey his hat and coat. *"Au revoir, Docteur.* Thank you for all your help." Vincent followed him into the hall, where I heard their voices, low and indistinct.

Vincent made a face when he came back into the studio. "He reminded me that I'm supposed to 'exercise restraint with women' for a while." His eyes narrowed. "Why do I think the good doctor would like to abandon restraint with you?" When I laughed and said he was being ridiculous, Vincent insisted, "I saw how he looked at you."

I had seen it too, but it didn't worry me. "I think we need

to change the subject, that's what I think. You work on your painting, and I'll make some supper."

"Supper's a poor substitute for what I really want," he grumbled and snatched up his paintbrushes.

By the time I'd gone shopping and cooked our meal, Vincent's new painting was nearly finished, and his grouchy spell had passed like a summer shower. I sighed happily as I made the stew and rearranged the kitchen to my satisfaction, brushing my hand over the dishes and utensils the way Vincent had done with the things in his bedroom and studio. I was glad to see his hearty appetite when I served supper; I'd spent extra for good beef. "I had a letter from Johanna," he said as we ate.

It took me a moment to remember who she was. "Theo's fiancée?"

He nodded. "A very kind letter, just a few lines. She seems charming and intelligent. And desperate for me to like her."

"That's not surprising," I said. "She's marrying your brother. I'm sure she'd like to be friends." How much did she know about Vincent's illness, I wondered. "Do you approve of the match now?" I asked cautiously.

He looked me straight in the eye. "I was caught by surprise, that's all. He's loved her a long time, and when he proposed before, she said no. It devastated him. Then after a year of no contact she appears in Paris, arranges a 'chance meeting,' and they're engaged ten days later? You must admit, that's suspicious." I had to agree, it was. "I feared she would hurt him again, but she seems to truly love him. It seems I was mistaken."

"It's natural to worry about Theo and want what's best for him." I stood to get Vincent more stew, and with my back turned, I said, "I did wonder if you were jealous."

"Jealous?"

"Thinking Johanna might come between you and Theo."

I heard him shift in his chair behind me. "Maybe. But I don't believe that now." I brought his bowl and took my seat again, and he added, "Rachel, when Gauguin said I was upset about the money—that's not true. Or at least not completely true. Naturally I can't help but think about it, but I'd never want Theo to be lonely because of me. I'm not the selfish bastard Gauguin made me out to be, and I wouldn't want you to think I was."

"I'm the last person to believe anything that man says," I said with a snort, then reached across the table to take his hand. "I just want everything to be all right again, Vincent."

"Everything will be," he promised.

After supper, he smoked his pipe and wrote a letter to Theo, while I did some of his mending, then read a book. When the clock tinged nine, Vincent looked over at me and patted his knee; I went to him and perched myself on his lap. "*Ma petite*," he said quietly, removing my hairpins so my hair fell over my shoulders, "I would like it if you stayed here tonight, instead of going back to the *maison*."

"You know I can't. The doctor said—"

"I don't mean that. I mean, stay and sleep in the other bedroom. I'd like knowing you are here."

He lit a candle to lead us upstairs and found me a clean nightshirt. He made sure I was settled, then kissed me before shutting the door between us. I climbed into bed and hugged my knees, listening to him move around his room, gazing at his paintings by candlelight. The golden sunflowers and green gardens whispered of happy days past and future, and I smiled to myself as I blew out the candle and burrowed under the covers. Vincent had come home. So had I.

★ ★ ★

*"NO!"*

Vincent's shout rang through the house, and I threw open the door between our rooms to find him writhing in bed. With trembling hands I lit the lamp on his dressing table, then softly said his name. He sat up with a gasp, and I took him in my arms. "I'm scared, Rachel," he said into my shoulder. "I'm so scared . . ."

He wouldn't stop shaking, even when I kissed his forehead and smoothed his tousled hair. "It was only a dream, dearest."

"What will I do, Rachel, what will I do if I wake up one day and I can't paint anymore?"

"That won't happen. You were painting this afternoon, weren't you?"

"A still life, that's all." His voice rose. "What if I can't paint Dr. Rey? What if I can't paint anything else?"

"Shhh, you can, *mon cher,* of course you can. Please don't excite yourself." I held him until his breathing calmed and his grip relaxed. It was like that night of the rain, I thought, and my stomach clenched. "I'll go downstairs and get you some water."

"Don't leave me."

"Only for a moment, dearest."

I left him the lamp and found my way in the dark. When I returned, he was clutching the sheet to his chest and staring into the empty fireplace. "Here, drink this. Now lie down and let me cover you up, you've kicked away all your blankets. Do you want the fire lit?"

He pulled the blanket up to his chin and shook his head. "Will you stay with me?"

"Of course, if that's what you want." I climbed into bed and guided his head back to my shoulder. "Nothing is going to hurt you. Go to sleep, you need your rest. Don't be afraid anymore."

Sleep didn't come for me until just before dawn. "Artist's fit"—what did that mean? What if Vincent wasn't as well as he seemed? What if his illness returned? Every time he stirred in the night, I felt his forehead to check for fever; any time he made a sound, I held him tighter and wished the spirits away.

He was gone when I woke. I found him in the studio, sitting on a stool before another canvas, the still life from yesterday already finished and set aside. The mirror that usually hung in the bedroom was propped against some books on his worktable, and he glanced from his reflection to the picture, palette and hands smeared with the brightest of pigments, puffs of smoke drifting upward from his pipe. He was painting a self-portrait.

"Up so early, dearest?" I said.

He didn't look away from his painting, only mumbled around his pipe stem, "I wanted to work."

I yawned as I lit the stove and brewed coffee, yawned again as I sliced bread and fumbled in the cabinet for jam. Vincent frowned a little at the interruption of breakfast but accepted the cup of coffee and wedge of bread I gave him. I eyed him warily. "How are you feeling?" I asked. "That nightmare of yours—"

He brushed it away. "It was nothing. Just a dream."

"Do you have bad dreams like that often?"

"Almost every night. Ever since . . ." He stared at the bread in his hand. "Dr. Rey says it'll pass. He gave me bromide of potassium to take."

"I'll make you a bedtime tisane out of some herbs Françoise

has, that'll help too. Lemon verbena and *millepertuis* chase the devil away, they say."

"Pagan superstition," he scoffed.

"It helps, it did me a power of good when—" I stopped myself. "When I wasn't feeling well, while you were sick."

He waved toward the canvas and said, "Working will help more than anything."

"Maybe you shouldn't work today. Maybe you should rest."

He scowled at me. "Rachel, I'm no invalid to be coddled. Good or bad, a dream is only a dream. Now stop worrying and look at my painting."

"Vincent van Gogh, you are the stubbornest man I ever did meet," I complained but went to the easel just the same.

This painting seemed no different, no less strong than any of the others. In it he wore his green overcoat and fur hat, like the day he left the hospital, but he'd shown himself with no beard and with eyes green as emeralds. Vivid red and searing orange divided the background, and the white bandage around his head stood out sharply against the color. He was not hiding what he'd done. If anything, he'd made the bandage more obvious, more prominent than it actually was. I'm still here, the portrait seemed to say. I'm still here, and I can still paint.

"I thought it'd be good practice before Dr. Rey poses," he said. "What do you think?"

"Complementary colors," I murmured. "Blue and orange, red and green."

"Excellent. What else?"

I studied the painting more before answering. "At first it seems the colors clash, that there's no harmony, but when you look closer, you realize there is. Your eyes are green to match the coat, and the red in your mouth matches the red in the pipe and back behind. The coat's green, but you put blue and orange in it to match your hat and the orange at the top."

I got a delighted smile full of teeth in response. "You've developed quite an eye."

"One doesn't have to spend much time with you to learn about colors," I said modestly.

"I suppose not." He tilted his head to study the painting alongside me for several minutes. When he spoke again, his voice shook. "Is that the face of a madman?"

I didn't hesitate. "No. It's the face of the man I love."

## CHAPTER SEVENTEEN

## The Doctor's Portrait

*I now intend to do a portrait of Dr. Rey and possibly
other portraits as soon as I am a little used to painting
again.*

—Vincent to Theo, Arles, January 1889

D id burglars break in and clean up?" I asked when I arrived
at Vincent's studio on Sunday. The empty paint tubes and
dried-up pots of ink had disappeared, the floor was swept free
of dust and canvas scraps, and his best armchair sat ready by the
window. Vincent looked as tidy as the room, with scrubbed-
clean trousers and a new artist's smock. "*Tiens,* you look nice,"
I said, straightening the tie of the smock and smoothing the
fabric across his shoulders. "You smell nice too. Like soap instead of turpentine."

He fidgeted under my hands and made a face. "I haven't
worn one of these since Paris. I need a long moustache to twirl
and some plaster casts lying around, like a pretentious Aca-

démie ass." I laughed and told him he looked very professional.
"If Dr. Rey is happy with his portrait," he continued, "perhaps
he'll recommend others to come. I'll wear a smock if it means
I can charge fees and earn some money."

"We'll give him a nice day. I'll start some tea. I don't suppose you have any biscuits?"

"Biscuits?" His eyes widened. "I should have biscuits?"

I laughed again. "The *boulangerie*'s still open, I'll buy a tin."

A knock announced the doctor's arrival not long after I
came back. I hurried to put the kettle on the stove and arrange
biscuits on a plate, then peeked into the hall to give Vincent
an encouraging smile before he opened the door. I'd left my
apron in the kitchen during an earlier visit, so I tied it around
my waist. Now we both looked respectable. "Good afternoon,
Doctor," I said when I met them in the studio. "Would you
care for some tea?"

"Good afternoon, Mademoiselle. Yes, thank you."

"I thought you'd like to see my latest work," I heard Vincent
say as I busied myself in the kitchen. "I made a concentrated
study of complementary colors in this self-portrait."

"Your command of your brush has not weakened at all," Dr.
Rey said.

I poured out the tea in Vincent's best blue china cups—the
only cups he had that matched—then placed everything on a
tray and swept into the studio with what I hoped was a hospi-
table smile. "I hope you will join us, Mademoiselle," Dr. Rey
said as he accepted a cup of tea and balanced two biscuits on
his saucer.

"But of course. Vincent?" I extended the tray to Vincent
before setting it on the table and taking up my own tea.

Vincent probably hoped we would discuss his paintings, but
instead Dr. Rey asked how he was sleeping and whether he had

any nightmares. Vincent frowned and fiddled with his teacup. "Not as many as before."

"Soon they will diminish altogether," Dr. Rey assured him. "Dizziness?"

Vincent shook his head, and the doctor asked about his appetite. Vincent's frown deepened, and I chimed in, "He's been eating well, Doctor. He's doing everything you asked him to do." *Including not sleeping with me*, I added in my head.

"Excellent," Dr. Rey pronounced. "Let's have you come twice this next week to keep a check on the dressings, and the following week we can take the bandage off."

"I'm in no hurry," Vincent muttered into his tea.

"It has to come off sooner or later," the doctor said gently. "We talked about this." Vincent's reply was something between a snort and a grunt.

I changed the subject. "Vincent tells me you were born in Arles," I said to Dr. Rey, "and did your schooling in Montpellier."

"Yes, Mademoiselle, both are correct. I've not actually received my full degree yet, though. I am completing my thesis soon, then I'll go to Paris to defend it."

"Will you move to Paris?" I asked. Vincent was still scowling, and I saw him twist his head toward the clock in the hall.

Dr. Rey smiled, and for once didn't look so much like a doctor. "Oh no, I belong in Arles. I want to serve the people of this region, and my family is here. I am living with my parents, in fact, until I marry."

"I'll give you the address of my brother's gallery in Paris, so you can call on him," Vincent broke in. "He is acquainted with several doctors as clients." Dr. Rey started to thank him, but he waved his hand impatiently. "*Ce n'est rien.* Now I'd like to begin your portrait, while the light is fine."

As Dr. Rey took his place in the armchair and Vincent set about posing him, I hastened with the dishes to the kitchen and back so I wouldn't miss anything. Vincent squatted, stood, backed away, came close. He had the doctor turn this way and that to test the light, move the chair, move it back. He made noises while lost in thought: "Hmmm. HMMM." Finally he was ready. "Rachel, do you see my pipe?" I located it in a jar of brushes, where it had migrated during his cleaning. Another minute or two of hunting followed, until he realized the tobacco pouch was in his trouser pocket.

"You're not smoking too much, are you?" Dr. Rey asked from the armchair.

"No. Hold the pose."

Vincent picked up his palette and squeezed paint from various tubes, using his knife to blend the colors as his eyes, and mine, stole to his seated subject. Dr. Rey had the jet-black hair of a true Provençal, fashionably slicked back with an equally fashionable goatee and upturned moustache. He'd dressed for his portrait in a handsome suit of quality fabric, topped with a blue jacket trimmed in red. He was a little pudgy—someone who enjoyed home cooking and didn't get outdoors much— but he had a pleasant way about him and wasn't unattractive. A courteous gentleman with money: why wasn't he married? Surely the bourgeois ladies of Arles would fall over themselves to match their daughters with a doctor. Maybe he never left the hospital long enough to meet any of them.

Dr. Rey caught me watching him. "Eyes to me," Vincent said irritably. "I realize Mademoiselle Rachel is more pleasing to look at, but she's not the one doing the painting." The poor doctor blushed to his ears at this remark.

Vincent muttered aloud while he painted, sometimes to Dr. Rey, sometimes to me, sometimes to himself. "I'm showing you from torso up, which I've found works best for a true character study," he'd say, or, "Damn it, that's too much red." At one point he stopped painting altogether and stared at the doctor. "Do you always wear a cravat?"

Dr. Rey's hand went to his throat. "Pardon?"

"Every time I see you, you're wearing a thick cravat. Doesn't it choke you?"

I tried to catch Vincent's eye—this was no way to woo a customer! But Dr. Rey smiled and said, "I'm accustomed to it."

"I can't remember the last time I wore a cravat like that." Vincent dabbed his brush in his paints and kept working, only to stop again and say, "I'll tell you what I've told my sister. It is not enough in life to only study. One must *live*. Enjoy oneself, have as many diversions as possible, fall in love." He waved his brush emphatically. "Cast aside your books and your cravat. What good is it to heal people if you yourself need healing?"

Dr. Rey looked amused more than offended. "That is good advice. Perhaps once I have my final degree, I will have more time to find diversions, as you say."

"Humph" was Vincent's answer, and he painted in silence for the rest of the session.

When the portrait was completed, he signed it in bold red against the blue of the doctor's jacket and presented it to Dr. Rey with a reminder to be careful, it wouldn't be fully dry for a few weeks. The doctor's face was unreadable as he examined the painting. "It's very fine," he said with a stiff smile and a quick glance at me. Then I knew—he didn't like it. And he didn't want Vincent to know.

"I'm glad it pleases you," Vincent said with a sigh of relief. "If you know anyone who would like to have their portrait painted, perhaps your parents or one of the other doctors—"

"I will keep that in mind," Dr. Rey said politely and con-

sulted his pocket watch. "I should return home. Mother has the
cook prepare a grand dinner on Sundays, and she'll be wondering where I am. Thank you for an enjoyable afternoon, Vincent, Mademoiselle."

"I'll see you out," Vincent said, and when he came back to
the studio, he was smiling. "That went well—perhaps this is
the beginning of some commissions!" He hummed a merry
tune as he wiped his brushes clean and put his paints away.
I didn't have the heart to tell him that the doctor's portrait
would probably wind up in Mother's attic. "Why don't I paint
you next?" he asked.

"Oh, Vincent, I don't know . . ."

"Don't tell me you're afraid!"

"I suppose I am," I confessed. "What you said to Dr. Rey
about how you peer inside people when you paint them . . .
what would you see if you peered inside me?"

He stopped arranging his paints to look at me. "You have
nothing to worry about, *chérie*. Please?"

It would make him so happy. "Someday soon."

"It'll be the most beautiful portrait I've ever done, I know
it," he said eagerly, rummaging again in his paint box. "I can
already see it in my head. Promise me?"

"Someday soon," I repeated. "I promise."

# Chapter Eighteen

# Whispers in the Place Lamartine

*Along with other young people I used to poke fun at this queer painter.*

—an unidentified Arlesian,
interviewed in the 1920s

The next time I visited the yellow house, raised voices greeted me through the half-open door. I pushed it open and hurried into the hall. "*Qu'est-ce qui se passe?* What's going on?"

Vincent and the potbellied man with him stopped arguing. "This is Monsieur Soulé, owner of the hotel next door and my landlord," Vincent said. Monsieur Soulé looked me up and down with a grin that said he'd like to get me into one of his rooms. "He's come to turn me out," Vincent added.

"What!" I stared from one to the other. "Why?"

"Monsieur van Gogue owes me two months' rent," Monsieur Soulé replied.

"Gogh," Vincent muttered through clenched teeth. "Damn

it, I told you I have the money." He disappeared into the kitchen, then returned with a handful of coins and bills. "*Voilà,* thirty francs. Now I have work to do, so good day to you."

"It's not that simple, Monsieur van Gogue," Monsieur Soulé said smugly as he tucked the money into his waistcoat pocket. "I've already rented the house to another tenant, a tobacconist who's opening a shop here. I told him he could move in at the end of the month."

Vincent glowered at him. "What'd you do that for?"

"Word around here a few weeks ago was that you weren't going to recover."

"As you can see, I have recovered, so you can find someplace else for your tobacconist."

"He'll be a more responsible tenant," Monsieur Soulé said in the same smug tone.

"Who paid to have the whole house painted, inside and out? Who arranged to have gaslights installed in the front room?" I put my hand on Vincent's arm, but he ignored me and kept shouting. "Christ, this house was a disaster when I moved in, and you want me out so you can charge somebody else higher rent? Thanks to *my* improvements?"

"Who's always late with the rent?" Monsieur Soulé fired back.

"I won't be late anymore, I swear!" Vincent ran his fingers through his hair and wheedled, "Please don't turn me out. I need this house to do my work. We had a deal when I rented it at the beginning of last May: one-year lease. Let me keep it until the end of April, then if you're not happy with the way I've been taking care of things, I'll go. *D'accord?*"

Monsieur Soulé frowned as he mulled over Vincent's plea. "*D'accord.* End of April. But I better not hear any more stories about you, or you'll be out."

"Yes, yes, thank you," Vincent mumbled. "I really do have

work to do, so please excuse me . . ." He ushered out Monsieur Soulé with a halfhearted "*Bonne journée.*"

"God damn it!" he exploded once he shut the door. "I wasn't expecting to give him the whole thirty francs today!" He stomped into the kitchen as I followed behind him. "Thirty francs to the charwoman," he ticked on his fingers. "Thirty francs to the hospital. Twenty francs toward the gas heater and the furniture I have on account. Twelve francs fifty for all the laundry. Fifteen francs for new brushes and to replace the clothes I ruined. Five francs for wood and coal. Now the rent! God damn it! And my *brother*"—he grabbed sheets of paper off the table and shook them—"only sent fifty francs! I have precisely twenty-three francs fifty left, how the hell am I supposed to live thirteen days on that? How am I supposed to get better if I can't afford food? I've already run up a new credit at the Restaurant Vénissat—"

I interrupted his tirade. "Don't do that any more, Vincent. I'll give you the money."

"Theo and I have a business arrangement. It's his responsibility, not yours. I was just writing to remind him of that fact." He glared at the pages in his hand and shook them again.

"But if you think about it, it'd really be returning your own money to you. All those three-franc visits from before—"

"I said no. I won't take your money." He collapsed into his chair by the fireplace with a sigh. "And now Gauguin wants my sunflowers."

"What?"

"Read that letter sitting on the table."

I picked up the letter and tried to read as Vincent kept complaining. Gauguin's handwriting wasn't much better than his, and I had to squint at some of the words. "First Gauguin goes to Theo and implies we were exploiting him," Vincent said.

"He insists that Theo owes him money, which is absurd. *Then* he tells Theo stories about what went on down here, most of which is *completely* exaggerated. After I *specifically* asked him to keep matters between ourselves."

My head jerked up from the paper. "Not things about me?"

"I don't think so, or I would have heard about it." Vincent rolled his eyes. "Gauguin told Theo that he'd prefer to work only with him on the business side of things, and keep me out of it. Did he think Theo wouldn't tell me?" His voice rose again with his aggravation. "Then he has the *gall* to write me that letter, overflowing with compliments about the paintings of mine Theo showed him in Paris. He's hung the self-portrait I gave him in his studio, etcetera, etcetera, then he drops what he really wants. My sunflowers."

Gauguin's letter was filled with good feelings and helpfulness on the surface but, knowing the writer as I did, flooded with greed and manipulation underneath. *"Un style essentiellement Vincent,"* he called the sunflowers, "an essentially Vincent style," and he minced no words about which painting he wanted either: the yellow-on-yellow sunflowers, the ones I loved most of all. He gave Vincent advice about caring for damaged canvases—hadn't we all had enough of his advice?—then closed the letter with a cheery *"Mes amitiés à tout le monde,"* wishes of friendship for everyone in Arles that only angered me more.

I lay the letter on the table. I wanted to wash my hands after touching it. "You're not going to do it, are you?"

"Of course not!" Vincent's mouth tightened into an obstinate line. "I'll send him his own paintings, I'll send him his childish fencing things upstairs in the closet, but never, ever will he get those sunflowers."

As much as I wanted to say "I told you so," I muzzled it.

"You need to calm down, *mon cher*," I said instead, kneeling next to Vincent and placing my hand on his. "Forget about the money, forget about Gauguin."

"If only I could sell a painting," Vincent groaned. "Just one goddamn painting. What the hell is Theo doing up there? Selling fucking Corots, that's what he's doing, instead of looking out for his own brother."

I sighed and rubbed his hand. "You know what would make you feel better? To paint outside a while. You haven't painted outdoors at all since you left the hospital. I could go with you. The almond trees are beginning to blossom—"

"I tried."

"What do you mean, you tried?"

He stared into the fire. "After I read Gauguin's letter yesterday, I packed up my gear and headed to the orchards. I wanted to get out of the house. But . . ."

". . . but what?"

"Some children found me." He fidgeted in his chair. "Well, older than children, a group of boys about twelve or thirteen."

"And? . . ."

"They said things."

"What things?"

"The kinds of things boys say to a crazy man." They made up a song, he said, singing it over and over as he tried to hurry away. He begged them to leave him alone, but their voices grew louder, until he gave up and came back to the yellow house. "They imitated the way I walk, Rachel. They wouldn't stop laughing, and they followed me all the way here." A tear rolled down the side of his nose. "One of them knew I went to the brothel when I . . . and he knew your name. He said it was in the newspaper. Is that true? Was there something about me—and you—in the newspaper?"

I didn't want to tell him, but I didn't want to lie. He put his head in his hands at the look on my face and murmured, "Christ. The whole town knows."

"It was a tiny article, dearest," I said, draping my arm around his shoulders. "Weeks ago. I doubt most people saw it."

"That explains everything. What Soulé said about stories about me, the way everyone stares, the way they whisper when I go to the restaurant or the café . . . I told myself I was imagining things, but I wasn't." His voice quivered.

"Ignore them, ignore them all," I pleaded. "As for those *catiéu mòssi* . . . they're just kids, they aren't worth the trouble."

"All I want is to work and get better in peace. Is that too much to ask?"

I didn't try to answer the question, because I couldn't. "Listen, why don't I buy some things next door and cook us a nice supper?"

"Your answer to all my problems is to feed me."

"It always cheers you up, doesn't it?" I smiled and gave him a squeeze. "We'll sit by the fire, I'll stay tonight if you want me to. . . . Forget about all that other nonsense."

He regarded me solemnly. "Of all the people in this town, the person who should be most angry with me, most afraid of me, is you. But here you are. Why?"

I ruffled his hair. "I think you know the answer to that."

Marguerite Favier next door at the *épicerie* had been friendly in the past, but that day she didn't smile, she didn't reply to my *bonjour*. Her eyes followed me around the shop. I lay the groceries I chose on the counter and announced, "I'm cooking Vincent a special supper tonight. He's very sad today about the way people have treated him."

She focused on the groceries and wouldn't meet my stare. "Oh?"

"His own neighbors have been avoiding him and saying nasty things behind his back." I clucked my tongue dramatically. "You haven't heard any of that, have you?"

"Oh no, I haven't heard anything." Her face had gone red. She was lying.

"Well, if you do, tell them he is doing much better. You'd think good Christians would know it's wrong to gossip and judge." I grabbed my basket and flounced out of the shop, wishing I'd been a man so I could have said or done more. Or even less of a lady.

# CHAPTER NINETEEN

## Sunflowers

*I am a man, and a man with passions;*
*I must go to a woman, otherwise I shall freeze or turn to*
*stone.*
                    —Vincent to Theo, Etten, December 1881

Vincent was still writing his letter to Theo when I returned, pages of tiny script that made him grumble and scowl. Not once did he comment on how good supper smelled, and when I served it, he picked at his food, drawing on his plate with his fork instead of eating. I tried to make conversation, but I had to repeat everything before he heard me and answered with as few words as possible. After supper he stared sadly into the fireplace and ignored the book in his lap, pipe hanging unlit from his mouth.

I told him I'd stay in the second bedroom, and as I changed

into his nightshirt and washed my face at the basin, I heard
him pacing in his own room, up and down the wooden floor.
I stared at his paintings in the candlelight, seeking comfort
from them as I always did. A poet's garden, that's what Vincent
called the public garden of the Place Lamartine, a garden of
love. The couples in the paintings would never stop holding
hands among the trees and flowers. They'd walk those paths
forever—around the firs, around the cypresses—with no one
to separate them. No one could.

I was just drifting into sleep when the door opened, and I sat
up with a start. "Vincent? Is something wrong?"

"I—I lit a fire in my room," he stammered. "I—I thought
you might like to sleep where it's warmer."

I pushed back the covers and climbed out of bed. "Are you
worried about nightmares?"

He traced the length of my arm with his hand. "No."

My heart started to pound. It'd been so long. So many things
had happened—"*D'accord,*" I whispered, nodding my head. I
didn't know what else to say.

I followed him into his room, and he shut the door so the
warmth of the fire would not escape. He tipped up my chin
with his fingers and gave me a kiss. Another. Another. Our
arms wrapped around each other, we consumed each other,
his hand roamed up my belly to knead my breast through the
nightshirt. Would he know my body had carried a child, I
thought wildly, would it hurt?

"Wait." I freed myself and backed away. "Stop, it's too soon."

His eyes were wide in the firelight. "You don't want me
anymore."

"No, that's not it, Dr. Rey said—"

"You don't want me because of this." He gestured to his
bandage. "And why should you? A broken man, a—"

"That's not true," I insisted and cupped his face in my hands. "It's what happened to you, it's not who you are. I know who you are, and I love you, I want you as much as ever."

"Truly?"

"Truly. But I think we should wait."

"I'm tired of waiting," he sighed, and pulled my hands from his face to press them against his chest. "Please, Rachel. I need you. I need to feel . . ." His words trailed away.

He didn't have to say it. I understood.

I didn't protest as he lifted the nightshirt over my head and I stood naked before him, oranges and yellows from the fire dancing across my skin. His hands trembled, then teased as they skimmed over, up, and down, and his mouth too, exploring me as if it had been the first time for us both. Everything about me felt weak, flimsy, as if he'd been a sculptor instead of a painter and I'd been clay to be molded and shaped by his touch. I let my shaking fingers glide over his chest, shoulders, face, until he lifted me and lay me on the bed, reaching impatiently for his own nightshirt.

I tensed when he entered me. "Am I hurting you?" he whispered.

"No," I whispered back, although it did hurt a little, and I hoped I wouldn't bleed. I clung to his neck, and the pain eased, my fear ebbed. To be together like this, when I'd come so close to losing him. . . . I savored the rhythm of his body, I closed my eyes so tightly that colors swirled behind my eyelids, a kaleidoscope of yellows, blues, pinks, greens. Then the colors were exploding within me, washing over me, drowning me in their brilliance until I gasped for air and called his name. From far away I heard his answering cry, and he collapsed against me, shivering as I shivered, holding me as tenderly as I held him.

Tears spilled over my cheeks. He smiled in the half-light and kissed them away.

For once, the breaking of dawn didn't lure Vincent to the studio. When I awakened, he was still beside me. I propped myself on my elbow to watch him sleep: the anxious lines on his forehead had smoothed, his features were peaceful. So many things flooded me in that moment—love, desire, gratitude, hope—that I nearly cried again from the joy of it.

I touched his cheek, and his eyes fluttered open. "I'm sorry I woke you," I whispered. "How are you feeling?"

His drowsy smile was the most beautiful thing I'd ever seen. "Alive."

"Whatever would the doctor say?" I teased.

"To hell with him. He lives with his parents, for God's sake." Vincent brushed a stray lock of hair from my face. "You have never looked lovelier to me than you do right now."

"Even with my hair all mussed?"

"Especially with your hair all mussed. I'd draw you if you'd let me."

I pressed my lips to the downy red thatch on his chest and let my hand creep down his stomach. "Don't you ever think of anything besides drawing?" I asked, still teasing.

His answer was to roll me onto my back and nudge my legs apart, nuzzle that place behind my ear that never failed to make me tingle. "Ohhh, I suppose you do," I giggled, greedily welcoming him inside me, and in the light of that morning we were resurrected, reborn. Alive.

The whistle of the Marseille-bound express train echoed through the Place Lamartine sometime later. "I have to work,"

Vincent said, swinging his legs over the side of the bed. "It's getting late."

"Damn train," I muttered, reaching out to trace his spine. "Don't go, stay with me. Just a while longer?"

He laughed as he pulled on his painting trousers. "*Petite coquette,* twice is all I can manage for a while. I'm not as young as I used to be."

I lay back onto the pillows and lazily watched as he finished dressing then disappeared into the other bedroom. But when I saw what he brought out with him, I sat up straight. "Where are you taking the sunflowers?"

"I'm making a copy."

"For who? Gauguin?"

He frowned at my accusing tone, then said patiently, "I have to sell something, Rachel. I figure Theo could get five hundred francs for a good sunflower picture, so I'm copying this one and the one with the blue background. The originals will stay here with me. With us." He paused and added, "If they don't sell, then Gauguin can take whichever copy he pleases to shut him up."

I climbed out of bed and fetched my clothes. "I don't understand you, Vincent. Why would you let that man have anything of yours?"

"I'm not as naïve as you think, *chérie*, nor as Gauguin thinks. If he has one of my sunflower canvases, then other painters will see it in his studio. With my name on it." I was about to ask who cared about that, when he continued, "More than one painter has accused Gauguin of lifting ideas. Not saying he'd try with my sunflowers, but . . ."

"But why not make sure?" He smiled a smile that said he knew exactly what he was doing.

By the time I ventured to the bakery and prepared our breakfast, Vincent's sunflower painting was well underway. He'd already traced the outline of the original painting on the new canvas and was starting to add the colors. "It's yellower than the first one," I observed when I handed him a cup of coffee and *une tartine,* bread slathered with butter and jam.

"Different paints," he said. "But I'm feeling the high yellow note especially well this morning, and that's part of it too." He gave me a naughty wink.

I winked back, then cleared a chair of drawings and started my own breakfast. "Vincent," I said, trying to sound casual, "I've been thinking. Maybe it's time to tell Theo about me. About us."

He raised his eyebrows over his coffee cup. "What brought that on?"

"Well . . . since Theo is engaged and so happy, perhaps he'll understand now. You could write him, and so could I, like Johanna wrote you. Then he'd see that I'm not like—"

"Sien." Vincent sat his coffee and half-eaten *tartine* on the table among paint tubes and charcoal sticks and walked back to the easel. "There isn't just Theo, you know," he said, picking up his palette and avoiding my eyes. "There's my mother, my sisters . . ."

"Imagine how much better life could be for you—for both of us. You wouldn't be alone anymore. We could have a real home. And if you get sick again—"

"I won't get sick again."

"But if you do, I could take care of you. Don't you see? I love you, and we could be so happy. And I"—my voice wavered—"I could give you children. We could have a family, a real family."

He gazed at the sunflowers, brush poised in his hand. "I've caused Theo so much trouble already . . . now he has to plan for a wife . . . he'd see it as an added burden, thinking he has to take care of us. He'd be angry that I've kept you a secret." He shook his head and declared, "It's not the time."

"Theo wouldn't have to take care of us," I protested. "I have money saved, and once my name is off the police register, I can get another job, maybe as a laundress—"

"No. That kind of labor would kill you."

"Then something else, in a shop or café—"

He shook his head again. "I don't want you supporting me. I want to be able to take care of you, like a man should."

"Only until your work starts selling. We could manage without troubling Theo."

"Then why tell him at all? Why is it so important to you?"

I took a deep breath. "Don't you love me? Don't you want us to be together?"

"Of course I do." He lay down his brushes and palette to take my hands in his. Yellow stained my fingers. "But right now we have to wait. I can't risk losing—"

"—Theo's money?" I snapped.

"You. I can't risk losing *you*." My face flushed, and I stared at the floor. "I know it's a lot to ask, but we must both be patient a while longer."

"Patience again," I sighed. "I suppose you'll tell me about the wheatfields next."

"I was going to tell you that winter will be over soon, and spring will come before we know it." He bent his head to kiss me, and I slid my arms around his neck. He's such a child, I thought, believing a kiss would distract me and make it all better. "Just a while longer," he murmured in my ear. "Please trust me."

A sound of laughter pulled my attention to the window. A trio of young boys stood on the sidewalk outside, poking each other and making loud kissing noises. Vincent spun to face them, and the boys grabbed their ears, their cries of "*fou rou, fou rou*" penetrating the glass. Crazy redhead. Crazy redhead.

I tore myself from Vincent's arms and ran into the kitchen to snatch up the broom. Throwing open the front door, I shouted, "Get out of here! And if you come back, I'll beat you until you're black and blue!" The boys' jaws dropped, and they scurried away.

Vincent was laughing fit to burst when I came back into the studio. "I think you scared them. You scared me!"

"You remember that!" I teased and waved the broom at him.

He fell serious again. "One day soon, Rachel. I promise."

"I think you're afraid to be happy, Vincent," I said, serious again too. "And I don't know why."

## Chapter Twenty

## Revelation

*From what I am told, I am obviously looking better;
inwardly my heart is rather full of so many feelings and
divergent hopes, for I am amazed to be getting better.*
    —Vincent to Theo, Arles, late January 1889

Once I'd been one of the *filles* most in demand at No. 1,
Rue du Bout d'Arles, but not any more. Saturday night,
the stream of customers was steady, and I sat alone at the bar,
the only girl without a single *mec* or a single franc. Jacqui'd had
three customers already, little Minette four—I'd been counting. So had Madame Virginie.

I'd started working again a few days after that night at the
yellow house. I couldn't keep taking Françoise's money, and
even with her help, weeks of not working had left a dent in my
box of coins. I needed to make more and fast, for my future and

Vincent's. But the francs didn't come as quickly as they used to. The first night, two of my former regulars had ignored my smiles, and I'd gotten the leftovers: a fat farmer who'd said to Madame Virginie in thick Provençal, "She the only one free? *Acord,* but I'm paying a franc." In my room he'd tried to bargain down to fifty centimes.

"What's wrong with me?" I asked Françoise after I took a bath to get rid of his smell. "You'd think I had spots or a disease!"

"Things'll pick up," she said, but I knew *Le Forum Républicain* had done its work. Nobody wanted to screw the crazy painter's whore.

Old Louis Farce stopped me on my way to the market the next morning and offered me a post in his *maison.* He pulled open the folds of my cape and said, "Nice *nénés,* not too small, not too big. We change your name, dress you up, you'll be a rich girl in no time." I tugged my cape shut and told him what he could do with that notion.

I didn't worry Vincent with my money troubles. I put on my best face during my daily visits to the yellow house: watching him paint, helping with chores, looking after him without coddling. Every day he seemed stronger, and I stopped searching for signs of weakness or reminding him not to work too hard. Another fifty francs from Theo raised his spirits, for he was able to catch up on his debts. He returned to the portrait of Madame Roulin he'd begun before his illness, signing it, with a flourish, *La Berceuse,* "the woman rocking a cradle." He was so pleased with it that he made a second version, then started a third. Pester him as I might, though, I couldn't persuade him to paint outside.

The door to the *maison* swung open, and I looked to see who Madame Virginie would push off on me. "Vincent!" I ran to him and grabbed his hands. "What are you doing here?"

"Dr. Rey told me that I'm nearly recovered. That calls for a celebration, *non?*"

I took him to a corner table, then went to the kitchen for coffee. Memories were flickering in his face when I returned, and his eyes darted nervously around the room. Other customers were staring at him, probably wondering if he'd do something crazy. "We don't have to stay here," I said. "We can go upstairs, or back to the house—"

"I can't hide forever," he said, and I took his hand with a smile. In that moment, I thought him the bravest person I'd ever known.

We talked softly together and drank our coffee until the other customers grew weary of staring and turned their attention back to the girls. Vincent had just whispered that he wanted to go upstairs, and I'd just responded with a playful squeeze of his thigh under the table, when Madame Virginie appeared. "Monsieur Vincent!" Her voice was louder than usual. "So nice to see you've recovered from your illness."

He blinked at her, as confused as I was. "Thank you, Madame, but I must apologize for my behavior during my last visit. I wasn't myself. It won't happen again."

"*Pas de problème,*" she said, then added conspiratorially, "everyone here goes cracked sometime—the mistral, you know. Well, I shall leave you to Rachel's company. *Bonne soirée.*"

Then something wonderful happened. One by one Madame Virginie's *filles* came to speak to Vincent, smiling and expressing delight on seeing him, wishing him well. Françoise even kissed him on the cheek. Vincent seemed overwhelmed by the attention, and I was filled with love for the girls, treating him with such compassion. We knew what it felt like to be shunned and condemned as an outsider. He was one of us.

Jacqui was the last to approach, and she took a seat without asking. "I want to apologize for how I acted to both of you," she said with a smile. "I'd like us to be friends."

"*Ce n'est rien,*" Vincent said, more generously than I would have. "Your apology is accepted."

"Thank you, Monsieur. But where's your friend?" Vincent told her that Gauguin had gone back to Paris, and she said, "That's too bad, he sure does show a girl a good time. Well, *salut,* I've got a fellow waiting for me." Jacqui rose and strolled away, then came back, as if she'd forgotten something important. "Oh, and Monsieur, I meant to say—"

Triumph gleamed in her eyes as she glanced at me. Suddenly I knew what was coming, and nothing I could do or say would stop it.

"—I'm sorry about the baby."

Vincent stared at her. "What baby?"

Jacqui put her hand to her bosom in feigned innocence. "Rachel hasn't told you? I wouldn't have said anything, but I was sure she . . . oh dear, I'm so sorry . . ." She backed away with an apologetic look on her face.

"Told me what?" Vincent asked me, fear in his eyes. "What baby, Rachel, what is she talking about?"

"Let's not talk about this here, *mon cher,*" I said hurriedly. "Let's go to the house."

How long Jacqui must have waited, silent and motionless like a cat watches its prey, waiting for the chance to strike. Vincent said nothing as we walked across the Place Lamartine, but I could imagine the suspicion racing through his head: that I'd gotten pregnant but had had an abortion rather than give birth to his child. The crazy painter's child.

He contained himself no longer once we entered the studio and I lit the gaslamps. He seized me and gave me a shake. "Tell me, Rachel—you must tell me!"

I glanced at the many faces of Marcelle Roulin, of her mother. *Maybe if I whisper the words, they won't hurt as much.* "Vincent, that night in December . . . I had a miscarriage."

He dropped his hands from my shoulders. "What?"

"I was pregnant. I lost the child."

"Was it mine?" I couldn't answer, I could only nod to the floor. "Oh Christ, oh dear God. Why, *why* didn't you tell me?"

"I didn't know I was pregnant. If I'd known, I would have told you, I promise."

"Were you ever going to tell me?"

I shook my head.

He paced in a tight circle, running his hands through his hair, looking at the paintings, the floor, anywhere but at me. He rushed to the easel and grabbed his palette, squeezed paint from the tubes, worked on the third *répetition* of Madame Roulin's portrait as if I hadn't been there. It was so quiet I could hear nothing but the tapping of his brush against the canvas and the ticking of the clock in the hall. I held my breath, watching him, waiting for the explosion.

"All those paintings I did of the baby," he finally said. "It's almost like I sensed it."

Tap, tap. Tick, tick.

"I painted Roulin for the first time after Marcelle was born. I asked him to pose because once I knew what it felt like, to be so proud and so happy. When Sien came home from the hospital with her baby, I watched him sleeping in his cradle for the longest time, and I drew him too. When he got bigger and could crawl, he'd tug at my coat or climb against my leg until I pulled him onto my lap, and he'd sit there for hours if I let him, watching me work. I thought I'd never feel anything like that again. If only I'd known—"

He hurled the palette against the wall, colors splattering in a rainbow against the stark white. Flinging his brushes after it, he fell to the floor to sob into his hands, and I knelt on the tiles to take him in my arms. He was muttering to himself, and at first I couldn't understand. Then when I could, his words cut like a razor to the heart. "It's my fault. I killed our baby."

"No, Vincent, you mustn't think that, it wasn't anyone's fault. It"—I stumbled over my own words—"it wasn't meant to be."

"I frightened you when I . . . If I had even suspected . . . I'm so sorry . . ."

I stroked his hair and tried to soothe him. "Dr. Dupin says I can have other children. There can be another baby one day."

"Not with me. It's too late."

"I don't believe that. There's plenty of time."

He looked past me to the paintings of little Marcelle. "You could have died, Rachel. If you had died . . ."

"I was sick for a while, but I'm well now. Françoise and Dr. Dupin took good care of me. I'm well now."

I held him until his weeping subsided. I could barely hear his next question, so softly did he ask it. "Why weren't you going to tell me?"

"I was afraid it'd hurt you too much," I whispered.

"But you've had to bear it all alone. All this time you've been grieving, and I—"

"It was more important that you get well," I started to say, but my strength left me. It was my turn to dissolve into sobs, his turn to comfort me and try to take the hurt away. We didn't speak any more but just held each other, with the ticking of the clock to break the silence.

# Chapter Twenty-one

# Relapse

*A wife you cannot give me, a child you cannot give me,*
*work you cannot give me. Money, yes. But what good is it*
*to me if I must do without the rest?*
— Vincent to Theo, Nuenen, February 1884

When I arrived at the yellow house the next morning, Vincent didn't answer my knock, and the door opened easily under my hand. I hadn't wanted to go back to the *maison*. I'd told him I'd stay with him, sleep in his bed or the other room—whatever he pleased—but he'd kept saying he wanted to be alone. As I'd walked away across the Place Lamartine, I'd glanced back to see him through the studio window, picking his brushes and palette from the floor.

He often forgot to lock the door when he went out. Perhaps he'd gone to the hospital to see Dr. Rey, I told myself, to the public bathing-house for a wash, or to the garden for a walk.

Just to be certain, I called his name as I went into the studio. No answer.

During the night he'd finished the third portrait of Madame Roulin. It stood on the floor, propped against the table where it would slowly dry, and already a new canvas waited on the easel. Sketchy charcoal lines and the beginnings of painting showed me what he'd be doing next: a fourth *répétition*. Four copies of the same picture. The same woman rocking a cradle.

His palette and brushes were heaped on the worktable where he'd left them. Dried paint encrusted the bristles, green from Madame Roulin's skirt and the wallpaper background, red from the floor, orange from her hair. Those brushes were fine sable, sent by Theo all the way from Paris. Vincent always cleaned them after working. Always.

"Vincent!" I ran into the hall and up the stairs. "Vincent, are you here?"

Soft singing stopped me on the landing. His singing, on the other side of the closed bedroom door—in Dutch, so I couldn't understand the words, but the lilting tune said the song was a lullaby. What had he done? I wiggled the knob, but it was stuck, and I pushed against the door with my shoulder to force it free.

The green shutters stood open to the winter, and Vincent sat before the window, rocking back and forth, humming that tune with his arms wrapped around himself. He wore no jacket, only a shirt and trousers, and his feet were bare. Red stained his fingers. Paint. This time it was only paint.

"I have to leave," he said before I could speak. He didn't turn around. "I have to go to Nuenen."

"Leave—why? Has something happened to your mother or sister?"

He kept rocking in the chair. "Theo says I belong with the family. Theo says I have to leave you."

I felt faint and grabbed the bedpost. How had Theo learned about me? Dr. Rey? Surely not Joseph Roulin, surely not Reverend Salles. Surely not Vincent himself, he'd been so determined . . .

Gauguin.

I could see him sitting across from Theo in the Paris gallery, his expression so concerned, his voice so earnest. "A whore down in Arles has your brother under some kind of spell. He wants to marry her, you best stop it before he ruins himself." Gauguin would say he was being a friend, that he only wanted to help. And Theo would believe him. He must have sent Vincent a letter, which had come in the early morning post, or a telegram, if he was angry enough.

"If I don't leave," Vincent said, "Theo will stop sending me money. I won't be able to paint."

I'd been wrong about everything. Wrong to think Theo would be sympathetic, wrong to think Vincent wouldn't leave me. "Your painting, always your damn painting!" I cried. "How could you do this, when you know how much I love you? How can you throw me away like another one of your whores?"

He turned to face me, eyes red, traces of tears marking his cheeks. "You mustn't worry. I'll send you something from time to time—"

"Send me something? What do you take me for?"

"—if I can do it without Father finding out. He's more cross than Theo about all this."

*Oh, God.*

"Vincent," I said slowly, "your father is dead."

He tilted his head to stare at me. "Nonsense. He came to visit us, don't you remember? I thought once he saw how happy we were, he'd understand, but he doesn't. None of them do." He walked to me and enfolded me in his arms. "Maybe after I've been there a while I can convince my family and come back to be with you. We can work out our problems, try again." He sighed against my ear. "I never meant to hurt you, Sien."

There was no letter from Theo, no journey to Nuenen. Gauguin hadn't said anything.

*He doesn't know who I am.*

Vincent held me tighter when he felt me tremble. "Please don't cry, Sien, my Sien. I promise I'll do everything I can, for you and the children too. I'm so sorry."

*Oh, God. No. No.*

I broke from his embrace. As calmly as I could manage, I said, "Vincent, dear, you look tired. Why don't you rest a while?" I pulled the window shutters closed, then helped him into bed.

He gazed up at me from the pillow. "In the middle of the night I watched the little one in his cradle for the longest time. The longest time. Will you stay with me, Sien?"

I winced at the name but tried to smile as I gave the blanket a last tuck. "Only if you rest." He closed his eyes, and I felt his forehead. No fever that I could tell. This was all my fault. If only—

I shut his door as quietly as I could and tiptoed down the stairs. Even if I hired a carriage, it could be thirty, forty minutes by the time I found Dr. Rey and brought him back with me. I couldn't leave Vincent alone for too long—

"Where's the fire, *bello chatouno*?" called an old man sitting in front of the Café de la Gare, as I ran through the Place Lamartine. I found Joseph Roulin in the postal headquarters near the station, sorting the latest mail delivery, and when I told him what was happening, he gave the work to someone else and sprinted into the street. "I'll fetch Dr. Rey," he said over his shoulder. "You go back to the house."

Vincent was asleep in his bed, tossing and moaning, but asleep. I stood at the window and watched for the doctor's carriage. Finally it came racing through the square, and I hurried down to meet him. "We'll take Vincent to the hospital, Mademoiselle," Dr. Rey said, striding into the house with his black bag in hand. He'd brought two orderlies, who carried a stretcher, and Roulin was with them too. The doctor stopped me before I could follow them upstairs. "You should stay here. Vincent's not likely to react well."

When the men entered Vincent's room, first there was quiet, then the furious cry, "I will not go back there! I will not be caged!" A loud crash and Vincent's voice again, spewing hateful curses I'd never heard him use.

I dashed up the stairs, calling his name, but Joseph Roulin hustled out and grabbed me by the shoulders. "You'll only make it worse."

"They're hurting him!"

"The doctor is trying to give him a sedative. Go downstairs and stay out of the way."

Another crash, now Dr. Rey's voice: "Vincent, we're your friends, we're trying to help you. Hold him steady!"

I squirmed to break free from Roulin's grasp. "I won't leave him! Let me in!"

"They'll be bringing him out, and they'll need to get down the stairs. Now get out of the way as I tell you, or I'll carry you myself!" Reluctantly I returned to my post downstairs in the hallway, and Roulin hustled back inside.

Finally it was quiet again, then Dr. Rey emerged, cautioning the two orderlies who followed him to be careful on the stairs.

Roulin brought up the rear. Vincent lay motionless on the stretcher, wrapped in thick white fabric so he couldn't move his arms or legs, face frozen into an angry snarl. I blocked the path to the door. "Why did you tie him up? He's not an animal!"

"It's to protect himself as well as those around him," Dr. Rey said. "We'll take it off when we get to the hospital." He raised his hand before I could object. "I wish to help Vincent as much as you do, Mademoiselle. Please trust me to do what is best."

I looked from Dr. Rey to Vincent's chalky-gray face and moved aside. Roulin followed the orderlies to help lift the stretcher into the carriage, while the doctor stayed behind long enough to say, "I feared he might relapse—he tried to do too much, too soon. I will do everything I can, Mademoiselle." I wondered if I should tell him about the news that had caused Vincent's collapse, then decided I would not. Our baby was our sadness, Vincent's and mine. I didn't want anyone else to know.

Roulin patted me on the shoulder as the doctor joined the orderlies in the carriage and they drove away. "Vincent pulled through this once, Mademoiselle Rachel, he'll pull through it again. The lad's got gumption." He cleared his throat and added gruffly, "I'm sorry I had to be rough with you inside. Shall I walk you home?"

"No, thank you, Monsieur, I'll stay here a while."

"I'll send word if I hear any news. Let me know if you need anything, *d'accord*?" I thanked him for his help before he tipped his cap and left for the postal headquarters.

Little things around the house—the barely begun painting on Vincent's easel, his pipe sitting on the chair together with the book he'd been reading—made me feel more helpless and empty. I had to do something, anything, so I carried the broom and dustpan up to his bedroom. In the scuffle he'd broken his porcelain pitcher and basin, and thrown things everywhere. His dressing table was empty, the bedding crumpled on the floor. All the pictures were gone from the walls, even his Japanese prints, their glass frames shattered into tiny pieces. Only the mirror hung untouched where it belonged.

Careful not to cut my hands, I swept up the fragments of porcelain and glass and stacked the prints on the chair. The paintings I hung back on the wall, then I brought a pitcher and basin from the other room and made the bed, straightening the covers and fluffing the pillows as I'd done many a time before. I retrieved Vincent's other things, his yellow straw hat almost making me cry as I hung it on a peg with his blue smock. That silly yellow hat, even more battered now than when I'd first seen it.

His razor lay in the corner. As I walked to the table to set it with everything else, I caught sight of myself in the mirror, holding it, and my hand shook. Had he looked in the mirror like this, that December night? Had it been a slow, deliberate cut or a sharp one, done in a flash? Had he cried out or borne the pain without a sound?

I flung open the window shutters and threw the razor into the street with all the force I had in my arm. A passing delivery boy looked hastily around before tucking the razor into his pockets and continuing on his way. I pulled the shutters closed, then pulled back the blankets on the bed I'd just made and crawled into them. Vincent's pillow smelled of paint and pipe smoke.

"Rachel, dear, wake up."

I opened my eyes to find Madame Roulin, hair caught up in a plaited bun, apron over her green dress, as if the portraits in the studio had come to life. "How long have you been here?" she asked.

I sat up and held Vincent's blanket to my chest. "Since they took him away."

For three days I'd been wandering the lonely rooms, sitting in the studio among his paintings or in the kitchen with cold cups of tea. Staring out the bedroom window into the Place Lamartine, staring at the sunflowers or the splashed paint on the studio wall. I'd jumped at every sound and run to look when the post had been shoved into the letterbox. Nothing from Joseph Roulin, nothing from Dr. Rey. Only a letter from Theo, which I'd left on the kitchen table for Vincent to find.

"Making yourself ill will not help him, dear," Madame Roulin said with a frown.

I shrugged and pulled my feet under me. "Forgive me, Madame, why did you come?"

"My husband told me what happened. I was away with the children visiting my mother in Lambesc. I came to clean things up, but it seems you already have." She glanced around the room, up at Vincent's paintings on the wall, then back at me. "Now we need to get you cleaned up, that'll make you feel better. Stay here and I'll fetch some water."

She returned with a full pitcher and poured fresh water into the basin. "Come wash your face," she said in a motherly way, as if I'd been young Camille. It felt good to scrub away three days' worth of dried tears. "Now sit." She dragged Vincent's comb through my tangled hair and clucked her tongue over the knots. "Where's the bath?"

"He doesn't have one. He goes to the hotel next door, or to the public bathing-house."

She clucked her tongue again. "Only a man could live without a proper washtub. They wouldn't wash at all if we didn't make them. Gracious, what pretty hair you have."

That's what Maman used to say. She combed my hair like that too, slow and careful from the crown of my head down the length of my back. She'd keep combing my hair even when there were no more tangles, to make it shiny, she said. Any worries I had, any bad things that happened that day, vanished while Maman combed my hair.

"Madame Roulin," I said quietly, "there's something you must know. Vincent and I—"

The comb made another sweep down my back. "I already do know, dear. Vincent told me everything the day I visited him in the hospital, after his first *crise*."

She'd been so kind to me in the Café de la Gare, was being so kind to me now. Kind to Vincent, coming to pose for him and cooking him dinner at her family's house. Did she know other things, did she know her husband had been with Fran-çoise that night and many other nights besides? "Oh, good-ness, don't cry," she said when she saw my hand go to my eyes. "Vincent needs you to be strong."

"No one has told me anything," I said. "I don't know what's happening."

"There's nothing new to tell. My husband learned this morning that Vincent still . . . sees things and hears things. But the doctor thinks he'll come out of it, take comfort from that." She patted me on the shoulders. "There, you look better already. Why don't you come home with me? You can have a warm bath, a good supper . . ."

Sitting around the table with the Roulins? Watching her hold Marcelle as the baby giggled and cooed? "*Non, merci,* that's kind of you, but—"

"You can't stay here forever, dear."

"I feel close to him here," I said numbly. "I can't leave."

Françoise was the next to find me. Roulin had told her the whole story too. "Making yourself sick isn't going to help matters," she said, sounding more like a bossy big sister than a soothing mother. "Come back to the *maison* and leave this place."

"I can't go back there, Françoise. If I see Jacqui—"

"Jacqui's gone." Françoise told the story with relish: how furious Madame Virginie had been after I'd left with Vincent, how she'd slapped Jacqui and called her an ungrateful bitch. I smiled with grim satisfaction as I pictured Madame flinging Jacqui's things down the stairs, Raoul pushing her into the street—my first smile in days. "She's working for old Louis," Françoise said. "Good riddance, although as far as I'm concerned that's too damn close." Her voice softened. "Madame and the girls are worried about you, Rachel. Please come home."

I agreed to return with Françoise to the Rue du Bout d'Arles. Everyone treated me with kindness, like I was some fragile, wounded bird, but I felt no peace. I sat awake in my room every night as I'd sat awake in his, waiting, waiting.

On the fifth afternoon, Roulin brought news. For three days Vincent had heard voices and hadn't been able to recognize anyone, not even Reverend Salles or Dr. Rey. He wouldn't eat—had said he was being poisoned—and he wouldn't sleep. On the fourth day, he'd been calmer and had recognized people again, and Dr. Rey had moved him from the isolation room to the main ward. Roulin had gone to see Vincent that morning, and he seemed much better. "He asked if you were all right," Roulin said. "He's worried about you." That was all I needed to hear, and I started toward the stairs to fetch my shawl. "Wait until tomorrow, Mademoiselle Rachel," Roulin called after me, "when he's feeling even better."

"No, Monsieur Roulin," I called back. "I'm going now."

I paid for a carriage to the hospital and took the familiar route to Dr. Rey's office, this time without anyone trying to stop me. He didn't appear at all surprised when I turned up at his door and announced, "I want to see Vincent."

"Good afternoon, Mademoiselle," the doctor said calmly, pulling a pair of spectacles from his nose. "Monsieur Roulin has spoken with you, I presume."

I felt myself blush: where were my manners? "I mean— Good afternoon, Doctor, I'm sorry to disturb you, but I really must see—"

"And you shall, Mademoiselle. Vincent's much improved. The hallucinations have stopped, he's been eating, he's much better. Monsieur Roulin's visit cheered him considerably." While Dr. Rey walked me to the main ward, he continued, "Vincent felt well enough to get out of bed this afternoon, so you might find him near the stove. You may stay longer this visit, because I think it will cheer him even further."

I walked past the rows of beds to the potbellied stove in the back, where Vincent sat alone, engrossed in a book. "What are you reading?" I asked as I sat beside him.

He looked up, and his face brightened. "It's Dickens, the Christmas stories. I know it's not Christmas, but they comfort me." He held the book to his chest, suddenly looking all the world like a boy who thought he was in trouble. "I frightened you again. I'm sorry."

"It's not your fault, dearest," I said. "You've had a terrible shock."

"Are you all right? Truly all right, you're not—?"

"You mustn't worry about me, *mon cher.* Let's worry about making you better."

His gaze moved from me to the book in his hands. "Dr. Rey

thinks that even when I do feel better, perhaps I should sleep and eat here at the hospital. I could go to my studio or out to paint during the day, then come back here at night."

"That might be a good idea, until you're stronger," I said with a smile and reached for his hand, toasty warm from sitting near the stove. "I can look after the house while you're gone, have it ready when you come back."

"You don't have to," he murmured. When I told him nonsense, I wanted to help, he fidgeted in his chair. "I mean, if you'd rather end things, I'd understand."

My smile faded, and I let go of his hand.

"The doctor says I should improve," he rushed on, "but what if I don't? I'd understand if you don't want to see me anymore, we can just—"

"Is that what you want?"

"Of course not. But I can't ask you to give up your life for me."

I tried to take him in my arms, to show him what I wanted, but he shied away, carefully keeping his left side hidden. It took me a moment to realize what was upsetting him. His bandage was missing.

His hand went to his ear when he saw the direction of my eyes, and his voice became a whisper. "Dr. Rey made me take it off. It's hideous. I'm hideous."

"May I see?" I asked, as gently as I could. "I promise I won't hurt you."

He didn't say yes, but he didn't say no. He didn't say anything. I circled to his side and knelt beside him as he pulled his hand away. The wound had healed, but what he'd done was there for everyone to see. He'd cut the lobe in a sharp diagonal, leaving behind a ragged flap of raw flesh at the top. The rest was gone.

I felt a wave of revulsion, not for how he looked so much as for the forces inside that had driven him to do this. Revulsion at the memory of that night, of his blood on my hands. I blinked and glanced away, then forced myself to look again. That night doesn't define who he is, I told myself, this does not define who he is. He is still my Vincent, who paints beautiful pictures and smiles at me with crinkles around his eyes and holds me and kisses me and calls me his little one. Nothing has changed. Nothing has changed.

*It's what happened to you, but it's not who you are. I know who you are.*

I reached out my hand to lightly trace the outline of the remaining skin. Every muscle in his body tensed, and he shook under my fingers. I gently—so, so gently—pressed my lips to him. "There's your answer," I said. "I'll never leave you."

# Chapter Twenty-two

## The Petition

*This so-called good town of Arles is such an odd place that it's with good reason that old Gauguin calls it "the dirtiest hole of the south."*
—Vincent to Theo, Arles, February 1889

A mere ten days after his collapse, Vincent had improved enough to return to the yellow house. But only to use the studio—he accepted Dr. Rey's suggestion that he sleep and eat at the hospital, at least for a while. I believed he would feel better at home, but I kept my opinions to myself. Monsieur Roulin whitewashed the studio wall so the splattered paint was no longer visible, and I went searching for new brushes, carrying Vincent's ruined ones with me for the shopkeeper to compare. Their quality wasn't as fine, but I hoped they would do for now. When he saw them standing in a jar next to his easel, Vincent kissed me on the cheek and told me they were perfect.

The first afternoon he drew quietly in his sketchbook, practicing with things lying around the house. He spoke little— ever since he'd gone back to the hospital, he'd spoken little, and his silence worried me. He never mentioned the baby or anything that had happened, but sometimes I'd catch him watching me, and the grief and regret in his eyes were plain to see.

The second afternoon I arrived to the smell of turpentine. "You've started painting again," I said as I walked into the studio. "What are you working on?"

"The fourth *répetition* of Madame Roulin's portrait," he said, frowning at the canvas on the easel. "The fourth *Berceuse*."

"Are you sure that's a good idea?"

"Why wouldn't it be?"

"You were working on the first one when you got sick the first time," I said hesitantly. "You'd finished the third one and started this one when you got sick the last time . . ."

"I didn't get sick because of the painting," Vincent said. "This is a comforting image, the kind of picture that lonely men would see and remember their own wives and mothers. I imagine it hung between two of the sunflower canvases to form a triptych of musical color—don't you think that would make a fine effect?"

"Yes, *mon cher,*" I gave in.

"You shouldn't be so superstitious," he added, and I let the matter drop.

He worked on the portrait a few days, then set it aside to make another copy of the sunflowers. Aside from the occasional grumble, he seemed satisfied as he worked, but something was missing: some fire, some passion that he'd never lacked before. The high yellow note, as he called it.

A week after he left the hospital, I told him he could paint me.

He was fiddling again with the fourth *Berceuse*. "Damn it, I can't get her hands—what did you say? Right now?"

His eagerness made him stumble over his own feet as he scurried around the studio to find a length of canvas and tack it to a stretcher. Then he dug in his jars and boxes. "I can't believe you've said yes," he said, a new flame blazing in his eyes. "I've waited for this since the day we met!"

He brought the armchair that he used for posing from the kitchen and positioned it between the windows to catch the afternoon sun. Taking a deep breath, I sat and arranged my skirts as he circled me and studied me the way he had Dr. Rey: crouching, standing, muttering to himself. I wasn't Rachel anymore. I was a collection of lines, curves, and colors, his challenge to capture in paint.

At last he nodded with approval and started to pose me, moving my hands and arms like a doll. "You're too stiff," he scolded. "I can't paint you like that."

"I'm sorry, Vincent. I'm very nervous."

"Don't worry, I promise I won't hurt you." He touched me under the chin, and I was his Rachel again. "Drop your shoulders. Place this hand in your lap and drape the other over the arm of the chair. Now you're relaxing too much. Don't slouch." He pressed his hand against my spine to force me straighter, then backed away, still giving instructions as he steadied the new canvas on the easel and prepared his palette. "This will be the most beautiful thing I've ever done, you'll see. It makes such a difference when the painter—"

"—is in love with the model?" I prompted with raised eyebrows. He blushed and told me not to smile so big.

His eyes flickered between me, paints, and canvas. His hand swept up and down, returning to his palette for a daub of color, then back to the painting as he outlined my figure and the shapes in the picture. There was a lot of blue on his palette, I noticed, the same rich blue he used for skies, and his favorite yellow, too. I wondered if he'd paint me wearing the yellow dress he liked so much instead of the pink one I was wearing today.

After a while my arm started to ache and my back to stiffen, but I hardly noticed. I could never tire of him looking at me like that, his gaze gliding over my body then meeting mine to send an electricity through me. With every stroke of his paintbrush it felt like he was touching me, making love to me right there in the studio. We were connected as one, and I was completely his at last.

A pounding at the door made us both jump. "Who the hell is that?" Vincent mumbled. "If that's Soulé, I'll— Hold the pose, I'll get rid of them."

His footsteps. The door opening. "*Oui*? Why, *bonjour*, Superintendent d'Ornano." I dropped my pose, sitting up straighter and straining to listen. "I'm working at present, but is there something I can do for you?"

"I'm afraid this isn't a social call, Monsieur van Gogh," the police superintendent said. "May we speak inside?"

"Of course. Come into my studio."

Superintendent d'Ornano removed his bowler hat with an uncomfortable "*Bonjour*, Mademoiselle" when he saw me in the armchair. I'd met him once or twice before in a nonofficial capacity; the *maison* was legal, after all. "Perhaps Mademoiselle Rachel should wait outside," he suggested.

Vincent and I exchanged glances, and Vincent said, "Anything you say to me she can hear as well. *Qu'est-ce qui se passe?*"

Superintendent d'Ornano produced a notebook while avoiding our curious faces. "Some of your neighbors, Monsieur van

Gogh, have submitted a petition to the police about your behavior."

"What behavior?" Vincent asked as we looked at each other
again.

The superintendent leafed through his notebook pages. "It's
said that you drink heavily in public and become unruly."

"I haven't had a drink since December," Vincent said. "A
glass of wine on occasion, but no absinthe, nothing like that.
Mademoiselle Rachel and Joseph Roulin can attest to it, as
can Monsieur and Madame Ginoux at the Café de la Gare." I
nodded from the armchair.

"There is concern about you being in the house after your
most recent hospitalization," the policeman continued. "It's
said you suffer from hallucinations."

Vincent drummed his fingers on the worktable. "I come
here only to work in the studio. I sleep and eat at the hospital
under Dr. Félix Rey's supervision. I've had no hallucinations
for nearly two weeks, and I have no reason to think they will
return. I'm certain Dr. Rey would gladly discuss my condition with you and verify what I have said." His firm, almost
haughty, tone filled me with pride.

The superintendent made a few notes, then cleared his
throat. "It's said that you —assault women."

"What?" Vincent and I both exclaimed.

Superintendent d'Ornano's cheeks flushed. "One of the
ladies in the neighborhood reports that you seized her around
the waist and made obscene remarks the day before yesterday.
Another lady reports that you touched her inappropriately."

I leaped up from the chair. "That's a lie!"

"Mademoiselle, please allow Monsieur van Gogh to respond
for himself."

"I can assure you that's not true," Vincent said. "I would never—"

"Indeed it's *not* true," I interrupted, crossing my arms and glaring at the policeman. "The only woman he touches is *me*."

"Mademoiselle, I beg you." The superintendent looked embarrassed. "The crux of the matter, Monsieur van Gogh, is that certain of the townspeople believe you unfit to live among them. In the petition they ask that you be returned to the hospital immediately or to the care of your family. The mayor has authorized me to escort you to the Hôtel-Dieu, where you will be confined until some permanent arrangement is made."

I rushed forward and grabbed Vincent's arm. "You can't do that! It's all lies!"

"May I know the identities of the townspeople who signed the petition, so that I can address these ludicrous charges more effectively?" Vincent asked. He was shaking a little under my fingers, but his voice remained steady.

Superintendent d'Ornano cleared his throat again. "Their identities are being kept confidential because of the delicacy of the case."

"You mean they're cowards!" I cried. "Self-righteous, hypocritical cowards!"

"Excuse us for a moment," Vincent said to the policeman and steered me into the hall. "Fetch Roulin as fast as you can," he whispered to me. "He's probably at the station."

"They can't take you away. I won't let them."

"Will you take a broom to the police superintendent, *chérie*?" He smiled and chucked me under the chin. "It's all a misunderstanding, and I can resolve it with Roulin's help. Don't worry. Now go."

Joseph Roulin was not at the station. The other postman there told me he'd gone home for the afternoon, to nearby

Rue de la Montagne des Cordes. "I need to see your husband," I gasped to Madame Roulin when I found the house and she opened the door. She asked no questions but disappeared inside, calling for him. I told Roulin the story as quickly as I could, and together we hurried down the Avenue de Montmajour to the yellow house. About two dozen people had gathered outside since I'd left, and two *gendarmes* were posted by the front door. News traveled fast in the Place Lamartine.

"Out of the way! Move!" Monsieur Roulin shouted as he pushed through the crowd. "Haven't you got anything better to do?"

"That's the *putain* the painter gave the ear to," I heard a man say as I followed Roulin, and from a reedy-voiced woman, "They should lock her up, there are too many whores in this town." I spotted Marguerite Favier from the grocery shop and Bernard Soulé from the hotel, women I'd seen around the Place Lamartine, men I'd seen in the Rue du Bout d'Arles. Those boys who'd heckled Vincent and me through the studio window. But what about the rest of Vincent's friends—why wasn't anyone else here to help him? Where were Monsieur and Madame Ginoux? The Café de la Gare was steps away, surely they saw the commotion.

Roulin had just walked into the house when a woman said, "That foreigner grabbed me and picked me up in front of Marguerite's grocery shop. *Quel fou!*"

I couldn't keep quiet and whirled to face her. "That's a lie!"

A man loomed over me; I recognized him as one of Minette's regulars. "Who do you think you are, calling my wife a liar?"

"Does your wife know you come to Madame Virginie's every Saturday night, or are you a liar too?" I retorted. "You're all hypocrites! Pretending to be such good citizens—you're nothing but vultures!"

The cackles and taunts got louder. "She's a spitfire, that one!" "Crazy as he is!" One of the *gendarmes* gave a halfhearted "All right, folks, let's settle down," but he was laughing with the rest of them.

I started to flee inside, but the door opened and Superintendent d'Ornano emerged, followed by Vincent and Roulin. "What's going on out here?" the superintendent barked. "You officers are supposed to be keeping order. The rest of you, move along!"

The crowd ignored him to jeer at Vincent. "It's the *fou rou!*" "You gonna give your whore your other ear?" "Go back wherever you came from and take her with you!"

"Hypocrites!" I shouted. "Bastards!"

Vincent took my arm and pulled me toward the house. "Wait, wait, yes, yes, just a minute," he told the frowning superintendent before leading me inside and slamming the door. "Rachel, acting like this won't help me, and it certainly won't help you. You'll only get yourself hurt or arrested."

I wiped away furious tears with my sleeve. "How can you be so calm? Why aren't you fighting back?"

"I have to stay calm so the police will see I'm not a madman. I've agreed to go with them to the hospital." I started to protest. "Listen to me, *ma petite*. Dr. Rey will talk to them and everything will be fine."

"Monsieur Roulin can send Theo a telegram," I said. "Theo can help!"

Vincent shook his head. "I'm not worrying my brother with this foolishness. I'm telling you, everything will be fine as long as I go without a ruckus. And you need to let me. I don't want anything happening to you because of me. You promise?"

Hard knocks came at the door. "Monsieur van Gogh?"

"You promise?" he asked again. I nodded, and he kissed

me on the forehead. "*D'accord,* let's go." He took my hand and opened the door.

"That was quick!" a man shouted. "She's got hot drawers, boys!"

Vincent clasped my hand harder at the roars of laughter, and I held my chin high as we walked to the *gendarmes.* Roulin was speaking with—more like speaking *at*—the superintendent, pointing his finger into the smaller man's chest. "Roulin, it's all right, *mon ami,*" Vincent said. "Please look after Rachel." I blinked away tears as I watched him vanish among the mocking faces to climb into the police carriage. The crowd began to scatter as they drove away.

I realized I'd forgotten my shawl in the studio, but as Roulin walked me back to the house, a *gendarme* blocked our path. "I have orders to lock up this house, Monsieur. No one goes inside." Behind him another *gendarme* was latching a thick padlock on the door.

"This is outrageous!" Roulin roared. "You can't do this to an innocent man!"

"I'm sorry, Monsieur, those are my orders."

"Your orders be damned! Come, Mademoiselle Rachel, I'll walk you home."

The sunflowers under lock and key. I felt sick and didn't speak until we'd crossed Place Lamartine and passed through the Porte de la Cavalerie. A few of the lingering townspeople gave me nasty looks, but no one dared say anything with burly Roulin beside me. "What's going to happen to Vincent, Monsieur Roulin?" I asked.

Roulin explained the procedure. First, the *gendarmes* would interview Vincent and the doctors at the hospital. The townspeople who'd signed the petition must file a formal complaint at the *gendarmerie* for it to be legally binding, then some of the same petitioners must give personal testimony to the police for a *procès-verbal*. The mayor would decide what to do after all the evidence was gathered and reviewed. I felt sicker and sicker. "Will Vincent have to stay at the hospital all that time?"

"It seems so," Roulin sighed. "I wanted to telegraph his brother, but he insisted I not."

"Who would say such dreadful things about him?" I hugged myself, chilly without my shawl. "It's not true, not a word of it."

Marguerite Favier and Bernard Soulé, definitely. That woman I'd heard saying things about Vincent and probably her husband too—how they knew him I had no idea. But who else? The widow Vénissat, owner of the restaurant where Vincent used to eat? I'd thought she liked him: she'd been sympathetic when he hadn't been able to pay his bill, and she'd made him special dishes to tempt his appetite. His former landlords at the Hôtel-Restaurant Carrel, almost certainly. Vincent had told me about the dispute he'd had with them over his room charges, how he'd won the case with the magistrate before moving to the Café de la Gare. I couldn't guess who else would sign that petition. Vincent had never hurt anyone. Only himself.

"I was just coming to find you," Françoise said when Roulin and I walked into the *maison*. News traveled as fast in the *quartier reservé* as it did in the Place Lamartine.

The other girls gathered around too. "Rachel, you poor thing!" "How could they?" "Did the police really arrest him?"

"Shush, all of you," Françoise ordered. "Give her room to breathe."

"Mademoiselle Rachel, if you need anything or if there's any trouble, come to my house, you'd be safe there," Roulin said. "Vincent's friend is our friend."

"Thank you, Monsieur Roulin," I said with a grateful smile.

"Come have some tea," Françoise urged, taking me by the elbow to lead me to Madame Virginie's parlor. Minette plumped up the pillows on the sofa so I'd be comfortable, Claudette threw another log on the fire. I let them fuss over me, but I thought only one thing: how much more could Vincent endure?

# Chapter Twenty-three

# Persuasion

*Unfortunately, the crazy act which necessitated his first hospitalization has resulted in a most unfavorable interpretation of anything out of the ordinary which this unfortunate young man may do.*

—Reverend Mr. Salles to Theo,
Arles, 2 March 1889

It's an abomination!"

I lost count of how many times Joseph Roulin said that in the first weeks after Vincent's arrest. Each time accompanied by a fierce bang on the table, usually followed by grumbling about policemen and bourgeois doctors.

What Vincent thought a simple misunderstanding was nothing of the sort. Instead of being interviewed at the Hôtel-Dieu, he was put into an isolation room and kept there. Dr. Rey had gone to Paris to complete his degree, and the other doctors denied Vincent any distractions, whether books or pen and paper to write letters, or any visitors save Reverend Salles. Nor would the doctors accept letters for him, so I and his other friends couldn't send even the briefest note.

The inevitable happened. He relapsed again, and his hallucinations returned. Roulin didn't want to tell me, but I made him: Vincent had tried to wash himself in a coal bucket and smeared soot over his face, babbling in Dutch all the while, then he'd chased a nurse when she brought his dinner. Reverend Salles told the doctors it resulted from how Vincent was being treated, but they'd hear none of it.

The investigation triggered by the townspeople's complaints continued. Roulin learned from a friend at the *gendarmerie* that Superintendent d'Ornano completed the required interviews with some of the petitioners, although Roulin couldn't find out who any of them were. The superintendent, the mayor, and the doctors of the Hôtel-Dieu concluded that Vincent belonged in an asylum, and it only remained to decide where to send him.

I kept waiting for Roulin to deliver the news that Theo had come to Arles to settle the matter, but no such news came. Theo and Johanna's wedding was rapidly approaching, but why wouldn't Vincent's own brother come to help? Perhaps Vincent himself insisted Theo stay away. Perhaps Theo didn't even know.

"Dr. Rey has come back," Roulin told me one day after his usual tirade. Vincent had been in the hospital nearly a month. "I spoke to him when I met with Reverend Salles at the Hôtel-Dieu."

"What did he say?"

Roulin sighed into his beer mug. "He insists the other doctors are his superiors, and he can't change their orders. Vincent has to stay in the isolation room until he's moved to another

institution." At my cry of dismay, Roulin added, "Vincent carried on a fairly long conversation with Reverend Salles yesterday, and he's feeling much better. He's pissed about being stuck
there, though, and even more pissed about this petition business. Another month in that room, and he really will be mad."
He glowered from under bushy eyebrows. "I've learned something else. The name of one person who signed that petition."

"Who, that fellow Soulé?" I said absently.

Roulin spat the name like a curse. "Ginoux."

"Monsieur Ginoux from the Café de la Gare? But Vincent
is friends with them, he painted Madame Ginoux back in the
fall!"

Roulin shrugged. "Well, he must want Vincent gone now,
because he sure as hell signed that petition." Roulin had run
into Monsieur Ginoux at the *gendarmerie* while making a delivery. Roulin had said *bonjour* and given the latest news of
Vincent, but Ginoux had seemed anxious to get away. "Gave
me a bad feeling," Roulin said, "so I went to my friend and
asked right out if Ginoux signed the petition. My friend's no
liar. Ginoux did, and he gave personal testimony to the police
for the *procès-verbal*." Roulin clenched his fists. "All the times
Vincent and I sat drinking in his lousy café, all the money we
spent! Wait until Vincent hears about this."

"Monsieur Roulin, you mustn't tell him," I said. "He con-
siders the Ginoux his good friends, it would hurt him terribly
to think he'd been betrayed."

"Don't you think Vincent should know the truth about these
so-called friends?"

"I think it'd do more harm than good. If the complainants'
identities will be kept confidential, then Vincent would have
no reason to find out. We should keep it that way, for his sake."
Roulin reluctantly agreed.

After he went upstairs with Françoise, and for the rest of the night, I thought hard about what could be done. Defy Vincent's wishes and write Theo? Go to the *gendarmerie,* speak to Superintendent d'Ornano myself? There must be something, there must be . . .

Then I knew what I could do. I alone, and nobody else.

The next morning, I drew from my armoire the brightest red dress I had, the one that showed ample *décolletage* and blazed like fire. I slipped a clean chemise over my head, hooked my corset, and studied myself in the mirror. This would never do. I needed more cleavage.

Quietly, so as not to wake the girls still sleeping, I tiptoed across the hall to Francoise's room and asked her to lace me tighter. "What are you up to?" she asked suspiciously, and when I told her my plan, she arched an eyebrow. "I see. Turn around." She tugged at the corset laces, and I winced as the steel frame nipped in closer around my waist. "How's that?"

"Any more and I won't be able to breathe."

Her fingers knotted the ribbons at the small of my back. "Men think they control everybody, but a girl can wrap any of them around her finger with a bit of bosom. Why don't you borrow a pair of my earrings? They tinkle a lot. He'll like that."

I took the earrings with a mumbled *merci* and crossed back to my room, where I pulled on my petticoat, then the dress. My breasts swelled nicely at the neckline now.

"What will you do when he comes here some night looking for you?" Françoise asked. She had followed me and was looking at me with concern.

I frowned at the dark circles under my eyes and reached for the rice-powder box. "I don't think he will. He seems too honorable, too much of a gentleman."

"But what if he does?"

"Then I'll spread my legs for him like the rest of them, won't I?" I snapped.

"Oh, Rachel, don't go, don't do this to yourself. Maybe I should—"

"Vincent needs me," I said firmly. "That's the end of it."

She left with a sigh and shake of her head, and I finished my preparations. A bit of rouge so I wouldn't look so pale, lips painted into a ruby-red Cupid's bow. A touch of rosewater behind my ears and between my breasts, Françoise's tinkly earrings. I stared at my reflection and remembered how Vincent once wanted me to pose for a brothel picture. That's exactly where the girl in the mirror belonged—she wasn't me at all, she was a stranger with a painted mask. And I hated her.

I couldn't let a policeman see me like this. I peeked down the stairs, then darted outside, pulling my cape shut to hide my dress and the hood up to hide my face. At that hour of the morning the streets of the *quartier reservé* were empty, so that was easy, and in the *centre de ville* I took a roundabout way to avoid snooping eyes. A *gendarme* walking the Rue Neuve gave me a fright; I pretended to examine a dressmaker's window display, praying all he'd see was my plain black cape. He passed without comment, and I ducked down the next street before he could look back. As I walked I tried not to think about what Vincent would say. I hoped he'd understand that anything I did was for him.

A smile and tinkle of the earrings persuaded the Hôtel-Dieu's gate porter to escort me personally to Dr. Rey. The nun on duty in the men's ward frowned but said nothing, probably thinking I was just another whore with the clap. Dr. Rey rose from his chair when I walked into his office, and he looked puzzled until I pushed back my hood.

"Mademoiselle Rachel! I'm sorry, I wasn't expecting you. Here, allow me." I untied my cape, and he hung it on a hat rack by the door. His eyes lingered on my bosom before he remembered his manners and gestured to a chair. "How can I help you?"

"I've come to talk to you about Vincent," I began, folding my hands together in my lap. "I'm worried about him."

"I'll be frank with you, Mademoiselle, so am I. As you know, there was nothing wrong when he was admitted, but now—"

"Monsieur Roulin told me he is in the isolation room, allowed neither visitors nor occupations. That alone would drive a man mad, Doctor." At Dr. Rey's nod of agreement, I opened my eyes wide and leaned forward. "Isn't there something you could do?"

He cleared his throat, obviously struggling to keep his gaze on my face. "I lack authority in this matter, Mademoiselle. Superintendent D'Ornano ordered that Vincent be isolated, with the support of Mayor Tardieu."

"You're Vincent's doctor."

"I am not in charge. Dr. Delon, my supervisor, is the one who admitted Vincent. He and the others listen to Superintendent d'Ornano before they listen to me. I'm sorry."

I fumbled in my reticule for a handkerchief, my act forgotten as I started to cry. A helpless look appeared on Dr. Rey's face. "I wish there *was* something I could do. I do not like seeing him in such misery." He paused, then added, "Or those who care about him."

Now was my chance. I swallowed my tears and dabbed at my eyes. "I'd be grateful, Doctor, if you could speak again to your superiors," I said and took as deep a breath as I could muster, to make my breasts heave under the red dress. "I would owe you a great deal."

He flushed at my careful words and moved some papers on the desk. "I know you would be grateful, Mademoiselle, I know all of Vincent's friends would be. Monsieur and Madame Roulin have been most persistent about helping him, as has Reverend Salles."

"Have you spoken to Vincent's brother?"

"Reverend Salles has been exchanging letters with him, and I myself will write him soon. Monsieur van Gogh is concerned that Vincent not be kept here without just cause."

I twisted my handkerchief in my hands. "Then will you help? *S'il vous plaît?*"

He looked at me then, and I forced myself to lock eyes. *For Vincent. For Vincent.* "I will try. And if you come back in two days, I will arrange for you to see Vincent, regardless."

I wanted to spring up and embrace him, but I only smiled. "Thank you."

Dr. Rey retrieved my cape from the hat rack, but instead of giving it to me, he placed it around my shoulders himself. His hands stayed there as I tied the ribbon around my neck—the first time he'd ever touched me—and I knew what it meant. I was wrong. Sooner or later, I'd be seeing him at Madame Virginie's.

When I arrived at the Hôtel-Dieu two days later, I half-expected Dr. Rey to have changed his mind. But the porter let me pass, and the nun in the men's building led me to the main ward as if she'd known I was coming. If she recognized me as the hussy who'd come the other day, she kept her thoughts to herself, explaining instead that Dr. Delon had given orders for Vincent to be taken from the isolation room. I sighed with relief. Dr. Rey had kept his promise.

Vincent was reading by the potbellied stove again, and he jumped from his chair to crush me in an embrace. "I can't believe you're here. However did you manage it?" I told him I'd talked to Dr. Rey, carefully omitting any details of the visit. Vincent studied me with raised, then furrowed, eyebrows, and I held my breath: had something in my voice given me away? "That was kind of him," he said slowly. "To allow you to come."

I tried not to fidget. "So you were moved from the isolation room this morning."

He took me by the hand and sat me beside him. "They leave me there for weeks, then take me out again without any explanation. Dr. Delon said I could have visitors, books, pen and paper . . . I can go to the house with an orderly, pick up some painting supplies, and work if I want." He shook his head. "The strangest thing."

"Perhaps it has something to do with the police investigation," I said.

He gave me another searching look. "Dr. Rey wants me to stay at least another fortnight. I don't know if he told you, but I had another attack. A short one, only a few days."

"Actually, Monsieur Roulin told me." I squeezed his fingers. "I'm sorry. Are you feeling better now?"

"I get very tired, and sometimes I feel quite muddled. Once I'm working again, that will help. Dr. Rey says in a week or so maybe I can go painting outside the hospital, as long as an orderly goes with me. He thinks being out of the isolation room will soon put things right." Vincent traced a pattern on the back of my hand. "I've worried about you, Rachel. Has anyone given you any trouble, the police, anybody?"

"No, everything's fine," I said brightly. "I want you well and out of here, that's all."

"So do I." He gazed into my face. "Why does it have to be like this? Why can't everyone just leave us alone?"

My bright tone melted away. "I don't know, *mon cher*. I don't know."

# CHAPTER TWENTY-FOUR

## Decisions

*He is entirely conscious of his condition and talks to me of what he has been through and which he fears may return, with a candor and simplicity which are touching.*
—Reverend Mr. Salles to Theo, 19 April 1889

At first Vincent was as eager to leave the Hôtel-Dieu as I was for him to go. He complained about being stuck inside when spring was coming, about having to take medicines and eat hospital food, about being around nuns and sick people all the time. The police had dismissed the charges filed by the petitioners—on whose authority Roulin couldn't find out—so he was free to leave whenever Dr. Rey deemed him well enough. The doctor reminded him that he shouldn't rush things, said he needed to stay a while longer.

"I'm not going back to the Place Lamartine," Vincent told me one day as we sat before the stove. "Soulé's probably rented the house to someone else anyway—our arrangement only goes to the end of this month. Reverend Salles thinks I could find something near the hospital." I offered to look at lodgings for him, but he shook his head. "I should look myself, so I can examine the light and space for my studio. Reverend Salles said he'd come with me, I'm guessing so he can help persuade a landlord to rent to the *fou rou*." He smiled wryly. "It's already the beginning of April. Surely I can leave here soon."

But once Dr. Rey gave Vincent permission to go outside and paint, his urgency about leaving seemed to fade. Now I was restless and pestering, asking every visit when he might be released. A fortnight passed, another week beyond that, and he sidestepped my questions—about a new apartment, about moving his things from the yellow house—with the vaguest of answers. "Soon, *ma petite,*" he'd say. "Soon."

One fine afternoon near the end of April, I came to the hospital to find Vincent painting in the courtyard garden. It was the warmest day so far that spring, and the flowers displayed all their colors, as if competing to see who was prettiest. The tidy flowerbeds surrounding the fishpond blended daisies, roses, all manner of blossoms, while a sweet aroma of herbs and orange trees perfumed the air. "Why don't you take a rest so we can talk a while?" I said.

Vincent frowned at his canvas, then wiped his brushes clean. "Looks like a shower," he said as we walked around the flowerbeds. "I need to get back to work in a few minutes."

I put my hand on his arm. "I have to talk to you first. I'm worried about you. You don't seem to want to leave here, and I really think—"

"I'm glad you mentioned that. There's something I need to discuss with you." He ran his hand through his hair. "Dr. Rey offered me an apartment up the street that his mother rents out. I went to look at it with Reverend Salles."

"That's wonderful!" I exclaimed. "Does it have plenty of space for your work?"

"It's only two rooms, but there's good light. Madame Rey will give me a reduction on the rent, so it won't cost much."

"Oh, dearest, I'm so relieved. I was afraid that you were giving up somehow." He didn't answer, and I could tell by his face—"Vincent, what is it?"

"I'm not taking the apartment."

I stopped walking and stared at him. "Are you going back to the yellow house?"

"Do you think the good people of Place Lamartine would allow that?"

"Then where will you go?" As soon as I asked the question, I thought I knew the answer. He was going to Paris to live with Theo and Johanna. Paris was so far away. . . .

He kicked at a pebble on the path. "I'm entering the asylum at Saint-Rémy."

The walls were closing in.

Vincent caught me before I crumpled to the ground, and he half-dragged, half-carried me to the low stone wall edging the fishpond. "Lean over, put your head between your knees," he instructed, then yanked up the back of my blouse and pulled at my corset laces. His fingers were warm through the thin cloth of my chemise. "Damn corset—there. Breathe deeply."

Slowly the world stopped spinning. "Can you sit up?" he asked after a few minutes. I nodded, and he dipped his hand into the cool water to pat my face. "I didn't know how to tell you. I thought about asking Reverend Salles or Dr. Rey to do it."

"Why are they sending you there?" I asked when I felt able to speak.

"No one is sending me. It was my idea," he said, dipping his hand into the pond again. "It'll only be for a few months.

I talked it over with Dr. Rey, and he agrees this is best. When I looked at the apartment, I realized I am terrified of living alone."

"You wouldn't have to be alone," I said. "I could live with you and help you—"

His jaw locked into the familiar stubborn line. "I won't force you to be my nursemaid. Rachel, please listen to what I'm saying. I need rest and calm to regain my strength, or one day I won't be able to work."

"Couldn't you stay here? Things are going so well . . . every day you seem better . . ."

"I need to leave Arles for a while." Reverend Salles and Theo had already arranged everything, he said, with Dr. Peyron at Saint-Rémy. Theo would pay for Vincent to have his own room, and Dr. Peyron said he could have a second room for a studio. As he spoke, I kept picturing the high walls, the cold stone walls that I'd seen as a child. He took my hand, his voice filled with sadness. "I am unable to look after myself right now—I'm different from what I used to be. You and I have been deluding ourselves for quite some time. I'm not well."

I knew he spoke the truth, maybe I'd known it for a long time, but that didn't make it hurt any less. "Will I be able to visit you?"

He looked down at our intertwined fingers. "Reverend Salles, Dr. Rey, and my brother are the only ones who would be permitted." The thought of him alone in that place was too much for me, and I fell into tears on his shoulder. "*Ma petite,* please don't. Three months, that's all it will be, I promise. Please try to understand."

It seemed important to him to have my blessing, even though the arrangements had already been made and everything was settled. I took the clean rag he offered me and blew my nose.

"I do understand, Vincent. It'll pass quickly, and it'll be worth it to have you back strong and well."

He kissed my forehead. "That's my girl. We'll spend some time together before I leave, and while I'm in Saint-Rémy I'll write you letters and draw you pictures, *d'accord*?"

"Promise? You won't forget about me?"

Something of the old sparkle leaped into his eyes. "How could I?"

Fifteen miles away, and Saint-Rémy might as well have been on the other side of France. I couldn't say the word *asylum*; it stuck in my throat. "Do you want to take these books with you to Saint-Rémy?" I'd ask as we packed Vincent's things, or I'd mention something we'd do "when you get back from Saint-Rémy," as if he'd been going on a painting expedition or summer holiday.

There was much to arrange that last week, and it helped distract me. Madame Ginoux offered to store Vincent's furniture and some paintings that weren't yet dry at the Café de la Gare, but she was charging him for the space, her husband's doing, I felt certain. Vincent's other things were divided between cases to send to Theo and a trunk to take to Saint-Rémy. He burned most of his papers. "Are you sure you don't want to keep those?" I asked as he tossed letters from his family and friends into the fireplace. He shrugged and said, "I never do."

Packing the paintings was the hardest thing to watch: Vincent carefully untacking each canvas from its stretcher, carefully rolling it up, carefully tying the bundles with twine. It must have broken his heart to see those weeks and months of work come down from the walls, out from their homes in the studio, sent away as the ultimate sign of his departure. Some of the paintings had been damaged while he'd been at the Hôtel-Dieu; the spring had been rainy, and with the house closed by the police, no one had been able to light a fire to dry out the air.

"Look how it's flaking," he said mournfully as he stared at a painting he'd done of his bedroom, back in the fall. "Theo will have to get it relined." He pressed newspaper to the painting's wounds and packed it with the others. When he brought the sunflowers downstairs and started taking them from their frames, I had to go into the kitchen. That I could not bear.

He'd dreamed so much in the yellow house. So had I.

"Where's the picture you began of me?" I asked when he finished bundling the paintings. I hadn't seen it since that day of the petition.

"I reused the canvas." At the look on my face, he added, "I had to, *chérie*, I was out. I couldn't have finished as it was, anyway. I'll start again another time."

My frown became a smile. "In three months it'll still be summer, you can paint me outside if you want." He smiled back and said that sounded like a fine effect.

Finally everything was packed. Monsieur Roulin helped Vincent move things to the café, and the cases for Theo were on their way to Paris via goods train. In the morning, Vincent would be going with Reverend Salles to Saint-Rémy, and we agreed to meet at the house one last time. "You're wearing my favorite dress," he said when he opened the door.

Of course it was the sunshiny yellow dress I'd worn his first night at Madame Virginie's. "I'll never wear it for anyone but you," I said and kissed him on each cheek.

He took my hand and led me into the studio. How strange it looked with everything gone and nothing on the walls, only the faintest scent of turpentine remaining. "I have something for you."

"You don't need to give me anything . . . ," I began, but

my words faded when he brought me the last painting in the yellow house, still in its frame. One of the garden paintings, showing the place where he'd found me.

He spoke softly, and his voice quivered a little. "The other afternoon, I drew that place in pen and ink—I wanted to draw it one more time—but it came out too melancholy to be right." A long pause. "Why were you crying that day?"

I looked up from the picture in my hands. "The day we met? You saw me?"

"I was painting behind the beech tree. You were crying so hard, I didn't want to disturb you. Why were you so sad?"

I sighed, trying to remember my life before he'd entered it. "I felt trapped. Lost, like no one could ever understand. But then I opened my eyes, and there you were."

"*Mon Dieu,* you were so angry with me," he said with a chuckle.

I laughed at the memory too. "I got over it. After all, if you hadn't drawn me, maybe we never would have met."

His voice grew serious. "You're not sorry?"

Suppose I had known what was going to happen, how much pain would mix with moments of joy. Suppose I could walk into the painting and relive that afternoon, have the chance to do everything differently. When I walked away from him down the garden path, would I still look back?

"I'm not sorry," I told him. "Not sorry at all."

# CHAPTER TWENTY-FIVE

## The First Letters

17 May 1889

Mlle. Rachel Courteau
c/o Mme. Virginie Chabaud
Rue du Bout d'Arles, no. 1
Arles-sur-Rhône

*Ma chère* Rachel,

I have done right to come here. The change of surroundings does me good, and slowly I am losing my fear of madness. It is a disease like any other, and I continue to believe I can be cured.

Dr. Peyron has not yet given permission for me to leave the walls of the asylum to paint. He says we must wait a few weeks to be certain my constitution can endure it, although I assure him it can. During my trip here, I saw that the country around is very beautiful, and I am eager to paint the olive trees. Until then, I spend many hours working in the hospital garden. But I am nearly out of paints and especially canvas, and have written Theo to ask for more.

Theo wrote to say my pictures arrived safely. He particularly liked the portrait of Roulin and the yellow-on-yellow sunflowers. When I think what else could have been accomplished in my little yellow house . . . But it is folly perhaps to dwell on such things.

May I ask something of you? I did not bring many books and will soon be depleted of things to read. If you could send something of your choice, I would be most grateful. I have asked Theo to send a Shakespeare so I may keep up my English.

My dear girl, I think of you often and miss you a great deal. You must write me and tell me how you spend your days. I, in return, promise to be more regular in my letters.

With a kiss in thought,
Vincent

19 May 1889

M. Vincent van Gogh
Maison de Santé de Saint-Rémy
de Provence
(Bouches-du-Rhône)

*Mon cher* Vincent,

I am relieved you are all right and well settled, and
I am so happy you are finding things to paint and
draw. I hope the doctor will soon let you leave the
walls to work—perhaps Theo can request it? I know
the fields and groves around Saint-Rémy very well,
and you would find much serenity painting there.

What is there to say of these days without you?
Even now I sit under the beech tree in the Place
Lamartine garden, wishing you were beside me.
I've been going on long walks into the countryside:
south as far as the Langlois Bridge, west to Trinquetaille on the other side of the river, east following
the Roubine du Roi canal and out to La Crau. The
wheatfields around Arles are turning from green to
gold, and soon it will be harvest time.

Everywhere I go, you are with me. I hear you
speaking the names of colors—ultramarine, cobalt
blue, malachite green, chrome yellow—and I imagine how you'd paint this or that. I tried sketching a
few times, thinking I'd send you a picture or two,
but I gave up. You'd laugh too hard at my pathetic
scribbles.

I'm glad Theo thought well of the new paintings—wouldn't it be wonderful if he found a way
to exhibit them? I know the thought of the yellow
house must sadden you, but what's happened has
happened. Let us think about the future instead.

I enclose a few books that I think you might like,
along with a jar of your favorite olives to give you

a taste of home. I know it makes you cross for me to say it, but don't work too hard. You must have a good rest so you can come back to Arles.

I send you all my love, and I embrace you in thought. Write me soon.

Ever yours,
Rachel

# CHAPTER TWENTY-SIX

# A New Customer

I pasted calendar pages from a cheap almanac on the inside of my armoire door and marked the days after Vincent's departure for Saint-Rémy. At first I drew the Xs with a shaking hand while blinking back tears, and a week after he left, the arrival of my monthly bleeding only made me cry harder. We'd made love that last night in his empty bedroom, and I prayed I'd be able to give him good news of a baby on the way. It was not to be.

As the Xs grew in number, my tears lessened, and the arrival of a pale yellow envelope never failed to cheer me. His letters weren't as gushing and emotional as mine, that wasn't his way. There'd be a paragraph about the weather and how he was feeling, several paragraphs about his work—his handwriting growing more untidy as he struggled to make his pen keep up with his thoughts—then, near the end, his reserve slipped and he said the things a lover should say. Those were the sentences

I read and reread in the lamplight before I went to sleep; those were the sentences that helped me through the day.

Everything was going as well as it could. Until one night in June, when Françoise and I sat at the bar in the *maison* and I received an unwelcome surprise. "*Merde,*" I muttered when I saw the latest customer to walk through the door.

Françoise turned on her stool to look as well, then chuckled. "Too honorable, you said."

Dr. Rey certainly attracted attention with his fine suit and expensive hat in hand. The Parisian *maisons* Jacqui had always boasted about—that was the sort of place suitable for a doctor, with elegant girls in elegant peignoirs, private *salons,* and champagne by the bucketful. Not Madame Virginie's house, which, well-kept as it was, catered to workers, soldiers, and farmers. Men for whom two francs was a splurge and champagne a bourgeois dream.

I'd never seen Madame Virginie move so fast. She practically sprinted to the door to meet the new customer: fawning over him, gushing about the quality of her girls, waving for Suze, a pert brunette from Toulouse who'd replaced Jacqui. Dr. Rey greeted Suze with gentlemanly courtesy but surveyed the room to catch my eye, indicating to Madame I was the one he'd come to see.

"This is a good opportunity for you," Françoise murmured. "Don't forget that."

I forced a smile as I approached the doctor and led him to a table. In a low voice he ordered our most expensive wine, the bottles of which usually gathered dust on the top shelf. When I went to fetch it, Madame Virginie caught my arm and told me to be nice. Do anything he wanted, get more francs if I could, get him to come back again. Shiny coins twinkled in her eyes. Served me right.

"I'm surprised to see you, Doctor," I admitted as I poured our wine.

"If I may be frank, Mademoiselle, I'm surprised to be here." He glanced uneasily around the room, at the prying looks of other customers. "I've never visited a *maison de tolérance* before, although naturally I have heard of such places."

"A bachelor like yourself—not even in Paris? Surely you don't hire a *courtisane* to come to your mother's house," I teased.

The composed surgeon of the Hôtel-Dieu disappeared as Dr. Rey blushed, shook his head, and picked up his wineglass to drink deeply. "Slowly, slowly," I said and put my hand on his arm. He jumped when I touched him. "Why don't we begin by you calling me Rachel? That feels more friendly, *non*?"

"Only if you will call me Félix," he replied, still rosy pink. "'Dr. Rey' seems inappropriate under the circumstances."

"Félix," I repeated and gazed into his eyes. I seldom laid it on this thick, but I wanted to get it over with. If Vincent ever found out . . . *I must not think about Vincent. I must not think about Vincent.*

The doctor cleared his throat and took another drink. "How does this transpire?"

"We have some wine, we get to know each other"—I eased my chair closer—"and whenever you're ready, we go upstairs. Unless you're ready now?"

"We can talk first, that's agreeable, Mademoiselle . . . I mean, um, Rachel."

I sipped my wine. He sipped his. He studied the room; I studied his elegant hat on the table and wondered if he'd bought it in Paris. Or did his mother choose his clothes for him?

"Have you been to see Vincent?" I blurted.

Dr. Rey hesitated before answering. "I visited him two days ago. Ever since he received permission to paint outside the asylum, his state of mind has markedly improved. He showed me some of his new canvases." Questions filled me, and I was about to ask them when the doctor stopped me. "Forgive me if I appear rude, but I did not come here to discuss Vincent."

I toyed with the stem of my glass. "I'm the one who's rude. I apologize."

"*Ce n'est rien.*" His voice was kind. "I know how difficult this must be for you."

Vincent's being in Saint-Rémy or my entertaining his doctor? I didn't know what to say, so I shrugged. Silence fell upon us once more.

"*Salut, Docteur!*" came a loud greeting from across the room, and a weathered man in clothes still dusty from the fields hurried to our table. "Never seen you here before. D'you remember me, Jacques Perrot? You fixed up my leg a couple of weeks ago."

Dr. Rey looked more embarrassed than I would have thought possible. "Yes, of course, Monsieur Perrot, good evening. How is your leg?"

"Right as rain," the man said and did a little jig. "Thank God too, 'cause the harvest just started. Don't know what we'd do if I couldn't help with the reaping. I sure do owe you." Dr. Rey murmured it was his pleasure, and Monsieur Perrot finished chatting with a hearty "Good seeing you, Doctor. You have yourself a good night, now." He winked at me, and I thought the poor doctor would bolt for the door.

"Mademoiselle, perhaps it's a convenient time to adjourn upstairs?" he asked once Monsieur Perrot returned to his own table and his own *fille.* "Forgive my haste, but—"

"It's all right. I understand." I stood and held out my hand, which he looked at curiously before taking. Plump and soft, this was the hand of a man who handled nothing but books and medical instruments. Not a man who hauled canvases and held brushes all day, and who had a permanent callus on his left thumb from clutching a palette.

"It looks like an ordinary room," Dr. Rey said in surprise when we arrived upstairs.

I laughed as I lit the lamp and pulled back the covers. "What did you expect?"

He smiled a little. "I don't know. One hears curious things about . . ." He coughed and reached in his waistcoat pocket. "Do I pay you now, Mademoiselle?" he asked, then apologized for sounding too abrupt.

"You can pay me now if you like. Five francs." No dithering, no bargaining, he just handed me a banknote and I gave him change. Three francs into my little box, two for Madame Virginie. "Why don't you sit down and make yourself comfortable, and tell me what you want."

He looked anything but comfortable as he took a seat. "The usual thing, I suppose."

I sat on his lap, and he flinched. "Now, now, you must relax," I urged as I untied his cravat and started unbuttoning his waistcoat. "You act like you've never been with a woman before." He turned as red as a nervous teenager. "Oh, gracious. Really?"

"I presume that poses no difficulty," he said stiffly, "but if you'd rather not—"

My hands returned to the business of undoing his buttons, and I gave him a reassuring smile. Why on earth hadn't I brought the wine upstairs? "I said, call me Rachel. We'll have a lovely time."

It was strange knowing he was a doctor. As I undressed for him, I tried not to think about the embarrassing twice-monthly examinations when Dr. Dupin checked us for diseases: *Knees up and spread your legs, please, Mademoiselle. Very good, you're healthy.*

*Next!* Surely Félix wouldn't be checking my health as we went along, but at the moment, he wasn't even moving.

I lay down and stretched my limbs, patting the bed as if I couldn't wait for him to join me. He allowed himself to touch me then, but in a clumsy, self-conscious way. If Vincent looked at me like I was a work of art, then Félix was looking at me like some bizarre laboratory specimen, something he'd read about in books but wasn't sure what to do with in real life. I showed him where and how he should touch me, gasping and moaning at the right places so he'd feel he was doing it correctly. He was a quick learner and managed just fine, but it was all rather clinical.

"*Merci, Mademoiselle,*" he mumbled afterward, clearly uncertain of the etiquette in such a situation but trying to be polite.

"That was very nice," I told him.

He looked as if he'd been given good marks in school. "May I see you again?"

I remembered Françoise's words about a good opportunity and thought fast: five francs a visit, three francs of it mine. Suppose he visited once a week, that'd be twenty-four francs before Vincent came home. Unless he visited more frequently . . . and what if Vincent needed his help . . . ?

"As often as you wish," I said with a stroke of his cheek. "I'd like that very much."

I felt a pang of guilt at the look on his face. Bless his heart, he believed me.

When Félix returned a few days later, he was not empty-handed. "You brought me flowers?" I asked in dismay. That was Vincent's job, Vincent's right. Vincent always picked his own flowers too, he didn't buy ready-made bouquets from the *fleuriste.*

"I—I thought all ladies liked flowers," Félix said in obvious confusion, his hand dropping to his side.

*Think about the money. Think about Vincent. This man can help Vincent.*

I confused him further with a dazzling smile as I took the bouquet in my arms. "I was surprised, that's all. No one brings me flowers anymore." He gallantly said he'd bring flowers whenever I wished, and I pretended to think that a good idea.

He was more relaxed that second visit, telling me stories about working at the hospital and his journey to Paris. Upstairs he surprised me with a new boldness—had he written notes in a case diary for further study? Looked things up in his medical books? I choked back a laugh at the thought. That night he wanted practice in helping a lady disrobe, and as he puzzled over the hooks and eyes of my corset, it occurred to me I was doing his future bride a tremendous favor, whoever she might be. Indeed, the arrangement benefited almost everyone, or so I told myself as I tucked away his five francs.

Until Félix's third visit, when he tried to kiss me.

"What's wrong?" he asked with concern when I turned my head on the pillow to avoid his mouth. I patiently explained that I didn't let customers kiss me, and his tone changed as he asked, "Does Vincent kiss you?"

"He's not my customer."

"I see," Félix said, and rolled off me to get dressed.

"You don't have to leave. There are plenty of other places where you can kiss me." He didn't respond, only kept dressing, and I sighed. "Do you want your money back?" He told me to keep it and was gone before I could say anything else.

I thought that was the end of Dr. Félix Rey. Part of me was relieved, but the rest of me fretted about the money—so much money! I even wondered if I *should* kiss him. No, I told myself firmly, only Vincent. This man will not buy me. Anyway, he won't come back.

But he did come back, and he brought another gift.

"A new hat!" I plunged my hands into the tissue paper and withdrew the bonnet from the gaily striped box. Oh, it was lovely, quite the loveliest hat I had ever seen. Dove-gray satin and pink tulle, soft pink feathers and a pink rose tucked to the side—he must have gotten it at the milliner's shop downtown near the Place de la République, he must have paid twenty or thirty francs. More money than most people saw in a week.

"I hope you like it," he said a little timidly, as if he wasn't sure what I'd say.

"Oh I love it, thank you, but it's so expensive, I'm not sure I should accept—"

"You would honor me by accepting it. Please try it on."

"My hair's not fixed right for a hat like this," I said but perched it on my head anyway.

He smiled. "It suits you. I must admit, I know little of ladies' hats, so the *marchande* in the shop was obliged to assist me." He dropped his voice so no one could overhear. "I'm sorry about what happened the last time. I hope you can forgive my insensitivity."

I took off the hat and held it in my hands, looking at it rather than him. "Félix, I must explain something to you. I—"

"Explanations are unnecessary. I know the nature of your relationship with Vincent. I do not seek to take you away from him, but I hope you will permit me to see you while he is in Saint-Rémy. You've brought something to my life that was sorely lacking." I asked what on earth that could be, and he replied, "Excitement, spontaneity . . . taking off my cravat and enjoying pleasant diversions instead of keeping my head in books all the time."

"When Vincent told you that, I don't think he meant do it with me."

"He need never know. May I keep seeing you?"

I stroked the satin of the hat, smooth and cool beneath my fingers. Such cunning feathers. Such handsome material. I imagined the *modiste* crafting the hat in the backroom of the shop, choosing from the bolts of fabric on the shelves, then from a collection of ribbons and flowers. The *marchande* putting it on a stand in the window, turning it just the right way to catch the light, later wrapping it in tissue paper just for me. *If I keep seeing Félix* . . . I pushed the thought away, but the truth remained: his money was useful, and so was he.

"Vincent *must* never know," I corrected. "And when he leaves Saint-Rémy—"

"It will be over. I understand. Will you honor me by accepting my company as you have my gift?" He kissed my hand at my softly spoken yes. No one had ever kissed my hand before. Not even Vincent.

After Félix left that night, I tucked the hat back in its tissue, then reached for pen and paper to write Vincent. I intended a gay, cheerful letter saying nothing of my new customer, but the stripes of the hatbox taunted me.

20 June 1889

M. Vincent van Gogh
Maison de Santé de Saint-Rémy
de Provence
(Bouches-du-Rhône)

*Mon cher* Vincent,

I've tried to be patient and brave, but it gets harder every day. I don't know up from down any more without you. Is there any chance I can visit you, any chance at all? Ask Dr. Peyron, I beg you. Tell him I'm your French cousin, the sister of a good friend, your fiancée, anything that might persuade him.

Oh, dearest, I think every day of the things we can plan and do when you're free—when we're both free. Everything that's happened, anything we've done won't matter anymore. Nothing will matter but you and me.

I wait anxiously for the words that will send me running to Saint-Rémy.

                                        Ever yours,
                                        Rachel

The ink on the page was smeared with tears. I crumpled the letter and threw it away.

## Chapter Twenty-seven

## Only for the Day

*You get very fond of people who have seen you ill, and it has done me a world of good to see again some people who were kind and gentle with me then.*
— Vincent to Theo, Saint-Rémy, July 1889

Vincent was coming back to Arles. Only for a day, only for a visit to collect the paintings he left to dry at the Café de la Gare, but that was all I needed: only to see him, only to hear his voice again. A letter arrived Saturday morning to tell me he would take the train Sunday, and that we should meet at the café around eleven.

"You're in particularly high spirits," Félix observed that night over drinks. When I told him the news, unable to contain my excitement, his tight-lipped reply was "I see." I scolded myself—I should have let him think *his* visit made me cheerful.

Félix had been visiting for three weeks now, thrice weekly, as regular as the post, early in the evening before the *salon* got crowded and my sheets got rumpled. Never on Sundays. His fine manners and presents would turn any girl's head, and they made me the talk of the house. "You spoil me," I'd reproach him as I unwrapped a bracelet or tasseled bottle of *eau de cologne*. "It's my privilege to spoil you," he'd reply.

But even as I enjoyed his company, our arrangement filled me with guilt. Guilt that I was betraying Vincent, guilt that I was leading this nice doctor down a flowery path. I saw how Félix's black eyes glowed when he looked at me; I knew the difference between a man screwing a woman and a man making love to her. I worried that Vincent would find out, and I thanked the saints that Joseph Roulin made his trips to the *maison* later at night, after his children went to bed. So many times I practiced a speech to deliver on Félix's next visit, telling him I couldn't see him anymore. Then he appeared with five francs, a gift, and a smile, and my resolve melted away.

*I won't think about Félix*, I told myself Sunday morning. *Today belongs to Vincent.*

The train was late, so I sat alone in front of the café, glancing toward the Avenue de la Gare at every sound. I dreaded seeing Monsieur Ginoux, but he wasn't there; instead Madame Ginoux brought me a coffee with no greeting and no expression. A trio of old men at another of the outside tables glanced my way. "*Bonjour,* Mademoiselle," one of them said as his companions grinned. "You free?" I politely told him I was waiting for someone—polite only because I was happy for Vincent's visit, and because the man was old enough to be my *grand-père*.

When Vincent at last rounded the corner, he wasn't alone. A shy young man accompanied him, looking like he'd rather be anyplace else. "*Bonjour,* Rachel," Vincent said with a kiss to each cheek. "This is Monsieur Jean-François Poulet from the hospital. Dr. Peyron thought he should join me today and make sure I returned safely. Monsieur Poulet, this is Mademoiselle Rachel Courteau."

Poulet. His sister and I had gone to school together in Saint-Rémy. I barely remembered him, but from the way he stuttered a reply to my greeting, it was clear he remembered me all too well. I held my head high. "Shall we have a coffee?" I asked them.

Monsieur Poulet muttered that he'd sit inside out of the way and disappeared. "That wasn't my idea," Vincent said when he'd gone. "Maybe we can get rid of him later."

"Maybe so," I agreed as Vincent took a seat and Madame Ginoux brought him a coffee, smiling at him in a way she hadn't me. "I don't care, anyway. I'm so glad to see you, you could have brought a priest with you and I wouldn't mind." I studied him, his face and arms ruddy from painting outdoors, the gaunt look from before mostly gone. "You look well, *mon cher*. They must really be helping you."

"Painting outside again has done more good than anything. I wish I could show you the new studies. The landscape around the hospital has inspired me." He reached for my hand. "And you—you've been well?"

"As well as I can be," I replied, hoping he couldn't read Félix in my face. "It's been two months. Will you be leaving soon?"

Surprise jumped into his eyes at the blunt question, followed by that look he got when there was something he didn't want to tell me. "I had a long talk with Dr. Peyron yesterday. He thinks it will be at least a year before I can call myself cured."

"A year!" I set down my coffee cup with a clatter. "You have to stay there a year?"

"We'll have to see how things go over the next few months." Vincent released my hand and calmly stirred his coffee, looking into it instead of at me. "I realized myself it would take longer to recover than I hoped. A month ago when I first went to the village, the sight of people and the noise of the town made me feel ill, like I was going to faint. It's better now—you see I am fine here—but I need to be cautious."

"You didn't say anything in your letters about having to stay longer." I heard the shrillness in my voice. "You didn't tell me about feeling ill."

"I didn't want you to worry. Dr. Peyron says if the visit today goes well, I can come back another time, perhaps stay overnight. That will help the time pass."

I had many more questions, but I knew he would not answer them. He'd keep things from me and say again he didn't want me to worry. Or else he'd become cross and obstinate. Didn't he understand that his silence worried me more than any truth could? Why did he always have to do this, why did he always have to hide?

"I thought we'd go for walks today," he was saying, oblivious to my distress. "Maybe out to La Crau if it's not too hot. I'd like to visit the Roulins too, Reverend Salles, Dr. Rey . . ."

The last name startled me from my thoughts: I couldn't visit Félix with Vincent! "I'd hate to be in the way while you are visiting your friends," I said hesitantly.

"What do you mean? Wouldn't you like to see Madame Roulin?"

"Yes, but . . . she's probably taken the children to church. You know Monsieur Roulin doesn't go." I hurried on, "I could pick up some things for lunch and meet you later for a walk and picnic." Vincent considered this, then agreed.

The three of us—we weren't rid of Monsieur Poulet yet— left the café and crossed the Place Lamartine. "Someone's already moved into my house?" Vincent asked when he saw lace curtains fluttering at the windows.

I'd been shocked myself back in May to see a young couple unloading things from a wagon, a little girl skipping around with her doll. Too shocked, too saddened to mention it in my letters. I looped my arm through Vincent's. "You can have a new house when you come back. A better one, maybe out in the country, with room for a flower garden."

"There are nice cottages along the road to Tarascon," he said and looked cheered at the thought.

Vincent and Monsieur Poulet headed toward the Roulins' house, while I went in search of an open *boulangerie* and *charcuterie*. The problem of Félix occupied me the entire way. As Vincent's doctor, he'd be sorry to hear that Vincent was staying longer in Saint-Rémy, but as the man who regularly visited me at the *maison,* he wouldn't be sorry at all.

By the time I finished my errands, Vincent and Monsieur Poulet were waiting at the Place de la République fountain. "I saw Roulin and Reverend Salles," Vincent said, "but Dr. Rey was with a patient. Did you know Roulin was being transferred to Marseille?"

"He told us at the house a couple of weeks ago," I replied. "He asked me not to say anything. He wanted to tell you himself."

Vincent frowned. "It's a damn shame, although it does mean a promotion and small increase in salary. I shall miss them."

"So will I." So would Françoise. She'd burst into tears and run out of the room at Roulin's announcement, a display of emotion that had surprised us all. "Perhaps we can visit them in Marseille after you come back. By express train it's not too far. Now, how about luncheon? Where should we go?"

"South to the orchards," Vincent said at once. "It's too late for the trees to be blooming, but it'll be shady and quiet." Vincent glanced at Monsieur Poulet, and I read his thoughts: *I wish we could be alone.*

We crossed the Boulevard des Lices, then the Canal de Craponne to the gathering of orchards: plum trees, apricot trees, all manner of fruit trees. I'd come here with Vincent in the springtime when they'd erupted with flowers and I'd sat with him while he'd painted. Today the trees were green with spreading leaves, and early plums dangled in the branches. Monsieur Poulet took the food I offered him and vanished out of earshot, while between us Vincent and I made short work of fresh bread, garlic sausages, cheese, and wine. As the *pièce de résistance* I'd brought a jar of Vincent's favorite olives, soaked in brine and herbs, and he exclaimed in delight when I produced it from my basket with a flourish.

"I'm surprised you didn't bring your painting things," I said as I collected the remains of our picnic, then laughed as he pulled a sketchbook from his rucksack. "I should have known."

He settled with his back against a tree trunk and started to draw, plucking olives from the jar to nibble then tossing the pits into the grass. I pointed to the spot beside him on the ground, and he spread out his jacket so I could pillow my cheek on his thigh. "I love working here," he said. "Last spring after I first arrived in Arles, I couldn't get enough of the trees in bloom."

I lay and listened as he chattered on—chattered like he hadn't had anybody to talk to for weeks. He told me what he'd been painting and drawing at Saint-Rémy: things he'd already told me in his letters, but his voice saying the words made them new. He described the garden of the asylum, where at first he'd spent all his time—wilder, more neglected than the Place Lamartine garden, with rosebushes that no one ever pruned and ivy that no one ever cut. "At the farthest corner," he said softly, pausing to erase something in his drawing, "a stone bench stands alone among thick pine trunks. Twisting, gnarled tree roots, all that green spotted with pink and violet . . . it's an eternal green nest for lovers, hidden in the midst of madness." He paused again, this time to touch my hair. "I've missed you, my love."

It was the first time he'd said it that day, and I felt the tears well up. "Now, now," he said, brushing at my cheek with his thumb. "No sadness. Not today."

He'd left a smudge on my face, but I didn't wipe it off. "What else have you painted?"

"After Dr. Peyron let me go outside the walls, I explored the landscape around the hospital and decided to paint some studies of olive trees . . ." He conjured up not only visions of his paintings but also remembrances of Saint-Rémy—the mountains, the farms with their patches of wheat, the old quarries dug in the foothills where Maman said I must never go with a boy by myself. I closed my eyes to picture lazy summer days when I'd take a book to an olive orchard and lay under a tree like this, serenaded by cicadas, rose beetles hopping on my skirt. Fishing at the canal with Philippe and the other village boys, jealous that when it got too hot they could jump in for a swim while I had to sit sweating on the bank.

"Am I putting you to sleep?" Vincent asked with a chuckle.

"Never," I replied, then turned onto my back and gazed up at him. "Do you realize it's been a year since we met? Almost exactly."

"Why do you think I wanted to see you today?" His fingers moved to my face, then my throat. "This necklace is pretty, I don't remember this."

He didn't remember it because Félix had given it to me. I gabbled that I'd gotten it at the market, making up some story about a Marseillais merchant and Françoise talking me into it. Vincent stroked the colorful beads and said, "*Millefiori* glass from Venice, if I'm not mistaken. You must have gotten a good price."

I sat up and brushed grass from my skirt. "Will Theo visit you at Saint-Rémy?"

"I doubt it. He has many other things to occupy him right now. Johanna's pregnant."

A knifelike pain stabbed through me. "So soon? They only married in—"

"April. The baby will come in January, and if it's a boy, they want to name him Vincent." He sighed. "It's not that I'm not happy for them, Rachel—I am. But . . ."

Our own child would have been born around this time. Sometimes I still thought about what it would have been like, watching my belly swell, getting ready for the birth, preparing the house . . . then, when the baby was born, we would have celebrated the way all Provençal births were celebrated. The women I knew would bring gifts of bread, salt, eggs, and matches—to ensure the baby would grow up to be good, wise, and straight as a match—and our friends would join us for a birth feast. Maybe right now we'd be together in the little yellow house: him painting, me rocking the cradle with my foot as I sewed little yellow clothes.

"Maybe we should head back to town," I said, standing and not looking at him.

Vincent didn't answer, only placed his sketchbook back in his rucksack, the empty olive jar back in my basket. Monsieur Poulet returned and complimented me on the luncheon in a quiet voice, then led the way toward Arles. "I wish Dr. Peyron had let me visit earlier," Vincent mused as we walked, "so I could have done at least one painting of the harvest."

"Next June you'll be here." I reached for his hand and turned it over in mine. I knew every line, every callus, every paint stain that seemed never to go away with any amount of scrubbing. "You can paint the wheatfields to your heart's content, then dance with me around the bonfire at the feast of Saint-Jean."

"Only if you teach me like you promised, so we won't fall *into* the bonfire." I laughed as he slipped an arm around my waist, then glanced into his eyes to find a look I recognized. He jerked his head toward a nearby thicket, and at my look of astonishment, he mouthed, "We have time." He called to Monsieur Poulet, who hurried back as if he thought something was wrong. "Monsieur, would you mind meeting us later at the café?"

The young man's cheeks flushed as pink as mine must have been. "I'm not supposed to leave you alone."

"I wouldn't be alone," Vincent said innocently, and I couldn't help but giggle.

Monsieur Poulet's cheeks flushed pinker. "Catch up when you're . . . uh . . . through," he mumbled, then set off down the road, pointedly not looking back.

"I think he's jealous," Vincent said with a naughty grin. "As well he should be." I laughed again as he pulled me off the road, deep into a green nest for lovers where no one could possibly see.

Monsieur Poulet made a show of checking his pocket watch when we dawdled our way back to the Café de la Gare. "We must hurry, Monsieur Vincent, if we're going to make the train. Dr. Peyron wanted us back at the hospital before supper."

"I need to get my paintings," Vincent said. "Rachel, will you help me?"

I followed Vincent into a storage room in the back of the café. "You've seen me do this before," he said as he pulled a ball of twine and a pair of scissors from a shelf. "I'll take the canvases off the stretchers, you roll them and tie them with the twine—very carefully, or the paint will flake. I'll pack them properly before sending them to Paris, but I need to get them to Saint-Rémy without damage."

It reminded me of those last days when we'd packed his things in the yellow house, and I tried to let the paintings distract me as we worked together in silence. But even this did not help. I could remember the day he'd painted the chestnut trees along a path in the public garden of Place Lamartine, how the spring sun had lit the leaves, the way two little girls in white dresses had smiled at us when they walked past with their *maman*. "Rachel, we need to hurry," Vincent said gently when he saw me staring at the painting.

I rolled the canvas and tied it with twine, the others too. Soon we finished all six canvases to be carried back to Saint-Rémy and then sent to Theo. Monsieur Poulet took them from my hands, and I walked with the two men down the Avenue de la Gare to the train station. "We have five minutes," Monsieur Poulet said, his tone still scolding us.

We reached the platform just as a whistle sounded and the train chugged into sight. *I will not cry, I will not cry.* "Take care of yourself," I told Vincent. "Do what the doctor says, and don't work too hard." He kissed me on the forehead, his eyes glistening.

Monsieur Poulet motioned out the third-class compartment door for Vincent to hurry, while the conductor paced the platform and called for everyone to board. "*Direction Tarascon! En voiture!*" He approached us and pointed to the platform clock. "*En voiture, Monsieur, s'il vous plaît,* we have a schedule to maintain."

The train lurched forward. Vincent clasped my hand once more before scrambling aboard and pulling the compartment door shut. He waved out the window with a smile, and I watched the train until it had faded from sight.

# Chapter Twenty-eight

## News from the Asylum

16 July 1889

M. Vincent van Gogh
Maison de Santé de Saint-Rémy
de Provence
(Bouches-du-Rhône)

*Mon cher* Vincent,

Don't fret about the delay in writing after your return to Saint-Rémy. I'm glad you've completed a shipment to send to Theo. How exciting that he showed some of your Arles paintings to the artists from Brussels—do you really think you'll get an exhibition invitation for next spring?

You asked how I'm feeling about the decision to stay longer at the hospital. Of course I'm disappointed, but I agree that your getting well is the most important thing. It doesn't stop me from missing you terribly, but as you say, it will pass quickly. This time next year it will all be behind us . . . and perhaps we'll be celebrating your success in Brussels!

Take care of yourself and be of good heart. Write me soon.

Ever yours,
Rachel

24 July 1889

M. Vincent van Gogh
Maison de Santé de Saint-Rémy
de Provence
(Bouches-du-Rhône)

*Mon cher* Vincent,

You haven't answered my earlier letter, which makes me wonder if it was lost in the post. Everything here continues much as before. It's very hot, and we're in dire need of rain. How is the weather in Saint-Rémy? Are you able to go out and paint? Don't forget to wear a hat so you won't get sunburned.

Joseph Roulin sends his best. The family will be moving to Marseille at the end of August, and I hope my path will cross Madame Roulin's before they leave.

Write me soon, and take care of yourself.

Ever yours,
Rachel

1 August 1889

M. Vincent van Gogh
Maison de Santé de Saint-Rémy
de Provence
(Bouches-du-Rhône)

*Mon cher* Vincent,

It's been over a fortnight since I've heard from you,
and Monsieur Roulin hasn't heard from you either.
I'm worried as can be—are you all right? I'm praying that you're busy working and have been forget-
ful about writing. Send word soon. I won't be able
to rest until I know you are safe and well.

Ever yours,
Rachel

3 August 1889

Dear Mademoiselle Rachel,

It's as we feared. Dr. Rey learned Vincent had another attack about a week after his visit here. Dr.
Rey went to Saint-Rémy yesterday, and the news is
not good. Vincent is very ill. But Dr. Rey says the
doctor there is a good doctor and will do his best to

help our friend. Try not to worry, though I know
it's hard.

My wife sends her best regards. She prays for Vincent every day.

Your devoted servant,
Joseph Roulin

3 August 1889

Dr. Félix Rey
Hospices civils de la Ville d'Arles
Rue Dulau

Dear Félix,

It's been over a week since you've come to see me.
Will you come tonight?

Rachel

I hurried Félix upstairs without even a drink and shoved
Roulin's note at him. "How long have you known?"

He read the few lines and sighed. "I should have guessed your
message had nothing to do with me." I repeated my question,
this time more harshly, and Félix sighed again. "Dr. Peyron
informed me by telegram two days after Vincent's collapse."

"Almost three weeks and you didn't tell me?"

"I thought it would upset you. I was waiting until he—"

"No, you thought I'd be too upset to screw you." Félix's

jaw dropped and his face turned crimson. "Isn't that why you bring me presents, isn't that why you came here tonight? Isn't that why you sent Vincent away, so you could get your hands on me?"

"Going to Saint-Rémy was his idea," Félix sputtered. "I can't believe you'd think—"

"If you'd taken better care of him, he wouldn't be there. You *knew* he'd get sick again, you knew it!"

Félix folded Roulin's note and laid it on my bureau. "Rachel, that is most unfair. I did all I could for Vincent, you know I did. Of course there was a risk he could relapse again, but I thought going to Saint-Rémy would help. As did he. I cannot understand why you are behaving this way."

I wanted Félix to yell back at me. I wanted to keep shouting at him because I didn't know who else to shout at. His calm tone shamed me into silence, then sobs. "You're in shock," he said and whipped a handkerchief from his waistcoat pocket. "Sit down, and I'll bring you a brandy. Shall I fetch Madame Virginie or Mademoiselle Françoise?" I shook my head.

When he'd returned with the brandy and I'd taken several sips at his urging, I said, "I'm sorry, Félix. I didn't mean those horrible things."

"I know you didn't." He patted my arm.

"I thought he'd be fine . . . he was fine when he came here . . ." Félix nodded at the glass, and I took another sip. "He told me he was staying longer than he thought, but he was feeling stronger . . . he was sad about Theo's baby, but—"

Félix's eyebrows raised. "He was sad about what?"

"His brother's wife is pregnant," I said softly. "He found out before he came to visit."

"Why should that make him sad?"

"He would like a child of his own," I said, more softly still, and that was all I could say. Félix knew nothing of the baby I'd once carried, and I was not going to tell him now.

Félix pulled a small notebook and pencil from his jacket pocket and started writing. "Interesting," he muttered to himself, then, more distinctly to me, "in December, Vincent had just learned of his brother's engagement. In July, his sister-in-law's pregnancy. Mental disturbance is not my area of expertise, but perhaps Dr. Peyron knows similar cases, when attacks were propagated by crises in familial relationships." He tapped his lips with his pencil. "Can you recollect anything relating to Vincent's brother that may have triggered his February relapse?"

I glared at him. "Vincent's not 'a case,' he's a human being."

"Of course he is. I'm sorry." Félix clapped the notebook shut and replaced it in his pocket. "As Monsieur Roulin told you, I went to Saint-Rémy yesterday to evaluate the situation. I believe the worst has passed."

"Is he having hallucinations?"

Félix wouldn't meet my eyes. "Occasionally, not as much as before. Although according to Dr. Peyron, he . . ."

"He . . . what?"

"Ate his paints. Fortunately one of the attendants saw him do it, and an emetic was quickly administered." At my questioning look, he added, "Something to make a patient vomit so he won't be poisoned."

I started to cry again, and Félix drew my head to his shoulder. "He didn't know what he was doing—that was just after it began. The doctors and attendants are taking excellent care of him, and he will recover soon. You must not worry, *ma petite*."

I pulled away. "Don't call me that. You must never call me that."

He tried to take my hand, but I wouldn't let him. "Rachel, let me try to help—"

"Please go. Leave me, I beg you."

"Tell me what I can do. Anything, I'll do anything."

He had the same helpless look on his face that he'd had back in March, that day when I'd gone to the hospital to see him. The day he'd done exactly what I'd asked him. The blood was rushing in my ears, and my voice sounded far away. "Take me to Saint-Rémy."

"I'm not certain that's a good idea," he replied, and the helpless look had gone.

"You said you'd do anything."

"I know, but—"

I placed my hand on his knee. "The only way I can visit him is if I go with you. I have to see him, Félix." My fingers moved higher up his thigh. "Please?"

4 August 1889

M. Vincent van Gogh
Maison de Santé de Saint-Rémy
de Provence
(Bouches-du-Rhône)

*Mon cher* Vincent,

Monsieur Roulin learned of your illness from Dr. Rey, and I spoke to Dr. Rey myself to find out how you were. I don't know if you're well enough to read this letter, but dearest, I send you all my love and my prayers that you will recover soon from this *crise*.

I asked Dr. Rey if I may come with him to see you. He doesn't think it wise now, but he promised he'd arrange a visit when you're stronger. Please fight, fight to get well, and as soon as I'm able, I'll be there.

Ever yours, ever, ever *yours,*
Rachel

# Chapter Twenty-nine

## To Saint-Rémy

*I am working like one actually possessed. . . . And I think
that this will help cure me.*
—Vincent to Theo, Saint-Rémy,
early September 1889

29 August 1889

Mlle. Rachel Courteau
c/o Mme. Virginie Chabaud
Rue du Bout d'Arles, no. 1
Arles-sur-Rhône

*Ma petite* Rachel,

My head is still quite disordered, and it is difficult
for me to write for very long, but I must tell you

how grateful I am for your many letters. The *crise* has mostly abated, although I have a swollen throat and disturbing dreams on occasion. I would have preferred that you not learn of my attack until I was better, but I should have expected you would find out somehow.

Dr. Peyron forbade me to paint, which caused me no end of distress, but Theo persuaded him to relent. Yesterday I began a study of the view out my window, and today, a self-portrait. I'm thin and pale as a ghost, but it's a fine color effect, dark violet-blue, the head whitish with yellow hair.

It is kind of Dr. Rey to bring you to visit. Seeing you would do me a world of good, and I hope the trip will come to pass soon.

Ever yours, as you are ever mine,
Vincent

After receiving Vincent's pencil-scribbled note, the first word in weeks, I pestered Félix about going to Saint-Rémy. "Not until Vincent's stronger," he insisted at my wheedles, pouts, and frowns. "We don't want him to relapse from too much excitement." But when Vincent sent another letter, claiming to feel recovered and asking again when I might visit, Félix had no more excuses. Or perhaps he wearied of my wrangling.

He tactfully suggested I wear "something suitable"—"suitable" meaning respectable, modest, even bourgeoise. He offered to buy me a dress, but that was an extravagance I could not accept. Fortunately Minette and Claudette had both been seamstresses before coming to Madame Virginie's; they had worked for one of the finest dressmakers in town, Madame

Chambourgon. Claudette rummaged in her dress patterns until we found one we liked, and Minette volunteered to help find fabric and trimmings. We chose a demure gray muslin at the grandly named Grand Magasin de Nouveautés Veuve Jacques Calment et Fils, and at the market, Minette impressed me with her flair for bargaining when selecting lace, ribbons, and buttons. Making the dress passed the time as we cut, pinned, fitted, and sewed a plain but handsome demi-polonaise dress with a high lace collar, row of buttons up the back, and just enough bustle for just enough wiggle.

"You look like a princess!" Claudette exclaimed when she buttoned me up for Saint-Rémy. "But you need some rouge."

"Don't be silly, ladies don't wear rouge," Minette said and poufed my bustle. "Oh, no! We forgot gloves! A lady doesn't go out without gloves!" The three of us dug in our rooms until I found an old black pair at the bottom of my armoire. They had a hole in one finger and were the wrong color, but they would have to do. The pink-and-gray satin hat emerged from its hatbox to be worn for the first time, and I had to smile at my reflection as Minette covered my head with hatpins. "Thank goodness there's no mistral today," she said, "or this hat would end up on top of a mountain. Just think how surprised Monsieur Vincent will be to see you!"

"And how pleased Monsieur Félix will be," Françoise said from the doorway, where she'd been watching the commotion. "He's not going to want to share, is he?"

"Gracious, you have to hurry or you'll miss the train!" Minette cried when she peeked at the clock on the landing. She and Claudette jabbered instructions as they handed me my reticule and hustled me down the stairs. "Mind you don't let that hem trail—"

"But don't lift it up too high, ladies don't show their ankles—"

"Hold your head up so the hat doesn't go crooked—"

"Don't squash your bustle—"

Then together, "Have fun! *À bientôt!*"

A real lady would take a hired carriage to the train station, but it seemed wasteful for such a short walk. Besides, I rather liked passing through the Place Lamartine garden in my fine new dress. The ladies seated under the trees, their children playing in the morning sunshine, had nothing to criticize today, and I glimpsed envy in their glances at my hat. Old men playing *boules* tipped their caps with a respectful chorus of "Good morning, Madame."

I arrived at the station platform with two minutes to spare, my stomach fluttering at the thought of both returning to Saint-Rémy and seeing Vincent. Félix was already waiting, and he wasn't alone. Clever man, he'd invited Reverend Salles to come along. How could I spend time with Vincent now? I pasted a smile on my face as I greeted them.

"Good morning, Mademoiselle, you're precisely on time," Félix said. "I've purchased your ticket." His eyes approved my dress and lit up when he saw the hat, although he could hardly compliment me in front of Reverend Salles. The Reverend greeted me as if unaware I was a *fille de maison* in disguise, although we both knew he knew better.

I started toward the third-class carriages when the train arrived, until Félix took my elbow and guided me to first class. First class! I tried to look like I rode in first class every day, but I secretly delighted in the plush seat cushions and wide aisles as we climbed aboard. Félix and the Reverend opened copies of *Le Forum Républicain* and began reading as the train pulled away, while I watched the countryside roll past, sneaking off a glove to caress the mulberry velvet seat. It was time for the grape harvest, when thousands of laborers descended on the vineyards around Arles, and the fields outside the window buzzed with activity.

We changed trains at Tarascon for the local line to Saint-Rémy, and as we neared the village, the landscape changed. Arles straddled the Rhône among flat plains that for centuries had needed constant drainage, and the marsh of the Camargue was a short distance to the southwest. But Saint-Rémy lay far from the Rhône and the marshes, tucked instead among the Alpilles—*l'Aupiho* in Provençal: bald, craggy peaks strung like a necklace through the countryside. At the sight of the mountains, my heart leaped, as if seeing old friends long apart, and my mind wandered to happy days from my childhood.

"Papa, tell me how you met Maman," chirped my seven-year-old voice as I sat on Papa's lap next to the fireplace.

"Rachel, you've heard that story a thousand times."

"Please?"

"*D'accord,*" Papa replied, catching Maman's eye with a smile where she sat sewing. "I'd come from Avignon to Saint-Rémy to be a schoolteacher, and there was a grand *fête* for the Assumption of Our Lady—"

"Like there is every year!"

"All the marriageable young ladies of the town danced in the square in front of the Mairie. Your Maman danced the *farandole* to the music of pipes and tambourines, and I thought I'd never seen such a beautiful girl."

"Maman was wearing a yellow dress, wasn't she?"

Papa glanced again at Maman. "Yes, and she looked like a sunflower dancing in the breeze. She smiled at me, and I knew in that moment I had to marry her." As he always did, he leaned in close and whispered, "She bewitched me." As I always did, I giggled.

"I have Maman's eyes, don't I, Papa?"

Papa took my chin in his fingers and pretended to study me. "Yes, *ma pichoto* Rachel, and someday a young man will fall in love with you like I did with your Maman."

I giggled again and whispered in his ear, "Does she still bewitch you, Papa?"

"Every day of my life, little one. Every day of my life."

He locked himself in a world of books and papers after she died, writing his own book about Saint-Rémy that would never be finished. Another day and another voice came back to me from those later years. "Rachel is not a little girl anymore, Papa." My sister Pauline, six years older and already married. I heard her through the nearly closed door of Papa's study. "You can't let her run wild over the countryside, there'll be talk. There is already."

My father's sigh. "She has her mother's spirit, Pauline."

"Spoiling her will not bring Maman back," Pauline said crossly, as if she'd been the parent and Papa the child. "She's fourteen years old! A young lady, and she must act like one. Traipsing around the olive groves with boys like a hoyden— Madame Vallès saw her!"

"I'm certain it was perfectly innocent. You do your sister an injustice."

"Who will marry a girl with a reputation, who acts like a gypsy?"

"That's enough," Papa replied. "I shall speak to Rachel. You're not to trouble her with your gossiping."

"It's not gossiping, Papa," Pauline insisted. "I'm trying to do what's best for the family, to keep disgrace from falling on us."

"Enough!" Papa rarely raised his voice, and it made me jump. "You worry about your husband and your baby, I shall worry about Rachel."

"Don't say I didn't warn you. She'll bring shame to us all

if you don't rein her in." Pauline's heavy footsteps flounced toward the door, and I scuttled away so they wouldn't know I'd been listening.

Félix brought me back to the present. "Mademoiselle Courteau, we've arrived." I hadn't noticed that the train had stopped, and I apologized as I picked up my reticule to follow him.

Stepping onto the platform and looking around the station flooded me with memories. The day the first train had arrived from Tarascon, after the station had been built, the whole town burst into cheers as smiling passengers emerged from the carriages. Papa hoisted me on his shoulders so I could see, and he bought me a strawberry ice before we went home. Years later, there was the last day, when I stood here with my valise in hand and vowed I would never return.

An orderly from the asylum met us, greeting Félix and Reverend Salles with respectful familiarity. "The hospital lies beyond the town, on the other side, where it's quiet," the Reverend said as we approached a waiting carriage. "It used to be a monastery before the Revolution, called Saint-Paul-de-Mausole because of a Roman ruin that stands nearby. It became an asylum early this century, and today Dr. Théophile Peyron is the director. Sisters of the Order of Saint Joseph de Viviers act as nurses, mainly for the women patients, and there are male attendants too. A Catholic priest acts as chaplain, Père Eugène de Tamisier, and on occasion I help minister to any Protestant patients."

"There are women in the hospital?" I asked.

"The hospital can accommodate fifty men and fifty women, although at present there are many empty rooms. The male and female patients are not allowed to see each other."

Reverend Salles pointed out places of interest and told me things I already knew about the history of Saint-Rémy as we took the ring road from the station around the *centre de ville*. His placid voice droned over the clip-clopping of the horses' hooves, and to be polite, I posed questions and pretended I was listening. There was the church of Saint-Martin, not my family's church, but where we'd sometimes gone to hear concerts on the organ. Down that street were the Mairie—the city hall—and the square where Papa had fallen in love with Maman as she'd danced the *farandole*. If you turned left from there and followed another street, you'd come to the school where Papa had taught so many years.

Our house, though, had not been in the *centre de ville*. Maman could not bear to be away from the fields and mountains, so Papa bought a small farmhouse just north of the village, near a meadow filled with sunflowers and red poppies. I could still see Maman on her knees in the garden, burrowing her hands in the soil and coaxing herbs and vegetables to grow. Papa taught me about the Romans, mathematics, and other things one learned at school, but Maman taught me how to cook, how to sew, and how to name the winds. Everyone knew the mistral, but there were other winds too, the eastern wind called the Levant, the western, Traverso, the southern, Marin that brought the rain, and dozens of others besides: the Biso, the Majo Fango, the Montagnero . . . Maman had told me about them all.

The carriage passed under the plane trees shading the ring road, then turned south from the village toward Saint-Paul-de-Mausole. Groves of gnarled olive trees lined the road now, with occasional rows of cypresses to protect crops from the mistral. The Alpilles drew nearer as the road sloped uphill, formidable Mont Gaussier standing ahead with the twin-peaked hill known as Les Deux Trous. Gray limestone they were, molded by the winds of time with trees covering their lowest slopes—but never truly gray, for the mountains stole the ever-shifting colors of the clouds and sky. Today they were lilac-tinged, with deep purple in the clefts. I could already smell the wild thyme.

Reverend Salles was still talking. "We're almost to the hospital, Mademoiselle. Observe to our right the Roman ruins known as Les Antiques, the pride of Saint-Rémy, a mausoleum with sculpted friezes and a triumphal arch. Not as complete as the arch at Orange, but a superb example of Gallo-Roman architecture."

I'd seen Les Antiques more times than it was possible to count, so I gave them barely a glance and barely a thought. I couldn't stop fidgeting as we drew up to the hospital's outer walls, straightening my hat when it was already straight and smoothing my dress even though there wasn't a wrinkle. Félix kept sneaking looks at me. He'd hardly said a word since we'd gotten off the train, and he was probably regretting the fact that he'd brought me.

The attendant leaped from the carriage to tug open twin wooden doors marking the entrance to the hospital, and we continued down the tree-lined drive. All my years living in Saint-Rémy, and I'd never had reason to come inside this place; I'd only heard the rumors and stories. We passed a chapel ("twelfth-century, same era as Saint-Trophime, part of the original monastery," intoned the Reverend), then continued to a newer series of buildings that formed the heart of the hospital and enclosed a large garden.

An old man with thick black spectacles awaited us on the front steps with another older man in a blue striped jacket. Félix introduced me to Dr. Peyron as Vincent's neighbor from Arles, and Dr. Peyron peered at me over his spectacles. The man in the striped jacket was presented to me as Charles Trabuc, the hospital's chief attendant.

"Where is our patient?" Reverend Salles asked. "I don't suppose he's agreed to come out to the garden today."

Dr. Peyron shook his head. "He still refuses. He is in his room, writing letters."

Good manners required me to be quiet, but I couldn't help myself. "*Excusez-moi*, Doctor, what do you mean, he refuses?"

Dr. Peyron gave me another look over his spectacles. "He has not gone outside for nearly two months, Mademoiselle. Not since before the *crise*." Poor Vincent. Just like in Arles.

I accompanied the men up the steps and into the vestibule of the building. "This is the men's wing," Dr. Peyron said to me, then added, "we will have tea in my parlor, then Monsieur Trabuc will take you all to visit Vincent."

"Pardon me, Doctor, but perhaps Dr. Rey and the Reverend have things they wish to discuss with you in private?" Monsieur Trabuc said. "I could take the mademoiselle to visit Monsieur Vincent now."

Félix and the Reverend looked wary, Dr. Peyron looked taken aback, and I must have looked suspicious. Dr. Peyron glanced at Félix and Reverend Salles, and when he saw no objection, he said, "That sounds like a fine idea. Unless, Mademoiselle, you wish some tea?"

I shook my head and smiled. "You would be able to speak more frankly about the patients if I weren't present." Félix knitted his eyebrows and frowned enough for me to see.

"This way, Mademoiselle," said Monsieur Trabuc, leading me to the right down a long hallway while the others turned left. Looking back, looking ahead, all I could see were low-vaulted corridors pierced with barred windows, everything gray, walls, ceiling, floor. Our footsteps echoed through the building, conjuring what spirits of the past, I did not know, and a musty smell filled my nostrils. "It is good you have come today, Mademoiselle," Monsieur Trabuc said. "Monsieur Vincent speaks of you often and will be happy to see you."

"You know who I am?"

"Yes, Mademoiselle. When he was ill, he asked me to read your letters aloud to him."

I blushed and looked at him in horror, wondering if he laughed inside at the silly *fille de maison* in love with one of the patients. But his eyes were kind—placid, dark pools that must have brought comfort to many who suffered—and I instinctively felt I could trust him. Had he been the one to save Vincent when he ate his paints? I wondered.

We mounted a twisting flight of steps and were following another corridor, when a loud howl startled me. "It is only one of the patients," Monsieur Trabuc said. "Some of them are easily agitated and shout for no reason. Monsieur Vincent cannot bear the noise, so Dr. Peyron placed him in a room far from the others."

The howls faded as we came to a sturdy wooden door at the end of the corridor. Monsieur Trabuc peeked in a little window set in the door, then knocked and said, "Monsieur Vincent? May I enter?"

The familiar voice responded, and my heart surged in my chest. Monsieur Trabuc ushered me inside with a surprising sparkle in his eyes before closing the door and waiting in the hallway. Vincent was writing at a rickety wooden desk in the corner with his back to me. "*Bonjour,* Vincent," I said quietly.

He whirled to stare at me, the paper clutched in his hand, then he nearly knocked over his chair as he jumped up and seized me in his arms. "It's like magic," he murmured into my ear. "I was just writing you again . . . asking when you might visit . . . and here you are."

I smiled into his chest. "Here I am. Dr. Rey and Reverend

Salles brought me to visit for the entire afternoon." I pulled back to look into his face. "How are you, *mon cher*? I've been so anxious to see you . . . so worried . . . I wanted to come sooner, but . . ."

"I'm better, much better. Come, let me look at you." He drew me to the bed to sit beside him, then frowned. "What the hell are you wearing? You don't look like yourself. You look like some *petite bourgeoise* with that *truc* of a hat."

My cheeks must have been as pink as the rose on my bonnet. "I had to look like a lady, or they wouldn't let me come."

"Humph. I don't think much of ladies. Ladies won't let you do this . . ." He pulled me into his arms again and tried to nuzzle my neck through the lace collar.

"No, we can't, Monsieur Trabuc is right outside the door. Besides, you'll muss me." I swatted him away and reached up to unpin my hat.

"You never minded me mussing you before." He ran his fingers up my back until I shivered. "How many buttons does a dress need?"

"Enough to make you behave, it seems."

"Apologies, Mademoiselle." His eyes twinkled. "May I have your permission to kiss you if I promise not to muss you?"

I primly pursed my lips, but there was nothing prim about his kiss. Nor mine. "Oh dear, my hat," I said when it fell off my head and rolled to the floor. I got up to dust it off before laying it on the chair by his desk. "So this is your room?"

Except for the red tile floor and faded green curtains at the windows, it was as gray as the rest of the hospital. The iron bed was narrow, the pillow thin, the mattress lumpy. A tapestry-covered armchair stood next to the window, faded and tattered with scratched legs, the remnant perhaps of some long-ago patient whose family had let him bring one favorite piece of furniture from home. A small washstand was squeezed next to the door, with a few pegs for hanging clothes. When I walked to the window and parted the curtains, I gasped to find iron bars.

Vincent came to stand beside me. "At least I have a lovely view."

Below lay a wheatfield, freshly tilled and waiting for seed, enclosed in a square gray wall. Beyond the wall, a small farm with a country *mas*, where a woman hung out laundry to dry. Beyond the farm, gatherings of trees sprinkled the foothills of the Alpilles. And far away, hundreds of miles away, the Alps themselves stood stalwart against the horizon, mountains like I'd never known at a distance I'd never traveled. A beautiful infinity of trees and earth and mountains and sky . . . but in between, stone walls and iron bars.

"I watch the sun rise every morning," Vincent said, "and I watched them plow down there in the field after my *crise*. Soon they will come to sow."

"Dr. Peyron says you won't go outside," I said, my eyes still on the distant hills.

He stiffened next to me. "Is this why they brought you, to persuade me to go outside?"

"Of course not, it was my idea to come. But why choose to stay in a tiny room behind bars, when you can be outdoors in the light and fresh air?"

He shrugged. "I don't know. I suppose being out there makes me feel lonely."

"What if I went with you today, just to the garden?" He shrugged again and didn't answer. I reached up to caress his face. "You can't let fear keep you from doing something you want to do. Didn't you once tell me that?"

"We'll see, *ma petite,* we'll see. But first I want to show you my paintings."

Down more hallways, past more barred windows Monsieur Trabuc led us, toward the room Vincent used as a studio. The noise of patients grew louder, and Vincent took my hand. A man wearing a top hat and silk cape over his nightshirt, carrying an ivory-topped walking stick, strode out of one of the rooms, then bowed and said in elegant French, "Madame, Messieurs, I bid you a very good day." Monsieur Trabuc and Vincent bowed, as if they were quite accustomed to it, and I followed their example with a curtsey. "He used to be a wealthy banker," Vincent whispered after the man passed us. "He thinks he still is one."

Along the way Vincent told me about life at the asylum. Even for the worst cases, he said, there wasn't any real treatment, aside from two-hour baths given twice a week to calm the patients' nerves. Vincent too had to don the long white robe and sit in a porcelain tub, waiting quietly until he was told he could get out. Violent patients could be kept in a bath the whole day, wooden panels clamped over the tops of the tubs so that only their heads and feet were exposed, their yells of protest bouncing off the stone walls. Monsieur Trabuc pointed out that conditions at Saint-Paul-de-Mausole were far better than hospitals of the past, and treatment far more humane, but Vincent rolled his eyes behind Monsieur Trabuc's back and mouthed, "It doesn't matter." When I asked what patients did the rest of the time, Vincent shrugged and said, "I have my painting and reading, but most of the others sit around and do nothing."

"Do they have visitors?" I asked.

"Sometimes, but I think most of them have been forgotten by their families."

I dropped my voice. "Do they frighten you?"

"The dangerous ones are in a different ward, so I don't see them. When I came here, yes, I was frightened of the howling and the fits the others had, but I've since realized there is a strange friendship among the patients. They don't frighten me any more. Ah, here we are."

We'd come downstairs to the ground floor of the wing where I'd entered. Monsieur Trabuc unlocked a wooden door and motioned Vincent and me inside before once more staying discreetly in the hallway.

The makeshift studio was as cluttered as the one in the yellow house, paint tubes and half-empty inkpots strewn everyplace from the windowsill to the floor. Here the barred window overlooked the garden out front, and generous afternoon light caught the colors of Vincent's paintings, propped and stacked around the room. I gratefully inhaled the familiar smells of paint and turpentine, glad to rid my lungs of that mustiness in the corridors. The other room where he slept—that gray, dull room—was the room of a stranger. This room was Vincent.

He was sorting through the canvases leaning against the walls. "I sent Theo a shipment a few days ago, so not everything is here. Did I already tell you, two of my paintings are in the fifth exhibition of the Indépendants in Paris? A painting of irises that I did in the garden here when I first arrived and the night scene I did by the river in Arles. Theo tells me the irises aren't hung as well as they could be, but the night picture makes a good showing."

I envisioned flocks of Parisians standing in front of our starry night, talking quietly about it, admiring its colors. "I'm so proud of you," I said, and I knew my eyes shone like the lights in the painting. "What of that exhibition in Brussels you wrote me about? Any news?"

"The invitations aren't sent until November, but Theo tells me another of the Vingtistes was in Paris recently and saw my work. Theo said he seemed interested."

"How could he not be?" I kissed Vincent on the nose and made him flush red. "Didn't I tell you everything would happen someday . . . and now it has!"

"Let's not be hasty. I know better than to raise my hopes too high." He turned back to the paintings. "I've had such a desire to do portraits lately, but it's nearly impossible to find models here. I do have this one . . ." He produced a portrait of Monsieur Trabuc, a good likeness that captured the man's quiet strength. Vincent's voice was filled with respect as he described the attendant's career before coming to Saint-Rémy, his work at a Marseille hospital during a cholera epidemic, his help during Vincent's *crise*. The word "cholera" made me shudder—my father had died from it—but the portrait comforted me, knowing that this good man was looking after Vincent.

The familiar rat-a-tat cadence grew in Vincent's voice as he brought out canvas after canvas, prattling about the wheatfields and cypresses, the ivy-strewn undergrowth and the silver-leaved olive trees. "I wish I could go out at night," he sighed as he showed me a scene of a peaceful village under a bevy of swirling stars, a cypress reaching flamelike to the sky. "I did this one here in the studio back in June, from my imagination." He shrugged at my exclamation of delight and set it aside to pick up another. "Theo likes it better when I work from nature. Now this you'll recognize."

"You painted your bedroom in Arles again? Why?"

"Theo sent back the original so I could copy it before he had it relined. Look at the pictures on the walls."

Four pictures hung on the wall above his bed in the new painting, two below, two above: a self-portrait of him to the left, and to the right—a dark-haired young woman in a pink dress, eyes cast demurely down, hair caught up in a chignon.

Me, looking the way he'd drawn me in the Alyscamps. "You are never far from me, Rachel," he said.

I burst into tears, and he set down the painting to hold me close. "I was so scared when I heard you were sick," I sobbed. "I thought it wouldn't happen again."

"So did I. So did I."

"Why did it happen again? Why?"

"I don't know. Dr. Peyron thinks it's epilepsy."

"Epilepsy!" A dread word, a feared word. "That means—"

"—I might have attacks the rest of my life. I know."

I clung to him even more tightly, as if to keep the illness from stealing him. "Will you have to stay here forever?"

"I can't, or I'll go mad for certain. I'll stay through the winter, then I'll have a decision to make. Try not to worry, *chérie*. Dr. Peyron could be mistaken."

He glanced around for a clean rag, but I'd brought a handkerchief in my reticule. "You don't think you're working too hard, do you?" I asked.

His brow furrowed in the familiar way. "Working is the only thing that does me real good. It's the only thing that drives away the abnormal ideas that fill my head."

"But—"

"Shhh, stop. No more." He kissed me, not the passionate kiss of before, gentle kisses of consolation. My mouth, my nose, my closed eyelids . . .

"There you are. I've been looking everywhere."

Neither of us had heard Félix open the door. "I wanted to show Rachel my paintings," Vincent said coolly as I backed away and wiped my eyes.

"Is that what you were doing?" Félix asked, equally coolly. I gave him a warning look.

"If you didn't want me spending time with her, you shouldn't have brought her," Vincent replied. "We were about to take a walk in the garden. Alone."

Vincent took my arm and led me past Félix into the corridor, where Monsieur Trabuc watched and waited. "Are you allowed to go without Monsieur Trabuc?" Félix asked, to Vincent's scowl and Trabuc's shrug. "Rachel, you left your hat in Vincent's room," he added. I doubled back to take it from him, refusing to look at him as I did so.

Vincent made no comment as I caught up with him, and we continued down the hallway. "We don't have to do this," I said. "We can go back to your room, or—"

"I want to do this," he said tersely. "To live out in the world, to win my life back, I must do this."

But his footsteps slowed as we reached the vestibule and the doors to the outside stood before us. With a determined sigh, he pulled one of them open, reaching behind him for my hand as we walked into the sunlight.

"Let me show you something," he said as he brought us before a tall pine tree. His voice had softened. "During my *crise* there was a terrible storm, much thunder, much lightning. Not until I felt well enough to return to my studio and look out the window did I know this tree had been struck. They had to cut the trunk, leaving this gaping wound." He touched the bark of the tree. "But look! That smaller branch curling upward, it's still alive. This giant is defeated, he's somber, but he's still proud. He's still here."

"He's still here," I echoed, a lump rising in my throat.

Beyond the pine tree and a row of pink rosebushes, a path led into the midst of the garden, passing a stone fountain that today stood silent, the dirty water filled with leaves and pine needles. How different this garden was from the lovingly tended flowerbeds of the Arles hospital—the grass here overgrown, ivy crawling up the trees, weeds bartering with wildflowers for territory and attention. "How much farther do you want to go?" I asked after we'd crossed one terrace and reached another. "Are you feeling all right?"

Vincent looked at my dress and smiled. "How much farther do *you* want to go? We wouldn't want to muss you."

"I'll go wherever you go."

We wound our way to the corner of the garden, where a stone bench stood among the pines, the very one he'd told me about, and the hospital building was barely visible. I suddenly longed for my own clothes, not this ridiculous dress with its tight bodice and choking collar. I wanted to toss the satin hat over the wall and all the hairpins with it, cast off the pinching shoes to touch the earth between my toes.

"I'd forgotten how beautiful it is out here," Vincent said as we sat. "I'll have to write Theo for more paints before autumn arrives."

He put his arm around me, and I nestled myself into the crooks and crannies of his body, as comfortably as if I'd never left. The branches of the pine trees arched over our heads like the vaults of a church, and I closed my eyes to listen to a persistent pair of birds, twittering to each other across the air. Once monks in their solemn robes had walked under these trees, saying the rosary and whispering prayers. Asking for forgiveness.

"Vincent, there's something I need to tell you."

He didn't speak, and I wondered if he'd heard me. Then, very quietly, "There's nothing you need to tell me."

"Yes, there is. I—"

"There's nothing you need to tell me," he repeated, his voice both tender and sad.

He already knew.

I wanted to ask how he'd guessed, how long he'd known. I wanted to protest that Félix meant nothing to me, and his silly presents were just that, silly presents. He can never take me away from you, I wanted to say. Instead I wrapped my arms around his neck, breathed in his pipe-smoke, turpentine scent and said, "I love you, Vincent. Only you."

He kissed my forehead. "I'm sorry I left you alone, I'm sorry I haven't taken care of you the way you deserve. Someday I will show you how much I love you—for I do love you, with everything that is in me. And I will look after you. I promise."

"Vincent knows about Félix," I told Françoise after I returned to Madame Virginie's.

Her fingers paused over the buttons on the back of my dress. "Are you sure?" After I told her what he said, she asked matter-of-factly, "Well, he didn't tell you not to see Félix anymore, did he?"

"He doesn't like it. I can tell."

"What the hell does he expect you to do? Starve while you sit around waiting for him?" She tugged at the stubborn buttons. "Until he 'takes care of you the way you deserve,' you have to think of your future. Félix pays you well, brings you presents, and in case you haven't noticed, looks at you like you hung the moon."

"Are you saying Félix will ask me to marry him one day? You know better than that."

"Of course I know better than that," she snapped as she freed me from the dress and I pushed it to the floor. "But he could set you up in your own place and give you a nice little life. Get you out of here like you've always said you wanted."

"Until he tires of me and pushes me aside." I went to the washbasin to sponge my neck and arms, sticky from a day beneath the muslin. "Vincent loves me."

"From behind the walls of an asylum! He may never get out, Rachel. Love could leave you alone and very hungry." Françoise snorted as she shook out the dress to hang it up. "I've told you that from the beginning."

I frowned at her in the mirror. "You never did like Vincent."

"It's not about liking him. It's about wanting you to be happy. I see it in your eyes, you're not the girl you used to be." Before I could retort, she sighed and said, "I don't want to fight with you. I'm telling you to use your head. Screwing Monsieur Félix is no worse than screwing any of these other *mecs,* and only a fool would throw him away."

Minette appeared at the door. "Rachel, this came for you."

I opened the box she handed me—fine Swiss chocolates—and the note, written in Félix's well-educated hand.

Dear Rachel,

I did not have the opportunity to speak to you on the train with Reverend Salles accompanying us, but I am sorry for how I acted today. It was wrong of me to be so presumptuous and rude. I hope you can forgive me. May I come to see you tomorrow night?

With regards,
Félix

I handed the note to Françoise, and she gave an indifferent shrug. "Do what you want. I've told you what I think."

Dear Félix,

I accept your apology. Yes, you may visit tomorrow night. I'll be waiting.

Rachel

# CHAPTER THIRTY

# Invitations

2 November 1889

Mlle. Rachel Courteau
c/o Mme. Virginie Chabaud
Rue du Bout d'Arles, no. 1
Arles-sur-Rhône

*Ma petite* Rachel,

The weather has been changing, the days becoming dreary and the rain growing more frequent. Theo offered to pay Dr. Peyron more so that I might have wood for the stove in my studio, otherwise my fingers would get so chilly that it'd be hard to paint.

Because of the bad weather, I have been working on translations from Millet into color, based on a bundle of prints Theo sent me. It teaches me and consoles me, for I long to paint figures. One I have just done you would like very much. A country man and woman sitting together before a fire and under the light of a lamp, a color scheme of violets and tender lilacs. His back to us, the man works busily weaving a basket, and his lady sews contentedly while their baby sleeps in his cradle just behind. It moved me to paint it. Johanna will enjoy it, for Theo wrote me recently that she begins to feel the child stir within her. Theo must himself feel deep in nature at this time, and I am very glad things have changed so for him.

Millet's *Angelus* sold for half a million francs at a sale in Paris this past July. Half a million francs for the work of a dead painter paid nothing of the sort when he was alive. It is extraordinary.

Still nothing from the Vingtistes in Brussels. It is of complete indifference to me whether I am remembered, although Theo remains hopeful. A Dutch critic named Isaäcson has written a short note about me in a journal called *De Portefeuille,* and I include a translation. No need to tell you I find what he says extremely exaggerated.

[then, in different handwriting as if he'd left the letter and come back—]

My dear girl, I have splendid news. Dr. Peyron has given me leave to return to Arles, alone and for an overnight visit. I'll have to wait for Theo to send money for the trip, but I plan to arrive on the morning train from Tarascon on 14 November. I count the days.

With a kiss in thought,<br>Vincent

★ ★ ★

Had it been nearly a year since we'd last sat on this café terrace in the Place du Forum? Vincent had arrived that morning on the train, and I'd met him at the station, wearing Françoise's Arlésienne dress and cap. Vincent thought I'd arranged for a room at the Café de la Gare, but I surprised him by steering him through the winding medieval streets to an auberge on the other side of town. I hadn't wanted to risk seeing anyone in the Place Lamartine who might bring bad memories and ruin our day.

He looked further surprised at the cheery greeting of the be-spectacled spinster behind the desk—"*Bonjour,* Madame Courteau, I see Monsieur Courteau's train arrived on time"—but didn't give us away. She offered to bring us tea, and I bit back a laugh as I said, "No, thank you" and pulled at Vincent's arm to lead him up the stairs. We were both cursing all the pins securing my hair and the lace *fichu* shawl not long after that.

I woke from a doze to the smell of Vincent's pipe filling the room. "You shouldn't smoke in bed," I said with a yawn and stretch. "Fine way to set yourself on fire."

"The best ideas come when one is smoking one's pipe in bed." He touched me under the chin. "You were smiling in your sleep."

I glowed under his eyes. "How can I help it? Oh, dearest, I don't want you to leave. You don't need that silly hospital—you need me!"

He smiled and kissed me. "We have tonight and all day to-morrow. Now, where shall we go to eat? You must be hungry, I certainly am. What of the café in the Place du Forum?"

"I'm not sure . . . ," I began, then stopped myself.

"Being around all the people won't bother me. That's over and done with. I'm so tired of lentils and chickpeas, I think I'll actually have a *bouillabaisse.*"

I wasn't thinking about his illness, I was thinking about Félix. On the way to the auberge I'd avoided walking past the Hôtel-Dieu and taken us the long way round, for that very reason. I had no notion where Félix's family lived, but it would be our misfortune that they lived near the Place du Forum.

And yet here we were, with no sign of Félix. The café was as lively and sociable as I remembered, waiters scurrying, customers chattering over the clanking of plates and clinking of glasses. No one gave us a second look, no one seemed to recognize Vincent or me. "It's odd to come back and know the Roulins are gone," Vincent was saying as he attacked his *bouillabaisse*. "Did you see Madame Roulin before they left?"

"Yes, we arranged to meet in the Place Lamartine garden. You should see how big Marcelle has gotten. She was able to say all kinds of words—" I stopped myself again. I didn't want to tell him how Marcelle had climbed into my lap and tried to pluck the feathers from my hat before her *maman* had whisked her back. How she'd smiled up at me and babbled as if she'd been telling me something very important. "Madame Roulin sent her kind regards," I said simply.

"I had a good letter from Roulin a few weeks ago. They've hung the portraits and painting of oleanders I gave them in the new house." Vincent looked up from his plate and tilted his head. "*Ma petite,* I've felt better lately than I have for a year. You don't have to worry about things upsetting me anymore." He speared a prawn with his fork and, as calmly as if he'd been saying we'd be having good weather tomorrow, he added, "I've received an invitation to the Brussels exhibition."

I let out a shriek that made the other diners turn to look. "We've been together the whole day, and you're only just telling me? Oh, I knew they'd invite you this year! How many pictures?" He replied there'd be room for six of his large paintings, and I clapped my hands. "Which will you choose? Oh, the sunflowers, please choose the sunflowers!"

He laughed. "I think you're more excited than I am."

I leaned across the table and grabbed for his hand. "You must be excited too!"

"I'll be more so when I settle my choice of canvases. The Belgians have tremendous talent. They make me feel my inferiority."

I waved my other hand, as if fending off scores of imaginary Belgians. "Nonsense. How many other painters will be in the exhibit?" He rattled off half a dozen names, some of whom I recognized as his friends from Paris: Paul Signac, Henri de Toulouse-Lautrec, Lucien Pissarro. He mentioned a painter named Cézanne from Aix, and pride filled me at the thought of a Provençal artist in the exhibition. Another man, a Monsieur Renoir, must have been very important, judging from the respect in Vincent's voice when he said that name.

I asked if Gauguin was invited, and Vincent raised his eyebrows. "No. Even if he had been, he probably would have declined. Our friend Émile Bernard did." I asked why, and he said, "They don't get on with Signac. They don't like the neo-Impressionist style he advocates, and they refuse to exhibit with him or others working in that style."

"Does Gauguin get on with anybody?" I mumbled.

Vincent set down his fork. "Rachel, you should have forgiven him by now—I have. What happened was as much my fault as his. I've been corresponding regularly with him and with Bernard about the work they're doing. I don't like all of it, but it's interesting, and I think it a shame they aren't showing at Brussels."

I shoveled the last bite of my *poulet rôti* into my mouth without comment. I couldn't help but think of Gauguin tonight.

When we'd last come to this café, he'd been living in the yellow house, and we'd been a few weeks away from disaster without knowing it.

I glanced up to find Vincent gazing pensively at me. "Do you suppose I should send only the yellow-on-yellow sunflowers," he asked, "or the ones with the blue background too?"

"Oh, both! Both!"

After we finished our meal and Vincent paid the bill, he suggested we walk along the river before returning to the auberge. I didn't know this *quartier* well, and neither did he, so we got turned around twice and laughed at our poor navigation. When we found the river, we climbed the steps to the high stone embankment, turning downstream toward the Trinquetaille Bridge before crossing the bridge itself, with its iron railings and trusses. Other couples were sneaking kisses in the moonlight, and we smiled at each other as we stopped to take in the view. Vincent draped his jacket around my shoulders before putting his arm around me to warm me up.

"Will your paintings be for sale at the Brussels exhibition?" I asked.

He'd fallen quiet as we'd walked, and his answer now was brief. "They always are. They just never sell."

"How much would they sell for, if they did?" Vincent explained that Theo set the prices, and they'd probably be marked at four or five hundred francs each. "Why, that'd be three thousand francs if they all sold!"

He made a face. "I'll consider myself fortunate if one sells."

"But what if they did? What would you do with three thousand francs?"

He thought for a moment, and when he answered, his tone was serious. "Stop taking Theo's money. Rent, maybe even buy, a house." He paused and gazed across the water. "Marry you."

I fumbled for the railing. "What did you say?"

He smiled and said it louder. "I'd marry you."

"But . . . but . . . you wouldn't have to." We'd never mentioned marriage before, not even once. "I'm . . . I'm not . . . good enough for you to marry."

"If I'm a good enough painter to exhibit in Brussels," he said solemnly, "you're a good enough woman to be Madame van Gogh."

Madame van Gogh. I'd never dared to think the name. "But your family—"

"If I earn enough money, I can tell my family to go to blazes."

I stared into the dark river, uncertain how to ask the question I needed to ask. "Why are you talking about this now? Before you always said it wasn't the time."

He turned me by the shoulders and made me look at him. "I've been selfish and cowardly far too long, that's why. I want a home with you, I want a family with you, I want *you*, Rachel. You and no other. Will you marry me in the spring when I leave Saint-Rémy?"

All the words I wanted him to say. The words I had longed to hear in the studio of the yellow house, his blue-walled bedroom, my own room at the *maison*. Right here, under the stars, over a year ago. I covered his face with teary kisses to the amusement of a passing *gendarme*. "Yes—oh, yes!"

"Then I must concentrate on doing well in Brussels, no?" He pulled a handkerchief from his trouser pocket and wiped my eyes. "Listen, even if nothing sells, we'll find a way. Maybe I can organize an exhibition in Marseille, Roulin could help with that, or try harder to get some portrait commissions—"

I thought of Félix's francs piling up in my bureau. By the spring . . . "We'll find a way, *mon amour*," I agreed. "We'll find a way."

# CHAPTER THIRTY-ONE

# Crisis

31 December 1889

Dr. Félix Rey, *chef interne*
Hospices civils de la Ville d'Arles
Rue Dulau
Arles-sur-Rhône

Dear Dr. Rey,

I feel it my duty to inform you that Monsieur van Gogh has been the victim of another attack. He fell ill without warning the evening of 23 December, the year anniversary of his first *crise*. He has suffered considerable despondency and once again tried to ingest his own paints.

Monsieur Trabuc tells me that Monsieur van Gogh was in an uncommonly cheerful mood in the weeks leading up to the latest *crise*: painting actively, eating well, engaging in lengthy conversations. His journey to Arles in November brought no ill effects, and in fact seemed to lift his spirits. Monsieur Trabuc reports that Monsieur van Gogh kept busy after this trip preparing a series of paintings for an upcoming exhibition in Brussels. He spoke optimistically about the possibility of selling his work there.

The only annoyance he seems to have experienced is that he wished to visit Arles again for the Christmas holiday, but I did not permit it. I felt it unwise given that Arles was the location of his collapse a year ago, and I am certain you would agree with that decision. This attack was considerably briefer than the previous *crise* during the summer, and Monsieur van Gogh has almost fully recovered. Nonetheless, it is disheartening that he should fall ill again.

I will keep you informed of further developments.

With regards,<br>Th. Peyron, Director<br>Maison de Santé de Saint-Rémy de Provence

25 January 1890

Dr. Félix Rey, *chef interne*
Hospices civils de la Ville d'Arles
Rue Dulau
Arles-sur-Rhône

Dear Dr. Rey,

Monsieur van Gogh has once more suffered a *crise*. He fell ill two days after a brief visit to Arles to see a sick friend, the wife of his former landlord, although it is my conviction that the sick friend was not the reason for the collapse. Did he also visit you in Arles? Do you have any suspicions why this attack may have taken place? Monsieur Trabuc believes the approaching confinement of Monsieur van Gogh's sister-in-law may have played a role, for Monsieur van Gogh has shown signs of anxiety over it. Monsieur Trabuc also reminds me that some of Monsieur van Gogh's pictures are currently on exhibit in Brussels, and says that Monsieur van Gogh has been anxious over that as well.

I admit to being perplexed over this situation. Unlike most patients here, he can be lucid and normal one day, in misery the next, only to be lucid and normal once more as the attack passes. I suspect a form of epilepsy to be the cause but am confounded how he might be helped, or indeed if there is help for such a case. Just now Monsieur van Gogh seems to be improving, but for the past few days he has been unable to do any drawing or painting, and has answered incoherently any question put to him.

I trust this will pass as before, but as Monsieur van Gogh's former physician, I would appreciate any insight you might offer into how such attacks may be prevented in future.

With regards,
Th. Peyron, Director
Maison de Santé de Saint-Rémy de Provence

30 January 1890

Dr. Théophile Peyron, Director
Maison de Santé de Saint-Rémy
de Provence
(Bouches-du-Rhône)

Dear Dr. Peyron,

What a disappointment to learn of Monsieur van
Gogh's latest *crise*. He did not come to see me during
his visit here, and in fact I have not seen Monsieur
van Gogh at all since my visit to Saint-Rémy in
September. I am inclined to agree with Monsieur
Trabuc that events in Monsieur van Gogh's family
or connected with this Brussels exhibition may have
taxed his mental faculties to their limit.

While I hesitate to criticize your decision to let
Monsieur van Gogh travel, perhaps he should not
make any trips in the near future. Arles is not far
from Saint-Rémy, and the journey is not strenuous,
but these visits may only exacerbate his existing dif-
ficulties.

With regards,
Félix Rey, *chef interne*
Hospices civils de la Ville d'Arles

18 February 1890

Mlle. Rachel Courteau
c/o Mme. Virginie Chabaud
Rue du Bout d'Arles, no. 1
Arles-sur-Rhône

*Ma petite* Rachel,

I have splendid news. Theo will be submitting ten of my pictures to the Salon des Indépendants in Paris this March—*ten*! Our friend Paul Signac is on the hanging committee, and he will ensure everything is well displayed.

Theo was unable to attend the opening in Brussels because of my little nephew's birth, but my friend Henri de Toulouse-Lautrec says my pictures make a fine effect. Everyone talks of them, especially the sunflowers. No word about any sales, but like Theo, Lautrec believes it a matter of time. The article Monsieur Aurier wrote about me last month, he says, has gotten much attention.

My dear girl, do you realize what all this could mean? It is almost too much, so that my head feels quite muddled, and I must rest my pen and take deep breaths to calm myself. How I am sure you will laugh, you who have said that good things would happen. As has Theo. A lucky man I am to know such faith from my brother and little wife-to-be.

I will close this letter, because my head is throbbing and I wish to lie down for a few minutes. It may only be the change of weather since a manner of springtime has come this week, but I rather think I am overwhelmed too. I hope to go to Arles soon, especially since I missed you during my brief visit a few weeks ago. If it weren't for that blasted cold I caught after I came back, I'd have returned sooner.

With a kiss in thought,
Vincent

"I'm sorry, but I can't see you anymore."

I stared in the mirror above the fireplace in Madame Virginie's parlor, took a deep breath, and tried again. "Félix, this is hard for me to say, but I can't see you anymore."

I should have done it long ago, after Vincent proposed marriage, but Félix's money kept me quiet. Every time I counted the stash of coins and bills in my bureau drawer, I thought about what it could buy: new dishes, flowery wallpaper, seeds for planting a garden. I lay in my bed and imagined a farmhouse out the road to Tarascon—not one of those grand farmhouses with grand pillared gates but a simple cottage with thatched roof and blackened chimney. With a light-filled studio where Vincent would paint color-filled pictures, and a field of sunflowers nearby where our children could play.

Vincent's letters fed my dreams even more than Félix's money. Ever since that November visit, his words were charged with such hope, such faith that I hadn't seen in him for a long time. Paragraph after paragraph about the new painting he'd done for the Brussels exhibition and how much Theo liked it, Theo's certainty that sales would come, how strong and well he felt, an article written about him in *Le Mercure de France*. He sent me the article itself, and I wept with pride to read what the critic, Monsieur Aurier, had said about Vincent's work. Now this announcement of a new exhibition.

A knock at the door of the parlor. "What's the occasion, for us to meet in here?" Félix asked as he kissed me on each cheek. I was relieved to see he'd brought no flowers, no gift.

"I thought we needed a quiet place to talk." I handed him a glass of cognac and gestured toward the settee before taking the armchair by the fireplace and folding my hands in my lap. Best do it quickly, before I changed my mind. "Félix, I can't see you anymore."

He stared at me wordlessly, then tossed back his drink in a way I'd never seen him do. He hunched over and stared at the floor. The look on his face . . . "This is difficult for me," I said. "I've enjoyed your company, and I haven't wanted to lose your friendship."

"Why?" he asked. "Why now?"

"Vincent and I are engaged to be married. We have been since November."

Félix pulled a handkerchief from his waistcoat pocket and mopped his forehead. "Then why didn't you tell me this in November?" I looked down at my hands and didn't reply. "As if I don't already know," he added bitterly.

"Félix . . ."

"I hoped you would come to care for me as you do for him. I should have known better."

"I do care for you, please don't think otherwise. Please don't make this harder than it already is." When he didn't answer, I said, "I've risked much staying with you this long. Vincent found out ages ago."

Félix's eyes widened. "When?"

"I learned he knew the day we went to Saint-Rémy."

"*Merde.*" I'd never heard Félix curse before. He reached for the bottle of cognac and poured himself another drink. "And he let you keep on? Did he *tell* you to keep seeing me?"

I didn't like what Félix was hinting. "He absolutely did not. I'm certain he thinks I stopped seeing you."

"If you're engaged, why hasn't he told you to leave Madame Virginie's employ? What kind of man lets his fiancée—"

I fidgeted in the armchair. "It's not that simple. We need money."

"And I was the best way to get it."

"Félix, please—"

"What makes you think he can look after you as a husband should?"

His tone made me wince. "Some of Vincent's pictures are in an exhibition right now in Brussels, and he has every reason to think some of them will sell. He had an article written about him last month in a Paris *journal,* and next month he'll be exhibiting more pictures in Paris. He's strong and healthy, it's been almost five months since his last *crise*—"

Félix took a swallow of cognac. "Rachel, Vincent has suffered two more *crises* in the past six weeks." I felt the color drain from my face. "One began December twenty-third, the anniversary of his first collapse—"

"That's not true, he wrote me that morning, he said he felt fine."

"— the other was in late January after he came to Arles for a visit. Did he see you when he was here?"

I shook my head. "He came to visit Madame Ginoux, and when he stopped here, I'd gone out for a walk. I didn't know he was coming, and he didn't have time to wait."

"Two days after that, he collapsed again. Both *crises* lasted about a week, so they were shorter than his previous attacks, but serious nonetheless."

"He's said nothing about any *crise*," I protested. "He caught cold a couple of times and was too ill to write, but—"

"He's been lying to you."

I jumped to my feet. "How do I know you're not lying to me?"

Félix pulled two letters from his pocket and handed them to me. "*Suffered considerable despondency and tried once again to ingest his own paints . . . normal one day, in misery the next . . . I am confounded how he might be helped, if indeed there is help for such a case.*" If indeed there is help. If indeed there is help . . .

"Why are you telling me this?" I asked. "To hurt me? To make me stay with you?"

"To warn you. So you would know fully what you are doing, if you choose to affiance yourself to this man."

I shook Dr. Peyron's pages at him. "You think this makes a difference?"

"It should. Please listen to me, before you make a tremendous mistake. Vincent—"

I crumpled the letters and threw them on the floor. "The mistake I've made is carrying on with you all this time. To think I felt sorry for you, when you only want to ruin everything."

"That's not true." He rose from the settee and stepped toward me. "I care for you very deeply and want only what's best for you."

"Who are you to say what's best for me?"

"Let me finish. I can't let you go without saying that I would have been delighted—would *be* delighted—to give you a life of security beyond this place. A life that, no matter what you say, he can't give you."

"Please don't—"

"My mother has an apartment that she rents. It's empty now, and it can be yours. I'd pay the rent in your name, take care of you. Spoil you." He smiled, but I didn't smile in return. "You wouldn't have to worry anymore. I'd look after you."

"Until the time came for you to find a wife," I said quietly. "Marry a suitable bourgeois girl, have suitable bourgeois children. . . . You can't marry me, isn't that so? Or would you keep me around to do the things your wife won't?"

He flushed and straightened the front of his waistcoat. "Rachel, please."

"Your mother would never allow the likes of me in your family. You wouldn't be able to tell her I even exist. I'd be the girl you keep locked away for your amusement, no different than any other whore."

"It wouldn't be like that," he said and took my hand. "You are correct that my position in society forbids me certain things, but I would always make sure you were taken care of."

"Even after you throw me away?"

He dropped my hand. "It wouldn't be like that," he repeated.

"How else could it be?" I asked, as gently as I could manage. "I'm sorry, Félix. I love Vincent, and I am going to marry him. Nothing you or anyone else says will change that."

We were silent then, Félix looking at me as if he hoped I would change my mind, me looking at him and wishing I'd never let myself be swayed by his money and his gifts. I'd played with all our lives in a way I'd had no right to do, and now I was paying for it.

"I should leave," he finally said, reaching for his hat. "I don't think there's anything left to say."

"I'm sorry," I said again. "I wish things had been different."

He bent to kiss my cheek. "As disappointed as I am, it was

my honor to spend many happy moments in your company. If
there is anything you ever need from me, anything I can ever
do for you, I hope you will call on me."

After he left, I picked up Dr. Peyron's letters from the floor,
smoothed them open, and read them again. And cried.

Two days later, I received a note from Vincent, telling me that
he would be arriving in Arles for an overnight visit the evening
of the twenty-second. That evening. *"I have asked Dr. Peyron for
special permission to visit, for there is something I must tell you. It's too
important to discuss in a letter."*

I read and reread Dr. Peyron's letters to Félix until I knew
them by heart. I read Vincent's old letters too, wondering if
I'd missed some sign. *"I am sorry for the delay in writing over the
holiday,"* he'd said just after the new year, *"but working outdoors
resulted in a cold . . . I have been laid up in bed unable to do much
except sleep and read until today."* He'd lied to me, just as I'd lied
to him by keeping Félix my secret. Could a marriage be built
on secrets, on lies?

The clock on the landing struck eight. The train from
Tarascon would be pulling into the station, Vincent would be
climbing down the third-class compartment steps. Outside in
the Rue du Bout d'Arles a band of Zouaves was singing some
army song, on their way to find *filles* as jolly as they were. I'd
begged off the night's work with a headache and whispered to
Minette to send Vincent upstairs when he arrived.

I heard his quick footsteps down the hall before his sharp
raps on my door, and I stood to smooth my yellow dress. "I
thought I'd find you in the *salon*," he said when I let him in.

"I didn't want to embarrass myself in front of everyone," I
said with a weak smile and walked into his waiting arms. He

was thin again. He'd been more filled out when I'd last seen him, but now he was thin again.

"Is something wrong?" he asked, peering into my eyes. "You look different."

"I've missed you, that's all. What's that?" I nodded at a wrapped painting he'd leaned against the bureau.

"A present for Madame Ginoux. I'll give it to her tomorrow morning, then I thought we'd take a walk out the road to Tarascon before I catch the train. We have to start looking for a house." I stared and he said triumphantly, "I sold a painting in Brussels, the one with the red vineyard. Four hundred francs."

I leaped back into his arms with a gleeful squeal. "Oh, Vincent! Oh, dearest!"

"It's not enough to do everything I wanted," he cautioned. "I can't support myself on only that. But it's a start."

"Yes, and you have the exhibition next month, too!"

He took my hands in his and squeezed them tight. "*Écoute*, even if nothing sells at the Indépendants, I'll tell Theo everything. Ask for his help so we can marry in the spring as we planned. I'm well and healthy, I'll leave the hospital and we can—" My face must have betrayed me. "What is it?"

"Vincent, I know about the two *crises*." His smile faded, and his eyes turned to ice. "Why did you hide it, *mon cher*? Before we go any further planning marriage—"

"What do you mean, 'before we go any further'?"

"I mean, we need to talk about this. Why didn't you—"

"*He* told you, didn't he?"

Without meaning to, I glanced at the letters sitting on the bureau, where I'd forgotten to hide them. Vincent snatched them up and read them before ripping them into tiny pieces.

"Are you still seeing him?" he asked, and I said nothing. "Answer me, damn it. Are you—"

"No. I broke it off."

"When?"

I stared at the bits of fallen paper. "Two days ago."

"You've been screwing the goddamn doctor all this time? After I—after we—" I groped for his arm, but he shook me off to pace the room. "You must have gotten a good price," he sneered. "How much?"

"Vincent, please listen—"

"How much?" he shouted. At my whispered answer, he reached into his pocket and tossed coins on the bed. "You raised your fee. I only brought two francs."

"It meant nothing, I swear! I took his money, that's all, money I've been saving for us, Vincent—us!"

"So you can play Madame van Gogh the way you've played the little bourgeoise?" He grabbed the striped hatbox and waved the satin hat at me. "Is this what you sell yourself for? A fucking hat?"

"What did you expect me to do, starve while I wait for you?" Françoise's words flew from my mouth. "I don't have a brother in Paris sending me money!"

Vincent flung the hat to the floor and gripped my wrist until I gasped in pain. "Take that back!"

"Stop, you're hurting me—"

"I said, take it back!"

"I didn't mean it, I didn't, please stop!"

Something cracked inside him at my pleas. I could see it bubble to the surface as his face crumpled and he relaxed his clutch on my arm. He slumped to the floor, rocking back and forth like he had that terrible day in the yellow house. "I'm sorry, I'm so sorry, I don't know what came over me—"

Françoise burst through the door, dress unbuttoned, a half-naked customer behind her in the hall. "What the hell is going on? Get out of this house, you—"

"No, Françoise, he's sick!" I dropped to the floor beside Vincent and wrapped him in my arms. "Shh, it's over, my love, it's over."

"What the hell did he do?" Françoise demanded. "If he's hurt you, I'll—"

"Forgive me, please forgive me . . . ," Vincent said, then started babbling in Dutch. Although I couldn't understand but a few words, I realized he was reciting from the Bible.

"Send for Félix," I ordered Françoise. "He'll be at the Hôtel-Dieu."

She'd stopped yelling and was looking at Vincent as if he'd been a beast in a menagerie. Her customer had fled. "Are you sure that's a good—"

"Go!" I screamed, and she ran down the corridor calling for Raoul. I held Vincent as he kept jabbering, then as his speech faded away. His eyes went glassy and unfocused, and his breathing was labored. "Stay with me, *mon cher*," I murmured. "I'll take care of you, you're going to be fine . . ." I couldn't tell if he heard me.

Félix appeared in the doorway about twenty minutes later, doctor's bag in hand. "You didn't tell me it was Vincent," he said to Françoise before striding into the room and kneeling to feel Vincent's pulse. "What happened, Rachel?"

"I told him I knew about the *crises*, he asked how I knew, we started arguing . . ." *About you*. The words hung unspoken in the air. "It came on him all of a sudden."

"Has he had any absinthe, any alcohol at all?" I shook my head, and Félix said curtly, "He must have been on the verge of an attack before he came here. I told Dr. Peyron not to let him travel—Vincent, can you hear me?" He caught sight of my wrist, still red where Vincent had taken hold of me, and although he frowned, he didn't comment. "Mademoiselle Françoise, I need Raoul to help me get Vincent down the stairs. We'll take him to the Hôtel-Dieu." I suggested we take him to Saint-Rémy, and Félix said in the same brusque tone, "There's no time. Mademoiselle Françoise?"

"*Oui, Docteur,*" Françoise said and vanished.

"Félix," I asked, "would you have come if you'd known?"

"Yes. It's my duty as a physician. And I made you a promise." He wouldn't meet my eyes. "Fetch some water, let's see if he will drink something."

I climbed to my feet to pour a glass of water from the pitcher on my washstand. Vincent stared into nothingness when I asked if he wanted a drink, but when I dipped my fingers in the water and patted his face, he shook himself from his stupor to glare at Félix. "What's he doing here?"

"I'm here to help," Félix said. "I'm taking you to the Hôtel-Dieu."

"Like hell you are." Vincent struggled to stand, and I cried out as he faltered on his feet. "You'd gladly lock me up, wouldn't you, Doctor?" I tried to take his hand, but he yanked it away. "I don't want anybody's fucking help!" He stumbled into the hallway and down the stairs, seizing the painting for Madame Ginoux on his way out.

I started after him, but Félix stopped me. "We can't let him go like that," I said.

"He won't get far. I'll take the carriage and fetch two orderlies from the Hôtel-Dieu. He could turn violent again, and I don't want you getting hurt."

Françoise stuck her head in the door. "Vincent went off toward Place Lamartine. Should Raoul go after him?"

"No—Mademoiselle Françoise, please stay with Rachel," Félix said as he gathered up his bag and rose to his feet. "Bring her a brandy." He handed her a franc, then glanced back at me from the doorway and smiled, a wistful smile that pitied me. "Don't worry. I'll send word once I've gotten Vincent safely to the hospital."

When the clock struck one and I'd heard nothing from Félix, I crept past the dozing Françoise, down the stairs and into the street. I held my shawl close around me as I ran between the towers of the Porte de la Cavalerie into the Place Lamartine, where there was no sign of the hospital carriage and no sign of Vincent. "*Salut, ma belle,* I was just looking for me a pretty girl," a drunken Zouave slurred as he lurched toward me. I ducked between the hedges of the public garden, where I prayed I'd find Vincent by the beech tree or the cedar bush, or that he'd find me. I didn't, and he didn't, although I waited until dawn.

Not until the next afternoon did I learn what happened. Once Félix summoned two orderlies, he looked everywhere he could think to look—the Café de la Gare, the embankment by the river, the train station—but found no trace of Vincent. After two hours' search, he gave up, stopping first at the telegraph office to send an urgent message to Dr. Peyron.

Monsieur Trabuc and Monsieur Poulet were on their way to Arles in the morning when they spotted Vincent, collapsed and unconscious under a cypress tree, near a thatched cottage along the road to Tarascon. They gathered him up in their carriage and hustled him back to the asylum. The painting for Madame Ginoux was never found.

# CHAPTER THIRTY-TWO

# The Road Back

*I am so pleased that Vincent's work is being more appreci-*
*ated. If he were fit I believe that there would be nothing*
*for me to desire, but it appears that this is not to be.*
— Theo to his mother Anna and sister Willemien,
15 April 1890

No carriages stood outside the train station of Saint-Rémy.
I trudged alone through the village along the ring road,
past the olive groves and Les Antiques to the walls of Saint-
Paul-de-Mausole. There'd been a dusting of snow that morning, a last breath of winter, enough to soak my shoes and stain
the hem of my dress. The wind migrating from the Alps cut
through my cape like a dagger, and the respectable gray muslin
dress, ideal for September weather, offered no further protection. The sight of Mont Gaussier and its steadfast companions
should have lifted my spirits, but they only made me sadder, for
the mountains looked gray and lifeless under the leaden sky.

A fortnight had passed since Vincent's collapse. Félix had sent me messages at the *maison* with the latest news from Dr. Peyron, although he'd never come himself, and the news had changed little. Vincent would barely speak, barely eat, and seemed lost in a fog where no one could find him. Unable to bear it any longer, I'd asked Félix for a letter that would persuade Dr. Peyron to let me see Vincent, and without argument, without rebuke, Félix had sent one back to me.

The porter at the hospital gates escorted me as far as the entrance to the men's wing before hurrying back to his post. I rang the bell and stood at the bottom of the steps, rubbing my hands through my thin black gloves. Dr. Peyron appeared, and when I asked to see Vincent, he said, "No visitors are allowed for Monsieur van Gogh save his pastor. Good day."

"I was here in September, perhaps you remember me? I have a letter from Dr. Rey—"

Dr. Peyron ignored the paper in my outstretched hand. "I remember you perfectly, Mademoiselle. The last time you came here, Monsieur van Gogh left the building without permission and without supervision. With you."

"Only as far as the garden," I said in surprise. "What does that have to do with—"

He peered at me over his spectacles. "And I'm told that on a previous visit to Arles, the two of you, again without supervision, engaged in most inappropriate behavior."

Why, that tattling Monsieur Poulet. "But—"

"Did or did not Monsieur van Gogh visit you on his most recent journey, prior to his collapse?" I didn't answer, and he said, "Each of Monsieur van Gogh's attacks has had some connection with Arles, either while he was living there or in relation to a visit."

"He came to Arles in November and didn't have an attack."

He ignored me again. "Therefore, I am forced to conclude that something or someone connected with Arles is the source of Monsieur van Gogh's troubles."

"You can't be suggesting his illness is my fault!"

Dr. Peyron stared from the top step like Christ in judgment on the portal of Saint-Trophime. "Young woman, I'm not suggesting. I'm declaring unequivocally that your presence is detrimental to his recovery. Remove yourself from this institution at once, or I shall summon the gate porter."

"Doctor, you don't understand, Vincent and I wish to be married. I beg you—"

"My understanding, Mademoiselle, is that you are employed at an Arlesian brothel. Such a woman makes a suitable wife for no man. Perhaps you have deceived the impressionable Dr. Rey, but you cannot deceive me. Good day."

"Wait, please—" It was too late. The door had closed.

I would not crawl back to Arles like a criminal, tossed out of Saint-Rémy by that self-righteous prig of a doctor. I'd stay there until someone let me in, and anything that happened could be on Dr. Peyron's head. I brushed the snow off a nearby bench, then sat and wrapped my arms around myself under my cape. If I were already Vincent's wife, I thought, I'd be by his bedside. If our engagement had been published in *Le Forum Républicain* and proclaimed aloud in church, I'd be there. But a mistress, a lover, a whore—she belongs in the snow. *Such a woman makes a suitable wife for no man.*

What if Dr. Peyron was right? I'd always blamed the first attack on Gauguin, but that last fight between Gauguin and Vincent had been about me. The news of my miscarriage had brought on the second attack. The third in the hospital at Arles had had nothing to do with me, but the fourth had happened just after his visit in July. All this time I'd blamed Gauguin, Theo, Johanna for getting pregnant, the townspeople of Arles for their petition. Vincent himself for working too hard. Everyone but myself.

*Your presence is detrimental to his recovery.*

"Mademoiselle Courteau? Why did you not ring to be admitted?"

I was so absorbed in my worries that I hadn't noticed Monsieur Trabuc emerge from the hospital. "Dr. Peyron wouldn't let me in," I replied, my teeth tapping against each other.

"Come with me," Monsieur Trabuc said and took hold of my arm. "If I escort you to the wing where Monsieur Vincent is housed, Dr. Peyron will not find you."

I followed Monsieur Trabuc inside the men's wing, down the corridors, up the stairs. Today it was even more quiet than it had been on my first visit, and I kept looking over my shoulder, afraid that Dr. Peyron—or someone else—might be watching. Monsieur Trabuc unlocked a door next to Vincent's room. "You can recover yourself in here. There's a warm blanket on the bed, and I'll return presently with tea and hot water."

I discarded my cape and damp gloves to wrap the woolen blanket around my shoulders. Where Monsieur Trabuc went so quickly I had no idea, but he was back, it seemed, right after he left. He poured hot water into a basin as I gulped at the tea, letting it steam through me.

"Will you permit me?" Monsieur Trabuc asked, gesturing at my feet. I nodded, and he knelt to remove my shoes and stockings, gently placing my feet in the water. "You could have been frostbitten or caught pneumonia, Mademoiselle. Making yourself ill won't help—"

"How's Vincent?"

He rubbed at my calves to warm my skin. "We thought he'd be up and about in a few days, but he's taking longer to recover this time."

"Has he asked for me?"

Monsieur Trabuc busied himself with wiping up a bit of water that had splashed on the floor. "No, Mademoiselle. When I asked if he'd like me to send for you, he said you wouldn't come, and I shouldn't bother." At the look on my face, he sighed and said, "It's not my place to pry, so I'm not asking what happened, but whatever it was, Monsieur Vincent is most sorry for it now." He took the empty teacup from my hand. "I told him not to go to Arles, but he said Dr. Peyron gave him permission and that was the end of it."

"Why did you tell him that?"

"Monsieur Vincent was high-strung for a good week before he took that trip. He was painting every day and seemed all right, but there was something . . ." He shook his head. "I couldn't put my finger on it then, and I still can't."

*"My head feels quite muddled . . . I wish to lie down for a few minutes . . . It may only be the change of weather since a manner of springtime has come this week, but I rather think I am overwhelmed too."* It was all there, in the last letter he'd sent. The exhibitions, the article, Theo's child, the sale of his painting . . . then Félix. It had all been too much.

I pulled my feet from the basin and wiped them dry with the towel Monsieur Trabuc handed me. "Dr. Peyron believes Vincent's illness is my fault."

"Mademoiselle, if I've learned anything in all the years I've worked with the sick, it's that you cannot explain things so easily."

"Do you think it's my fault?" I pressed him.

"If I thought you shouldn't be here, I wouldn't have let you in," he replied sensibly. "If you'll put on your shoes and stockings, I'll take you to see Monsieur Vincent."

At Vincent's door, Monsieur Trabuc tugged open the little window to peek in. "Still sleeping, as I expected," he said in a low voice, then produced his ring of keys and unlocked the door to lead me inside. "He was overexcited this morning, so I gave him a sedative."

"Why does it smell of camphor?" I asked in panic. "Is there cholera about?"

"Not so loud, Mademoiselle. It's to help Monsieur Vincent sleep. A little camphor on the pillow soothes the mind."

Vincent was curled into a ball under a heavy blanket, and I knelt to peer into his face and stroke his cheek. He seemed to have aged years in the weeks since I'd seen him, new lines on his forehead, gray hair at his temples I hadn't noticed before.

A flicker of blue drew my attention to a painting hanging at the foot of the bed. A *Pietà*—a large, colorful *Pietà*. The limp body of Christ slumped against a rocky outcropping, while his mother gazed at me with a pleading expression, dressed all in blue, eyes hollowed from weeping. "Did Vincent paint that?" I whispered, although I knew he had.

"Back in the autumn after the first attack he had here," Monsieur Trabuc replied. "When he had the *crise* at Christmas, he asked that I hang it where he could see it from his bed."

"It's a Catholic picture. He's not Catholic."

Monsieur Trabuc went to Vincent's desk and handed me a print of the same picture, faded, creased, torn in one corner. "Monsieur Vincent had this hanging in here until he tore it down in a fit and poured lamp oil over it. He was so sad about it when he recovered that he made his own painting."

I gave Monsieur Trabuc the print and stared again at the *Pietà*. I knew the Virgin's face, I understood it, that lost look of having done everything you could to save someone only to have them slip away. Christ's face was in shadow, but hers gleamed in the light, the tilt of her head mimicking his and the lines of the rocks besides. Behind them a thunderstorm was subsiding, violet-blue clouds moving swiftly through the sky, the wind ruffling the Virgin's robe. Beyond the storm shone the golden rays of the Easter sun.

Words from old prayers bubbled inside me, prayers I hadn't said for a long time. *Ave Maria, gratia plena, Dominus tecum.* Papa had given me Maman's rosary when she'd died, but now it collected dust in a drawer at Madame Virginie's. *Benedicta tu in mulieribus, et benedictus fructus ventris tui, Jesus.* I remembered passing the beads through my fingers, feeling their smooth roundness, hearing the way they clicked against each other. I remembered Maman's voice too, rising and falling with the Latin words, leading us in prayer by candlelight. *Sancta Maria, Mater Dei, ora pro nobis peccatoribus, nunc et in hora mortis nostrae. Amen.*

"How can a Protestant paint such a picture?" I mused aloud.

"Monsieur Vincent said that when he was a young man and very religious, he loved church so much he went to all the Sunday services where he was living, whether Protestant or Catholic. He said he believed God to be in all of them."

I gazed at Vincent's sleeping face. "He never told me such things."

Monsieur Trabuc lay his hand on my shoulder. "Monsieur Vincent is a good man with a good heart. Only his illness fills him with darkness." He glanced at his pocket watch. "I shall leave you with him for a time. Ring that bell sitting on the desk if you need help."

When he'd gone, I pulled the armchair close to the bed and sat with Vincent, holding his hand. "There are so many things about you I still don't know," I whispered. "I'm sorry about what happened. I'm sorry I lied to you, I'm sorry for the hateful things I said." I kissed his hand and held it to my heart. "Please forgive me. Please come back to me."

*My room in Saint-Rémy. I am saying the rosary with Maman's beads and trying to reflect on the Sorrowful Mysteries, but I keep seeing my father's face, twisted in pain.*

*My sister Pauline's footsteps, coming to my room. "It's cholera," she says briskly and snatches up my valise. "Help me pack, you're living with me for a while. It's a wonder you aren't sick too."*

*I rise from my knees. "I won't leave Papa. I'll stay and help take care of him."*

*"You should have taken care of Papa to begin with. Letting him go to school when two of the children had the cholera—"*

*I am horrified. "I didn't know that, how could I have known?"*

*"Not sending for the doctor when he first felt ill two days ago—"*

*"Papa said it was only a stomach ailment and not to worry!"*

*She glares at me as she yanks open my bureau drawers and tosses clothes into the open valise. "Maybe if you spent less time with that Philippe—"*

*My eyes fill with tears. "I haven't seen Philippe in a week! I'm going to Papa." I start for his room, but she grabs my arm and says the doctor forbids it. I pull myself free and say I don't care.*

*I run down the hall and throw open the door of Papa's room. It reeks of camphor, it reeks of death. Papa's face is white as he tosses on the pillow, the doctor's face is grim. "Rachel, you shouldn't be here," the doctor says. "I told Pauline—"*

*"Rachel?" Papa opens his eyes to look at me. I take a step, but he shakes his head.*

*I want to hold Papa. I want to stay and look after him. "No," Papa says when I take another step. "Not you. Not you."*

*"He doesn't want you to catch the cholera," the doctor explains, then hands me a bottle. "Tincture of camphor. Take three drops twice a day, well diluted with water, for a week. I've given your sister some for her family, too. Now you must go."*

*"I want to tell Papa good-bye," I whisper. I know it will be for the last time.*

*"Tell him from the doorway," the doctor replies gruffly. "Unless you want to get sick."*

*Papa smiles, and I can tell it hurts him to talk. "Do not worry, little one. Your Maman will take care of me."*

*"I love you, Papa," I say and cry harder.*

*"I love you, my little Rachel." He closes his eyes. I wonder if he has died in front of me, but his chest is still heaving.*

*"Good-bye, Papa," I tell him, but I don't know if he can hear. I turn and walk down the hall, where Pauline waits to take me away.*

"Rachel? . . . "

I jerked myself awake in the tattered armchair. Vincent was lying on his side and watching me under heavy eyelids. "Did Trabuc send for you?" he asked, the sedative slowing his words. "What happened in Arles . . . I didn't mean . . ."

I knelt beside him. "We both said things we didn't mean. Let's forget it."

"I knew it would happen again," he whispered, his brow drawn into knots. "Pride, too much pride."

It took me a moment to understand. "You think you're being punished for the article and the sale in Brussels? For being happy about them?" His lower lip trembled, and I said firmly, "Vincent, your paintings are a gift from God, not a punishment. You shouldn't be afraid of success, not when you've worked so hard." I smiled and nodded toward the *Pietà*. "Gracious, what a Protestant you are. Even if you did paint a Catholic picture."

The faintest light in his eyes, the faintest smile. "It's the only one I can bear to have in here. It's Delacroix." The name came out as a long, weary breath.

A tap on the door, then Monsieur Trabuc entered with a tray, looking pleased to see Vincent awake and talking. "Would you like some soup, Monsieur Vincent?"

I asked what time it was, thinking of the train back to Arles. Monsieur Trabuc said it was a bit after four, and I hurried to pull on my cape. "Oh goodness, I need to start back to town. I wish I could stay longer, but I have to go."

"Will you come again?" Vincent asked, and I glanced at Monsieur Trabuc, who nodded his permission with a smile.

On my way to the hospital gates, I passed the chapel where the hospital sisters said their prayers and the priest looked after his flock. No Last Judgment stood above this portal, no terrifying vision of the Apocalypse with fierce angels and fearsome demons. Mary stood there instead, arms outstretched in greeting and solace. *Come in, come in,* she seemed to say. Ignoring the time, I slipped through the door under her waiting arms.

It was a simple place for simple prayers. No grand paintings, no grand tapestries. I didn't feel afraid or unwelcome—I felt peaceful, as if the Presence in the chapel liked me being there and wanted to listen. As I drew near a placid statue of Mary beside the altar, I felt I could talk to her the way I had always talked to my mother, or Françoise, or even Madame Roulin. I told Mary everything, and before I left, I spoke the words of her prayer, imagining Maman's rosary beads in my hands.

Vincent's *crise* lasted for two months, the longest of his attacks. I made the journey to Saint-Rémy whenever I could, and some nights, when Dr. Peyron was away, kind Monsieur Trabuc let me sleep in the room next door. The gray bourgeois dress stayed in Arles; I wore old clothes that could stand the chores of nursing and brought clean aprons in my basket. Monsieur Trabuc taught me how to care for Vincent: how to change the bedsheets without making him get up, give him a shave without cutting his chin, help him eat without making a mess. "And I said I wouldn't force you to be my nursemaid," Vincent said ruefully one afternoon as I gave the red floor tiles a better scrubbing than they'd had in months.

I sat back on my heels and put my hand on my hip. "Get better and I wouldn't have to be," I teased, and he managed a chuckle before sinking back onto the pillow.

Some days were very bad. In fits of melancholy, Vincent would refuse to speak, lying in bed staring at the ceiling or turning on his side to gaze toward the window. Those days I patiently read to him, and although he gave no response, I hoped it calmed him to hear the words. He had no hallucinations in my presence, although Monsieur Trabuc told me privately that sometimes at night, he started babbling in Dutch and needed a drop of sedative.

As quickly as a thunderstorm might materialize on a summer day, his quiet somberness sometimes gave way to violent weeping, and I set aside the book I was reading to hold him as he sobbed. I never knew why he grieved so, what memories or thoughts haunted him. I only knew he suffered, and it took everything I had not to collapse into tears with him. I stared over his head to the *Pietà* and asked the Virgin Mary for strength, for if I gave way to despair, then Vincent and I would both fall. Only when I was back on the train to Arles would I permit myself to cry into my handkerchief, when Vincent could not see.

Other days—the best days—I arrived to find him nearly himself, however weak. We talked as he lay in his bed and I did the mending or other things that needed doing, or simply sat with my fingers entwined in his. Ironically those days felt like a blessing, as if we were forging bonds between us that we hadn't attended to for a long time. Vincent told me things about his past that I never knew—things I will never repeat to a living soul—and I told him secrets from deep inside my heart. With each of those afternoons I knew with ever-growing certainty that I wanted to be his wife, that I was willing to bear any darkness for those precious minutes of light.

One afternoon, he said he wanted to draw. Monsieur Trabuc found a pencil and sketchbook in the desk; I helped Vincent sit up and watched as he took the pencil in his shaking hand. "It feels strange," he said, and furrowed his brow as he contemplated the blank paper. "I want to draw my foot," he said then, and I pulled the sheet free so he could see his toes. Scratch, scratch went the pencil. With each stroke the crinkles in his forehead deepened, until he cursed in frustration and snapped the pencil in two. "Damn it! It won't come right!"

"Maybe it's too soon," I soothed. "You can try again another day."

The next afternoon he asked again for his sketchbook and a pencil. "Only if you promise not to break it," I said after

Monsieur Trabuc sharpened the tip with his pocketknife. This time Vincent wanted to draw his soup bowl, and this time he went more slowly, taking deep breaths with every line he made. When he finished, I asked him if he wanted to rest, but he insisted on drawing his mug and spoon before surrendering the sketchbook. Each day after that he asked for his drawing things, and the pictures kept him occupied when he didn't feel like talking.

"*Souvenirs du nord,*" he said when he'd been drawing for about a week and wanted me to see his sketches. "Memories of the north. During all my attacks, I've seen again and again my life in Holland, especially my childhood in Zundert and the time I spent painting peasants in Nuenen."

I flipped through the sketchbook to find, along with drawings of the furniture in the room, shaky drawings of country people digging in a field or walking beside snow-covered cottages. "You must have been happy there, to keep remembering it so."

"When I feel well enough to write again, I'll ask Theo to send me the old drawings. I'd like to rework some of them, maybe redo a few of my old paintings too." He sat up straight when I turned a page. "That sketch you're looking at now, I did that from memory of my most ambitious picture from Holland, of a peasant family eating their dinner by lamplight. That's one I would really like to do again."

I frowned at him. "Vincent—"

"I mustn't rush things. I know."

I turned one more page. Here a man and woman walked a road in the rain, arm in arm, she with dark hair, he with a countryman's hat. A man and woman I'd seen before. Pencil-scribbled clouds gathered above them, but they seemed not to notice. The woman held up her skirt with her other hand so it would not drag in the mud. The man held the hand of a small child, toddling along beside them, and both gazed toward the little boy.

"If I draw it, maybe it will happen," Vincent said quietly. "Like magic."

I could not speak. I closed the sketchbook.

The next week Vincent announced he was ready to paint. When Monsieur Trabuc cleared his throat and said Dr. Peyron had forbidden it, Vincent said irritably, "I'm not planning to eat my paints, if that's what you mean."

"You can't even get out of bed," I protested.

"I can if you help me."

He'd nag until he got what he wanted, so I pulled Monsieur Trabuc aside and suggested he fetch Vincent's easel, paint box, and a canvas. Vincent hauled himself out of bed, and I supported him as he made his way to the chair beside the open window. He inhaled the spring breeze and smiled. "You see, *ma petite*? This is good for me."

His eyes were as bright as a boy's at Christmas when Monsieur Trabuc reappeared. He told us how to set up the easel, and once we arranged it to his satisfaction, he opened his paint box and pulled out his palette. "I won't overdo it, I promise," he said to my worried eyes as he pawed through paint tubes.

I helped squeeze paints, pour a little turpentine into a jar, set the canvas on the easel. He took a deep breath and dipped his brush into a puddle of green paint, sighing as if he were the happiest man in the world. I let him be as he worked, although I kept glancing at him while I changed his sheets and dusted his books. When he finished—Monsieur Trabuc had brought a very small canvas—he tilted his head and studied what he'd done, and I peeked over his shoulder. He'd painted a row of green-roofed cottages under a hot yellow sun, waving green grasses, a stiff-legged man strolling among them with a spade over his shoulder. "It's not quite right," Vincent declared, "but something's there."

"He has exhausted himself," Monsieur Trabuc complained as we walked to Vincent's room on my next visit, his tone cranky and unlike his usual placidity. "I tried to tell him he should stop drawing and painting for a few days and rest, but would he listen? Now he's back in bed, unable to do anything at all. And he wants his pipe. I told him no."

"If we didn't let him paint, he'd only get upset," I said. "He's stubborn as they come, we can't stop him." Monsieur Trabuc snorted and grabbed a broom to sweep the corridor.

"*Bonjour, mon cher,*" I sang out as I opened Vincent's door, then walked to his bed to kiss him on the cheek. "Why, you've nearly got all your color back."

"That's because I've been working. I've made myself tired now, but I feel stronger than I have in weeks. Look at that drawing on the desk." I studied his sketch of a chair beside a fireplace. "The perspective is almost perfect. It's coming back, my girl, it's coming back."

"Very good," I said and lay down the drawing. "But let's not hurry things, *d'accord*? What are we reading today?" I picked up the yellow-covered novel Monsieur Trabuc had left on the armchair: *L'Oeuvre,* by Émile Zola.

"Actually, Theo has sent a package. Would you open it and read his letter to me?" He'd never let me read any of Theo's letters before, and when I asked if he was sure, he nodded his head vigorously. The package contained prints, which he exclaimed over in delight. "Theo always knows what I like. *The Raising of Lazarus*, isn't that fine." Jesus stood in the center of the picture, lifting his hand to draw the weakened Lazarus from his tomb.

"Rembrandt," Vincent said, pronouncing the name with the solemnity of a priest.

"Rembrandt. He did the painting of the surgeon that you showed—" I stopped myself.

Vincent didn't seem to notice. "A genius. In Amsterdam and The Hague I spent hours in front of his paintings. Read the letter, please."

I tried not to rip the envelope, and I was careful too unfolding the fine paper. The address of Theo's gallery appeared at the top, and the name Goupil & Co., Tableaux, Objets d'Art, Boussod, Valadon, & Cie., Successeurs was stamped in an elegant design. "Theo's handwriting is better than yours," I said. "He writes like a gentleman."

"That's because he always did what he was supposed to in school. I didn't."

I started to read. " 'My dear Vincent, how happy I should be if I could go to you and shake your hand on the festive occasion of your birthday.' Oh! When was your birthday?"

"A few days ago, March thirtieth."

"You never told me. So you must be . . ."

He arched an eyebrow. "Thirty-seven, if you must know."

"Thirty-seven," I teased with a click of my tongue. "My goodness. 'Will it be a festive occasion for you, or is your condition still such that you are unhappy? What do you do in the daytime, and do you have something to divert your mind? Can you read, and do you get everything you want? After your last letter I hoped that you had entered upon a period of convalescence, and that you could have told me soon after that you were feeling better. My dear brother, how sad it is for us to be at such a distance from one another, and to know so little what the other one is doing.' How nice Theo sounds. Why doesn't he come to visit, I wonder?"

"It's a long way, and it's expensive. He's got work and the baby to think of."

The next sentences swallowed my voice. *For this reason I am very happy to be able to tell you that I met Dr. Gachet, that physician Pissarro mentioned to me. He gives the impression of being a man of understanding. Physically he is a little like you. As soon as you come here we are going to see him; he comes to Paris several times a week for consultations. When I told him how your crises came about, he said to me he doesn't believe it had anything to do with madness, and that if it was what he thought, he could guarantee your recovery, but that it was necessary for him to speak with you in order to make a more definite statement. He is a man who may be of use to us when you come here. Have you spoken to Dr. Peyron about it, and what does he say?*

"What is it?" Vincent asked anxiously. "Is something wrong with the baby?"

I didn't want to ask questions, not when Vincent was sick and easily upset. I skipped the passage about Dr. Gachet and continued with the rest of the letter. " 'I have not yet gone back to the Indépendants, but Pissarro, who went there every day, tells me that have achieved real success with the artists. There were also art lovers who discussed your pictures with me without my drawing attention to them.' That's good news," I said, trying to perk myself up.

"No sales?"

"It seems not." Vincent frowned and asked me to keep reading.

Theo said more about the exhibition, gave a description of springtime in Paris, some news of Johanna and the baby, and closed the letter: " 'My dear brother, I am anxious to know whether you are feeling better, and to receive particulars about your health. Be of good heart and cling to the hope that things will soon take a turn for the better. I am sending you some reproductions of etchings by Rembrandt; they are so lovely. A cordial handshake, and believe me to be your loving brother. Theo.'"

"He truly does sound nice," I said. All this time I'd pictured a prudish sort of man, cold and unfeeling, but Theo didn't sound that way at all.

"He'd have to be nice to put up with me," Vincent replied.

I set aside the letter and package to pick up *L'Oeuvre*. On that particular day, the story of obsessed painter Claude and his long-suffering mistress/wife Christine was the last thing I needed, and my voice started to shake as I read aloud. "I'm sorry," I stammered. "It's such a sad story."

Vincent's eyes were probing me. "Maybe we should stop reading today."

I lay the book on the floor. "Which paintings are in the Paris exhibition? You never told me which ones Theo chose."

"I wanted a mixture of work from Arles and Saint-Rémy . . ." I pretended to listen while my mind teemed. Who was Dr. Gachet, and why had Theo contacted him? What did Theo mean, "when you come here"—had Vincent made plans to go to Paris without telling me?

"Are you certain you're all right?" Vincent had stopped talking and was looking at me. I answered that I was just tired, and he said unhappily, "You've worn yourself out on my account. I told you that you didn't need to come so often—"

"That's not it. I like visiting you, I love spending time with you." My voice started shaking again.

"Come here, *ma petite*." He sat up in bed to hold me, the first time we had embraced each other since his collapse. I normally kept my distance for Monsieur Trabuc's sake. "Now, what's this fretting? I'm better today than I've been in a long time. I'll be up and about soon, I know it."

*Up and about in Paris*, the thought sneaked into my head. "Monsieur Trabuc said you've exhausted yourself with working. I'm worried about you getting worse again."

"Is that all? I'll slow down if that'll make you feel better. No more painting for a while, and very little drawing. Not until I'm well enough to get out of bed. *D'accord?*"

I smiled into his shoulder. For today, it'd have to be enough.

It was another three weeks before Vincent's *crise* fully passed. A bad day here, a few good days there, his mood and strength wavered and wobbled without pattern. Then, one afternoon near the end of April, I returned to Saint-Rémy after a few days' absence to learn that Vincent had left his bedroom and was working in his studio. Had been working there three afternoons in a row. My arms filled with pink spring roses I'd picked along the road, I opened the door to find Vincent standing in front of his easel.

"Come in, I'm just finishing," he said. He'd painted a bouquet of irises: blues, purples, and greens against a background as yellow as his sunflowers. Yellow like I hadn't seen him use since he'd left Arles. "You brought me roses! How delightful, thank you. These irises are nearly wilted, let's put them in here." He set down his brushes and palette to toss the irises to the floor, then tucked my roses into the jug, tenderly arranging the stems. "I'll paint these next."

"Does this mean you're well?" I asked in confusion.

He picked up brushes and palette again to dab blue on his irises. "Winter has passed, leaving only the spring. Not only have I felt like working but I've been writing letters again, and yesterday I packed a shipment of paintings for Theo that dried during my *crise*."

There was something else. I could feel it behind his breezy

reply, I could see it in the nervous lines of his body and the way he looked at the canvas instead of me. Just like that day a year ago when he told me about Saint-Rémy. When he spoke again, his voice was grave. "You already know about Dr. Gachet, don't you, *chérie*?"

I nodded to the floor.

"When I felt well enough the other day to read my letters, I saw the paragraph you didn't read aloud. That's why you were shaken that afternoon, wasn't it?" I nodded again. "And that's why you've seemed . . . not yourself lately."

I poked at one of the discarded irises with my foot. "Are you leaving? Are you going to Paris to live with Theo?"

"To Paris to visit Theo, then to a village called Auvers-sur-Oise, about an hour outside the city. Old Camille Pissarro told Theo about Dr. Gachet, a doctor living there who specializes in melancholia and collects paintings."

Outside in the garden those irises enchanted him. He plucked them, brought them to his studio, smiled at them while he painted—for that time they were the only things in his world. Until the next painting came along, then he didn't need them anymore. I gathered them up and lay them on a chair. "How long have you been thinking about this?"

"Theo first mentioned it back in the autumn."

"Why didn't you tell me?"

He put down his painting things to hold my hands. Blue and yellow stained my fingers. "I thought I'd have no need of another doctor. But you saw what Dr. Gachet told Theo, he believes he can help me. Isn't that what we both want?"

"Yes, but . . . I don't want you to go."

Vincent stared at me, then burst into a hearty laugh. "No wonder you looked so sad! I want you to come with me, my girl, to marry me like we planned!"

"But what about Theo? You didn't sell any paintings at the Indépendants. We can't afford to thumb our noses at him."

"I have the four hundred francs from Brussels. Anyway, he's bound to approve once he meets you."

"What if he doesn't? I have money too, but it's not enough to begin a life together."

Vincent dropped my hands to sweep the wilted irises to the floor and sink into the chair. "I thought you'd be eager to go. I thought you'd want to jump on the first train."

"I do want to jump on the first train, dearest," I replied and sat on his lap. "But you were always right when you urged patience. Maybe I shouldn't go to Auvers right away. Maybe you should speak to Theo first."

He ran his fingers through his hair, then proposed a plan. He'd go alone and visit Theo and Johanna for a few days before continuing to Auvers-sur-Oise. In Auvers he'd stay in a cheap auberge to save money and write the Ginoux to send his furniture, so he could begin looking for a cottage. At first he wouldn't say anything about me to Theo, not until he was settled in Auvers and had paved the way. When the time was right . . .

"Do you think you'll get sick again?" I asked quietly.

"I might. We can't pretend otherwise. But I believe I'll regain my balance in the north, and with Dr. Gachet to help me, I believe I'll be fine."

"When we're married"—I smiled and tweaked his nose—"we'll be so happy you'll have no reason to fall sick. You won't need any silly Dr. Gachet."

He smiled in return at the thought. "By the end of the summer at the latest, I'll send for you. Then, finally—"

"Monsieur and Madame van Gogh," I murmured and kissed

him soundly, before pushing away his wandering hands and sliding off his lap.

He put the finishing touches on his irises while I looked at the few paintings remaining after his latest shipment to Theo. "I'll have Trabuc send those after I get to Auvers," Vincent said. "They won't be dry by the time I leave, and I want to do a few more studies."

A small canvas caught my eye. *"The Raising of Lazarus,"* I said.

"I liked the print Theo sent me so much, I decided to try a painting from it."

Vincent had painted only part of the scene. Saved by an unseen Christ's healing powers, the weakened Lazarus was struggling to open his eyes after being brought back from the dead. His two sisters were reacting in shock at the sight, one drawing the cloth away from his face and throwing out her arms, the other at his feet with raised hands. A bright sun—a round, yellow sun not in the print, Vincent's own sun—watched the three figures with the hopeful dawn of resurrection.

Lazarus had red hair and a red beard. In the guise of the saved man, the healed man, Vincent had painted himself.

## Chapter Thirty-three

## The Trains of Tarascon

12 May 1890

Mlle. Rachel Courteau
c/o Mme. Virginie Chabaud
Rue du Bout d'Arles, no. 1
Arles-sur-Rhône

*Ma chère* Rachel,

Dr. Peyron had no objections about my leaving and agreed that a change of climate can do me good. Theo sent 150 francs for the journey, and I've begun packing. Theo at first insisted that I be accompanied the entire way, for he worries the strains of travel will bring a *crise* on the train. I told him each of my attacks has been followed by a period of quiet, and that I feel the utmost calm at present. Is it fair to have me accompanied like a dangerous beast?

I would like it if you met me at Tarascon station
on the 16th—I shall take the early afternoon train
from Saint-Rémy—so we can spend some time together. Will you?

With a kiss in thought,<br>Vincent

I prowled the station at Tarascon, the waiting room, the platform, the waiting room again, jumping at every steam whistle.
At last Vincent's train arrived, and I hurried to help as he descended from the third-class compartments. As usual he was
laden with any number of things: easel and stretchers on his
back, artist's box in one hand, valise in the other. "Always a
porcupine," I teased as I reached for his valise. He wore his
black velvet suit and nicest hat, ready for the streets of Paris, but
his shoes, in need of a polish, carried Provençal dust.

He chuckled and pressed his lips to mine, oblivious to anyone
watching. "*Bonjour, chérie.* Come, let's check the train schedule
before we do anything else."

Inside the waiting room Vincent consulted the chalkboard
listing the afternoon departures, then walked to the ticket
window, where the clerk leafed through a thick ledger. Vincent
nodded at what the clerk told him, then produced money to
buy tickets. He was smiling when he came back to me. "The
train to Lyon is at six, and there I change for Paris."

I glanced at the waiting room clock. It was nearly one.

"We could have luncheon and go for a stroll around Tarascon," he said, "or we could make a concentrated study of one
of the local hotels. Which do you think?"

"I'm not hungry. Are you?"

"We'll eat later."

A trio of cheap hotels stood in a row outside the station, and Vincent led us to the one that looked the least run-down. I wondered how many lovers came here for a last tryst. "How many nights?" asked the woman behind the desk, and when Vincent said it was only for the afternoon, she plunked a key on the counter. "Two francs. Room three, top of the stairs."

"Can you please send someone to knock at four-thirty?" Vincent asked as he paid the money and signed the register. I peeped over his shoulder and smiled at the scrawled *M. et Mme. V. van Gogh*. My future, in black and white for everyone to see.

The room wasn't much to speak of—the sort of room that smelled of stale smoke, with mousetraps in the corners—but at least it was clean. I helped Vincent take everything off his back and prop it neatly against a timeworn chair. He lay his hat on a table by the window, drew the curtains, then we stood and stared at each other. "We need to do this more often than every six months," he said, and we both laughed.

"Just wait until I come to Auvers."

We made love with a tenderness that honored our nearly two years together. I knew he was painting my portrait in his mind, lips and fingers brushing every line like sable bristles against canvas. He whispered colors into my skin to make me giggle, shades of this, tints of that he'd use for each shoulder, each breast, each leg, and made me swear that someday he'd have his chance. "When we're married," I told him, and he declared I always did drive a hard bargain. I sketched him in my head as best as I could as well, the red-gold of his eyelashes, the tawny freckles sprinkling his nose, his smell, his taste. His wounded ear, long since healed, long since accepted.

We fell asleep in each other's arms, curled together like kittens. In the haze of waking, I thought about how the next time would be in Auvers-sur-Oise. *Auvers. Auvers.* The very name a lazy river flowing across the tongue, a place where at last we'd find peace. I reached up to touch Vincent's face, and his cheeks were wet. "What's wrong?" I asked in alarm.

"Rachel, I want to tell you—" He swept my hair from my face and let the strands trickle through his fingers. "These past two years have been the most difficult of my life, but they've also been the happiest. You've given me so much of yourself, a gift I've hardly deserved. I shall miss you, *ma petite*."

"It won't be long until we're together," I reassured him with a kiss. "A few months."

"I know, but . . ." He looked toward the window, and his sentence trailed away. Then he sat up. "Let me draw you."

"Like this? Let me comb my hair and wash my face."

"No. As you are right now."

I pulled the blanket up to my shoulders. "Not naked. Not until—"

"We're married. I know. *Zut*, you weren't always so bashful." He smiled and slipped from the bed to find his trousers, find his sketchbook, and open the curtains.

"How many women posed naked for you before we met?" I asked as he sat cross-legged on the bed and started to draw.

He raised his eyebrows. "Ah, you've never asked me that before."

"I know of one, that Italian in Paris . . ."

"Very few beyond her. I've not been as successful as I'd like in persuading young ladies to part from their clothes in the name of art." He chuckled as he erased something in his picture.

"What's funny?"

"Before I went to Paris to live with Theo, I spent a few months in Antwerp and joined an art academy where I could draw from live models. But the students hardly ever drew from real women, they drew from plaster casts of statues. One afternoon, the drawing teacher brought a cast of a nude Venus. I thought her too skinny, so I gave her more curve in the breasts and hips in my drawing—like I like my women." The wicked smile returned. "When the teacher saw what I did, he tore my paper in two. Said I turned a classical Venus into a Flemish housewife."

"No! What did you do?"

"Jumped up from my stool and roared, 'You must know nothing of women, or you'd know a real one has hips and an ass!'" We laughed like we hadn't laughed for a long time. "I stormed out of the damned place and never went back." I giggled as his pencil played over the paper a while longer. "There—*j'ai fini*. Do you want to see it?"

I shook my head. "It's yours." He smiled at the page and closed his sketchbook, and I asked, "What time is it?"

"Must be close on four."

I patted the bed beside me. "I believe we have another half hour."

"I do believe you're right."

When the knock came at the door, a quiet voice saying, "*Seize heures et demie, Monsieur*," Vincent was hooking my corset as I laughed and squirmed. "I can't do this if you don't stand still," he scolded, which only made me laugh harder.

He tried pinning up my hair, but that didn't work, so he settled for kissing my neck while I stood in front of the mirror. "I can't do this if you don't stop," I said. His response was to slip his hand up my petticoat and stroke my thigh. I sighed and leaned against him. "We'll never get you on the train at this rate."

"Come with me," he murmured, his beard tickling my collarbone.

"Don't tempt me. We made a plan."

The woman downstairs didn't look up from her account book when we descended and Vincent returned the key. "There's a café across the street," he said as we walked outside. "Let's have an early supper."

The food smelled good, but I could only stare at my plate, my playful mood fading faster with the sound of every approaching train. Vincent prodded me to eat something, and to oblige him I took a few bites of my *omelette du jour,* but I couldn't taste a thing.

At the station, he stepped into the telegraph office to wire Theo, while I paced the rows of benches in the waiting room. Travelers were gathering for the evening trains, trains to Lyon, trains to Marseille, trains all across Provence. My train to Arles, which, according to the chalkboard, would leave at six-thirty. A paunchy man got a panicked look on his face, then sighed with relief at finding his ticket in his trouser pocket. A young woman nestled against a uniformed soldier, head on his shoulder, hand on his arm—he must have been on his way to Marseille, likely North Africa beyond that. She probably wondered if she'd ever see him again.

I beckoned to a passing flower seller and bought a single yellow posy. When Vincent joined me, I tucked it into one of his buttonholes. "What time do you arrive?" I asked.

He smiled down at the flower. "Ten in the morning at the Gare de Lyon. Theo will meet me, and I bet he won't sleep a wink all night."

"Will you write or send a telegram when you get there?"

"I'll try to send a telegram in Paris, then I'll write a proper letter when I get to Auvers."

Five minutes to six, read the clock overhead. "We should go to the platform," I said, my heart wilting within me.

A crowd followed us, everyone craning their necks for the

train. What would happen if I did climb aboard with him? I suddenly thought. What would happen if Theo saw me descending the compartment steps with his brother—would he confront Vincent then and there, or have the good manners to wait until we reached the apartment? Would Johanna regard me with scorn, would Theo order us from their home? If I went with Vincent to Paris right now instead of waiting for him to ease the way, what was the worst that could actually befall us?

Far more than I wanted to risk. I had to let him go.

The whistle sounded from up the track, and the waiting passengers started collecting their bags, telling their loved ones good-bye. Vincent set down his valise and artist's box to take my face in his hands, his eyes blazing with a fierce determination. "I will see you again."

"Say the word, dearest," I whispered, "and I'll come to you."

He kissed me on the forehead. "At summer's end. I'll be waiting."

He picked up his things just as the train pulled to a stop, slung his stretchers and easel over his back. The crowd was jostling us, the conductor was shouting, "*Direction Lyon! En voiture!*" and blowing his whistle, there was no time, no time, never enough time. We touched hands, then Vincent was gone, climbing into the third-class carriage with a glance out the window and a wave. I kissed my hand to him and waved back with a wobbly smile—kept waving until I couldn't see his train anymore. Then I crossed the empty tracks to the empty platform opposite, to await the train to Arles.

# Chapter Thirty-four

## Seventy Days in Auvers

25 May 1890

Mlle. Rachel Courteau
c/o Mme. Virginie Chabaud
Rue du Bout d'Arles, no. 1
Arles-sur-Rhône

*Ma petite* Rachel,

I spent three days in Paris and am now in Auvers. Seeing Theo, as well as making the acquaintance of Johanna and my little namesake, brought me much delight. Jo is sensible and cordial and charming, my nephew a treasure. Theo is well, although I found him paler than when I last saw him and with a rack-ing cough. It has pestered him for many years but is worse, and his appetite is less than I would hope. I encouraged him to visit the physician again and proposed the whole family spend their upcoming holidays here to benefit from the country air. Theo insists that a visit to Holland is long overdue so the child may see his grandparents, but I insisted a shorter journey would be better.

In Theo's apartment I had the opportunity to see my canvases from the beginning. So many that some are rolled and kept beneath the beds! Other of my paintings are being stored with Père Tanguy, who owns a color shop where I have long obtained paints and canvas. A bit of a *trou au punaises,* a bug-infested hole, and not entirely suitable. I brought four canvases from Saint-Rémy to keep me company and to show Dr. Gachet, but that is all I have room for at present. I reside in the attic of a friendly auberge across from the *mairie,* the city hall. It costs three francs fifty a night, more expensive than I would like, but such are things here. After some discussion, Theo agreed to maintain the 150 francs/month allowance.

Dr. Gachet seems an eccentric character with a nervous disposition. His face shows the lines of grief from his wife's death some years ago, but any mention of painting brings a smile. He has an extensive collection, which he has already been good enough to show me: a very fine Pissarro, two fine flower pieces by Cézanne, among many others. He invited me to paint at his house Tuesday; he has a fine garden which will offer good effects, and I hope I can induce him to pose for a portrait.

When I asked about my illness, his response was that I should work boldly on and not think at all of what went wrong with me. He is a homeopathic doctor, knowledgable about tinctures and herbs, and said if I find the melancholy too much to bear he can lessen its intensity. But at the moment all is well, and I have no need of anything.

There is a great deal of color here. Middle-class country houses covered with flowers, more modern villas, and for me the prettiest of all, moss-covered thatched cottages which sadly grow more rare with the passage of time. It does not take much effort to imagine *une petite famille van Gogh* living in one of them, and I work boldly on (as Gachet says) with that vision planted firmly in my mind. I wait in eagerness for your letters, which will brighten my days and bring the South up to me. Here is the address:

V. van Gogh
chez Ravoux, Place de la Mairie
Auvers-sur-Oise
(Seine-et-Oise)

> With a kiss in thought,
> Vincent

PS. I have heard nothing from the Ginoux regarding my furniture, this despite the fact I wrote them twice and made clear I shall repay any expenses. I may prevail upon you to visit Madame Ginoux and see about it.

28 May 1890

M. Vincent van Gogh
chez Ravoux, Place de la Mairie
Auvers-sur-Oise
(Seine-et-Oise)

*Mon cher* Vincent,

Françoise and I just returned from Saintes-Maries-de-la-Mer, where we took part in the yearly pilgrimage festival in honor of Saints Marie Jacobé and Marie Salomé. We traveled by diligence for five hours through the Camargue, along a desolate road that trails through marshes and sandy plains of grasses. Thousands of people filled the village for the festival, attending Mass then gathering on the beach as the statues of the saints were launched onto the sea in their little boat. I've never seen anything like it, the singing, the weeping, the hope in the eyes of the faithful. I lit candles in the church and prayed that the blessed ladies might touch you in Auvers and your healing continue. I send you a *carte postale* from the festival so that you may keep it in your room. Perhaps you think it superstition—or perhaps you don't—but I figure, any help we can muster is good help.

    Then what do I find when I return to Arles? A

letter from you that fills me with joy! I'm so happy
you're finding Auvers a peaceful place, and feeling
strong and well. It sounds like Dr. Gachet is confident in your recovery, which makes me wonder if
the Maries are already listening.

At Saintes-Maries I walked to the beach in the
middle of the night to stand alone with my feet in
the sea. I looked up to the stars to think of you far
away, my longing to be with you so strong that it
was a pain within me. I feel it even still, and I count
the days until we'll stand together to watch the stars
above Auvers and our own little mossy cottage.

Ever yours,
Rachel

5 June 1890

Mlle. Rachel Courteau
c/o Mme. Virginie Chabaud
Rue du Bout d'Arles, no. 1
Arles-sur-Rhône

*Ma petite* Rachel,

Your letter moved me near to tears, the thought of you
bouncing in the diligence over that rough road so you
could pray for me being more touching than I could
bear. I placed the *carte postale* on my desk so I may
think of you whenever I sit to write. My *Pietà* hangs
in my room as well, so I have a trio of blessed ladies in

Auvers, and one very dear girl back in Arles, to look after me. Which makes me a blessed man indeed.

Ideas for work come to me without stopping. I rise each morning around five and am in bed by nine. The people where I am staying are most kind, and I eat well of nourishing food.

I have become great friends with Dr. Gachet. Last week I painted two studies at his house, an aloe with marigolds and cypresses, then last Sunday some white roses, vines, and a white figure in it. I presented these to him to show that even if I cannot pay him in money for help he gives me, he can be compensated in pictures.

Sunday we dined with his son, about sixteen, and his daughter, a little younger than you. Dr. Gachet insists on having the housekeeper prepare elaborate four- and five-course dinners, although I tell him it is not necessary to go to such lengths. As I desired, I completed a portrait of the good doctor: the head with a white cap, the hands a light flesh tint, a blue frock coat and a cobalt blue background, leaning on a red table, on which are a yellow book and a foxglove plant with purple flowers. He was most pleased with it, and I think I will make a copy for him to keep.

Theo, Johanna, and the baby will spend a week of their holidays here before proceeding to Holland. Dr. Gachet visited Theo at his gallery to tell him I am entirely recovered, and to say he sees no reason why the attacks would return. I feel so calm and so much a master of my brush that I cannot help but believe him.

Two days ago I painted a picture I know you would like very much: a study of the village church, an effect in which the building appears to be violet-hued against a sky of a simple deep blue color, pure cobalt. The stained-glass windows appear as ultramarine blotches, and the roof is violet and partly orange. In the foreground some green plants in bloom, and sand with the pink glow of sunshine on it. This very old church sits on a hill above the town as if presiding over it, while above it still lie wheatfields on a plateau.

How I look forward to sharing this place with you, *ma petite!* The more I see Theo this summer, the easier it will be to broach the subject of our marriage with him. When the opportunity presents itself, I shall seize it.

With a kiss in thought,
Vincent

13 June 1890

Mlle. Rachel Courteau
c/o Mme. Virginie Chabaud
Rue du Bout d'Arles, no. 1
Arles-sur-Rhône

*Ma petite* Rachel,

Theo, Johanna, and my nephew came to Auvers this past Sunday for a luncheon at Dr. Gachet's, and we spent a splendid afternoon. Dr. Gachet and his children got on well with Theo and Johanna as I knew they would, Theo having met the doctor before and Mademoiselle Gachet being old enough to be a good companion to Johanna. I introduced *le petit* to the animals in Dr. Gachet's yard to his great amusement and mine as well. After luncheon we went for a long walk along the banks of the Oise, and Theo came to the auberge to look at my paintings.

I have done more studies of houses among the trees, a study of vineyards, and just yesterday a size 30 canvas of a landscape in the rain: fields as far as the eye can reach, all different kinds of green growth, a little carriage, and a train in the distance. Soon I hope to paint Mademoiselle Gachet, perhaps at her piano. I continue to feel strong and healthy, my mind more quiet than it has been in a long time.

I had a letter from Madame Ginoux. Monsieur Ginoux was seriously wounded by a bull when he was helping a friend unload animals from a wagon, which is why I had not heard sooner. Madame Ginoux assures me that my furniture will soon be on its way.

Take care, my girl, and I look forward to reading more of your news soon.

With a kiss in thought,
Vincent

16 June 1890

M. Vincent van Gogh
chez Ravoux, Place de la Mairie
Auvers-sur-Oise
(Seine-et-Oise)

Dear Vincent,

How nice that you are able to enjoy these leisurely
lunches and strengthen ties with the Gachet family.
I imagine Dr. Gachet could prove quite useful with
his art collection and Paris connections. Useful too
that Theo and Johanna have made the acquaintance
of the Gachets and are becoming friendly with them.
Perhaps when they take their holidays in Auvers, Dr.
Gachet and his daughter would be interested in hosting them. I don't suppose you've taken any chances
to speak privately with Theo about the future?

I am surprised you wish to paint Mademoiselle
Gachet—I thought you didn't care for *petites bour-
geoises* and their fripperies. I suppose she has lovely
manners and lovely clothes, and plays piano most
charmingly as a well-brought-up young lady should?
Presides over the tea table with elegance, dressed all
in white? No doubt she can speak quite intelligently
about art and painting, having grown up surrounded
by her father's collection. That will surely make for a
stimulating afternoon, when the time comes for you
to paint her.

Rachel

20 June 1890

Mlle. Rachel Courteau
c/o Mme. Virginie Chabaud
Rue du Bout d'Arles, no. 1
Arles-sur-Rhône

My dear girl,

I do believe your impatience is getting the better of you. Theo and I have not had the opportunity to discuss things privately, but I assure you I am sowing the seeds. *Chérie,* was it not you who urged patience this time? Said we must not thumb our noses at Theo?

In Arles I imagine the wheat in the fields is gold and ripened as harvest time draws near, but in Auvers the harvest is several weeks away, and the wheat only begins to turn yellow. *Things must proceed in their own time,* or we risk everything. Do you think I am not also impatient? I lay in my attic room every night, looking for the moon out the window and thinking about how happy we will be *when the time comes.*

As for my painting Mademoiselle Gachet, do I detect a certain *rivalité féminine*? I am not sure whether to be amused or cross at the implications— or pleased, if one takes the view that jealousy is a barometer of affection. *Ma petite,* to paint portraits one must have models. Did I not paint Madame Roulin and Madame Ginoux? Madame Trabuc at the *maison de santé*? I have just finished a portrait of the daughter of the people with whom I am staying (in blue against a blue background), and I should like to find a country girl to pose for me among the wheat. They are models, only models all.

It will please Dr. Gachet for me to paint his daughter, and I will offer him the portrait in thanks for his friendship. It is not for me. If I remember correctly, I asked you to pose many times before you agreed, and I still have not had the pleasure of finishing a painting of you.

All this to ask you to trust me.

My work and health continue well. I have begun painting in a new format, canvases 40 inches long and only 20 inches high, which excites me. Already I have completed a study of the wheatfields, another of the chateau at sunset, and the third an undergrowth with two figures passing through a forest, a man and woman with arms linked. As I painted this new study, I assure you Mademoiselle Gachet was nowhere in my mind.

With a kiss in thought,
Vincent

26 June 1890

M. Vincent van Gogh
chez Ravoux, Place de la Mairie
Auvers-sur-Oise
(Seine-et-Oise)

*Mon cher* Vincent,

I suppose jealousy and impatience did carry me away, and for that I am sorry, but I cannot help it. I am five hundred miles away from you, and I worry more and more, every day, that something will go horribly wrong when we are so close to happiness. I do trust you, please don't think otherwise, and I know you are doing what you can to plant the seeds in Theo's mind before speaking with him outright. It's just so hard, my dearest. It seems like it has been for far too long.

The day will come when you will have no need of another woman to pose. In the wheat, at a piano (although I have no notion how to play), on your bed . . . anywhere you want me, I am yours. I do not think Mademoiselle Gachet would say that!

With all my love,
your Rachel

2 July 1890

Mlle. Rachel Courteau
c/o Mme. Virginie Chabaud
Rue du Bout d'Arles, no. 1
Arles-sur-Rhône

*Ma petite* Rachel,

I have had a disturbing letter from Theo. The little one has been gravely ill, caused perhaps by an infection from cow's milk. Johanna herself has been sick for over a week, too sick to nurse, and the surrogate milk seems to have acted badly on the baby. The doctor told them the child will not die, but nonetheless Theo and Johanna are most anxious, and so am I. Theo says *le petit Vincent* wails incessantly and cannot be comforted.

The rest of the letter is unlike my brother, normally so calm and composed. He is contemplating leaving his gallery and starting one of his own with financial help from Dries Bonger, Jo's brother. What can he be thinking with this idea? It can only bring failure and ruin. I refuse to believe Jo supports this plan, although Theo does not say. I can only hope it is born of worry and will fade away as the little one's health improves.

Theo does say something that for us is very interesting: "I have, and I hope from the bottom of my heart that you too will someday have, a wife to whom you will be able to say such things." Is this the opportunity we have been waiting for?

I would like to go to Paris to be of what assistance I can, but Theo says I should not visit until Jo at least is feeling better. I plan to insist again that they spend their entire vacation in Auvers, as travel to Holland may be too much for Jo and the baby.

I am glad things between you and me are where they ought to be, even if impatience overwhelms us both. I shall take you up on your promise to pose for me, so prepare yourself for many hours of sitting—or lying—perfectly still while I indulge myself in looking you up, down, over, and under, and painting your figure until we are both satisfied.

The portrait of Mademoiselle Gachet is finished. The dress is pink, the wall in the background green with orange spots, the carpet red with green spots, the piano dark violet. Her father has promised to make her pose for me another time at a small organ to continue the musical theme.

Take care, *chérie*. I shall keep you abreast of any developments with Theo.

A kiss in thought,
Vincent

5 July 1890

M. Vincent van Gogh
chez Ravoux, Place de la Mairie
Auvers-sur-Oise
(Seine-et-Oise)

*Mon cher* Vincent,

How distressing, this news about your nephew. Perhaps he's just teething, and it is nothing more sinister than that? I hope both he and Johanna recover quickly. Please try not to be too anxious about them or about Theo's ideas of starting his own gallery. I know what must be in your mind, and I beg you again and again not to worry. We will manage no matter what Theo decides.

At the risk of sounding like a terribly jealous fiancée, could you indulge me by not painting Mademoiselle Gachet again?

Ever yours,
Rachel

7 July 1890

Mlle. Rachel Courteau
c/o Mme. Virginie Chabaud
Rue du Bout d'Arles, no. 1
Arles-sur-Rhône

*Ma petite* Rachel,

Yesterday I went to Paris to visit Theo and Johanna, and while I am glad to say the little one is much better, it was a most trying and difficult day in other respects. I intended to stay for a few nights, but found myself needing to flee almost immediately.

Such storms hang over us all that I feel very sad, as if my life is threatened at the root and my steps are wavering. I fear more than ever that I am a burden to Theo, that I stand between their family and true happiness. I would tell you all of what happened, only it pains me to think of it, and believe me when I say it would only upset you.

Today I tried to work although the brush almost slipped from my fingers. I painted vast fields of wheat under troubled skies, and I did not need to go out of my way to try and express sadness and extreme loneliness.

What is to be done?

Vincent

9 July 1890

M. Vincent van Gogh
chez Ravoux, Place de la Mairie
Auvers-sur-Oise
(Seine-et-Oise)

My dearest Vincent,

I cannot bear thinking of you in such a state, and I am terrified of what may have taken place between you, Theo, and Johanna to cause it. Is it Theo's idea of leaving his gallery? Or, God forbid, did you talk to him about us and have it go badly?

Shall I come to Auvers now? I can get the fare. Please don't give in to this sense of despair, and know that I love you with everything I have.

Ever yours,
Rachel

## TELEGRAM—14 July 1890

To:       Vincent van Gogh, chez Ravoux,
          Auvers-sur-Oise
From:     Rachel Courteau, Rue du Bout d'Arles
          no. 1, Arles-sur-Rhône
Message:  Have not heard from you. Fear
          another *crise*. Please send word.

14 July 1890

Mlle. Rachel Courteau
c/o Mme. Virginie Chabaud
Rue du Bout d'Arles, no. 1
Arles-sur-Rhône

*Ma petite* Rachel,

I am sorry to worry you, please forgive me. I have not suffered another *crise,* although I feared for a time one might be simmering. Jo and Theo have both written this past week about the matters we discussed in Paris, and although our problems are not resolved, we are drawing closer to an understanding.

Theo asked Messrs. Boussod and Valadon for a raise in salary, with the proviso that if it is not granted, he shall resign. That discussion took place on the 7th, so we all wait with bated breath to discover the outcome. It will determine many things.

I did not discuss you with Theo during the visit to Paris, please alleviate yourself of that anxiety. It was not the time.

Selfishly I long to tell you to board the train for Auvers, but I beg you to remain in Arles until we learn what will happen with Theo's position. He and Johanna are coming to visit for a week. I expect many things to be discussed and settled during that time, after which we can move forward as we planned.

I wait for the day when these storms have passed.

With a kiss in thought,
Vincent

### CARTE POSTALE

15 July 1890

Mlle. Rachel Courteau
c/o Mme. Virginie Chabaud
Rue du Bout d'Arles, no. 1
Arles-sur-Rhône

*Ma petite* Rachel,

Theo and Johanna are not spending any of their holidays in Auvers. They are going straight on to Holland, where Jo and the baby will stay for three weeks, and Theo will remain only one before going back to Paris. I cannot tell you how disappointed and yes, furious I am that they should change their plans so swiftly and leave me high and dry. I cannot imagine what they are thinking.

Yours,<br>Vincent

18 July 1890

M. Vincent van Gogh
chez Ravoux, Place de la Mairie
Auvers-sur-Oise
(Seine-et-Oise)

*Mon cher* Vincent,

Please let me come to you so we can weather the storms together. I'm certain Theo's decision had nothing to do with his feelings for you. Have patience with him and do not let this disappointment act upon you in ways it should not.

Dearest, always remember how much I love you. You are not alone.

Ever yours,<br>Rachel

26 July 1890

Mlle. Rachel Courteau
c/o Mme. Virginie Chabaud
Rue du Bout d'Arles, no. 1
Arles-sur-Rhône

*Ma petite* Rachel,

I am sorry to once more delay in writing, but there
has been much to think about.

Theo has returned to Paris, but I imagine has had
no news yet from Messrs. Boussod and Valadon, or
else he would have told me in his most recent letter.
I feel oddly calm about the situation, even as this
waiting remains difficult, and continue to think it
best that you stay in Arles until all this is settled.

I enclose some sketches of things I worked on this
week: one of the painter Daubigny's garden (he once
lived in Auvers, his widow is still here) and two sketches
of size 30 canvases representing fields of wheat after
the rain. The wheatfields are a rich gold and on some
farms, the harvest has already begun. I have written
Theo to ask for more paints, as I am nearly out.

My dear girl, my love for you is as deep and strong
as it ever was. These days it carries me through when
other things seem to fail me. May we soon find our
own harvest when all things come to fruition.

With a kiss in thought, I am forever yours.
Vincent

GOUPIL & CO.
TABLEAUX—OBJETS D'ART
BOUSSOD, VALADON, & CIE., SUCCESSEURS
19, BOULEVARD MONTMARTRE, PARIS

1 August 1890

Mlle. Rachel Courteau
c/o Mme. Virginie Chabaud
Rue du Bout d'Arles, no. 1
Arles-sur-Rhône

*Chère Mademoiselle,*

I write to you on behalf of my brother, Vincent, with news I wish I did not have to send.

I am sorry to tell you he is no longer with us. The evening of the 27th he injured himself at Auvers-sur-Oise and passed away a short time later. Before his death, he told me of your kindness to him and spoke of you with great affection. He asked if I would do something for you in his name, so I send the enclosed four hundred francs in the hope it may be of some assistance. Vincent earned this from the sale of a painting in a recent exhibition in Brussels.

Please accept my family's condolences for what must be a terrible shock for you, as it was for us all. If there is anything further I can do, please do not hesitate to contact me at the above address or at my home: 8 Cité Pigalle, Paris.

With regards, Mademoiselle,
Théodore van Gogh

## CHAPTER THIRTY-FIVE

## Paris, August 1890

I couldn't save him.

None of us could. Not Theo, not anyone in Vincent's family, not Félix or the other doctors who hemmed and hawed and pretended they knew what to do. Injured himself, that's what Theo said, but I knew it was no accident. Had Vincent drunk turpentine or eaten his paints? Taken a razor to himself and this time bled to death? Had another *crise* gripped him, alone in his attic room? Had Dr. Gachet done anything to help Vincent in those last weeks, or had he blithely insisted that Vincent only paint?

Why had Vincent wanted to die?

Four days after Theo's letter, I bought a bottle of laudanum at the apothecary's shop, to help me sleep, I told the clerk in a shaking voice. "Only a little each time," he cautioned, "or one morning you won't wake up."

The bottle was smaller than I expected, but it would be

enough. To the public garden of the Place Lamartine I went, to sit in the shadow of the cedar bush. Another hot day, but a quiet day, with not even the laundresses nearby to disturb me. The oleanders were beginning to bloom, and the summer cicadas droned an invitation. *Sleep, Rachel. Sleep.*

I uncorked the bottle and sniffed the laudanum inside. Would it be like absinthe, I wondered, strange at first, then sweeter as I neared the bottom? Should I drink it all in a gulp, or slowly, to savor the moment? Dying was like taking the train to someplace new, so Vincent said that night by the Rhône. If I drink this, I thought, soon I'll stand on a station platform in that new place—a busy platform like the one at Tarascon. I'll search across a sea of people, and there he'll be in his yellow straw hat. He'll meet me filled with smiles and laughter, he'll take my hand, and we'll begin again. Only this time, with no end.

*I'll go wherever you go.*

How bitter the laudanum smells.

A memory reached me then. Vincent in the Arles hospital after his first relapse, when his bandage had been removed and he looked like a lost little boy. His wide eyes, his words. *I can't ask you to give up your life for me.*

I corked the bottle and put it back in my reticule.

The next morning, I told Françoise I was going to Paris, to find Vincent's brother and learn the truth. "There's nothing you could have done," she said as I tossed clothes in my trunk. "You gave him all the love you had."

"I could have gone to Auvers," I replied. "Maybe he'd still be alive."

"He was sick, it was beyond your power. It's a blessing he no longer has to suffer."

I couldn't believe what I was hearing. "A blessing! A blessing he killed himself, a blessing he's dead? What do you know of his suffering, you who never liked him and wanted me to break from him?"

She took me by the shoulders and looked me in the eyes. "His spirit can be at peace in a way it never was when he was alive. You know that."

"Is he at peace?" I demanded. "The Church would say he's in hell for what he did."

"Is that what you believe?"

"I don't know what I believe anymore." I pulled away to bury my face in the yellow dress he'd liked so much, the one he'd always said looked like the sun. "I didn't get to say good-bye. I'd give anything to tell him I love him one more time."

She lay a hand on my arm. "He knew, dear. He knew."

"Then why? Why did he leave me?"

"His illness must have been too much for him." We were both quiet, then I wiped my eyes and kept packing. Françoise helped fold things and asked, "Will you come back?"

"No. If I must begin again, I'll do it in Paris. Not as a *fille de maison,* God no, with a respectable job and an honest living."

"You don't know anything about Paris," she said with a frown. "You've never been to a big city like that."

"I have to do this, Françoise. Everywhere I go, everywhere I look, I see only him and the life we could have had. If I stay in Arles, I'll go mad. Or die."

Madame Virginie was not surprised when I asked her to go with me to the *gendarmerie* so my name could be removed from the prostitution register. She wished me good fortune in Paris and, to my shock, pressed a fifty-franc note into my hand after I paid for my freedom. I gave my most revealing dresses and most gaudy jewelry to other girls in the *maison,* but they insisted on paying me. All that, plus what I had left from Vincent's four hundred francs and the money I'd saved, meant I had more than enough for the train fare, more than enough to sustain me until I could find work.

The evening before my departure, I wandered to the river's edge and the place where Vincent had painted. I watched the sun sink into the horizon, the stars flicker into brightness. "How do you call the stars in Provençal?" Vincent asked that night, just before he kissed me and I knew he loved me.

"*L'estelan*," I whispered now to the river, then took the laudanum bottle from my reticule and threw it with all the force I had in my arm. At the sound of the splash, I turned and walked to the Rue du Bout d'Arles for the last time.

To travel by train from Arles to Paris takes fifteen hours. The hard benches of the third-class carriages hurt my back the entire trip, and I was grateful for the breeze through the open windows that hid the stench of unwashed August bodies. The further north we went, the sky changed from the brilliant blue of Provence to a silvery gray, and I wondered if Paris itself would be as gray as Vincent always said it was.

A man with a northern accent tried to make conversation with me after we left Lyon. It was obvious what lay behind his comments about the weather, and I feared something of my old life clung enough for him to glimpse, despite the lady's dress, hat, and gloves I wore. Once I would have kept the talk going, seeing two francs ripe for the taking, but that day I informed him I was en route to Paris to meet my fiancé. His amused eyes said he didn't believe me.

Everything I owned was either in my trunk in the luggage car or on my person. Tucked into my valise were Theo's letter, all of Vincent's letters from Saint-Rémy and Auvers-sur-Oise, and the *santon* he'd given me the night of the *pastorale*. His painting of the Place Lamartine garden I'd wrapped in brown parcel paper and kept with me rather than surrender it to the luggage porter. It would have been easier to carry had I removed it from its frame and stretcher and rolled up the canvas, but I could not bring myself to do it.

When the train jerked to a stop at the Gare de Lyon in Paris, I climbed down the compartment steps to an extraordinary sight: the soaring glass-and-steel canopy covering the station, clouds of locomotive steam, pigeons flying about in a frenzy. More people than I'd ever seen in one place, everyone trying to get where they were going at once, bumping and jostling each other with hardly a *Pardon*. I clutched the handle of my valise and held Vincent's painting close as I maneuvered to the luggage car, where I spotted the man who'd tried to talk to me on the train, staring at me with the same insolent smirk. He saw there was no one waiting for me. He saw I was all alone.

A porter loaded my trunk onto a cart to wheel it out of the station. With him beside me to lead the way, I felt safer, and I looked in wonder around the *gare*. A grand-looking restaurant stood at the end of the platforms under an immense clock, huge signboards listed arrivals and departures, and conductors strode the platforms shouting the names of far-flung places: Marseille! Chamonix! Venice! Rome! *En voiture, mesdames et messieurs, en voiture!*

At a row of carriages outside the station, an old man leaped with surprising agility from a driver's seat and helped the porter load my trunk. "Where to, Mademoiselle?" I admitted that I didn't know, and the southern lilt of my French made him smile. "*Vous êtes Provençale?*"

"Yes, from Arles." I smiled back at his friendly tone. "This is my first visit to Paris."

He gave me a hand up into the carriage. "Hop in, Mademoiselle, and we'll get you settled. Are you visiting someone?"

"Not until tomorrow. Today I need to find an auberge—somewhere in Montmartre, I think? The person I'm visiting lives at 8, Cité Pigalle."

The driver took his seat and picked up his whip. "That's just below Montmartre. I know a place further up the *butte* suitable for a lady on her own. Clean, not too expensive." I thanked him before sinking back into the cushions, then I smiled to myself. He'd called me a lady.

With a flick of the whip, we were off, and Paris began to sweep over me. So many carriages, so many streets. I saw my first omnibus, crowded with people inside and on top—how could two horses pull it all by themselves? The driver noticed me looking left and right, left and right. "Paris must seem strange to a young lady from the south," he said.

"It's like nothing I've ever seen. How many people live here?"

"A couple of million, I should think, but few nowadays are true Parisians." The old man thumped his chest with pride. "My family has been here for centuries. My *grand-père* was one of the first inside the Bastille when it fell. Many changes since I was a boy, though, Mademoiselle. My *maman* and *papa,* God rest their souls, would not recognize Paris today."

We turned onto a wide boulevard that stretched as far as I could see, lined with graceful trees and modern buildings of gray-white stone. Throngs of people crowded the sidewalks and café terraces, strolling and strutting as if on parade. I gaped at richly dressed ladies with their pert bustles and stylish hats, clothes they must have bought at one of the *grands magasins* or else had made-to-order at one of the city's many *couturiers.* Huge signs told me I could look like them if I shopped at one of the department stores: Le Moine St-Martin, Le Bon Marché, La Parisienne. "*La plus grande maison de confections pour dames,*" one of the signs trumpeted, "the greatest store for ladies' clothes!" *Robes et manteaux! Peignoirs, jupes, et tournures! Chaussures! Chapeaux!* Once I'd thought Parisian elegance intoxicating, but now it frightened me and made me shrink in my seat. I'd already learned what trouble a fancy hat could cause.

"I'll drive you past the Cité Pigalle," the old man said, "so you can see where your friend lives." He rattled off the names of roads as we went along, pointing with his whip in this direction and that direction, saying things like, "That way is the Gare Saint-Lazare, if you want to go out to the *banlieues*," or "The Opéra is down that street." I couldn't possibly remember everything he was telling me, but he was so eager to be helpful that I nodded or commented whenever he spoke.

"*Voilà*, the Cité Pigalle," he said and gestured to a dead-end street. "We are on the Rue Pigalle right now, near the Boulevard de Clichy. It's not a far walk from where I'm taking you, but I'd hire a carriage just the same. You can find one in the Place des Abbesses."

The veneer of respectability surrounding the Cité Pigalle faltered when we reached the Place Pigalle up the way. Decent-looking cafés and shops circled the *place,* but the gaily dressed, gaily painted women loitering at a round fountain gave it another air entirely. They looked curiously at our carriage as we passed, and I recognized those hopeful glances, eager for a few francs to buy some supper. "Don't worry, it gets respectable again," the driver reassured me. "Girls come here hoping artists will hire them as models. They call it the Monday models' market. Other days, well, it's another kind of market." He chuckled, then apologized.

We climbed the *butte Montmartre* and rambled our way through a maze of streets that mixed modern apartments and shops with older, more run-down buildings. Some streets looked villagelike, with vineyards, kitchen gardens, even a few windmills. The people up here looked different, more like folks back in Provence, and colorful posters advertised not department stores but dance halls and cabarets: Le Divan Japonais, Le Chat Noir, Le Moulin Rouge. *Tous les soirs! Grande Fête! Entrée Libre!* Oh, certainly, free entrance, but once inside you'd be lured to spend all you had on drinks—even a country girl like me knew that.

"Montmartre wasn't part of Paris until about thirty years ago," the old man explained. "It was a separate town, and you had to pay a toll to go off the *butte* into the center. The true Montmartrois will still tell you they're not Parisian."

"Where's the Rue Lepic?" I asked, recalling the name of Vincent's old street.

"Back that way, a couple minutes' walk. You'll find the Moulin de la Galette there, a dance hall that's a hopping place on Sundays." Shortly after that, he pulled the horses to a stop. "*Et voilà,* Rue de Ravignan and the Hôtel du Poirier. I think you'll find it to your liking."

He gave me his hand to help me down, and as he went into the auberge I stayed and looked around me. We'd come to a square that sloped gently down the hill, where a series of streets met. A fair number of people milled about—merchants carrying things to and from their shops, old men resting on benches under chestnut trees—but it wasn't a large square, not even half the size of Place Lamartine.

The carriage driver reappeared, accompanied by a plump woman wiping floury hands on her apron. "*Bonjour,* you looking for a room?" I told her yes and gave her my name, and she said, "I'm Madame Fouillet. It's three francs a night room and board, and that includes one glass of wine with dinner. Laundry's extra." She gave me a stern look and added, "I don't mind letting to a young lady by herself, but this is a decent house, Mademoiselle. I won't tolerate strange men slinking about the place."

I felt myself flush. "*Oui, Madame.*"

"Not that you look the type, but you'd be surprised what happens to nice girls from the country once they meet a smooth-talking city man." She nodded toward the wrapped painting under my arm. "You an artist?"

"No, Madame. My . . . a friend painted it."

"Lots of artists in the *quartier,* and soon there'll be more. Monsieur François, who owns that building across the way"— she waved toward the other side of the *place*—"just turned it into studios. That'll change things round here, more *mecs* looking for easy girls." She sighed, and I flushed again.

"Jacques!" Madame Fouillet bellowed, and a long-legged youth scampered out. "Help Monsieur Pierrot with the young lady's trunk. Room ten. My son Jacques, Mademoiselle, he'll help you with things if I'm not around. My daughter Amélie works with me in the kitchen and does the cleaning."

Madame Fouillet prattled like a magpie as I followed her up three flights of stairs to my room. "There's a washroom at the end of the hall. Call down the stairs if you need hot water at a special time, otherwise one of us will bring you some at seven each morning. I'll bring you some now after we get you settled, I'm sure you'd like a wash. There's good drinking water out in the *place* at the *fontaine Wallace*—"

"Excuse me, the what?"

"That iron contraption with the women on it. Clean linens once a week, but you make your own bed, *d'accord*? Dinner's at seven sharp each evening, breakfast at seven-thirty each morning. I'll leave you to your unpacking."

I had barely sputtered a *merci* and given her twenty-one

francs for the first week when she was gone. The room was simply furnished with an iron bed, chest of drawers, desk, and washstand, but I opened the shutters to find a spectacular view across the housetops of Montmartre, down into Paris. Back in Arles I liked climbing the tower of the Roman arena to look across the countryside; it was easy to see where the town began and ended. But Paris didn't seem to end at all. Vast and intimidating, it went on and on, to the very horizon. Would it ever feel like home? Or would I tire of it as Vincent had?

I unwrapped Vincent's painting and set it on the desk. Madame Fouillet hadn't brought the hot water yet, so I decided to take off my hat and make the bed. I tried to be cheerful as I shook out the sheets and tucked them into place, stealing glances out the window, but the topsy-turvy day overwhelmed me. I sank onto the mattress, sobbing and clasping the pillow to my chest.

I didn't hear Madame Fouillet's tap on the door, and I didn't hear her open it. "Now, honey," she said as she poured hot water into the pitcher on the washstand, "you're not the first girl to be homesick, and you won't be the last. Where you from?"

"Arles, down south in Provence."

"Bless your heart, you're tired, that's all. Have a wash and a nap, then come down for a good dinner. Everything will feel better in the morning. My word, would you look at those colors!" She'd spotted Vincent's painting. "Your friend painted that? What's his name?"

"Vincent van Gogh. He used to live here, on Rue Lepic."

"Don't know him. Where's he live now?"

I stared at the floor. "He died a few weeks ago."

"Oh, honey, I'm sorry." She patted me on the shoulder like Françoise would have done, or Madame Roulin. "I'll light a candle for him in Saint-Pierre. You and he had an understanding?"

"We were going to be married."

"I'm sorry," she repeated with a long sigh. "I lost a man twenty years ago during the Commune. Shot by the soldiers. Oh, in time I married someone else, had children, but . . ." Her eyes returned to the Place Lamartine garden. "Did he paint a lot of pictures, your fiancé?"

It was the first time anyone had called him my fiancé. I looked at her and smiled. "More than you could imagine."

## Chapter Thirty-six

## 8, Cité Pigalle

*It is a sadness which will weigh upon me for a long time
and will certainly not leave my thoughts as long as I live.*
— Theo to his mother, 1 August 1890

At four o'clock the next afternoon, a respectable hour for
visiting, I hired a carriage in the Place des Abbesses to take
me down the *butte Montmartre* to the Cité Pigalle. The driver
offered to drop me at Theo's front door, but I descended where
the Cité met the Rue Pigalle, figuring the few minutes' walk
would help me gather my thoughts. As I picked my way over
the paving-bricks and looked over each door for number 8, I
became less conscious of the noise of the Rue Pigalle behind
me and more conscious that I was being watched by several
pairs of eyes from behind lace curtains. The Cité Pigalle didn't
seem like a street that saw many strangers.

Number 8 was last on the right, tucked behind an iron fence
woven with green ivy. No sooner had I approached the gate

than the *gardienne* pounced. "*Vous cherchez quelqu'un?*" she asked in the thickest Parisian accent I'd heard yet.

I almost said "No, thank you," and hurried back the way I'd come, but I squared my shoulders. "Monsieur and Madame van Gogh, please."

"*Troisième étage, numéro six,*" she said brusquely and opened the gate.

I crossed a little garden planted with lilacs, heaved open the front door, then mounted the twisting stairs to the third floor. With each step I grew more nervous. Maybe it was bad manners to appear like this without sending a note. Maybe Theo and Johanna had no interest in Vincent's Arlésienne *amoureuse*. Maybe they wouldn't even be home.

A small woman with short dark hair, enormous dark eyes, and a black dress answered the door of apartment number six. "*Bonjour,* Madame, I'm sorry to disturb you," I said, my breath coming fast from the climb. "I'm looking for Monsieur and Madame van Gogh."

"I am Madame van Gogh," she replied with a smile. "May I help you?"

"My name is Rachel Courteau. I was a friend of Vincent's in Arles, and I've come to pay my respects to your family."

She recognized my name, I could see it in her eyes. Her smile evaporated, then returned just as quickly. "Come in— won't you please join me for tea?" She stood aside to let me pass into the corridor. "I'm afraid my husband will not be home until later this evening." Her French was not as correct as Vincent's; a strong Dutch accent flavored her words, and she spoke with some hesitation.

"Thank you, that would be lovely."

She led me into a small *salon,* where the sight of Vincent's paintings made me gasp. A harvest scene of the plains of La

Crau shone rich with yellows above the fireplace, while above the piano hung a painting of an almond tree, delicately blossoming against a blue sky. Pink and peach blossoming orchards of Arles on another wall, and above the settee, the starry night over the Rhône. It had been over a year since I'd laid eyes on it.

I could feel Johanna studying me as I studied the paintings, not with contempt, with curiosity. A lady like her would see prostitutes from a distance, from the safety of a carriage seat if at all, and she certainly would never have spoken to one before. How much did she know about me—how much had Vincent told Theo, how much had Theo seen fit to tell his wife? God forbid, did she think I'd come to Paris to ask Theo for more money?

"May I take your hat, Mademoiselle?" Johanna asked with another smile. I unpinned the demure black bonnet I'd bought in Arles, handed it to her, then turned back to the starry night. "That one was shown at the Salon des Indépendants last September," she said. "The almond tree over the piano he painted when the baby was born. Now please make yourself comfortable"—she gracefully indicated an armchair—"and I'll return soon with our tea."

I settled myself and gazed around the *salon*. Shelves of books lined the walls, mostly literary and art books from the titles I could see, and sheet music stood ready at the piano. The furniture was handsome but not extravagant. Even Vincent's paintings weren't in fussy gilded frames, but plain white ones that showed the colors to their best advantage.

"Your husband works at the gallery of Boussod & Valadon, *n'est-ce pas?*" I asked as Johanna returned with a tray and set it on a low table.

"Vincent must have told you. Messrs. Boussod and Valadon actually have three galleries here in Paris, and others abroad.

My husband manages the Boulevard Montmartre branch, and he's been in that position for nine years. He works very hard. Too hard." A shadow passed over her face.

So I was right in thinking Theo hadn't left his employers; the letter he'd written me had been on Boussod and Valadon's notepaper. Had they given him the raise he'd asked for, or had he proven too anxious about the future to quit? As of the last letter he'd sent, Vincent hadn't known. Had he ever found out? I couldn't ask Johanna, so I simply said, "You have a lovely apartment, Madame."

Her expression brightened. "Would you believe my husband did the decorating? I lived in Amsterdam until we married, so Theo found the apartment and got it ready. The letters we exchanged with such exciting discussions as the colors of the curtains and wallpaper!" She laughed as she poured our tea into Japanese-style cups. "When I came here, it seemed everything I admired the most was chosen by Vincent when he and Theo lived together. That vase on the mantelpiece, for example, or this jug on the tea table. 'Vincent found that,' Theo would say, or 'Vincent thought that was so pretty.'" Her smile faded once more. "Hardly a day passed that we did not speak of him. Even still."

I walked to the mantelpiece to see more closely the vase she'd mentioned, a delicate, rounded shape with a little foot, blue as a robin's egg. It wasn't difficult to imagine Vincent at a *marché aux puces* or some dingy Montmartre shop, smiling at his discovery as he pulled the vase from a shelf. Proud of his prize, he probably filled it with flowers and painted a picture. When I picked it up and turned it over in my hands, I noticed a chip on the rim that looked like it had been there a long time. Vincent wouldn't have minded. Its flaws would only have made him love it more.

I felt Johanna studying me again, her unasked questions floating between us. We both had things we wanted to know, but etiquette required us to speak in harmless pleasantries. "Vincent said it was agreeable to have family so near while he was in Auvers," I said as I replaced the vase and came back to the table. "Did he visit you often?"

"Only twice. The first time for three days when he came up from Saint-Rémy. I'd never met him before, and I was surprised how cheerful and healthy he seemed after a year in the— He looked more healthy than Theo. He was so pleased to see us and visit his friends. The morning after he arrived, Theo and I found Vincent roaming the apartment in his shirtsleeves, pulling out all his paintings to look at them. Some of them he hadn't seen for years."

"Like a father gone too long from his children," I said and had to smile, thinking of that day when he'd returned to the yellow house after his first *crise*.

Johanna smiled in return. "*Exactement.* We went to see him in Auvers one Sunday, to have lunch with Dr. Gachet and his family. When Vincent met us at the train, he brought a bird's nest for the baby." A bird's nest. Like the one he'd given me. "He refused to eat until he showed *le petit* all the animals the doctor had: cats, dogs, rabbits, chickens, even ducks. Vincent wanted us to join him in Auvers for our vacation, but we needed to go to Holland instead to see my parents. We planned to visit him later on, but . . ." Her smile became a frown.

"Vincent wrote me that he painted a portrait of Dr. Gachet."

"Yes," she said, "and it's very fine. Theo has it somewhere." She extended a plate with little cakes. "We owe a great deal to Dr. Gachet. He was the one who sent word to Theo when . . ." She frowned and stopped herself again.

I wanted to hear what had happened, but not yet. I glanced toward the piano. "Vincent also said he painted Mademoiselle Gachet."

"Marguerite? Yes, but he gave that one to her father. I've never seen it." Johanna paused and crinkled her forehead. How I'd said the name must have given me away. "There was nothing between them, Mademoiselle," she said gently.

She knew exactly who I was. She couldn't tell me she did—ladies didn't discuss such things—but she knew that I wasn't just another whore, that I'd meant something. She continued, "Marguerite may have been infatuated, Theo thought she was, but Vincent certainly was not interested in her. She's a well brought-up girl, very innocent. Not his sort of woman." She flushed when she realized what she'd said. "I'm sorry, I didn't mean—"

"It's nothing," I reassured her. "You said Vincent visited you twice . . . ?"

"He came at the beginning of July but stayed less than a day. It was not a good visit." She pursed her lips and stared at her teacup. "You knew him a long time, didn't you?"

"For two years."

"Then you know how he could act sometimes," she said wryly, "how stubborn he could be." She sighed. "I wish I could have seen him one more time, to tell him how sorry I was for being impatient. It was not a good visit."

Johanna sipped her tea, and her face reflected some turmoil inside her head. Had Theo and Vincent quarreled about Theo's desire to leave the gallery? Had Johanna quarreled with Vincent, said things about his dependence on Theo to upset him? *"I fear more than ever that I am a burden to Theo, that I stand between their family and true happiness,"* Vincent had written after that day.

A loud wail from another room broke our silence. "Oh, gracious, please excuse me," Johanna said before bustling out and returning with the baby. Vincent's nephew. His flesh and blood. "This is little Vincent, hungry and ready for his supper. Would you mind holding him while I warm a bottle?"

To my relief, *le petit Vincent* didn't complain as I walked him around the *salon,* didn't mind a stranger's arms. He had red hair like his uncle, light wisps against his pale skin, and his blue-green eyes regarded me solemnly. In front of the blossoming orchard paintings, I'd have sworn he tilted his head to study the colors. I crooned a Provençal cradle song under my breath and was rewarded with a crooked grin that made me both happy and sad.

A voice like Vincent's in the hallway startled me. "Jo?"

"Hello, dear," Johanna answered from the kitchen. "You're home early."

"Monsieur Valadon vexed my patience today. I couldn't wait to leave." Slow, deliberate footsteps, not quick and restless like his brother's. "I'm trying to convince him to let me do another one-man show of old Pissarro's work. He kept saying the Raffäelli show wasn't reviewed by *Le Figaro,* so what's the point. He misses the point—no vision at all. I'm not going to bother asking him to show Vincent's work. Durand-Ruel remains my best hope."

"I'm sorry you didn't have a good day, dear," Johanna broke in, and her cheeriness sounded forced. "You're home now, just forget about it."

"You're right, my love, as always. Where's my little man?"

"In the *salon.* We have a guest."

Johanna and Theo entered the *salon,* and Johanna introduced me before returning to the kitchen. Theo had the same reddish hair as Vincent, more auburn than coppery blond, as if he seldom saw the sun. The same eyes, piercing and curious. But he was taller and more lanky, certainly more tidy with his neatly clipped moustache, carefully pressed suit, and shiny polished shoes without a speck of dirt. The perfect portrait of a successful businessman, until I noticed how loosely his jacket hung on his hunched shoulders, and how haunted his eyes were.

"*Bonjour*, Mademoiselle," he said, and I extended my hand, still clutching the baby in my arms. "Welcome to our home, I am pleased to make your acquaintance. I see you've met the most important member of the household already." He smiled at the baby, who held out his arms and cooed for papa. I passed little Vincent to Theo, and for a second the haunted look disappeared. "Please, let's sit down."

I felt shy in the presence of this man who'd been so central in Vincent's life. "I am pleased to meet you as well, Monsieur van Gogh. I came to pay my respects, first to tell you how sorry I am for your loss, and secondly to thank you for the help you provided me."

He kept gazing at me with those eyes so much like Vincent's. Was he surprised at the look of me, surprised I had good manners and was nothing like Sien Hoornik? "Thank you for your condolences. I am aware it is your loss too, so please accept mine in return." I inclined my head gratefully. "As for my helping you, it is my honor to fulfill one of my brother's final wishes. When did you arrive in Paris?"

"Yesterday."

"Where are you staying?"

"The Hôtel du Poirier on the corner of Rue de Ravignan, in Montmartre."

"A good choice. You came all this way to see me?"

"No, Monsieur. I've decided to leave Arles and start over."

His brow furrowed. "What will you do?"

"Find work, to begin with, Monsieur. This morning I saw a lovely flower shop near the auberge with a sign looking for a salesgirl. I thought I'd inquire there first."

"Not the *fleuriste* on the Place des Abbesses?"

"Why yes, that very one."

Theo smiled nostalgically. "That shop's not far from where Vincent and I used to live. He went there most afternoons to look at the flowers. The owner, Madame Hortense, always felt sorry for him not having any extra money, so she gave him the leftover bouquets to paint, the ones nobody wanted to buy. She's a kind woman, and would be a fair and just employer."

The coincidence struck me mute. A warmth passed through me, and I suddenly felt as if I was being looked after. As if I wasn't alone after all.

Balancing the baby on his knee, Theo reached into his waistcoat pocket and handed me his visiting card. *Th. van Gogh*, it said in graceful script, *Boussod, Valadon, & Cie., 19 Boulevard Montmartre*. "Please give my name and best regards to Madame Hortense. I am certain she remembers both Vincent and me, and would consider you favorably for the position."

"Thank you. That is most kind."

"My brother would be so pleased, Mademoiselle. He wanted you to have a good life."

"Thank you, Monsieur," I repeated, looking at the card in my hands.

Johanna returned to the *salon*. "The baby's bottle is warmed. Why don't I feed him in the kitchen, so the two of you can continue talking?" Her smile looked brittle, as if it would chip at the edges.

"Here you are, my little man," Theo said, handing the baby to Johanna. "I'm going to pour myself a cognac, would you care for an *apéritif*, Mademoiselle?" I politely refused.

Theo brought a glass of cognac from the dining room, then settled himself in the armchair again. As he reached in his jacket pocket for his cigarette case, a fit of coughing seized him, so fierce that he had to set down his glass. "Are you all right, Monsieur?" I asked, wondering if I should call for Johanna.

"This blasted cough has plagued me for quite some time," he said with a last wheeze and shaky smile. "I can't seem to get rid of it. Rheumatism, too. I must be getting old." He took a sip of cognac, and his hand trembled.

I put together what I was seeing with things Vincent had said about his brother's health, and I knew. Johanna knew too, although I doubted Theo ever admitted to his well-bred wife what truly ailed him. Syphilis was a fickle thing. Some led fairly healthy lives after being treated for the symptoms, while others had no future except pain, paralysis, and the madhouse. Theo had probably caught it years before, long enough ago to avoid infecting his wife and baby, and he'd probably quietly consulted the doctors and quietly taken the mercury treatments. But to no avail. I feared it would not be long before Theo van Gogh followed the brother he loved so dearly.

Theo retrieved a cigarette from his plated cigarette case. Crossing his legs, he closed his eyes to blow out the smoke, the way Vincent always had. "Do you want to know what happened?" he asked. "Isn't that partly why you're here?"

He could read me as well as his brother. I nodded, my heart starting to beat very fast.

"There's no easy way to tell you," he said slowly, "although I wish I could spare you the shock. He shot himself in the abdomen. At dusk on a Sunday, in a wheatfield at Auvers."

Vincent with a revolver in his hand, looking across a sea of gold. Watching the sunset, thinking it would be over soon. Vincent falling to the ground. Vincent alone.

There wasn't a breath of air in the room.

Theo was pressing the glass of cognac to my lips. I gulped at it, letting its heat burn through me, hot like a July sun. "Where did he get a revolver?" I managed to say.

Theo retreated to his chair and lit another cigarette. He must have stubbed out the first one. "Nobody knows, or at least no one would admit giving it to him. No one could even find it. He dropped it someplace before he went back to town."

"Went back to town? He didn't die there?"

Theo stared at the burning cigarette in his hand. "He must have fainted, but he revived and dragged himself back to the auberge where he was staying. Monsieur and Madame Ravoux discovered what he'd done and sent for Dr. Gachet. Gachet sent me word at the gallery, because Vincent wouldn't give him my home address—he told Gachet I shouldn't be troubled. I went to Auvers once I received the note the next morning, and he was still alive. We spent about twelve hours together.

"It was peaceful, Mademoiselle, you need to know that. He lay there smoking his pipe, and we talked. About our child-hood in Holland, about Jo and the baby, his paintings . . . and he told me about you. How important you were to him and how he wanted to marry you." A long silence, as if Theo was summoning the strength to continue. "Sometime after mid-night, he said very quietly, '*La tristesse durera toujours,*' closed his eyes, and it was over."

The sadness will last forever. His last words.

Theo walked to the mantel, where he stared at the painting of the harvest at Arles and lightly fingered Vincent's blue vase. He tossed his cigarette into the fireplace and murmured, "I blame myself."

"It wasn't your fault." Johanna had reappeared in the door-way. "You did everything you could to help him."

He spun to face her. "What if I'd told him how I settled things with Boussod and Valadon, that I wasn't leaving the gallery after all? I told you, I told Mother, why the hell didn't I think to tell him? One more letter, and he could still be alive—what was I *thinking*?" His voice rose with each question, and he looked more like Vincent than ever.

"Stop! Please, stop!" Johanna pleaded, then changed to Dutch. I couldn't understand the flurry of her words, but I understood her tone and the tears in her eyes. With a mumbled apology to me, Theo took her by the elbow and led her down the hall.

He returned several moments later, and I could still hear her sobs from their bedroom. He apologized again and said, "All this has been an incredible strain. Especially for Jo, with the baby to look after."

"Perhaps I should go."

"No, please, I want to talk about Vincent with you. We shouldn't pretend that nothing has happened, we should talk about him. Jo fears it's worse for me to keep dwelling on it, but she's wrong." His jaw tightened into a stubborn line. Just like his brother.

I stared at the now empty glass in my hand. "Where is he?"

"The cemetery at Auvers-sur-Oise. I knew he'd want to stay in the country." Theo gazed past me to some faraway place. "It's a sunny spot on a hill, in the middle of the wheatfields he painted. The day we laid him to rest, friends came from Paris together with the new friends he made in Auvers. We placed his coffin in a downstairs room at the auberge, and I surrounded it with his paintings, his easel, his paints and palette, even his pipe. His friends brought bright golden flowers . . . it was a hot day, but a beautiful day. A day made for him."

"Theo?" Johanna's voice, small and sad, came from the *salon* door. Her face was puffy from crying, and she carried a basket with the baby inside. "I'm taking Vincent for a walk. He needs some fresh air."

"That's a fine idea, my dear." Theo crossed the room to kiss her forehead and touch her under the chin. "Be careful on the stairs."

"It was a pleasure to meet you, Mademoiselle," Johanna said. "I hope you'll come again."

"I would like that. I'm happy to have met you, Madame van Gogh." I smiled at her, trying to show her I understood—I understood everything. She smiled back at me, she knew what I was telling her. Then she was gone.

"Would you like to see Vincent's paintings?" Theo asked. "There are so many that they aren't all here, but I'd be honored to show you what I have. The rest are stored at Père Tanguy's shop on the Rue Clauzel."

Walking through the apartment and looking at Vincent's paintings was like falling in love with him all over again. The parts of his life I knew, the parts of his life I didn't, all mixed up there at 8, Cité Pigalle: small canvases, large canvases, calm colors, wild colors. Theo told me about the paintings, but it was Vincent's voice I heard, little whispers tender in my ear.

"Let me tell you about Holland," the voice said as I studied pictures of the country, dusky peasants digging in the fields, weavers working at their looms. Baskets of fruit, a family gathered around a table under a glowing lamp, eating a simple meal of potatoes. Broad strokes of brown, gray, beige, and black, the colors of the earth itself. "Vincent said he wanted to make a picture that speaks of manual labor," Theo said, "of honest people earning their food. He said a peasant picture should smell of bacon, smoke, and potato steam."

"Now let me tell you about Paris," Vincent's voice whispered. Bouquet after bouquet of bright flowers, probably from the shop where maybe someday I'd give leftover bouquets to a hungry painter. A sultry woman seated at a tambourine-shaped table, cigarette in hand, mug of beer in front of her—Agostina Segatori, the Italian, it had to be. Vincent's own face stared at me from many canvases, no two alike. Here he was a somber soul trying to fit into Parisian life with his black suit and felt hat, there the busy artist at work, standing before his easel with brushes and palette. Twice he'd painted himself in the yellow straw hat, which after all this time could make me smile. Only the eyes were the same in every painting. Questioning, searching.

"You already know about Arles, *ma petite*." The pictures I knew and loved—the yellow house, his bedroom, portraits of his friends—pictures that called up so many things within me. The sunflowers. My yellow sunflowers. "Do you remember?" asked the voice. "Do you remember?" Theo watched my face, and I knew he wanted to ask me things about my life with Vincent. I also knew he wouldn't.

"It's strange," Theo said as we paused before the three paintings of the Place Lamartine garden. "He talked about four paintings of this garden in his letters, and he even sketched the fourth for me. But he sent only three."

"He gave it to me," I said quietly.

Theo didn't answer for a moment. "I'm glad."

From Arles to Saint-Rémy. I'd seen some of these, but many he'd sent to Theo before I'd been able to. Olive grove after olive grove, cypress after cypress. When I saw a cypress tree in a wheatfield, I gasped at the sky and said, "He painted the wind." At Theo's puzzled look, I added, "On a day of mistral, that's how it feels when the wind comes through the Alpilles. Swirly." I fluttered my hands to try and explain, fearing

I sounded like a country fool. But Theo didn't look at me like I was a fool. Not at all.

One small painting astonished me more than the rest. Vincent had imagined a twilight scene, the sky green, yellow, and orange with a slender crescent moon. Spiky cypresses stood among plump olive trees with cool blue mountains in the distance, and a couple strolled among the trees. The man was dressed all in blue, but no hat this time; his red hair and beard were there for everyone to see. He guided the woman through the grove, holding her arm so she wouldn't stumble. She wore a bright yellow dress.

"Vincent painted that one at Saint-Rémy, I don't know when exactly," Theo said. "He never mentioned it in his letters. It appeared in a shipment one of the attendants sent after Vincent came to Auvers. I meant to ask him about it."

This was how Vincent had seen us. Walking together forever, under a moon that spoke of consolation and infinity. Frozen in paint. Frozen in time.

Theo leaned forward to look at the painting more closely, then looked at me. "I wish he'd told me about you sooner," he said softly. "I used to say to Jo, I want Vincent to find a woman who'll love him so much that she'll try to understand him—although I knew such a woman would have to be someone very special and very patient. I know why he thought he couldn't tell me, but he was wrong. Things weren't what they were before."

I placed my hand on his arm. "It wasn't your fault. None of us could have known what would happen." Theo didn't reply.

"Do you have any of the paintings from Auvers?" I asked as we returned to the *salon*.

"Only one. I gave some to Dr. Gachet for his collection, the rest are at Père Tanguy's." Theo disappeared into the dining room and brought back a painting, which he propped on the settee. "Vincent experimented with the double-square format while he was at Auvers. He never stopped growing in his work, never stopped trying new things."

A crossroads in a golden wheatfield under a brilliant blue sky, three roads twisting into the distance to some destination as yet unseen. Black crows, a whole flock of them, descending—or were they taking flight? I didn't understand this painting, I didn't understand what Vincent was trying to say. In front of this painting, the voice was silent.

"Did he tell you about his exhibitions this year?" Theo asked, his eyes shining. "Les Vingt in Brussels in February, the Salon des Indépendants here in March. Jo and I attended the opening of the Indépendants, and you should have seen the effect his pictures made. Everyone was talking about them. Our friend Paul Gauguin said they were the highlight of the show, and Monsieur Claude Monet pronounced Vincent's work the best in the exhibition."

I smiled up at him. "Yes, Vincent told me."

"I've received so many letters, Mademoiselle, and not just from family and friends. Monsieur Monet never met Vincent in person, but he sent a kind note. If Vincent could have seen the respect which so many have shown for him and the things they say about his paintings . . ." His eyes lit up the way Vincent's always had when a new idea was brewing. "I'm planning a retrospective show with all the finest work. Paul Durand-Ruel, one of the most important dealers in Paris, was here the other day to discuss the possibilities."

"Vincent would have loved that," I told him with another smile and touch to his arm.

The shadows of dusk were stealing into the room, and Theo lit two lamps on the mantelpiece. "Would you like to stay for dinner? Our housekeeper is out for the day, but Johanna will cook a good Dutch meal. She'll be home any minute."

"Thank you, but I've taken enough of your time."

"Then I hope you will visit us again, any time you want to see his paintings—oh, I almost forgot, please wait here." Once more he disappeared into the dining room, this time bringing a bundle of letters, clumsily tied with a yellow ribbon. "These are for you."

All my letters from when Vincent was at Saint-Rémy and Auvers. "Thank you."

"I was surprised to find them with his things at Auvers. He seldom kept letters." Theo smiled wistfully. "I'm the opposite. I kept almost every letter he wrote me, hundreds of them over many years, I don't know why. Now I read them to feel close to him again." He paused, and his next words were a whisper. "He was so much my own brother."

That night I untied the bundle of letters by lamplight and read the pages I'd written, smiling at some, crying at others. The last letter I'd sent to Auvers was worn and crumpled, as if Vincent had folded and unfolded it many times, perhaps carried it in his pocket. I caressed the paper with my fingers, comforted that the last touch had been his. At least he'd died knowing I would have crossed the miles—the world—for him if he'd asked me. I still would.

# CHAPTER THIRTY-SEVEN

# The Crossroads

*We climbed the hill outside Auvers talking about him, about the daring impulse he gave to art, of the great projects he was always thinking of, and of the good he had done all of us.*
— artist Émile Bernard to critic G. Albert Aurier, Paris, 31 July 1890, writing about Vincent's funeral

On Sundays, cityfolk probably crammed the train to Auvers-sur-Oise, flocking to the countryside to enjoy picnics, boating, and socializing. Ladies in their summery frocks, men in their *canotier* hats, everyone eager to leave the trials of the week behind. But not today, not an ordinary Wednesday. I sat alone in the third-class compartment, gazing out the window as Paris transformed itself into trees and fields.

An hour or so after the train had departed the Gare du Nord, I alighted at the little Auvers station with its twin platforms.

The church was easy to find, looming as it did on a hill above the village, but how to get there? Was the town cemetery up that way, too?

I turned left from the station and followed what appeared to be the main street through the town. Auvers couldn't be less like Paris or Arles—I passed not one but two street sweepers in just a few steps. The white-walled Hôtel de Ville looked more like a candy box than a staid government building, and a pair of bored *gendarmes* lounged under the trees. I was about to ask them for directions when I saw the Café de la Mairie, its painted signs proclaiming it a *Commerce de Vins/Restaurant* and advertising *Chambres Meublées*, furnished rooms for rent. I knew it at once as the place where Vincent had lived. And died.

Local people occupied two tables in front of the auberge, sipping coffee and munching brioches. Their eyes sized me up as a stranger to town even as they nodded a wordless greeting. Were they regulars here; had any of them known Vincent? Windows in the auberge roof let light into attic rooms, the *chambres meublées* of the sign. Which had been his? Did someone else sleep there now, or would that room be shunned forever as the death-room of a suicide?

A young girl with a white apron over her blue dress was clearing a third table. A pretty thing, the owner's daughter I supposed, with a turned-up nose and blue ribbon in her hair. From her face she couldn't have been a day over fourteen, although she had the figure of a girl much older. Her papa probably had a time of it fending off the village boys. "May I?" I asked and pointed to an empty chair.

She gave the table a last wipe with her cloth. "*Je vous en prie.* May I bring you something, Madame?"

"Tea, please." When she returned, I asked, "Is it true, Mademoiselle, that many artists have come to Auvers-sur-Oise?"

The locals at the next table were straining to listen. "*Oui,* Madame, some of them have stayed here at my papa's auberge. We've got two now, a Monsieur Hirschig from Holland and a Monsieur Valdivielse from Spain." She stumbled over the foreign names.

"Have other artists stayed with you recently?"

She dusted invisible crumbs off the seat of the chair opposite me. "*Oui,* Madame, Monsieur Vincent. He was a nice man, well respected at our place."

"Did you know him well? How long did he stay?"

"About two months, Madame, but I didn't know him well, no." Her papa probably forbade her to have much to do with their male guests. "Mostly kept himself to himself, a quiet man. He took all his meals here, never refused a dish. Always smiled and thanked me when I brought up the clean sheets. At night after supper, he drew pictures for my baby sister Germaine to make her laugh. He liked playing with her. She's two."

"He painted a lot?"

Her eyes widened. "Oh, yes, more than any of us thought possible for one man to do. Every morning he went out in the countryside, he came back at noon for lunch, then in the afternoon he worked in the room Papa lets the artists use or went outside again." She lifted her chin with pride. "He painted me once."

I remembered that from his letters, and now that I'd met her, I wasn't surprised. I felt myself smile. "He did?"

"One morning when I was hanging up laundry, out of the sky he says, 'Would it please you if I did your portrait?' He said hardly two words to me before, I couldn't believe it. I said to him, and I was sure to be nice about it, Sir, I'll have to ask my Papa. He said, I wouldn't have it any other way, Miss, you ask your Papa. Papa said it'd be all right, 'cause he was a good gentleman and wouldn't try things he shouldn't. Monsieur Vincent didn't talk while he painted my picture, but when he finished he praised me for not having moved once."

"Did you like your portrait?"

She hesitated. "It wasn't what I expected, Madame. But I like that he painted me in a blue dress—this dress—and made the rest of the picture blue too. I have it upstairs in my room. He gave Papa a picture too, of the Hôtel de Ville on Bastille Day." She waved her hand toward the city hall across the square.

"What happened to Monsieur Vincent?"

She dropped her voice so the other customers couldn't hear. "He died, Madame, upstairs in his room. Shot himself in the wheatfields behind the chateau. How he got himself back here we don't know, but he did, and Papa sent Monsieur Hirschig for the doctor."

"Dr. Gachet."

She looked surprised I knew the name. "No, the village doctor, Dr. Mazery. But he'd gone to Pontoise to see a patient, so instead Monsieur Hirschig fetched Dr. Gachet. Dr. Mazery came later." She dropped her voice even lower. "I heard them arguing about what could be done for Monsieur Vincent. Dr. Gachet said it was hopeless, bandaged Monsieur Vincent's wound, and went home. He didn't come again until after Monsieur Vincent died, then he took many of the paintings away."

"What do you mean, took them?"

"Monsieur Vincent's brother came from Paris to be with him—a nice man too, such sad eyes you never did see—and after Monsieur Vincent passed on, he said we could choose paintings to have. Papa didn't want to be greedy and said he was content with the two Monsieur Vincent gave our family. He said Monsieur Vincent's brother should have the other paintings. But Dr. Gachet and his son wrapped up a whole parcel of them, after the funeral when Monsieur Vincent hadn't been an hour in the ground."

The girl's frown told me exactly what she thought of that, and resentment rose in me as well. If Dr. Gachet had wanted Vincent's paintings so much, why hadn't he paid for them when Vincent had been alive, when he'd known Vincent's circumstances and known the money would have been welcome? Would things have been different if he had?

"Did Mademoiselle Gachet come too?" I asked.

The girl took my empty teacup and shook her head. "They say she seldom leaves the house. *Alors*, it's a strange family. They're not from here, they're from the city. Would you like another?" This time she brought not only a fresh cup of tea but a crusty brioche as well. "Forgive me if I'm being impertinent, Madame, but"—she hesitated again—"are you a friend of Monsieur Vincent's? He told Papa he'd been in the Midi, and you have a southern accent."

I tried not to sound too sad as I replied, "Yes, I am."

"Were you his sweetheart?" I nodded, and she clapped a hand to her mouth. "Oh, Madame, I've been going on and on—"

"*Ce n'est pas grave,* Mademoiselle," I told her with a smile. "I wanted to know what happened. That's why I came."

Tears glittered in her eyes. "Monsieur Vincent never told us he had a sweetheart. I'm so sorry, Madame."

"Thank you," I said gently. "Thank you, too, for being so kind to him. He said nice things about your family in his letters." That made her smile. "May I ask, Mademoiselle, do you know anything about why he . . . did what he did?"

She wiped her eyes with her apron. "No, Madame, he seemed satisfied to be here. He did keep to himself, but we never imagined he was unhappy. It was the shock of our lives when he . . ." She paused, then asked in a quiet voice, "You've come to see him?"

I could only nod.

"If you turn right at the end of our building, you'll see the Rue de la Sansonne. Take that and go up the stairs in front of you. The road winds up the hill through the *quartier de l'église*, then you go up more steps to the church. The cemetery is a short ways past."

"Thank you, Mademoiselle. What is your name?"

"Adeline Ravoux, Madame. And I'm truly sorry. He was a good man."

Mademoiselle Ravoux scurried into the auberge at the sound of her mother's voice calling her name. I left some centimes on the table, then started down the road, making the turn she'd indicated. The narrow Rue de la Sansonne led uphill past a manor house, and I wondered how many Parisians kept country houses here. Dr. Gachet must have been one of them— another day, another time, I might have asked Mademoiselle Ravoux where he lived. I might have stormed through the door and confronted him, railed at him for not taking care of Vincent like he should have. But not today. Even Marguerite Gachet, who'd filled me with such jealousy when I'd first read Vincent's letters, meant nothing to me now.

The tidy whitewashed cottages along the road with their colorful flowerboxes, the fresh country air that cleansed the lungs, made it easy to see why Vincent had liked Auvers. I caught glimpses of rolling hills in the distance, mist clinging to them even this late in the morning. Down there somewhere lay the Oise, surely a more peaceful river than the Rhône, hosting Sunday pleasure boats instead of Marseille-bound coal barges. Something lovely everywhere you looked—Vincent never would have run out of subjects for pictures. Even in his last letter, he'd said he'd asked Theo for more paints. He hadn't planned to die, I was sure of it.

Ahead lay the stairs leading to the church. It was very old, the church, at least as old as Saint-Trophime but not so large, with thick stone walls and a sturdy bell tower. I walked around the back but couldn't find the cemetery. Mademoiselle Ravoux had said it was a little ways past, but which way? The nearest path led further uphill through a thicket of trees. Lifting my skirts in my hands, I started up it, and when I did, the church bells startled me with bold rings calling across the valley, ten of them altogether following me as I climbed over the stones.

I emerged from the shadow of the trees to a plateau covered with wheatfields. When Vincent arrived in May, this wheat would have been young and green. He would have watched it ripen over his time here until it had turned richly gold, as gold as in the painting Theo had shown me. Now the harvest was over. The reapers had done their work, and the bundled sheaves of grain resembled women in yellow dresses, dancing gracefully under the blue expanse of sky.

Something told me to keep climbing into the very midst of the fields, and at the summit of the plateau, I came to a crossroads. The crossroads from Vincent's painting.

He had walked the same path, canvas and easel strapped to his back, face hidden by his straw hat. He set up his easel where I stood, saw the crossroads as I saw it. He sat on his folding stool and touched brush to canvas, hands smeared with blue and yellow paint. Once in a while he stopped to look around, tilted his head, pulled off his hat to run his fingers absently through his hair. He nodded and smiled when he saw what needed to be done next and returned to his work.

The vision in my head was more real than anything I'd felt since the day he died, so real that I expected him to turn and find me. But today no crows swarmed overhead. The sky was free of storms, and the sun caressed the earth like a lover. A beautiful day. A day made for him.

With no sound around me but the whispering wind, I felt drawn to something larger than myself, something Vincent would have called infinity. I pulled the pins from my hair to let them fall to the ground, let my hair tumble down my back. I closed my eyes and stretched out my arms to whirl round and round in a circle like a child might do—faster, faster—letting dizziness carry me, the sweet smell of harvested wheat envelop me. Shards of golden yellow pricked my eyelids, and in those spinning seconds I wanted to embrace the sun itself.

*I am not alone. I am not alone.*

I opened my eyes to find myself facing the stone walls of the cemetery at the end of the road. I could still leave, I thought as the giddy feeling drained from me, I could still turn back. Away from Auvers-sur-Oise—far away, if need be—I could pretend he had not truly gone, that it was all a dream from which I would someday wake to find him lying beside me.

I stood there at my own crossroads, and I let the wind tell me which way to go. There was no leaving. Vincent was waiting for me, at summer's end like he promised. There was no turning back.

*Ici repose Vincent van Gogh, 1853–1890.*

In the cemetery I knelt before the newly carved headstone, the freshly turned earth, and I covered my face with my hands. Thirty-seven years. Hundreds of pictures he'd made, but how many remained unpainted? How many days and nights together remained unlived, how many words would always be unsaid? Images darted through my mind, one after the next: his loving eyes in Tarascon, his pale face in the hospital, the touch of his hand when all was brightness and light, his smile under the stars. The sunflowers. His eternal sunflowers.

Piercing the silence like a messenger, a crow called, then

called again. Shaken from my grief, I gazed at the sky, but I saw nothing except swirling clouds.

I know you are here.

I feel your presence, as warm and real as if you are sitting beside me. The wind lifts my hair and strokes my cheek like you used to do, so softly, so gently. I whisper your name, and I know you can hear me. If I reach out my hand, I imagine you will touch me.

*Mon cher,* I have come too late, how I wish I'd been there to hold your hand and soothe you to sleep. Thank God Theo was with you so you would not be afraid, so the last thing you'd see would be a face filled with love.

To lose you like I'd lost everyone was too much for me, and I thought of joining you. I came so close, but something stopped me. Something made me throw the laudanum into the river, something told me it's not my time. I know the voice murmuring in my ear was yours. Even in death you still speak to me.

I came here to try and understand, I came here looking for answers. Maybe I haven't found them—maybe I never will—but this quiet place under the sun makes me believe that whatever drove you to take your life, you are at peace. Your sadness will not last forever. Your sadness is gone, and even now you walk these fields with your brush poised to capture all you see. I know it. I feel it.

I kiss my hand to you, my love, as I did that day when you boarded the train and I saw you for the last time in this life. I press my hand to my heart and say to you not good-bye but *au revoir.* I will see you again.

Wait for me.

# Author's Note

Surviving historical sources reveal next to nothing of the real Rachel. The brief article about van Gogh's breakdown in the 30 December 1888 edition of *Le Forum Républicain* (included in Chapter 15 in partial translation) provides her first name, occupation, and address, and identifies her as the girl Vincent asked for at the brothel, then presented with the fragment of his ear. A brief notice in another news clipping (see Bailey 2005 in Further Reading) calls her only "a café girl," while in a letter to artist Émile Bernard not long after that night, Paul Gauguin mentions "a wretched girl." (Gauguin's account in his 1903 autobiography, *Avant et Après,* changes the story to have Vincent give the packet to "the man on duty.") An Arlesian police officer named Alphonse Robert, recounting in 1929 what had happened, stated a prostitute known as Gaby gave him the ear and said Vincent "had made them a present"; however, it is not clear whether Robert meant "Gaby" was the same girl to whom Vincent actually gave the ear. Robert's account does give the name of the brothel's madam (Virginie), recently verified by Martin Bailey as Virginie Chabaud (Bailey

2005, p. 36). The city's files on brothels from 1871–1891 are sealed until 2042, so if records provide Rachel's last name (or real name, if she was using a pseudonym), age, etc., scholars have not examined them.

In his letters, the historical Vincent says little about his visits to what he called "the street of the good little women" and gives the names of none of the girls. One of his few references to the "ear incident" comes in a letter to Theo of ca. 3 February 1889 (LT 576), when he says, "Yesterday I went to see the girl I had gone to when I was out of my wits," in other words Rachel, presumably to apologize. He adds, "She had been upset by it and had fainted but had recovered her calm." That Rachel not surprisingly fainted at receiving van Gogh's "gift" is further attested in Gauguin's letter to Bernard.

This novel was born from the question, Who was Rachel? To have asked for her that night, Vincent must have known her, but how well? Had he just been another customer, had she just been another prostitute—or not? I imagined a relationship on the premise that if there *had* been something between the historical Rachel and historical van Gogh, Vincent would have likely kept it secret from Theo, fearing disapproval after the disastrous affair with Sien Hoornik.

I have tried to faithfully situate the fictional story of Rachel within the historical framework of the last two years of van Gogh's life. I have remained largely true to the chronology of Vincent's paintings and to events that took place at Arles, Saint-Rémy, and Auvers-sur-Oise. I have also tried to remain faithful to the historical Vincent's personality as I have interpreted it from his letters, artworks, and other archival sources. Such events as the number and length of Vincent's attacks between December 1888 and May 1890, the petition of the Arles townspeople, his arrest by the police, and, of course, the "ear incident" are historical actualities, although I have viewed them through a novelist's lens.

A few exceptions exist with regards to chronological accuracy. Joseph Roulin was transferred to Marseille in late January 1889, his family following him a few months later; I keep them in Arles until August for dramatic convenience. Van Gogh's visit to the *pastorale* at the Folies Arlésiennes took place in January 1889, not December 1888, and he would not have attended with Joseph Roulin, who had already left for Marseille. I likewise moved van Gogh and Gauguin's visit to Montpellier up by a few weeks; their trip seems to have actually taken place on December 16 or 17, only a week before Vincent's breakdown.

Most characters are inspired by real people, with the following exceptions: Françoise, Jacqui, and the other girls of the *maison* (but not Madame Virginie, the true *patronne* of No. 1, Rue du Bout d'Arles); Raoul the bouncer; old Dr. Dupin; Madame Fouillet in Paris; and assorted nameless characters. Bernard Soulé, Marguerite Favier, and Joseph Ginoux were indeed among those who'd signed the petition against Vincent, as highlighted recently in Martin Gayford's book, *The Yellow House* (see Further Reading).

The letters Vincent writes Rachel in the novel are my creations, although readers familiar with the historical van Gogh's letters will notice I borrowed phrases here and there for verisimilitude. The letter from Theo that Rachel reads in Chapter 32 is the only letter I have used word-for-word from an original: letter T31 from the current standard English translation, dated 29 March 1890. The quotes that open chapters are from surviving letters and documents.

As for the "ear incident," accounts differ as to what actually happened. Gauguin's version as written in *Avant et Après* is thought by many to be exaggerated: he speaks, for example, of

Vincent charging at him with a razor in the darkened Place La-martine, when he does not in earlier descriptions of that night. I have avoided using Gauguin's account for that reason, although I did use his version of what Vincent says to Rachel ("You will remember me") rather than the less romantic line recounted in *Le Forum Républicain* ("Keep this object carefully"). Martin Bailey, in his 2005 article (see Further Reading), postulates on good evidence that Gauguin and Vincent learned of Theo's engagement to Johanna Bonger the morning of 23 December, and that it might have pushed Vincent over the edge.

What was "wrong" with Vincent van Gogh? Many theories exist, ranging from a form of epilepsy (the diagnosis favored by his own doctors), lead poisoning from his paints, a strain of syphilis (unproven for him but definite in Theo van Gogh's case), absinthe poisoning, and so on. Martin Gayford makes a good case for bipolar disorder in his 2006 book, a diagnosis shared by Dr. Jean-Marc Boulon, current director of the asylum of Saint-Paul-de-Mausole in Saint-Rémy. I discussed van Gogh's symptoms and circumstances with Dr. Susan Toler, professor of psychology at the University of South Florida St. Petersburg, and she also arrived at a bipolar disorder diagnosis. In the novel, Dr. Félix Rey makes a connection between Vincent's attacks and events in his relationship with Theo, al-though historically there is no evidence he did so; I did this for the reader's benefit, since now many do see a connection. The emotional trigger I created for Vincent's first relapse in Febru-ary 1889 is, of course, fictional.

The work of many art historians, art critics, and scholars in other fields has proven invaluable. The reader is encour-aged to look at the partial bibliography provided in Further Reading, but I would like to single out here the scholarship of Martin Bailey, Anne Distel and Susan Alyson Stein, Douglas

Druick and Peter Kort Zegers, Martin Gayford, Jan Hulsker, Leo Jansen, Hans Luijten, Ronald Pickvance, Debora Silverman, Judy Sund, Bogomila Welsh-Ovcharov, and Carol Zemel as especially helpful. I eagerly anticipate the newest edition of van Gogh's correspondence, to be issued by the Van Gogh Museum in 2009, the culmination of fifteen years' work by the Van Gogh Letters Project.

# Acknowledgments

My story of *Sunflowers* began in May 2006 where Rachel's ends: at Auvers-sur-Oise, with a quiet walk in the wheatfields and solitary moments at Vincent's grave. At first my scribbled musings were just that, thoughts on a page, until slowly they became something more. The journey would take me through van Gogh's letters and paintings, up to the Netherlands, down to Provence on a crowded train, and back to Auvers-sur-Oise—a journey of heart, mind, and pen.

So many people helped make this book possible. First, my family: my mother, Janie Bundrick, who has always encouraged me to be creative and take risks, and who acts as my cheerleader when I need it; my sister Chantel DiMuzio, herself a beautiful writer, who faithfully read every sentence of every draft and provided important feedback; my father, Wyman Bundrick, for his love and support; my brother-in-law, Adam DiMuzio, for making me laugh; and my nephew Anthony, our little ray of sunshine, born during the writing of this book. I'd paint him a picture of flowering almond tree branches against a crystal blue sky if I could.

To friends and colleagues who read drafts or part of drafts and gave me essential input, thank you so much: Jennifer Palinkas, Anne Jeffrey, Susan Toler, Patrice Boyer, Laura Wingfield, and Julianne Douglas. Special thanks to Dr. Susan Toler for all the discussions about Vincent's psychological landscape. To other friends who knew what I was up to and supported me—too many to name—many mercis. Kudos to the wonderful library staff at the University of South Florida St. Petersburg!

Very special thanks to Barbara Braun, my agent and fellow art historian, who took a chance on an academic-turned-novelist. Very special thanks as well to Lucia Macro, my editor at Avon Books/HarperCollins, for believing in *Sunflowers* and giving it a good home. Everyone at Avon—a special thank you to Esi Sogah, assistant editor—has been amazing.

And finally, to Vincent van Gogh, whose art, words, and un-flagging spirit have inspired not only me, but millions around the world. Fond as he was of sentimental novels, I'd like to think he would enjoy this one.

**A<sup>+</sup>**

**AUTHOR
INSIGHTS,
EXTRAS &
MORE...**

FROM

**SHERAMY
BUNDRICK**

AND

**AVON A**

# Discussion Questions for Reading Groups

1. Why do you think the author decided to have Vincent and Rachel meet in a garden? What significance does nature have in the story?

2. Perception versus reality is a theme of *Sunflowers*. What perceptions do strangers have about Vincent and Rachel? What perceptions do Vincent and Rachel have about each other when they first meet? How do their—and other people's—perceptions change as the novel proceeds? Do you feel your perception of van Gogh and his work has changed as a result of reading the novel?

3. When Rachel goes to the Café de la Gare to watch Vincent paint, she expects to see a beautiful picture. Why is she disappointed? Why do you think the author chose to have the first painting Rachel sees be "sinister and brooding"?

4. Why is Rachel reluctant to visit Vincent's house/studio at first? How does their relationship change when she does decide to visit? She remains reluctant to pose for him for most of the novel. Why do you think this is? Why does she change her mind?

5. Discuss Rachel's reaction when seeing Vincent's painting of sunflowers for the first time. Why does it hold such emotional appeal for her? Have you reacted strongly when seeing a work of art in a museum, whether by van Gogh or another artist? What is your favorite painting by van Gogh, and why?

6. Discuss the character of Paul Gauguin, remembering that we see him through Rachel's eyes in the novel. How do Rachel's feelings about Gauguin contrast with Vincent's? Why is she so wary of him? Are her suspicions justified?

7. Vincent's mental illness (believed by some scholars today to be bipolar disorder) manifests itself over the course of Gauguin's stay in Arles. Do you see hints of his illness before Gauguin's arrival that Rachel does not notice? What factors made it worsen, do you think?

8. How does Rachel cope with the dramatic and tragic events that happen in December 1888 and afterward? Twice in the novel before those events, she refers to girls "braver than I"—but is she braver than she thinks? Vincent is surprised Rachel continues to stand by him. Were you surprised? Was there ever a point in the story where you feel you would walk away?

9. Discuss Vincent's relationship with his brother Theo, which is "off-camera" for most of the novel. What perception does Rachel have of Vincent's brother? Does her perception change when she finally meets him?

10. In chapter 19, Rachel says, "I think you're afraid to be happy, Vincent. And I don't know why." Why is Vincent so reluctant to reveal his relationship with Rachel to his family, even at that stage? Fear torments both Vincent and Rachel over the course of the novel: what are Vincent's greatest fears? Rachel's?

11. Discuss two pairs of characters important in Vincent and Rachel's story: Joseph Roulin and Félix Rey; Françoise and Madame Roulin. How do they compare and contrast with one another?

12. Discuss Rachel's relationship with Félix. Do you agree with her decisions about him? Why does she turn to Félix at that point in the story? How does Vincent react?

13. The theme of containment (or imprisonment) versus freedom is important in *Sunflowers*. In what ways is this theme expressed?

14. "Working is the only thing that does me real good," Vincent tells Rachel while he is in the asylum at Saint-Rémy, when she worries he works too hard on his painting. Do you agree? Why is Vincent so driven to create, even when he is most ill?

15. Why do you think the author chose letters between characters as a way to communicate key events? Did you find this method effective—why or why not?

16. Why does Rachel feel it so important to go to Paris and then Auvers-sur-Oise at the novel's end? Would you have done the same? What does she learn there?

17. Why do you think the author chose to call the novel *Sunflowers*?

## Selected van Gogh Paintings
## Referenced in the Novel

All paintings and drawings described or mentioned in the novel exist except Vincent's three sketches and half-finished painting of Rachel. This list presents some of the mentioned paintings by van Gogh, which amount to a fraction of his actual output. Their historical dates are consistent with the time frame given in the novel, with a few minor exceptions where I moved something a few days up or few days back. The order in which the various versions of *La Berceuse* were painted is debated; I follow the chronology developed by Kristin Hoermann Lister (see Further Reading), although I do not mention the fifth version, painted in late March 1889 (now in the Kröller-Müller Museum).

The historical Rachel may appear in *The Brothel*—the girl to the left in the yellow dress—although this is unconfirmed. Van Gogh intended to paint a brothel picture based on *The Brothel* oil sketch, but it remains unknown why he did not. The painting that Vincent gives Rachel in the novel is *Poet's Garden II*. Although the historical Vincent provided Theo a letter sketch of this painting, it was never sent to Paris, and its whereabouts have been unknown ever since. Van Gogh gave some of his paintings to friends as gifts, and likely he did the same with *Poet's Garden II*. We just don't know to whom.

### Chapter 2

| | | |
|---|---|---|
| *Portrait of Joseph Roulin* | July 1888 | Museum of Fine Arts, Boston |
| *La Mousmé* | July 1888 | National Gallery of Art, Washington |

## Chapter 3

| | | |
|---|---|---|
| *Night Café in the Place Lamartine* | Sept 1888 | Yale Univ. Art Gallery |

## Chapter 4

| | | |
|---|---|---|
| *Public Garden of the Place Lamartine (Poet's Garden I)* | Sept 1888 | Art Institute of Chicago |
| *Portrait of Patience Escalier* | Aug 1888 | Private Collection |
| *Coal Barges* | Aug 1888 | Private Collection |
| *Self-Portrait as Japanese Bonze* | Sept 1888 | Harvard Univ. Art Museums |
| *Café Terrace at Night* | Sept 1888 | Kröller-Müller Museum, Otterlo |
| *Sunflowers* | Aug 1888 | National Gallery, London |

## Chapter 6

| | | |
|---|---|---|
| *Starry Night over the Rhône* | Sept 1888 | Musée d'Orsay, Paris |

## Chapter 7

| | | |
|---|---|---|
| *The Yellow House* | Sept 1888 | Van Gogh Museum, Amsterdam |
| *The Green Vineyard* | Sept 1888 | Kröller-Müller Museum, Otterlo |
| *Sunflowers* | Aug 1888 | Neue Pinakothek, Munich |
| *Public Garden with Round Bush (Poet's Garden II)* | Sept 1888 | Whereabouts unknown since 1888 |
| *Public Garden with Couple and Fir Tree (Poet's Garden III)* | Sept 1888 | Private Collection |
| *The Lovers (Poet's Garden IV)* | Sept 1888 | Whereabouts unknown since WW II |

## Chapter 8

| | | |
|---|---|---|
| *Les Alyscamps* | Oct 1888 | Kröller-Müller Museum, Otterlo |

## Chapter 9

| | | |
|---|---|---|
| *The Brothel* | Oct 1888 | Barnes Foundation, Pennsylvania |
| *Nude Woman Reclining (Agostina Segatori?)* | early 1887 | Kröller-Müller Museum, Otterlo |

## Chapter 16

| | | |
|---|---|---|
| *The Sower* | Nov 1888 | Van Gogh Museum, Amsterdam |
| *The Sower* | Nov 1888 | Bürhle Foundation, Zurich |
| *Portrait of Madame Ginoux* | Nov 1888 | Musée d'Orsay, Paris |
| *The Red Vineyard* | Nov 1888 | Pushkin Museum, Moscow |
| *Portrait of Joseph Roulin* | Nov/Dec 1888 | Kunstmuseum Winterthur |
| *Portrait of Camille Roulin* | Nov/Dec 1888 | Museu de Arte de São Paulo |
| *Portrait of Camille Roulin* | Nov/Dec 1888 | Philadelphia Museum of Art |
| *Portrait of Camille Roulin* | Nov/Dec 1888 | Van Gogh Museum, Amsterdam |
| *Portrait of Armand Roulin* | Nov/Dec 1888 | Museum Boymans-van Bruningen, Rotterdam |
| *Portrait of Armand Roulin* | Nov/Dec 1888 | Museum Folkwang, Essen |
| *Madame Roulin with Baby* | Dec 1888 | Metropolitan Museum of Art, New York |
| *La Berceuse (Madame Roulin)* | Dec 1888/ Jan 1889 | Boston, Museum of Fine Arts |

## Chapter 29

| | | |
|---|---|---|
| *Irises* | May 1889 | J. Paul Getty Museum, Los Angeles |
| *Starry Night* | June 1889 | Museum of Modern Art, New York |
| *Portrait of Charles Trabuc* | Sept 1889 | Kunstmuseum Solothurn |
| *Van Gogh's Bedroom at Arles* | Sept 1889 | Musée d'Orsay, Paris |

## Chapter 30

| | | |
|---|---|---|
| *Night (La Veillée), after Millet* | Oct 1889 | Van Gogh Museum, Amsterdam |

## Chapter 32

| | | |
|---|---|---|
| *Pietà (after Delacroix)* | Sept 1889 | Van Gogh Museum, Amsterdam |
| *Thatched Cottages in the Sunshine (Reminiscences of the North)* | March 1890 | Barnes Foundation, Pennsylvania |
| *Still Life with Irises against a Yellow Background* | late April/ early May 1890 | Van Gogh Museum, Amsterdam |
| *Raising of Lazarus (after Rembrandt)* | May 1890 | Van Gogh Museum, Amsterdam |

## Chapter 34

| | | |
|---|---|---|
| *Church at Auvers* | June 1890 | Musée d'Orsay, Paris |
| *Mademoiselle Gachet (?) in the Garden* | June 1890 | Museé d'Orsay, Paris |

# A Few Words About Places . . .

A plaque marks the site of Vincent's yellow house on the Place Lamartine in Arles, destroyed by Allied bombs in 1944. Bernard Soulé's hotel still stands, but the buildings that once housed Marguerite Favier's grocery shop, the Restaurant Vénissat, and the Café de la Gare were damaged in the bombing and eventually demolished. Most of the public garden in the Place Lamartine is now a parking lot. The Rue du Bout d'Arles is now the Rue des Écoles; the building that once housed Rachel's brothel lies in ruins. In downtown Arles, one can visit the Roman arena, church of Saint-Trophime, public garden on the Boulevard des Lices, and relax at a café on the same spot as the one Vincent painted in the Place du Forum. The Alyscamps is a protected historical site and accessible to visitors.

In Saint-Rémy, the asylum remains a working hospital, today home to about 100 female patients, who engage in art therapy under the auspices of the Fondation Valetudo. Part of the hospital is open to visitors, including the chapel and a reconstruction of Vincent's room. The buildings that housed Vincent's actual room and his studio are reserved for patients and their visitors; so, too, the garden where he drew and painted. Around the asylum one can see olive groves evocative of those in Vincent's time; a relatively new addition is the Roman archaeological site of Glanum next door to the hospital, excavated beginning in the 1920s. Vincent was standing on an ancient town when he painted Mont Gaussier and didn't know it.

In Paris, the Gare de Lyon remains the gateway to southeastern France. A street adjoining the station is now called the Avenue van Gogh in the painter's honor. In Montmartre, the former Place

Ravignan is now the Place Émile Goudeau. The Hôtel du Poirier that stood here in the late nineteenth and early twentieth century housed many artists and writers, among them Albert Camus and Amedeo Modigliani. The studios in the square referenced by (the fictional) Madame Fouillet, converted in 1890 by the building's (real) owner, Monsieur François, were later nicknamed the Bateau Lavoir and are best known as the place where Pablo Picasso painted *Les Demoiselles d'Avignon* in 1907. Vincent and Theo's apartment at 54, Rue Lepic remains a private residence. Theo and Johanna's apartment at 8, Cité Pigalle is likewise a private residence. My descriptions of the latter are based on letters between the couple during their engagement, as compiled in *Brief Happiness* (see Further Reading).

The inn in Auvers-sur-Oise where Vincent lived and died, known as the Auberge de la Mairie in his day, later became known as the Auberge Ravoux after the former innkeepers. Today, after an extensive restoration, the Auberge Ravoux (also known as the Maison de van Gogh) welcomes visitors to its restaurant once more. One can see the attic room where Vincent died, never occupied again because he was a suicide. Like Arles and Saint-Rémy, Auvers has plaques marking van Gogh sites for visitors: at the church, for example, and at the crossroads from *Crows over the Wheatfield*.

Vincent's grave is in the town cemetery of Auvers-sur-Oise; a law passed in 1881 decreed that all could be buried in the same cemetery regardless of religious belief or manner of death. Theo van Gogh—who died in January 1891 of complications from tertiary syphilis—lies next to his brother, his remains moved from Utrecht in 1914 at the request of Johanna van Gogh-Bonger. Johanna is buried in Amsterdam next to her second husband, Johan Cohen Gosschalk. Johanna deserves recognition for her significant contribution to the propagation of Vincent's legacy, along with her son, Vincent Willem van Gogh, who, among other things, worked with the Dutch government to create the Van Gogh Museum.

The house of Dr. Paul Gachet in Auvers-sur-Oise is recently restored and open to the public. Much of the Gachet collection, including some of the family's van Gogh paintings, can be found in the Musée d'Orsay; Paul Gachet *fils* and his sister Marguerite sold other van Goghs in the first half of the twentieth century (including *Marguerite Gachet at Her Piano* to the Kunstmuseum Basel in 1934—see Distel and Stein 1999 in Further Reading). The core of the van Gogh family collection, including the majority of Vincent's letters, a host of other archival materials, and paintings by Vincent and other artists of his and Theo's acquaintance, forms the Van Gogh Museum collection in Amsterdam. Over the years, paintings and drawings by Vincent have scattered to museums, galleries, and private collections all over the world. Today they fetch prices that would shock and bewilder the artist who made them.

# Further Reading
## (Partial Bibliography of Works Consulted)

Bailey, Martin. "Drama at Arles: New Light on Vincent van Gogh's Self-Mutilation." *Apollo* 162 (September 2005): 30–41.

Carrié-Ravoux, Adeline. "Les Souvenirs d'Adeline Ravoux sur le sujet de Vincent van Gogh à Auvers-sur-Oise." *Les Cahiers de Van Gogh* (1956): 7–17.

Cooper, Douglas. *Paul Gauguin: 45 Lettres à Vincent, Théo, et Jo van Gogh.* La Bibliothèque des Arts, 1983.

Corbin, Alain. *Women for Hire: Prostitution and Sexuality in France after 1850.* Translated by A. Sheridan. Harvard University Press, 1990.

Distel, Anne, and Susan Alyson Stein. *Cézanne to Van Gogh: The Collection of Doctor Gachet.* Exhibition catalogue. The Metropolitan Museum of Art, 1999.

Dorn, Roland, et al. *Van Gogh Face to Face: The Portraits.* Exhibition catalogue. Thames and Hudson, 2000.

Druick, Douglas W., and Peter Kort Zegers. *Van Gogh and Gauguin: The Studio of the South.* Exhibition catalogue. Thames and Hudson, 2001.

Gayford, Martin. "Gauguin and a Brothel in Arles." *Apollo* 163 (March 2006): 64–71.

——. *The Yellow House: Van Gogh, Gauguin, and Nine Turbulent Weeks in Arles.* Little, Brown & Co., 2006.

Gogh, Vincent van. *The Complete Letters of Vincent van Gogh.* Introduction by V. W. van Gogh. Preface and introduction by Johanna van Gogh-Bonger. 3rd ed. Bulfinch, 2000.

Harsin, Jill. *Policing Prostitution in Nineteenth-Century Paris.* Princeton University Press, 1985.

Homburg, Cornelia. *Vincent van Gogh and the Painters of the Petit Boulevard.* Exhibition catalogue. Saint Louis Art Museum, 2001.

Hulsker, Jan. "Critical days in the hospital at Arles: Unpublished letters from the postman Joseph Roulin and the Reverend Mr. Salles to Theo van Gogh." *Vincent* 1, no. 1 (1970-71): 20–31.

——. *Vincent and Theo van Gogh: A Dual Biography.* Fuller Publications, 1985.

——. "Vincent's stay in the hospitals of Arles and St-Rémy: Unpublished letters from the Reverend Mr. Salles and Doctor Peyron to Theo van Gogh." *Vincent* 1, no. 2 (1970-71): 21–44.

——. "What Theo Really Thought of Vincent." *Vincent* 3, no. 2 (1974): 2–28.

Ives, Colta, et al. *Vincent van Gogh: The Drawings.* Exhibition catalogue. The Metropolitan Museum of Art, 2005.

Jansen, Leo. *Van Gogh and His Letters.* Van Gogh Museum, 2007.

Jansen, Leo, Hans Luijten, and Nienke Bakker, eds., *Vincent van Gogh—Painted with Words, The Letters to Émile Bernard.* Rizzoli, in association with the Van Gogh Museum, 2007.

Jansen, Leo, and Jan Robert, eds. *Brief Happiness: The Correspondence of Theo van Gogh and Johanna Bonger.* Van Gogh Museum, 1999.

Jirat-Wasiutynski, Vojtech. "A Dutchman in the South of France: Van Gogh's Romance of Arles." *Van Gogh Museum Journal* (2002): 78–89.

Leaf, Alexandra, and Fred Leeman. *Van Gogh's Table at the Auberge Ravoux.* Artisan, 2001.

Lister, Kristin Hoermann. "Tracing a Transformation: Madame Roulin into *La Berceuse.*" *Van Gogh Museum Journal* (2001): 63–83.

Luijten, Hans. *Van Gogh and Love.* Van Gogh Museum, 2007.

Pickvance, Ronald. *Van Gogh in Arles.* Exhibition catalogue. The Metropolitan Museum of Art, 1984.

——. *Van Gogh in Saint Rémy and Auvers.* Exhibition catalogue. The Metropolitan Museum of Art, 1986.

——. *'A Great Artist is Dead': Letters of Condolence on Vincent van Gogh's Death.* Edited by S. van Heugten and F. Pabst. Van Gogh Museum, 1992.

Silverman, Debora. *Van Gogh and Gauguin: The Search for Sacred Art.* Farrar, Strauss and Giroux, 2000.

Stolwijk, Chris, and Richard Thomson. *Theo van Gogh, 1857–1891.* Van Gogh Museum, 1999.

Sund, Judy. "The Sower and the Sheaf: Biblical Metaphor in the Art of Vincent van Gogh." *Art Bulletin* 70 (December 1988): 660–76.

——. *True to Temperament: Van Gogh and French Naturalist Literature.* Cambridge University Press, 1992.

——. *Van Gogh.* Phaidon, 2002.

Tilborgh, Louis van. *Van Gogh and the Sunflowers.* Van Gogh Museum, 2008.

Veen, Wouter van der. " 'En tant que quant à moi': Vincent van Gogh and the French Language." *Van Gogh Museum Journal* (2002): 64–77.

Vellekoop, Marije, and Roelie Zwikker. *Vincent van Gogh Drawings, vol. 4: Arles, Saint-Rémy, and Auvers-sur-Oise, 1889–1890.* Van Gogh Museum, 2007.

Walther, Ingo F., and Rainer Metzger. *Van Gogh: The Complete Paintings.* Taschen, 2006.

Welsh-Ovcharov, Bogomila. *Van Gogh à Paris.* Exhibition catalogue. Musée d'Orsay, 1988.

——."The Ownership of Vincent Van Gogh's 'Sunflowers.'" *Burlington Magazine* 140, no. 1140 (March 1998): 184–92.

Whitney, Charles. "The Skies of Vincent van Gogh." *Art History* 9 (1986): 351–62.

Wolk, Johannes van der. *The Seven Sketchbooks of Vincent van Gogh*. Thames and Hudson, 1987.

Zemel, Carol. *Van Gogh's Progress: Utopia, Modernity, and Late Nineteenth-Century Art*. University of California Press, 1997.

Photo by Brandi Image Photography

**SHERAMY BUNDRICK** is an art historian and professor at the University of South Florida St. Petersburg. She grew up in the Atlanta area where she earned her Ph.D. from Emory University, and spent a year in New York as a research fellow at The Metropolitan Museum of Art. The author of scholarly publications in the field of ancient art yet a longtime lover of Vincent van Gogh, Sheramy tries her hand at historical fiction with *Sunflowers*.

Sheramy Bundrick